SHE WOULD RISK HER INNOCENT
SOUL FOR A DEVIL'S KISS!

"YOU LITTLE FLIRT," HE GRATED.

He wasn't thinking, he was only feeling. "A man's kiss," he cried. "You want a man's kiss?"

She frantically shook her head no.

His mouth came down hard and brutal upon hers. He was savage in his attack, plunging relentlessly into her mouth, again and again.

"Jane," he whispered, agony in his voice. She was clinging to him, her hands caught in his hair. He pulled her closer, stroking down her back to her waist, hips, and the delicious curve of her buttocks.

He needed her desperately.

He wanted her with every fiber of his soul and being.

In horror, he saw them then. The depraved brute and the innocent schoolgirl. She was moaning . . . clinging . . .

With supreme willpower he threw her to the ground.

Jane lay panting, face uplifted. "Nicholas," she begged.

He stood staring down, more horrified than he had ever been in his life. More afraid.

"God, what am I doing?" he cried into the night. And then he turned and ran.

Also by Brenda Joyce

THE CONQUEROR

THE DARKEST HEART

LOVERS AND LIARS

Dark Fires

♨♨♨

BRENDA JOYCE

A DELL BOOK

Published by
Dell Publishing
a division of
Bantam Doubleday Dell Publishing Group, Inc.
666 Fifth Avenue
New York, New York 10103

ISBN: 0-440-20610-3

Printed in the United States of America

Published simultaneously in Canada

June 1991

10 9 8 7 6 5 4 3 2 1

OPM

For Prince Eliyahu—I love you.

With the utmost, heartfelt thanks
to Tina Moskow and Leslie Schnur
for their wonderful warmth
and incredible support.

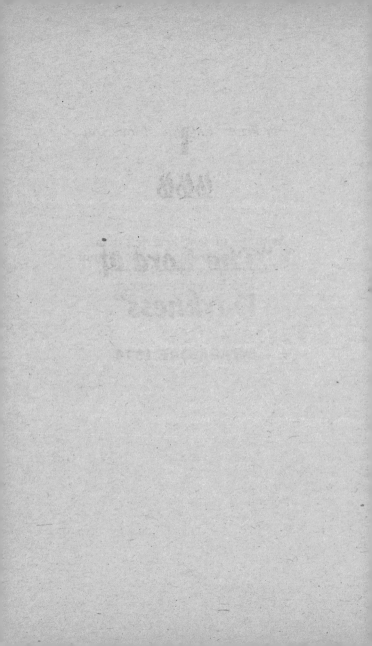

I

"The Lord of Darkness"

DRAGMORE 1874

1

🔥🔥🔥

He wasn't in a particularly good mood.

But then again, the Earl of Dragmore wasn't particularly well-known for his good moods.

Nicholas Bragg, Lord Shelton, stood staring out of the French doors his wife had insisted on, a letter dangling loosely from his hand. The vista that greeted him was spectacular: endless lawns of emerald green carefully, faithfully manicured, thick beds of pink roses, a long, curving graveled drive, and beyond, sweeping green hills framed by oaks in the last of summer's lushness. The earl was not soothed. His hard mouth was twisted into an even harder line; the tendons in his powerful brown hand tightened, and he crushed the letter. "Damn!"

The word was an explosion, and simultaneously he jettisoned the letter in one violent movement.

He began pacing.

The earl was clad, as usual, in soft, form-fitting

breeches, high black boots, a fine cotton shirt carelessly tucked in and open to midchest, ignoring the dictates of Victorian decorum. As he moved, it became evident that a barely restrained power coursed through his muscles, like that of a cougar or a panther. He paused to stare down at the crumpled letter on the floor, feeling the childish urge to crush it under his heel. But that would not make the letter go away. Nor would it make *her* go away.

A ward.

He cursed his wife, now dead, with no remorse.

The earl strode to the windows, raking a hand through impossibly thick and impossibly black hair—so black it shone blue in the sunlight. He had too much to do to play nursemaid to some ward, for God's sake. He didn't need this complication in his carefully constructed life. The harvest was about to begin and he was on his way to Newmarket to look over some breeder bulls. His stallion, No Regrets, was racing Sunday next, and by damn if he'd miss that. He'd intended to spend the following fortnight in London, assuming everything went smoothly on his estates until then. *Damn.*

How the hell old was she?

The earl savagely retrieved the letter, tearing it as he unfolded it. His face was nearly expressionless except for the blazing anger in his gray eyes, so pale as to appear silver at times, all the paler because of the dark, coppery cast to his bronzed skin. She was seventeen. Seventeen, for God's sake, and according to her aunt Matilda, a handful of trouble—which was why they were coming to him.

The earl cursed. "I'll put her in with Chad," he decided grimly. "She can be of some use in the nursery." He briefly questioned the wisdom of this, a seventeen-year-old girl with his five-year-old son, then dismissed the issue.

His wife had been seventeen when they had first been introduced.

His rage and, it seemed, frustration, grew. He would not think about that lying, deceitful bitch, who, if the Christians were right, was at this very moment burning in hell. He laughed, feeling no compassion. He did not believe in hell—or in God, for that matter.

His stallion was as dark and big and powerful as its owner. The grooms of course were used to their lord. No one batted an eye when Nick leapt up onto the stallion's broad bare back and urged him into a gallop. He tore down the drive. It was graveled and meticulously raked every day; his wife had ordered it so, and the orders still stood, four years after her death, because he did not care enough to change them. The drive wound for four miles through Dragmore before reaching the main thoroughfare to Lessing and then London. The earl urged the stallion off the driveway and across a carefully groomed lawn. He knew his gardeners thought him ignorant. They thought he did not know that every time he raced his mount across the lawn he tore it up and that they frantically repaired it with sod before he could see the damage. Nick smiled. It was his lawn. He'd tear it up if he wanted to.

They took a fat, high stone wall fearlessly, the horse and rider flying effortlessly over as one being. It was a harmony of motion, a ballet. Yet on the other side the earl instantly checked the steed into a canter, careful to skirt the sheep—his sheep —and later, in the next pasture, careful not to upset the mares with their frolicking foals. He did not ride through the cornfields. He never had, he never would.

Just the goddamned lawn that required fifteen gardeners.

He returned to the stable, his shirt soaked with sweat and sticking to his powerful torso, his mount blowing heavily. Grooms came running out to take the stallion. The earl waved them away. He walked his horse for thirty minutes, until the two of them were cool and dry.

The head groom, an old man named Willard, watched from a distance, chewing tobacco. His nephew, Jimmy, twelve and new to Dragmore, also watched his lord, wide-eyed. "Is it true?" the lad whispered. "Is it true what they say? Is he the devil, then?"

Willard spat another wad, watching the earl, whose hand was on the stallion's velvet muzzle, his head bent low, near the horse's ears. It was impossible to see if the man spoke or not, yet the way he walked, it was as if he were in low conversation with the beast. Willard knew one thing for sure. The stallion was Satan's own. "Maybe," he muttered. "Maybe. But don't be caught talking that way, boy."

The earl left the stallion and moved swiftly back to the house. It was a huge affair, with forty or fifty rooms, yet modest compared to the Duke of Marlborough's manor. It was hewn of dark-gray stone, with turrets and porticoes and many crystal-paned windows. Roses crept here and there and everywhere—again, his wife. He'd always preferred the ivy, now long since cut away.

The south wing had been gutted by a violent fire. Blackened walls, only partially erect, rose up over charred stone and timbers. Here there was no roof, no turrets, just one lone tower with gaping holes where the windows had been. It remained a tragic sentinel amid the crumbling, burned-out ruins. The earl did not even glance at the ashes.

He entered his study through the French doors, thinking about a whiskey and some correspondence from his Braddock tenant-farmer. He had never acquired a taste for brandy. He paused in the threshold, his gaze held riveted by an overly lush female derriere. The maid was bending over, apparently retrieving the letter.

The very faintest of smiles touched his lips. It was the barest curving up at the corners of his mouth, so faint as to be indistinguishable except for the instant softening of his features and, especially, his eyes. Yet this was the best smile the earl could offer.

For a moment he just watched her.

Then he reached the maid in a soundless stride, grasped her hips, pressed his own arousing tumescence against her, and as she gasped, jerking upright, he nipped the nape of her neck.

"You scared me," she scolded breathlessly without turning, relaxing visibly.

"Did I?" He was pulling her firmly against his body, wrapping his arms around her, throbbing against her buttocks. He rubbed himself lazily, then urgently, there.

"Y-yes." She gasped. Despite her passion, it flitted through her mind to tell him that he frightened her more often than not. That it was only when they were making love that she *wasn't* afraid of him. She knew she would never say so.

The earl pressed his face into the side of her neck and ran his palm over her groin, again and again, until she was thrusting against him and he was thrusting against her.

Sullenly he pushed her onto her belly on his desk, flipping up her skirts. He entered her abruptly and she cried out—yet it was clearly in pleasure, not pain. She was wet and hot and he groaned in undisguised pleasure.

"Harder, my lord." She gasped. "Harder!"

The earl held her hips and thrust. A moment later it was over. He did not even try to contain his own release—he did not care to. He rested a scant minute, his weight upon her, letting her finish, then he withdrew and fastened up his breeches. He moved to the sideboard and poured himself a whiskey. He was aware of the maid, Molly, fixing her skirts behind him. His mind was elsewhere. It had been foolish to ride No Regrets like that just now, with the race just around the corner. Very foolish. He sipped the drink and resolved not to do so again. His gaze drifted to the open French doors and the lawns beyond. Molly, daring a quick glance at him, left without a word. He barely noticed her.

His foul humor returned. His gaze found the crushed letter, now lying upon his desk where the girl had left it. She had tried to smooth it out. A ward. Christ! Just what in hell was he going to do with a seventeen-year-old ward?

He cursed again, viciously.

The Earl of Dragmore was furious.

2

❦❦❦

I will not be afraid.
  I am not afraid.

It was a refrain that Jane kept repeating, with a kind of desperate determination, the closer they got to Dragmore. She sat stiffly glued to the seat of the hansom they had rented at the rail depot in Lessing. Her hands, gloved in fragile white lace, twisted miserably in her lap. Her blue eyes barely focused on the rolling meadows, the treetops framing them vividly against the dismal August sky. A fine English mist covered the countryside. She did not see the beauty of the Sussex landscape. She could only feel the tight, tense beating of her heart.

Oh, whatever had possessed her to do something so stupid as dress up in dead Charlotte Mackinney's clothes and haunt the school bully, Timothy Smith? The whole plan, inspired by her vivid imagination and her desire to scare the pants off the boy, who deserved at least one good

setdown for all his cruel, bullying ways, had
backfired, and soundly. Charlotte Mackinney was
Tim's aunt and dead one month. Jane *had* scared
the daylights out of Timmy, floating into his room
at night like that, lingering, beckoning, just like a
ghost—after all, she was an actress. She relished
the part. She played it to the hilt. Timmy had been
whiter than her own fair complexion, as white as
the whites of his eyes. He'd been frozen stiff. Jane
had so gotten into the role, drifting around the
doorway of his bedroom, that she hadn't heard
anyone coming down the corridor. She had
nearly jumped out of her skin and Charlotte
Mackinney's dress when a woman behind her exclaimed, "What's this!"

It was pitch black in Timmy's bedroom, except
for the glow of the full moon, and near pitch in
the hall. Jane found herself face to face with Timmy's mother—Charlotte's sister. Abigail Smith
saw Charlotte's dress and flaming hair and fell
dead in a faint at her feet. Jane managed to stifle
a scream. She picked up her hem and ran. In her
haste she went smack into the door jamb, stub-
bing her toe smartly. She cried out in pain. That
was the beginning of the end.

"You ain't no ghost!" Timothy shouted.

Jane threw him a look. Timothy was beet red,
whether from embarrassment or fury Jane didn't
know. But he was a mean fifteen-year-old bully,
six feet tall and twice her weight, and Jane suspected she was in dire straits. She ran.

Timothy caught her.

Now Jane blinked back a sudden tear. Everything had gone so well until Abigail Smith had
come along and fainted. Damn damn damn her
impulsive, reckless behavior! If only Abigail had
picked another time to go to bed, if only she,

Jane, had enjoyed her performance less and quit sooner, while she was ahead, if only she hadn't thought of the stupid idea anyway . . . If, if if!

They called him the Lord of Darkness.

Jane shuddered. She told herself not to be silly, to stop thinking like a moron. He was no devil. He was just a man. She was not afraid.

She shot her aunt a despairing glance. She knew there would be no sympathy from that stiff-backed widow. Matilda sat ramrod straight, eyes turned out of the carriage to the countryside. Jane had to try.

"Aunt Matilda, are you sure you won't reconsider?" Her voice broke. She couldn't control it.

Matilda turned her plump, unsmiling face to her niece. "We are almost there. Don't you dare pull any of your ill-mannered, thoughtless stunts, Jane. I'm warning you. You had it easy when Fred was alive, that you did—twisted him around your finger, you did, with those big blue eyes. An' these past six months you've run free, you did, with me grievin' an' all, God bless his departed soul. But the earl ain't a foolish country parson. He won't put up with any pranks from you." Matilda shook her finger. "No stunts, you hear!"

Jane turned her pale, gamin face away, biting her full lower lip. Matilda had never liked her, never cared. Her uncle, Fred, who had died last winter of a heart attack—he had liked her, a little, anyway. Maybe it was for the best. She would go crazy living with the stern, no-nonsense Matilda. She had never seen the woman smile, not once.

She had considered running away. After all, she was seventeen, soon to be eighteen. But Matilda's decision to pack her off to Dragmore had come so suddenly, she hadn't the chance to formulate any plans. Yet she could still do it. A surge of warmth

filled her heart, and Jane thought about her
friends—her real family—left behind four years
ago in London. The King's Acting Company of the
Royal Lyceum Theatre.

If only Robert had never made her leave.

Her mother had been Sandra Barclay, the famous actress. Jane had grown up in theaters
across the country. As an infant a nurse had
rocked her in her mother's dressing room. Jane
had fallen to sleep soothed by the sounds of the
standing ovations her mother received on stage.
As a toddler she had seen her beautiful blond
mother sweeping into the chamber clad in elaborate costumes, glittering and sequined, then
sweeping out again, in a different dress, to the
roar of applause and whistles and shouts. As a
young child she had watched, wide-eyed, her
mother on the stage, gesturing, crying, laughing,
even dying—only to stand up again and receive
one thunderous ovation after the other. Roses
were strewn at her feet. Again and again.

"Your mommy is wonderful, isn't she?" her father would say, hugging her and letting her ride
his shoulder. Jane, beaming, agreed. "Almost as
wonderful as my little angel," he would say, stroking her fine platinum hair. "My blue-eyed angel."

Jane would laugh and pull his hair. Then her
mother would appear, impossibly beautiful, radi-
ant in the aftermath of her performance. Jane
called out. Sandra, seeing her, instantly softened,
and took her from her father's arms, hugging her
fiercely. "Darling! Darling! Mommy is so thrilled!
Did you enjoy the show?" And her mother nuzzled
her soft cheek.

She was Sandra Barclay, considered one of the
finest actresses of her time, renowned throughout
London. He was Lord Weston, the Duke of

Clarendon's third son, the Viscount Stanton. To this day Jane had such wonderful, vivid memories of the three of them together, always in one theater or another, until her father died when she was six.

It was a terrible time. Her mother would see no one and Jane did not recognize the pale, gaunt woman who turned away from her. Her uncle, who was not really her uncle but the manager of the troupe, explained carefully to Jane that Daddy had gone to heaven. Jane knew about heaven, so now she demanded, "Tell him to come back!"

"I can't, Jane," Robert Gordon said softly. "But he is in heaven with God, and he is happy."

"Has Daddy died?"

Robert hesitated, surprised, then stroked her hair. "Yes, angel. But don't be afraid. One day you will see him again."

Jane clutched his shirt. "I want to see him now!" she cried imperiously. "Tell him to wake up!"

"I can't," Robert said, agonized.

"Yes, you can," she said, sobbing, desperate. "Mommy dies all the time, but she always wakes up to come home!"

At first Robert didn't understand. Then he realized that she was thinking of her mother's dramatic performances. "Honey, this time is different. Your mother only plays at going to heaven. Your daddy really has."

Jane could not understand. She didn't believe Robert. Her daddy would come back. She tried to tell her mother this, but Sandra only wept. Wept with her daughter in her arms, hugging her fiercely, as if Jane could ease her pain. And then one day Jane knew the truth. He wasn't coming back—not ever.

Her mother came out of mourning after a year to take her place in the theater again. Her own personal tragedy had made her better than ever, the critics said. Her performances were haunting. No one who saw Sandra Barclay on the stage could ever forget her.

Sandra refused to send Jane away to school, but hired a tutor instead. Jane learned to read and write mostly in her mother's dressing room, or sitting in the huge, empty auditorium, or, sometimes, from the study of her mother's London town house in Chelsea. When Jane was ten her mother became very ill, and three months later she passed away. The doctors never had an explanation.

At ten Jane had been too old and too worldly not to understand exactly what had happened. This was no act. Her mother had died and was never coming back. Robert and her mother's friends—actors, actresses, musicians, stagehands —would not leave her alone to grieve. Their grief was shared, and Jane found comfort from everybody. Robert soon gave her her first role as an actress to distract her. She played a little boy in the production of *The Physician*. She only had five lines, but—stepping out on the stage as someone else, becoming someone else, playing someone else for a thousand people—it was the most exciting event of her life.

And afterward, when she came to take her bow with the rest of the cast, the applause was thunderous. Jane, holding hands with an actress and actor, bowed again and again to the standing ovation. Her face was wreathed in smiles. Her heart was expanding to impossible dimensions.

Someone shouted, "It's the Angel's daughter! It's Sandra's girl!"

And the actress pushed her forward. "Take your own bow, Jane, they want you," she cried. Jane found herself alone on the stage, bowing. The crowd went crazy for the little blue-eyed blonde.

"Angel, Angel!" they screamed, applauding wildly. She soon became London's darling of the stage. They called her "Sandra's Angel."

"Jane, stop your daydreaming—we're here!"

Jane jerked out of her sentimental memories at the sound of Matilda's intrusive voice. She had tears in her eyes, both from joy and pain, and she brushed them away. She found herself staring at the dark-gray stones of the neo-Gothic manor looming before them. She had expected something dark and gloomy and menacing. She wasn't disappointed. All that was missing was overgrown ivy—the creeping pink roses and the carefully tended lawns were incongruous to the dark, dismal castle. As her gaze traveled along the immense, turreted outline of Dragmore, she came to the south wing, jagged and blackened and gutted grotesquely from a fire. Apparently it had been left that way for years. An irreverent testimony to the past—or was it some sort of macabre reminder? Jane shivered, her heart lodging in her throat, as they entered the circular drive going round in front of the house. And then she saw him, standing in the ancient stone arch of the barbican, his body partly turned to them, tall and powerful and darkly forbidding. In that moment, as he stared at them, he appeared to be the resurrected ghost of one of his ancestors, an indomitable pagan lord from another time and place.

The Lord of Darkness.

Oh, how the title suited him.

They said he had killed his wife.

3

🔥🔥🔥

It had to be she and he wasn't pleased.

The earl was in the process of entering the manor. He paused at the sound of the carriage approaching, clearly discernible despite the frantic barking of the hounds. Vast irritation filled him, and he abruptly crossed the courtyard and stalked into the house, past the butler. "Show them in," he said through gritted teeth.

"Which room shall I show them to, my lord?" Thomas asked politely. He was in his fifties, white-haired, balding, his face always bland. The earl thought that he could run around in a loincloth and moccasins with full Comanche warpaint and the old man wouldn't bat an eye. Nick actually, secretly, liked him.

"How the hell would I know? You can take them to the stables for all I care." The earl strode across the marbled foyer, oblivious to the fact that he was tracking mud and manure through.

He began bounding up the curved mahogany stairs.

"Shall I serve them tea and crumpets?" Thomas called after him politely.

"Serve them spitted catfish heads," he said with a growl.

"Yes, sir," Thomas said.

The earl paused on the first landing, his hand turning white on the banister. His cold glance locked with Thomas's bland one. He almost smiled. At least Thomas knew when to take him literally, unlike his wife's man. That imbecile had actually served the closest thing he could find to catfish once upon a time, when the earl had been forced to host friends of Patricia's in her absence. It was hard to say who had been more shocked, his guests or Nick, at the sight of the spitted, grilled fishheads served with the tea. Nick had actually laughed once he recovered. His wife, Patricia, had not found the episode the least bit amusing.

The earl stomped into the master suite. There was no valet there awaiting him; he did not have one. That had caused another, albeit minor, scandal, not that the earl cared. Until his wife's death four years past he had suffered with a valet, which he found ridiculous. He was a grown man and he was capable of dressing himself. The lack of privacy bothered him as much as the inanity of it, and after the trial he had dismissed the valet immediately. He would have discharged two-thirds of the household staff as well, except that he worried about turning them out of their jobs. The earl was well aware that most agricultural laborers, when unemployed, moved to the towns, where there were jobs aplenty in the factories. He did not have the heart to consign these people,

whom he knew, to such a cold, dismal fate. Born
and raised on a west Texas ranch, for Nick such
an existence was hell on earth.

His shirt was wet with sweat, and the earl removed it, flinging it to the floor. He had been
working with the laborers building a new stone
wall in one of the south meadows. He had enjoyed the task—gathering the rocks from the
fields and adding them to the growing wall. Unlike some of his neighbors, whose acreage was
going from corn to grass without grazing live-
stock, the earl was increasing the use of land on
all fronts. The new meadow would be turned to
hay to feed his increasing herds. He was aware
that agriculture was in a precarious state—he
sensed the beginning of its decline. He knew he
must be careful, yet Dragmore, under his efficient
policies, was thriving. Nick understood that to
compete with the vastly cheaper American agriculture, he would have to increase Dragmore's ef-
ficiency. It was a challenge, a task he threw his
entire heart into, one that kept him going from
dawn until dusk.

They were waiting.

The earl grimly buttoned a fresh shirt. He could
not put it off. They were waiting. Not for the first
time, he regretted the day he had ever married
Patricia Weston.

She heard him coming.

Jane took a breath. The wait had been unbearable. And very rude too. She had seen him turn
his back on their carriage as they entered the
drive. He hadn't even remained to greet them as a
host should. Now they had sat in the yellow parlor for a good half hour, and there was still no
noble presence. Jane had scanned her environs

out of sheer boredom and the need to occupy herself. She had instantly noted that the parlor appeared to not have been used in a long time—or cleaned, for that matter. While everything was in perfect order, there was a thick coat of dust everywhere, and cobwebs hung in the corners of the ceiling above the heavy brocade drapes. The walls were covered in faded, aging, quite garish gold damask. Cherubs and nymphs and God only knew what else flew above them, painted on the ceiling amid blue sky and puffy clouds. The room was the epitome of bad taste. Matilda was unperturbed, sipping her tea and eating three crumpets in rapid succession. Jane had tasted the tea—foul stuff. She preferred coffee as her mother had. As for the pastries—she would never be able to get one down.

She stared at the door, hearing the soft footfall, and then it swung open. Her gaze locked with his.

Her heart stopped, jolted by his presence, then began to beat anew.

Before she had just gotten a glimpse of blue-black hair and broad shoulders. Now she was ensnared by frosty silver eyes without the least bit of warmth in them. His presence was vast, threatening. So dark. He filled the doorway. He was bronzed the color of teakwood. It made his pale eyes startling, even eerie, in the harsh, high planes of his face. And he was big. Taller than Timothy, and filled out, broad of shoulder, his hips small but strong. Jane saw, shocked, that he wore only a linen shirt casually tucked into his breeches, no vest, no jacket, no tie, and it wasn't even buttoned all the way. She could see the flat plane of his chest, a sprinkling of black hair. His breeches were pale, tight doeskin, covering large, powerful thighs and stained with dirt and grass.

His boots were muddy. He was obviously the one who had tracked the filth into the house.

He was uncouth. He was a barbarian. He was everything they said. He was so dark, she understood now where he had gotten his name. And he was staring back at her.

This realization, that he was staring back as rudely as she had been staring, made her blush hotly, and she abruptly dropped her gaze to her lap. But she could still feel his, cold, menacing— yet somehow hot too.

"I am Jane's aunt by marriage," Matilda was saying. "I trust you received our letter?"

"I did."

"I'm so sorry if I've given you a jolt, but with my dear husband passing on, I just can't keep Jane, and you—"

"I have no time for a ward."

His words were hard and curt, and Jane gasped in surprise. Their gazes met again. Color flooded her. His cold eyes slipped from her face to her waist, but so rapidly she thought she must have imagined it. He turned back to Matilda. "I am sorry," he said. It was a dismissal.

Matilda stood, growing red, but not intimidated. "I cannot handle her alone. I am an old woman. She is a trying handful, she is impulsive, reckless, always in mischief. I am returning to the parsonage. Without Jane."

"How much do you want?"

Matilda grew redder. "I didn't come for money! But we cared for her for almost four years, since she was fourteen. If you have the charity to pass something on, I can use it. But I cannot handle Jane," Matilda cried with obvious conviction. "If you don't take her I will toss her out onto the streets!"

Silence greeted this. Both pairs of eyes turned to Jane. Jane was too hurt by Matilda's words to be enthused with the prospect of escaping both unwanted guardians, for if neither one wanted her, this was her chance. "It's all right," she bravely said, attempting a fragile smile. "I will go to London. I have friends there."

"Friends! Bah!" Matilda spat. "That theater trash your mother was a part of!"

The earl wasn't listening to Matilda. He was staring at Jane. She had the voice of an angel. He liked this situation less and less with every passing moment. He hadn't expected this—beauty and innocence and those big blue eyes. And—she was a child. To send her to London alone would be to doom her to a life of prostitution. The factories if she was lucky. He cursed aloud. "Damn Patricia."

Matilda gasped. Jane's big eyes went bigger, like saucers. He looked at Matilda. He did not care what these two thought—he had long since ceased to care what anyone thought of him. Not since the trial had he given a damn about gossip. "Are you certain there are no other Westons?" But even as he spoke, he knew that, with his wife's death, there was no one else on the Weston side to take the girl in. "What about her mother's family?"

"There is no one but you and me," Matilda said firmly. And then, angrily, she proceeded to tell him about Jane's last escapade. The earl's expression did not change, but he stared again at Jane. "Abigail Smith almost had a heart attack," Matilda finished triumphantly. "How can I control the likes of her? I'm an old woman!"

He did not think the offense serious; in fact, had he not been so angry about the entire situation, he might have been momentarily amused.

Grimly he said, "I am not equipped for this. I know nothing about raising a girl."

"You have a son," Matilda pointed out, smiling now, sensing victory. "He has a governess. Jane will fit right in. And, my lord, in your position you can find her a husband, quickly if you wish. Then Jane will be settled and everyone's conscience will be relieved."

Nick stared at Jane. She was seventeen, she was beautiful, she was a Weston. He knew very few details, other than that she was the old duke's granddaughter. But these bare facts were enough. He could find her a husband easily. And his life would return to normal.

"Very well," he said. "She can stay. And I will find her a husband immediately."

"I don't want to get married!" Jane cried.

Both heads whipped toward her. Matilda was furious, the earl surprised. His surprise faded to what appeared to be amusement, while Matilda became threatening. "What you want is of no concern," she hissed. "Be quiet!"

Jane opened her mouth to protest—and met the earl's intense gray stare. She swallowed her denials. She knew, in that instant, that what she wanted did not matter in the least. The earl would have his way—with them all.

4

Matilda had left.

Jane suddenly, abruptly, felt alone and abandoned. She managed a bright smile for the servant who had carried up her bags, and then he too was gone, closing the heavy rosewood door behind him. An immediate, heavy silence descended.

Jane felt it, the stabbing of hurt, of grief, of aloneness and homesickness. She swallowed the lump choking her and walked past the four-poster, silk-canopied bed to one of the crystal-paned windows. She looked outside.

The lawns stretched away in perfect lush harmony. The drive glittered like diamonds as it snaked through Dragmore, catching the reflection of the sun piercing through the heavy drizzle. Rolling hills, slick and wet, studded with sheep, cows, waving corn and wheat, undulated to the gray horizon. Heavy clouds scudded above. She could see the glimpse of a steeple—the chapel at

Lessing, perhaps? And she wondered how much of all of this was Dragmore.

She was not going to get married.

She was going to become a famous actress, like her mother.

Jane turned away from the window, only to notice the black dust covering her hands from where she'd leaned on the sill. She frowned. He had an army of servants, she'd seen them, but what did they spend their time doing? Of course, it was no business of hers, and they had arrived suddenly, barely with any warning.

Had he really killed his wife?

There was a knock on the door, and Jane felt her spine stiffen, her heart freeze—thinking it was he. She was assailed with an image of his dark, harshly chiseled face and his pale, pale eyes, and then a maid poked her head in, smiling. "Hello, mum, I'm Molly. He says you're to take your meals with Chad and Randall in the nursery."

A hot flush swept her. He would resign her to the nursery, would he? "And where is it?"

"It be just down the end of the hall." The pretty, plump maid pointed. "Jake is bringing you some hot water for a bath and fresh tea. They be eatin' at six, mum."

Jane nodded. "All right, Molly, thank you. Please forget the tea, and bring me some coffee." Molly's eyes widened, but she nodded and backed out. Grimly Jane turned to face the full-length mirror standing in its walnut frame in a corner of the room. Did she appear such a child, then? She stared at herself, the crimson still staining her cheeks.

Jane was of less than average height and very petite. What she saw was her tiny figure and a white, triangular face that could have been that of

some little lost urchin. Her cheekbones were
high, her nose small and tipped, her lips too full
for her small face. Her eyes were huge, wide now,
and the bright blue of bluebells. In her plaid high-
necked dress, which she wore without the customary bustle, and the blue bonnet, she looked
like a twelve-year-old. Jane yanked off the bonnet
and threw it onto an overstuffed chair. Piles of
waving platinum hair the color of champagne
spilled down her back. There was too much hair
for her small frame.

And she still looked twelve.

There was no denying it, and Jane felt a sudden, intense frustration. She pictured him—the
earl. The darkness, the intensity, the power. She
could almost feel the heat of his presence behind
her, and Jane hastily darted a glance over her
shoulder. But of course the room was empty, of
course she was alone. Yet she could still see him,
still feel him, and something Jane could not de-
fine swept her. A frisson. Of fear . . . or excitement?

She turned to the mirror again. There was a
bright flush upon her cheeks now. She stared.
This was how he had seen her, in the frowsy,
childish dress with the small, childish body. But
she wasn't a child. She was seventeen.

And suddenly it became of overwhelming im-
portance that the earl should see her as a grown
woman.

The earl paused on the landing to the third
floor. The rich, bell-like sound of a woman's
laughter rang out merrily, deeply. Jane Weston.
His response was instant—a tightening of every
fiber in his body. He heard his son's childish giggle in response. His surprise died. He had, after

all, ordered her to the nursery. But, he thought as
he approached silently, Governess Randall had
never laughed like that.

Nick paused in the open doorway, without a
sound. He was purposeful in being quiet. He had
been raised on a ranch, and his father was half
Apache; his mother had been a Mescalero squaw.
Derek had also been a captain in the Texas Rangers, and he had taught all his children, even
Nick's sister, to track and hunt and to move
soundlessly. It was a part of their heritage, Derek
had always said. And one day, maybe such skills
would save their lives.

The earl felt the old, old stabbing then, an anguish so deep and intense that if he didn't cut it
off immediately he wasn't sure what would happen—he would cease to be a man. He did cut it
off. And he corrected himself, silently, with a bitter twisting of his lips in the mockery of a smile.
Not his father. His father hadn't raised him, his
father was dead. Killed violently by the man who
had raised him and called himself his father—the
man Nick had adored as his father his entire life.
Until he had learned the truth.

He shook it all away, but he could not shake the
self-hatred and self-disgust. It was all one big
joke. He was not Nicholas Bragg, Lord Shelton,
the Earl of Dragmore. He was nothing more than
the grotesque product of a violent rape.

He was glad Derek had killed his real father,
the Comanchero Chavez. Because if he hadn't,
Nick would have.

His stunning, dead wife's image loomed. Her
face was white, so carefully painted that it appeared natural. Rich blond hair was coiled atop
her head. Her expression was one of horror.

He hadn't even shared the terrible secret. He

had started to. He had only gotten as far as confessing his Indian heritage. And she had recoiled . . .

Abruptly he shoved his morose thoughts away. And saw his son. Nick softened.

Everything went soft. His face, his eyes, and the tension in his body drained away. Chad was almost five, with dark-brown hair and a medium complexion and his mother's green eyes. He was giggling, although trying to be serious. The earl watched as Jane filled a wineglass with water, then lifted her own. "To you, my lord," she said in a high, false voice. "To the Lord of Dragmore." Governess Randall, a big, stocky horse-faced woman, frowned disapprovingly and harrumphed.

"To you, my lady," Chad mimed, and they drank their toasts.

The earl smiled.

"My lord, I fear there is some urgent correspondence awaiting you in your library," Jane continued. "If you have finished, perhaps we should see to it."

"I am finished," Chad announced. "Do we go downstairs?" His adorable face screwed up quizzically. "Papa may be in the lib'ry!"

"But my lord," Jane cried, standing with dignity and gesturing grandly to the corner of the nursery. "Your library awaits you there."

Chad stood, imitating her graceful, regal movements. The earl was no longer watching his son. He was watching Jane. She had changed out of her schoolgirl's dress and was wearing a simple skirt, sans crinoline or bustle, and a silk, striped blouse with a lace collar. Her hair hung in a braid as fat as his arm to her buttocks. He had seen a few wisps before, peeking out from the bonnet, so the pale, champagne color did not surprise him. She had beautiful hair. The tail teased the small of her back. It was a saucy, impudent curve of derriere, high and round, and realizing what he was eyeing, he abruptly jerked his gaze away. *What the hell was wrong with him?*

"Papa!" Chad shrieked.

The earl caught his son as he charged into his arms, lifting him high and swinging him around. He slipped Chad to his feet, ruffling his thick hair. "How was supper, son?" He was squatting.

"Jane and me, we played a game," Chad cried excitedly. "I was lord and she was my lady! That's our lib'ry. Want to come in?"

The earl knew how to play with his son. He had taught him how to ride, fish, and hunt, how to track. *The way Derek had taught him.* Now he was uncomfortable, with Chad pulling on his hand, trying to drag him into the "library." He felt the heat of the skin on his face. "Maybe later," he said, his hand in the boy's hair. It lingered there. Chad was not disappointed. He gazed up at his father with adoration.

Nick met Jane's glance. It was soft and surprised and curious. A blush stained her cheeks. He didn't like her regard, and he shot her a quelling look. In return, she gave him her fragile smile and cast her eyes away.

As she stood there in the blue serge skirt without the crinoline, he realized her legs were very, very long.

"My lord," Governess Randall interrupted. "I really think these games, at the table, are quite inappropriate. Chad should learn his manners, not—"

"I think Chad can both learn manners and play games with Jane," the earl said abruptly. His gaze strayed of its own accord from Randall to Jane. She was poised like a bird about to take wing; then she relaxed and smiled a true, wide smile. It was warm, it was light and laughter, it was happiness. Nick felt the surge of an answering warmth in his own heart. Confused, he stared at her. And he became aware of her gazing back and the heat building slowly in his loins.

He recoiled. *What the hell was wrong with him?*

She was a child, his ward.

But the heat grew. And he was afraid, so very afraid, that he knew what was wrong. Abruptly he wheeled and left the room, for once not even hearing his son calling after him. His strides were long, hard, fast. As if he could outrace the thought forming in his mind.

But he couldn't.

He was thinking of his father, the Comanchero Chavez.

5

The sooner she got this over with, the better.

Jane took a deep breath, for courage. She was standing outside the massive teakwood doors of the library, which were closed and highly forbidding. She knew, already, that this was the earl's solitary, private domain. She had sensed that even his son was hesitant to venture forth there. She knew he was within. Not that she had asked his whereabouts—she could feel his presence.

It was tangible.

Jane hesitated, remembering hotly how he had found her playing childish games with his son in the nursery. She once again regretted her impulsive behavior and her flyaway imagination. She was confirming his first opinion of her—that she belonged in the nursery. Gnawing her lip, she resolved to control herself. To be graceful, dignified, adultlike. She knocked.

There was no response.

Jane hesitated, more sure than ever that he was

within, afraid now to incur his displeasure, or worse. But she did not believe in procrastinating. She had to get this over with. Bravely she knocked again, harder this time.

The door opened so abruptly and without any warning that Jane, leaning against it, fell forward and against his body. She did not have to look up to know it was he. He was so tall and so hard, harder than she believed possible. He caught her, exclaiming, "What the hell!" She gasped and looked up. His hands dropped from her shoulders as if he'd been burned. For an instant their gazes met, his so pale yet so dark. He was angry.

"I'm s-sorry," she stammered. She regretted now her foolishness in seeking him out. It was like bearding a wolf in his den. Her heart was thundering in her breast.

"I take it you want something," he said, arms crossed.

"May we speak?"

He nodded and turned his back on her and paced to his desk. He sat behind it. Jane slowly crossed the room, so nervous that she didn't pay attention to its size, the plush carpets, the thick, gleaming mahogany walls. The desk was overly large—it suited him. She couldn't help but notice the endless piles of paperwork, ledgers, and books. She felt like a supplicant at the royal throne.

She wasn't sure whether to stand or sit, so she stood.

"Well?"

"My lord." She took a breath, looked him in the eye. "I cannot marry."

Not an emotion crossed his face. "No?"

"No."

"Why not?"

"I am an actress, sir."

It was said with such seriousness, such conviction, that Nick felt the corners of his mouth trying to lift. He fought the urge to smile. "Indeed?"

"Yes." Calmer now, Jane smiled. It was so sweet the earl felt the stabbing all the way to his gut—and he didn't like that. His jaw clamped, but she went on serenely. "You know, don't you, that my mother was a famous actress, Sandra Barclay. And I, well, I had my first role at ten at the Lyceum Theatre." Her eyes shone. "I was on the stage until I was fourteen," she said, as if that explained everything.

The earl was stunned and disbelieving. "Your mother was an actress? I find it impossible to believe that the blue-blooded Westons would allow such a woman into their noble midst."

Jane grew slightly pink.

"You are a Weston?"

She didn't respond, pinker still.

"You are somehow related to the family? I was led to believe you were the dear, dead duke's grandaughter."

"I am," she squeaked.

"I see," he said, leaning back, his face ferocious-looking now. "A bas—illegitimate?"

She was red. "My father, the duke's third son, Viscount Stanton, loved my mother to distraction. And she loved him."

"But they weren't married."

Jane was both upset and angry at his prying. "He could not marry her, sir," she said clearly.

He raised a brow.

"He already had a wife," she managed.

"Ah," Nick said. "I see."

Jane swallowed, hard. Some time before he had died, her father and mother had carefully explained that they weren't married, although they loved each other completely, and that her father already had a wife from the time before he'd known and fallen in love with Sandra. Jane knew they loved each other and was so secure in this fact that the truth had not upset her. It was only much later, after her mother died, that her father's marriage and her own illegitimacy suddenly became an issue—with her newly found fame as London's darling of the stage.

The earl felt sorry for her. He fought the unfamiliar sympathy. He concentrated on his smoldering anger—he had been tricked, deceived. Marrying the chit off would be no simple task. It would be nearly impossible, no matter how pretty she was. She was the bastard of an actress—her mother might as well have been a prostitute for all the difference it would make to Society. He would have to give her an incredible dowry—and then some.

And it wasn't exactly as if his reputation was spotless, either. He almost laughed, then, thinking of the irony of it—the man who had stood trial for the murder of his wife, in one of the century's most shocking courtroom dramas, trying to arrange a "respectable" marriage for an actress's bastard. How appropriate.

"He loved her very much," Jane said. She was staring at the floor. "It's the truth."

He eyed her.

"Those were the best, most wonderful times." She looked up, eyes wet. "Daddy and I would watch Mother on the stage. He'd hold me in his arms, up high, so I could see. He would always tell me how wonderful she was, how beautiful. Then he'd tease me, telling me that one day I'd surpass even her. And she was wonderful, she was beautiful. She always performed to standing ovations—the audiences couldn't get enough of her. And the men. They all fell in love with her. But she wanted no one except my father."

Even if it were true, it made no difference to Nick. He supposed they were lucky, to have shared something special, even if for a short while. He thought of Patricia. He thought of the day he had learned the truth—the day she had left him and Chad and run away with her lover. He looked at the fragile child standing in front of him. "Your mother died when you were fourteen? And you were sent to your aunt's?"

"Mother died when I was ten. Robert—the manager—let me stay on with the company until I was fourteen." Suddenly she blushed and gazed at the floral carpet. "Something happened," she mumbled. Recovering, she met his gaze with a faked shrug. "He decided I had best go to relatives."

It was unbelievable—a child raised by a troupe of actors. "What happened?"

She blushed again. "One of the actors, someone new . . ."

He studied her, at seventeen still so young, and imagined her at fourteen—nearly sexless, a mere child, a wraith most likely. He felt hard, hot anger. "Did he hurt you?"

Jane shook her head. "Scared me, is all. He wouldn't have . . . I'm sure he wouldn't have . . . He only kissed me, touched me. He wouldn't have hurt me. He was my friend."

She believed it. Whoever had molested her had been depraved, but she, to this day, thought him her friend. She was utterly innocent. He imagined, with some horror, what would happen if she was allowed to go to London to the stage. A lamb among wolves. She would be slaughtered. The earl stood abruptly. "It's late."

She smiled tremulously. "Then you understand? I won't have to get married?"

The one thing the earl understood was his duty, his responsibility. And she was now his ward. "You will be married as soon as I find a suitable prospect," he said firmly, moving to the door and opening it.

Her eyes were wide, distressed.

"Good night, Jane." He watched her. She wanted to argue. He waited, and it came.

"I won't get married." Her full lower lip pouted, trembling.

He smiled slightly. "We shall see." It was a dismissal. He watched her leave, trying to ignore the tumult rising within him. There was no choice, he *must* marry her off. The problem loomed, like a five-foot stone wall before his Irish-bred hunter. Just how in hell was he going to find her a suitable husband when he had not been among Society since the murder trial?

And he felt it then, anguish, dread.

But with iron control, he shoved both feelings deep, deep inside.

6

Jane passed a sleepless night. She tossed and turned, both miserable and angry. She would never give up her dreams, yet she sensed that the earl would be as immovable as a stone wall. Again and again their conversation replayed itself in her mind. The words became lost among the images. Mostly his image, dark and threatening. He had not a jot of compassion in his entire large, hard body. His eyes were silver ice. If she wasn't careful, she would probably be married within the fortnight.

Knowing him now, as little as she did, sensing the dark, hot anger pulsing within him, she thought that perhaps what they said was true, perhaps he had killed his wife. After all, where there's smoke there's fire, and he had been on trial for the murder—the trial of the Earl of Dragmore had been sensationalized by the press, making headlines every day for a week. It had only been three and a half years ago. Jane had seen

some of the papers. That particular week Matilda
and the parson had argued vehemently once over
whether he was guilty or innocent, Matilda certain he had done the grisly deed. She had won
that battle. But he had been acquitted. Some time
during this period he had gained the popular title
the Lord of Darkness.

And then she remembered his hands.

She saw them clearly, big and powerful, hands
that could kill. Yet how could a murderer's hands
stroke a little boy's hair with such tenderness?
Jane was assailed with the memory of how, earlier, in the nursery, Nick had not been able to
take his palm out of Chad's thick hair. The power
had been cowed by gentleness, such gentleness . . .

Jane hoped he hadn't killed his wife. Suddenly
she wished she could remember the details of the
case. She had only been fourteen, and she hadn't
read the papers, just glanced at the headlines and
listened to Matilda and the parson fighting.

When she finally fell asleep she dreamed. But
not of the murder. She dreamed of his hands, big,
gentle, stroking Chad's hair. Except the hair
changed from brown to blond. And he was stroking her hair. His warm hand, throbbing with life,
slid to her neck, cupping it. And across her
shoulder, down her arm . . . The pleasure was
unbearable. She awoke stretching like a cat, sensually, languidly, a smile on her lips. Her breasts
felt full and aching, and her nipples were small
and hard, rubbing against the thin lawn of her
nightgown. Jane did not want to wake up. She
touched her breast, a small caress, held it, then
her hand drifted to her belly and paused. Her
gown was twisted up around her thighs, which
were spread open, sprawling lasciviously. She re-

called then, in a flash of clarity, that she had been dreaming of his touch, and she went pink. Yet it had been so real.

She would never dream that dream again!

Thank God he would never be able to read her mind!

Jane leapt from the bed and washed and dressed in a plain blue-striped dress. She wished now that she had brought her crinoline, but because she hated it and never wore it at the parsonage she hadn't. She wondered if he expected her to take her breakfast in the nursery as well. She was seventeen, not six. She would not—even if he thought her a child. Still, as she went downstairs she was soundless, purposefully, and outside the doors to the breakfast room she hesitated, momentarily unsure, even afraid to enter. The room was empty.

Relief was vast, but there was a tingling of disappointment too.

The sideboard was still graced with hot, covered serving dishes and platters. His place was empty, the plate gone but the setting still there, left in disarray. Jane could still feel his presence, or so she imagined. There was no setting for her. With determination, she went out and into the kitchen. A dozen servants stood about, gabbing. Food being prepared for the earl's next meal lay about on what appeared to be a dirty countertop, the mutton unwrapped, not even on a plate. Jane was aghast. Dirty pots were piled in the sink. The floors were filthy, both dirty and stained. The walls, usually white and now gray, needed a washing as well.

"Mum, can I help you?"

It was Molly. Jane smiled. "Yes. Please set me a place at the table in the breakfast room. I will be taking"—she hesitated—"breakfast there from now on." She wanted to take all her meals with him, but decided she had better go inch by inch. "Molly, why is that counter like that?"

"Excuse me, mum?"

"Who is in charge here?" Jane asked.

"I am," said a chubby man in a chef's white uniform. He smiled back at her, thinking he had never seen such a sweet angel-like doll in his life. "I'm Frankel, ma'am."

"Frankel—" She searched for the words. "Would you please remove that mutton to the dogs and find his lordship something else for his dinner?" She smiled encouragingly. "Would you please have the counters cleaned before you do another thing?" She paused, to see if she had offended him. Her smile was quick, warm. "This kitchen needs a woman's touch!"

"That it does, miss!" Frankel agreed wholeheartedly. They beamed at each other.

"After you have fixed the earl's dinner, can you see that all the counters are washed down, the floor swept and mopped? And the pots and pans should be done immediately." There was more, so much more, but Jane knew she would have to stand there and supervise personally to see it done. "Do you need more staff?" she asked innocently, knowing that he did not.

"No, miss." Frankel began barking out orders, puffed with pleasure, the general with his army performing for the lady. It had never occurred to Jane that she would not be obeyed. She was used to winning people with her smile, beauty, and good nature.

But Molly hadn't moved. She was watching her nervously. Jane turned to her inquiringly. "Mum, did his lordship say it's all right?"

Jane fought the blush. "His lordship will not mind."

Molly gave her a glance filled with doubt.

In the breakfast room Jane waited for Molly to set her a place. That was when she saw him.

Through the tall, arched windows she watched him come galloping around the corner of the house. Galloping. Across the beautiful, perfectly tended lawns. Clumps of grass and dirt actually flew up and hit the windowpanes. His stallion was as black as the devil. He sat bareback. They appeared unnatural, like some ungodly creature, or something out of mythology, a Centaur, perhaps. The earl went galloping away, riding like a madman. In his wake he left an endless gash of mud and dirt.

"He is mad." Jane didn't realize she'd spoken aloud until she heard herself. "He'll kill himself!"

"Oh, no, mum, there's no one who can ride like he can."

Jane glanced sharply at Molly. There was no mistaking the pride in her tone and, now, the shining of her eyes. Why, Jane thought, startled, she's half in love with him! "But look what he's done to the lawn!"

Molly shrugged. "He don't care."

Jane thought of the mud she'd seen in the foyer yesterday and the dust in the parlor, the state of the kitchen. No, he didn't care. "Molly, how long have you worked for his lordship?"

"Just a few months, mum."

Jane was disappointed. "Are the stories true?"

Molly's face lit up. "About his wife?" she whispered.

Jane bit her lip. She shouldn't be gossiping with the servants, but . . . "Yes." She was whispering too.

"He could have killed her," Molly said. "He's so angry. And so strong."

"Yes, I think . . ." Jane stopped, looking at Molly. "How do you know he's strong?"

Molly actually blushed.

Jane was no fool. Molly was pretty and plump, the earl a handsome man. She felt the hot hurt balloon in her heart and told herself she was being a ninny. Many lords dallied with servants. It was not unusual. Why had she felt such a rush of tears? She turned away, to look back out the window. To her shock, she saw an army of gardeners, a dozen of them in their baggy knickers with shovels and spades—and they were patching the vast runnel he had made with pieces of sod right before her very eyes. Jane gasped.

"He never comes back this way," Molly explained. "He'll be gone until dinner. When he returns, it'll be as good as new."

It was unbelievable. "Where do they get the sod?"

"They buy it every week, keep tons of it out back. He does this every day."

The amusement faded. The man was insane, she decided, and it was incredibly arrogant of him to treat his home with such disdain.

"Thomas was here when it happened," Molly confided, low.

Jane whirled. "The butler?"

"Yes'm. You know, she died in the fire."

"No, I didn't know."

Molly nodded toward the south wing, just visible through the window, the walls black and crumbling, the windows gaping, jagged holes, like toothless open mouths. "They think he set the fire —to kill her?"

Molly nodded. "He almost killed her lover. You

know about that? Crippled him, he did. The
Earl—"

"Molly! That's enough. You have duties upstairs."

Both girls whirled, Molly curtsying, Jane flushing. Thomas stood, arms folded, watching as
Molly ran off. Jane managed a good morning, her
ears pink. Thomas replied politely, but his eyes
were all-seeing, his expression reproving.

7

By two in the afternoon Jane knew what she was doing. She was hanging about the downstairs foyer, waiting for him to appear, as if she were some smitten schoolgirl. She wasn't smitten, oh, no, not in the least. She was just . . . fascinated.

She had gleaned all sorts of information from Molly as the plump maid had done her chores upstairs. The earl took coffee, not tea, and eggs, steak, and potatoes, all fried, at six in the morning. He did not eat kippers or smoked salmon and he hated kidney pie. He read the papers while he ate, then rode his stallion out to oversee his vast acreage. Almost invariably destroying the lawns. He returned between two and two-thirty for dinner, then spent the afternoon in his library taking care of the business of the estate and his own private affairs. Supper was at eight. He often took whiskey, not brandy, before. Some evenings he retired and some he went out.

Molly had been a gold mine of gossip. Jane

learned that the earl was American, not English. His mother had been the old earl's daughter, and she had married a rancher in Texas. The earl had been raised there. He had come to England upon his majority to take over Dragmore and had dutifully married Patricia Weston. Patricia had been the duke's eldest son's only issue; her father had been killed in a hunting accident before the duke himself died of natural causes and old age. She was Jane's cousin although they had never met. Patricia was the last of the Westons; Chad would inherit the duke's title and estates. Patricia had been a blond, green-eyed beauty who could have had any peer in the land. Yet, Jane thought, she had chosen the Earl of Dragmore. Apparently it had been a love match.

Yet a year after Chad's birth Patricia had left her husband, running away with a lover. Molly told her that Patricia had been afraid of the earl, afraid he would kill her for her infidelity. He had chased them down and challenged her lover, the Earl of Boltham, to a duel. Boltham had been crippled—to this day he walked with a limp.

"After that he hated his wife," Molly told her eagerly. "*Hated her.* Locked her up. Wouldn't let her leave Dragmore. Hit her, he did. *Raped her.*"

"Molly!" Jane protested. "This is all gossip—and it's terrible of you to be saying such unkind things about his lordship!"

"It's true," Molly cried. "Believe me, mum, I *know* him. He's the kind who'll take what he wants, when he wants it—if you get my meanin'." Molly winked.

Jane did, indeed, understand. She refused to think of the earl with Molly, taking what he wanted when he wanted it, and she was not going

to even consider that he had raped his poor, per-
secuted wife.

Molly shrugged. "Anyway, he just got tired of
her one day an' set the fire an' she died."

"The courts found him innocent," Jane said.

"Wasn't enough evidence that it was murder,"
Molly replied. "But he wanted to kill her, he'd
said so plenty of times, plenty of folks heard him
say it. An' the judge said the fire was set. If he
didn't set it, who did?"

"Are you sure the courts found the fire to be
arson?"

Molly nodded. "Ask Thomas. He knows. If he'll
tell you."

"Then why did they acquit him?" Jane found
herself getting exasperated.

"He had an alibi." Molly grinned, dimpling. "He
was with a whore all night. She testified. A famous London madam. But everyone knows how
easy it is to pay those birds off, mum."

That he had, or might have, consorted with a
prostitute seemed to bother Jane as much as anything. She turned away, telling herself that she
had gotten what she deserved for gossiping with
the smitten maid. It was all just rumor, not even
secondhand.

Could he have killed his wife?

She did not believe it. She would not believe it.

It was two-fifteen and there was no sign of the
earl. Jane caught her reflection in a Venetian mirror in the hall. Her face was pink with a healthy
flush. Her blue eyes were bright, shining. But,
with dismay, she thought she still looked like a
schoolgirl in the high-necked, plain blue dress.
Maybe she should be wearing crinolines. The
braid definitely had to go. And then she saw his

reflection behind her in the glass. She whirled. She hadn't heard him approach.

He eyed her.

Jane bit her lip, her heart pounding furiously. She felt like a thief caught red-handed, which was ridiculous, for she hadn't been doing anything wrong. Their gazes locked.

He was damp with perspiration. It trickled on his brow. His black hair was wet. A drop ran from one very high cheekbone and down to his strong, hard jaw. The cords were visible on his neck, as strong as the rest of him, and slick, too, with sweat. She could smell him—man mingled with horse and leather and cut hay. Her fingers nervously smoothed her unwrinkled skirt.

His gaze followed her hands.

Jane took the opportunity to look at his chest. His shirt was, unbelievably, open almost to his navel. His chest was broad, the chest muscles thick, sprinkled with black hair. She could see a taut, copper nipple. His torso below was flat and crisscrossed with sinew. It moved as he breathed. His breeches, skin tight, clung to his hips and groin. His sex was heavy and prominent. Jane instantly yanked her gaze to the floor, burning. She remembered her dream, vividly, how she had imagined him touching her, how she had felt upon awakening. The burn, the yearning. She felt that way now. She couldn't breathe.

They had been standing staring at each other for only a few seconds, but it seemed like an eternity. Jane dared a glance at his face. His was rigid, as if he were controlling anger. Briefly, grimly his gaze scorched her. He nodded abruptly and strode past her, without a word.

Shock at his rudeness was replaced with hurt anger. He did not even notice her, could not even be civil, did not care to even say good day! She stared after him, blinking furiously at the tears that welled. Molly appeared at the end of the hallway, curtsying and giggling. He didn't stop. He disappeared into the dining room.

Shock rose again. Wasn't he going to wash and change before his meal?

Had Jane a proper wardrobe, she would change for every meal, including tea, into the appropriate costume. She would also change for riding or an outing in the carriage. This was the norm for all ladies and gentlemen. It was unbelievable that the earl would come in from the fields, dressed like a field hand, and dine that way.

He had also tracked dirt down the entire hallway.

It *was* unbelievable.

Then she recalled that he had been raised far from civilization, among savages, most likely, in the wilds of Texas. She couldn't stay angry. He just needed to learn the social graces. She imagined teaching him. And just as quickly shoved that disturbing thought away.

Her mind raced. What if she just appeared at the table and joined him? What could he do? Yell? Quell her with a freezing look? Order her away? He would do the last, she thought with dismay. Order her to the nursery, and the humiliation would be unbearable. But . . . if she didn't try she would never know.

Impulsive, Jane, an inner voice chastised. Do not be impulsive—look at the trouble it always gets you in.

She ignored her logical self. Lifting her skirt, she tiptoed down the hall. She paused near the open doors, listening, but he made no sound. Then Thomas asked him if he would like more

wine and he grunted some reply. Jane winced at
his manners. He needed a wife, she thought. A
wife would never let him be so uncouth.

And she imagined herself dining with him as
his wife.

In her fantasy, she was as gorgeous as her
mother, not petite and slender but lush and voluptuous and dressed in satin and jewels. And the
earl—he was dressed in a black evening suit with
tails, looking magnificently handsome, and he
was adoring her with his eyes, hanging onto every
word she spoke, every trill of laughter.

She peeped inside.

He sat alone at the head of the vast table, which
was long enough to seat thirty or forty guests. His
solitary presence in the large room was suddenly
significant and wrenching. Never had a man
seemed so alone. Jane had never been lonely in
her entire life until she had been forced to leave
London and go to the parsonage. The contrast
then had been gruesome, making her understand
loneliness better than anyone who had never experienced the warmth of love and family. Now
she watched the earl and felt tears rise—tears of
compassion for him. In that instant, she knew,
with some timeless, ageless instinct, that the earl
was more than alone, he was unbearably lonely.
She felt anguished.

He lifted his head, stopped his chewing, and
stared at her.

Jane felt a surging of hope, and she waited for
him to ask her to join him. She even smiled, tentatively.

He stared and said nothing.

Her courage failed. Jane turned and fled.

8

There was no way he could sleep.

It was late that night, and the Earl of Dragmore reigned alone in his library. One solitary lamp lighted the room from the corner of his desk. He stood in the shadows by the stone hearth, brooding, whiskey in hand. From outside, a hound howled, the sound aching with its loneliness.

Nick downed the whiskey abruptly.

He moved to refill his glass. He could not shake Jane's image from his mind. He was angry because of it. He did not want to be haunted by her angelic face and innocent eyes; he did not want to see that fragile smile as she hovered uncertainly in the doorway of the dining room, waiting, he knew, for him to invite her in. He hadn't, and now he felt like the lowest kind of heel. He had seen her face crumble before she turned and left. He had also seen her slender shoulders proudly squared.

And he had seen a lot more.

He had seen the way she looked at him in the hallway. Christ! He knew she had no idea of how she'd been looking at him—and where. Her perusal had been intent, mesmerized—and undeniably sensual. She had stared at his chest, his belly, his groin. With a sharp, indrawn breath, Nick reached down and tugged at his breeches to ease his discomfort.

Shit.

This was all he needed. To be the object of a schoolgirl's crush. She *was* a schoolgirl. She was seventeen. Only seventeen.

And old enough to be married.

"She's my goddamn ward," he cried aloud, frustration welling. His grip on the snifter in his hand tightened. It shattered. Cursing, he let the shards fall to the floor. He ignored the cuts, the burning of the whiskey. He poured himself another drink.

He would have to put an end to her going without a crinoline. He was too experienced; he easily could imagine her endless legs beneath her skirts when he saw her thus. Now he vividly imagined them, white, slender, impossibly long. And fantasizing made him recall her soft, graceful hands—sliding down her hip beneath his regard. Did she know what she was doing, touching herself like that, so sensuously? Did her skin flame beneath her own touch? Was she inviting him to touch her like that? Did she touch herself when she was alone—while thinking of him?

He was going to explode.

He drank more whiskey.

It eased his groin. He knew damn well she wasn't teasing him, had no idea of her effect on his libido, knew she didn't masturbate and fantasize about him. He debated fucking Molly, or any one of a dozen passable maids in his employ, but decided the self-inflicted torture was welcome—he deserved it for his depravity. He must find her a husband immediately—and get her the hell out of his house and his life.

By the time he had finished the glass of whiskey, he had an overwhelming urge to see his son. Just thinking of Chad, upstairs, asleep, well fed, well cared for, and loved, brought a rushing warmth to his insides, something the whiskey could never achieve. In case Chad awakened, Nick wrapped his hand in a linen handkerchief, so as not to scare him with the blood. He silently moved upstairs, ignored her closed bedroom door, quelled the thoughts that tried to rise, and entered his son's room.

Chad lay sleeping on his belly, his face turned toward the door, his breathing deep and even. Nick didn't want to awaken him, but the need to touch his son was uncontrollable. He dropped to his knees beside the boy's bed and gently let his hand slip into the child's hair. Chad stirred, sighed contentedly, but did not awaken.

Nick felt the anguish then.

He was here, where he did not belong, and he had no choice. But this, all of this, all of Dragmore and all of Clarendon, would one day be Chad's. This made his own life bearable. This made it worth it.

Yet the fantasy was incipient but tangible. He pictured Chad in dungarees and bare feet running in the Texas woods. He pictured him running with his cousins, his sister Storm's children. He pictured him sitting on his grandfather's knee, being regaled by tales of Apaches and Texas Rangers and grizzly bears, in the house where he had been raised. By the man who had raised him.

Raised him, loved him, lied to him.

Shit, Nick thought, caressing his son. The anguish was worse now. Well, regardless of what Derek and his mother had done (he just couldn't think, much less say, *my parents* anymore), one day Chad would have to go to Texas to visit. It was his heritage as much as Dragmore.

And just the thought of taking his son to Texas brought something hot and hard to his chest. Something choking. It had been so long since he'd been home. What would he say to Derek? Derek, to this day, did not know he knew the truth. Nick had seen him only once since he had found out, in late '65, right after the War Between the States, while he was on his way to England and his new life.

He didn't want to think about any of it. Not about the blood and stench, the death and dying, of the war. He didn't want to think about the day he'd left, ridden off to fight—which was also the day he'd learned the truth about his father. It was amazing. He'd just made love to his girlfriend, the daughter of a neighboring rancher, a kind of farewell. And then she told him. Told him his mother'd been abducted by a Comanchero who'd raped her. Told him how his father—not his real father, but Derek—had hunted the Comanchero—his real father—down and killed him. Miranda had been married to Derek for only a short time before the raid; she had been mourning her first husband. Her marriage to Derek had been in name only, hastily conducted a few weeks after her husband's death because of an oath made between the two men, who were blood brothers. Derek had sworn to take care of her. When she gave birth to Nick nine months after her abduction, there was no question that the father was the Comanchero.

Shocked, Nick asked her how she knew, but even in the midst of the trauma, he recognized the truth. Because the truth was in his appearance. He was different from them all. His father was a golden man like his own Nordic father; so were his brother and sister. His mother had sable hair and ivory skin. He, Nick, had blue-black hair and dark copper skin.

His girlfriend told him it was no secret.

So everyone in the territory knew the truth—except him.

Yet he thought of all the times he'd been alone with Derek, hunting, on the trail, riding cattle, in the fields. He thought of the warmth and camaraderie they'd shared. Derek had cared for him. That he didn't doubt, not now, when the trauma of the truth had receded, replaced with some degree of objectivity. But love him as a son? Impossible—because he wasn't his son, he would never be his son, he was the bastard of a raping, murdering half-breed Comanchero.

Nick looked at his son with fierce, fierce love. He did not believe in God. But if he had, he would have said thanks that his son would never go through what he had gone through. That Chad had been young enough when Patricia had run away not to even notice, and young enough to get over her death without a tear.

The earl got up and left, closing the door gently. In the hallway his eyes found her door of their own will. He stared at it. In his emotional state he didn't give a damn if he thought improper thoughts. She was in bed, asleep. Probably naked except for a thin nightgown. He imagined her breasts, small, too small, but perfect. He imagined her hair, thick and untamed and coming to her hips. He imagined her naked, her hair streaming down over her bare body, over her breasts, tangling between her legs. He walked downstairs.

And in his bed he lay on his stomach, hard and throbbing against the mattress. His chest was tight, his breathing heavy. What if he went to her door, opened it, watched her? What if she awakened, smiled sleepily? What if he went to her, and she was naked, her body white and pink, nipples small and tight, and he touched her, touched her breasts, firm and hard, touched her waist, slid his hand between her legs and touched her . . . He was moving his hips restlessly against the mattress. With a cry, he ground his thick erection into the bed, rhythmically, fiercely. He was alive and desperate, his rigid organ pulsating . . . Nick grabbed the headboard. He gasped as his seed erupted, warm and wet on his belly, again and again.

He lay very still. He'd nearly broken the headboard. Damn. Worse. He was truly depraved. He was fantasizing about a schoolgirl. About his ward. He was depraved.

He was just like his father, the Comanchero Chavez.

9

Jane was nervous.

She told herself that she was being foolish, acting like the child he thought she was, but that did not soothe her emotions. She hovered in the hallway between the kitchen and the dining room. He was coming; she had seen him riding across the field toward the stables. It was just past two.

She had overslept and missed him that morning and had taken her breakfast alone downstairs. She had no intention of doing so again. She had skipped lunch at noon in the nursery on purpose. In the dining room two places were set. Molly had been wide-eyed when Jane had ordered her to do so, but Thomas had hidden a smile. Now Jane hugged her arms to her body and waited. She never heard his footsteps—he was as soundless as a tomcat. But she heard the doors drifting shut. And then she heard him. "What the hell!"

Before Jane could move, he opened the door to

the back corridor where she stood. It was hard to say whom was more surprised when they came face to face, she or the earl. She tried not to appear cowed. She let her arms fall to her sides.

"Is Amelia here?" he asked.

Who was Amelia? "I do not know," Jane answered breathlessly.

His gaze pinned her, then slid, quickly, below her neck. He turned abruptly away with a muttered curse and wheeled back into the dining room. She heard his chair grating against the floor as he yanked it out. Swallowing, Jane entered as gracefully as possible. She sat down at the place on his right.

His eyes went wide. He recovered; they narrowed. He said nothing. He just stared.

Jane reached for the little silver bell. Her hand, damn it, shook. She rang it. He was still staring. His presence was overwhelming. Jane felt tiny—worse, like the child he thought her to be. She was starting to regret what she had done. And still he said nothing.

Thomas entered, followed by two servants with platters of food. He seemed to be hiding another smile upon his bland face. "Wine, my lady?"

Jane opened her mouth.

The earl's hand rudely covered her glass. Jane noted that it was clean—unlike the rest of his work-dampened body. "She is not my lady," he said distinctly.

Thomas was unperturbed, turning to the earl. "My lord?"

The earl gazed at Jane, hard. "Am I to understand," he said sarcastically, "that you seek the pleasure of my company?"

Jane blushed. For some awful reason, the cat had her tongue.

He laughed. He removed his hand and nodded at Thomas, who filled his glass with a rich French Bordeaux.

Jane peeped at him. He was being served a lamb stew and vegetables, and he was ignoring her—or he was actually oblivious to her presence. She could not believe she had succeeded in attaining her goal so easily. And then, as he started to eat, not waiting for her to be served, she felt indignation rise. She couldn't help it. She said, "My lord?"

He paused, fork raised, barely looking at her.

"Usually one waits for everyone to be served before starting one's meal."

A small, ugly smile started, and then he resumed eating. "This is your choice," he said. "Not mine."

She gasped.

With his fork, he pointed at her, still smiling. "But don't you dare to criticize me."

He ate savagely, not sparing her another glance. Jane wanted to cry. She understood, then, that he hated her. How had she not realized this before? And now, to sit at his table and be ignored after being so put-down. . . . This was worse than being ordered away. She numbly thanked the two servants who had served her and stuck her fork into a piece of lamb. She would not cry. He was the one at fault, not she. He was rude and insufferable. He was the boor. He even smelled. It was the height of boorishness.

"Shit," the earl said with a growl, throwing down his silverware. "If you start crying . . ." He stared at her grimly.

Jane blinked at him fiercely. She would not shed a single tear in front of this man, not ever.

He scowled and reached for the decanter of wine. He filled her glass, without looking at her.

Jane knew then, astonished, that she had just won some small kind of victory—that he was, in some brutish way, trying to atone for his earlier rudeness. It didn't matter that she did not want any wine, what mattered was what he had done. Her appetite returned. She began eating slowly. He wolfed his meal. The silence was complete, not companionable, the tension thick and awkward, but Jane was no longer completely dismayed. Yet she had learned her lesson, and she did not dare to attempt to converse with him. Other than peeping at him cautiously a few times, she concentrated on her food with determination.

The earl threw down his linen napkin and, hands braced on the table, started to lunge to his feet. Jane froze, her fork in midair. The earl froze too. The tension increased, as taut as a high wire between them. Then he sat back down, hard. He toyed with his wineglass, watching her.

Jane would have been devastated if he had been rude enough to leave her alone at the table to finish eating. She realized, keenly, that he was not trying to be rude; rather he had never learned etiquette or else had lived alone for so long he was sorely out of practice. So this seemed another small victory, and she smiled sweetly. "If you wish, you may leave."

"That's right." He leaned back lazily. "I can do any damn thing I wish."

She decided she had eaten enough, and she carefully placed her knife and fork side by side. He had left his utensils sprawled out, as if he were in the midst of dining. His gaze narrowed. "Your manners are so proper."

Jane looked at him. "My mother was a lady."

He had the grace not to respond, but she sensed he was skeptical of that statement. "Finished?"

She nodded. He bolted. With long, hard strides he left the room.

Jane collapsed in her chair, exhausted and trembling, not sure whether to be exultant or insulted. The earl was not just difficult, he was frightening. But . . . he wasn't hopeless.

The manor's foyer was vast. It was as large as half the parsonage. Jane surveyed it with satisfaction. The black-and-white marble floors gleamed. There was not a speck of dust on the tawny stone prayer table, and the ornate mirror above shone. The scrolled Tudor chairs and the rest of the furniture, mostly Regency, ringing the perimeter of the entryway glistened with polish and wax. She watched two servants cleaning the windows that were on the second-story level. They stood atop ladders, rubbing the panes industriously with soapy water.

The hounds were baying. Jane moved to the open drapes and saw a hired curricle come up the drive. The earl had a visitor. She smiled, for the timing was almost perfect. At least the foyer was clean the way it should be. She turned to alert Thomas, but he must have surmised the situation from the howling hounds, for he appeared to open the front door. "Madame." He bowed slightly.

A woman with vivid auburn hair, resplendent in emerald-green silk and black cording, swept in, parasol dangling from her hand. "Hullo, Thomas. Is the earl in the library?"

She was smiling. Jane had a bad feeling. The woman was gorgeous, big breasted, full hipped, with a tiny waist. She was near the earl's age. She did not wait for an answer, but started across the foyer. Then she stopped, seeing Jane.

Jane was instantly aware of the contrast between them. She felt like an ugly orphan next to this elegant, sophisticated woman. She regretted the braid she wore, the dirt on her nose, the dust on her hands, and her plain blue dress. Mostly she wished desperately that she was not seventeen and skinny. She had a terrible feeling.

"Hello," the woman said slowly, no longer smiling. Her glance swept Jane from head to toe. It was a calculating, critical perusal. "Are you a new maid?"

"I am Jane Barclay," Jane said coldly.

"How nice," the redhead murmured, and then she was gone, gliding down the corridor toward the library, her red heels clicking on the stone floors. Jane watched, with growing dismay, as she knocked once upon the door then let herself in without waiting for a response. She felt a strange urge to cry, but would not. Hopefully, desperately, she waited for the earl's anger to erupt. But it never did.

She looked at Thomas glumly. "W-who is t-that?"

He gave her a kind, commiserating look. *"That* is the Lady Amelia Harrowby. The widow Harrowby," he added significantly.

"Oh" was all Jane could manage, her chest choking her.

She blinked up at the servants, who were watching her strangely, and with compassion, it seemed. She forced a smile for their sakes. "Please finish the windows, and thank you very much." The last words broke.

Jane didn't go upstairs to her room. She slowly

walked down the corridor toward the library. The door was still open. She paused there, looking in.

Lady Harrowby sat on the earl's desk, while he sat behind it. She was leaning over, her breasts practically falling out of her bodice. Her face was close to his, and she was smiling, laughing actually. Jane really couldn't see the earl's face, but it looked like it was stony. Then the widow took a finger and traced it over his cheekbone, down to his jaw, and up to his mouth.

Jane must have made a sound, because Lady Harrowby jumped off of the desk and the earl leapt to his feet. His gaze found Jane's. She turned and ran, but not before she heard the redhead saying peevishly, "Who is that, darling?"

There was no reply.

10

The earl was not particularly pleased.

He sipped a whiskey in his study, feeling, in fact, profoundly agitated. Normally he did not care when Amelia chose to just pop in. She never stayed for more than a few days, as the country "bored" her. She knew he would tolerate no disturbances during his work day, and what she did to occupy herself then, he never knew and did not care to know. At night she amused him, sufficiently well, to say the least. Then she would return to her London town house on Warwick Way.

Today, however, the earl was disturbed. He had been planning on going to Newmarket tomorrow to look at those breeder bulls. Now he would have to postpone his trip. Because of Amelia's untimely arrival; it had nothing to do with Jane. And when the thought occurred to him that he could take Amelia with him, as they would have to stay overnight, he shoved it abruptly away. No, he would not go tomorrow, maybe next week. And this was the cause of his current agitation, nothing more. It certainly had nothing to do with the blue-eyed girl who had stood in the library doorway looking so devastated that afternoon. Or so Nick kept telling himself.

"Damn it!" he exploded.

It was for the best, he thought savagely. He was a man, with a man's needs. Amelia was his mistress, one of many, so what? Jane was a schoolgirl and his ward and the sooner she realized this, the better. The sooner she got over her little schoolgirl's crush, the better. Right, damn it?

"Right!" he roared.

"My, we are in a mood," Amelia said from the doorway.

He glanced at her.

She smiled and moved to him, undulating gently. She wore a low-cut, sleeveless crimson evening gown, the better to show off her magnificent breasts. For some reason, tonight she reminded Nick of a schooner, a top-heavy schooner crashing through the waves. He smiled slightly at the imagery.

"That's better, darling," Amelia purred. "Did you miss me?" She clung to his arm. Her bosom pressed there invitingly. The earl was, surprisingly, not in the least interested.

"Amelia, please, spare me the cute dialogue." He shook her free.

"Damn you," she hissed.

He turned to her, lifting a brow. "Too late, I fear I'm already on my way to hell. Or maybe," he mused, "I'm already there. Care for a shot?" He raised the decanter of whiskey.

"You are in a worse mood than usual," Amelia stated.

"True." He poured them both large snifters. "If

you don't like it," he said, handing her a glass, "leave."

She stared.

He stared back.

She put her drink aside and tried a smile, touching his arm. "I'll make you feel better, darling, I promise," she finally said.

He looked her in the eye. "I doubt it."

She could hide beneath the covers of her bed, or she could get up and get dressed and go downstairs for supper.

Jane was a fighter. It wasn't in her personality to weep and be morose. Besides, he was a man, he was her guardian, he was almost old enough to be her father, and so what if he had that floozy redhead as a mistress? Did she care? Of course she didn't!

But, Jane swore, she would not go downstairs dressed like some schoolgirl. Oh, no. She could be every bit as elegant as Lady Amelia Harrowby. She had a few of her mother's evening gowns, which she had never even considered throwing away. She would wear the bold purple, the most elegant, expensive one of the lot. And she would have Molly put her hair up. No more braids for her! And a bustle, she would have to find a bustle. And he would look at her and be stricken by her beauty and . . .

Jane smiled. She ran to the door, flung it open, and yelled for Molly.

When the earl saw that three places were set in the dining room, he actually smiled. Then, of course, remembering their meal together at noon, remembering his purposeful rudeness, he felt a tide of shame rising.

"Who is joining us?" Amelia cried in dismay.

"I am" came a sweet voice from behind them. They both turned. Amelia gasped, and for an instant, the earl's mouth hung open.

What in hell had she done?

Jane's hair was piled high on top of her head. She was so small and fragile and she had so much hair that the effect was unbalanced and ridiculous. She wore a vibrant purple gown, sleeveless and low-cut. The color was all wrong for her—she was too pale, she should be wearing pastels. And the gown and oversize bustle were meant for a woman built like Amelia. On Jane it didn't just reveal that she was slender, in fact, it made her look breastless and hipless when Nick knew damn well she was not.

Amelia started to giggle.

The earl shot her a look with imminent murder on his mind. Her smile vanished. Nick said, "This is the Duke of Clarendon's grandaughter, Jane. She is my ward."

That truly shut Amelia up. She stared, eyes narrowed now.

The earl turned to Jane. She was staring up at him with such a hopeful look that he had the urge to lift her in his arms, carry her away on a white horse, and be her knight in shining armor. Which was, of course, impossible. He was no knight in shining armor. He would not carry her away to a happy fairyland, he would ruin her and hurt her and toss her aside. After all, he was a depraved son of a bitch. Even his wife, whom he had once stupidly loved, had thought so.

The earl gestured for both women to precede him in. He saw Jane's fallen look. What had she been expecting? Him to tell her she looked beautiful while swooning at her feet? He started after them. Amelia paused so she could cling to him as they rounded the table. He saw Jane surreptitiously tugging up the bodice of her dress, which looked to be in imminent danger of falling to her waist. *I will have to get her some clothes,* he thought grimly.

Amelia whispered loudly, "You must do something about that poor child's wardobe, darling. Perhaps I can be of assistance."

The earl froze. Jane, of course, had heard. Calmly he said, "But I don't want her dressing like a whore."

Amelia gasped.

Jane had frozen, and she was white, tears threatening to spill down her cheeks.

Nick wished fervently that he was anywhere but there. He found himself taking Jane's arm, his grip firm but gentle. He seated her. He knew she was surprised at his sudden manners, but what wrenched at him was how damn fragile she appeared, how bravely she was fighting the tears. Her mouth trembled. He wanted to kiss her wildly.

Amelia was clearly furious. Nick didn't care. She was a bitch for what she had done. He refused to seat her, standing instead, impatiently waiting for her to take her seat or leave. She finally accepted defeat and sat. Nick signaled to Thomas, indicating he should pour Jane's wine first. He knew she was gazing at him gratefully, adoringly, so he ignored her.

Supper was a silent affair.

And Jane was kicking herself for coming.

She had known the dress was wrong the instant she had looked in the mirror, hadn't she? But Molly had encouraged her. Molly had watched, wide-eyed, awed by the expensiveness of the gar-

ment. Molly had told her she looked elegant.
What did a maid know? She didn't look elegant,
she looked like a clown, or a little girl playing
grown-up, which was worse.

His mistress had been laughing at her.

Jane had known, by the shock on the earl's
face, that she was a disaster. But for once he was
kind. He hadn't said a thing, he was treating her
like an adult, he had even cut Amelia to the quick.
But still, it was too late. Jane wanted to cry. She
was a skinny, hopeless thing, and she could not
compete with the lush beauty of his mistress. She
wanted to run to her room and hide. But she
would not.

She was not going to leave them alone together.
Not if she could help it.

She could not eat. She didn't even try. The wine
alleviated some of her misery. It started to soothe
the hurt. She found that she could not take her
eyes off of the earl's handsome profile. He was
magnificent. Looking at him thrilled her. And he
was kind. He had been kind tonight. He had been
kind to her.

Then, after the main course, Amelia broke the
silence and began flirting with the earl. It sickened Jane. It brought back the misery, and something more: jealousy. The earl did not respond.
His answers were monosyllabic, more grunts
than anything else. That did not stop Amelia, who
laughed and chattered gaily, as if he had not practically called her a whore to her face. She stroked
his hand, he removed it. She pushed her breast
against his shoulder. This time he did not move
away, but responded to whatever nonsense she
was asking him. Jane wished lightning would
strike her plumed headdress and sizzle every hair
off of her red head. Leaving her bald.

"Amelia," Nick finally said curtly, "I do not care about the goddamn Arlington's ball."

Amelia was silent.

He looked at Jane, to find her studying her full plate. He scowled. If Amelia was not there he would have cut her off from the red wine a long time ago, but he didn't want to treat her like a child in front of the other woman. Not after what she'd done. He hoped she wasn't drunk. She didn't seem drunk. And, thank God, she was no longer making calf's eyes at him.

"Shall we adjourn?" he asked, rising.

Amelia touched his hand with a laugh. "That's my line, darling."

He ignored her. He watched Jane stand and saw her sway slightly. She moved unsteadily away from the chair, bumped into the table. Amelia was watching too, wide-eyed and definitely gleeful. "Nick! She's—"

The earl clapped his hand over Amelia's mouth before she could utter another word. "Go to the drawing room, Amelia, and await me there," he said softly.

She stared at him.

He wondered if he should throw her out now, or if he should use her to alleviate some of his own physical distress and then throw her out. He took Jane's arm. "I'll see you to your room."

Jane gazed up at him with those big blue eyes, filled with infatuation. She smiled. It was beautiful and sweet and she was beautiful and sweet and Nick felt the terrible stabbing in his heart. "Awright," she said, slurring softly.

They started to walk and her hip bumped his. He pretended not to notice. They moved past Amelia, who was red with anger. Jane was very unsteady on her feet. In the doorway she tripped

on the Persian rug. The earl instantly did what his
instincts had been clamoring for him to do: he
swept her up into his arms. She weighed nothing.

She gazed at him.

He pounded up the steps. She was soft and
warm and she smelled fresh and sweet. She clung
to him. Her hair was spilling from its coif. He felt
it tickling the back of his hands, softer than silk.
Nick would not look at her. He didn't dare. Another glimpse of her lovestruck eyes and he
would be lost . . .

He was getting hot. His groin was aching, swelling. Just from the feel of her in his arms . . . he
was in serious trouble.

Not that he would ever touch her.

He nudged open her door with his shoe and
laid her atop the white, lacy covering of her bed.
As he did, his gaze fell to her face. Her eyes were
half closed, lidded with the sensuous look of a
woman about to be bedded. She was as aroused
from being in his arms as he was excited from
carrying her. He was stunned. Slowly her head
fell back to the pillows, her darkened gaze on
him, lips parted, wet and full. His hands were still
beneath her. It was reflexive—his glance roamed
down, and he froze. Her bodice had fallen, revealing her breasts.

He couldn't move. She was fuller than he'd
imagined, actually voluptuous for a petite girl,
each breast round and high and a perfect handful. Her nipples were the pink of a virgin. Pink
and pointed, tiny and tight. She moaned, her head
going back, offering him her lovely throat and
lovelier breasts.

He wanted to touch her. He didn't.

She turned her head to look at him, nostrils

flared, eyes hot and bright. She lifted a hand, imploring. "Please," she said throatily.

"Damn," the earl croaked, leaping up from the bed. He had to get away from her. Because if he didn't, he would touch her, kiss her, take her.

"Oh, God!" Jane cried, her hand flying to her forehead. "Don't move like that!" And then she leapt up herself, her face green now, sliding to the floor and staggering to the chamber pot. She began retching.

Desire fled, sympathy and concern welled. Nick found himself beside her, kneeling, supporting her. When she had finished vomiting all the wine, she started to weep.

"Are you in pain?" he asked anxiously. "Let me take you to the bed."

She shook her head, sobbing.

He thought she was finished, so very, very carefully, he lifted her and carried her to the bed. "Jane, don't cry," he ordered helplessly.

"Oh, God, how could I make such a fool of myself . . ." She rolled onto her stomach.

She kept crying. He wanted to touch her but was afraid to. Not because of desire, for he was now under control. Still, she was just a child, little different from Chad. He ignored the image of her young, ripe breasts that immediately taunted his mind. Shakily he reached out and tangled his hand in her hair. He gasped from the sheer pleasure of it.

"How quaint," Amelia said through gritted teeth from the doorway.

Nick withdrew his hand as if he'd been burned, standing.

"Are you blushing?" Amelia asked incredulously.

The earl knew he was. He spoke quietly to

Jane's back. "I'll send up Molly with water and some toast. It will be here on your bed table. You will probably be thirsty and hungry in a few hours."

There was no reply. She was asleep. The earl turned away, to his mistress, who was waiting.

11

♨♨♨

Jane felt miserable.

Somehow she had dragged herself out of bed and had managed to get dressed. It was just past noon. She was suffering from acute nausea and a headache and, worse, complete recollection of the night before. In the act of brushing her hair, tears welled in her eyes and she could not fight them. They spilled down her cheeks.

She had shown him just what a child she was.

The humiliation was unbearable.

The purple gown that Sandra had worn with such aplomb lay draped on the chintz chaise. Jane hated it. She wasn't her mother, didn't even look like her mother, would never be her mother. Her mother had been stunningly beautiful and perfectly curved. Her mother had had hundreds of men dying for her love. Her mother had been an actress . . . Jane was nobody.

She crumpled onto the chaise. She would never forget the look of malicious delight on Amelia's

face when she had seen Jane in her mother's
finery; worse, she would never forget the earl's
shock. And she had thrown up while in his arms!

When she had been determined to gain his attention, she had never meant to do it like that!

She could not, would not, face him.

Jane made her way to the nursery where Chad
and Governess Randall were having lunch. The
odor of baked cod turned her insides upside
down. The little boy leapt up to greet her with a
squeal of delight. Jane patted his shoulder. She
could not eat. She needed air.

Then she became aware of his presence.

Before Jane even turned to look at the doorway, she knew he was there, filling it with his con-
siderable magnetism. Dread and something else,
something nameless, swamped her. Her heart began thundering. Her face went red. Oh, no, why
now? She moaned silently.

"Papa!" Chad shrieked, lunch forgotten. He
raced to his father who swung him up and
around.

"How are you feeling?" the Earl of Dragmore
asked over his son's shoulder.

Jane stared at her hands, twisting them nervously. She prayed he would be as kind as he had
been last night—that he would just go away. She
lifted her gaze. "Not quite the thing."

"You're an unusual shade of chartreuse," the
earl said.

Jane's stomach roiled. She knew she looked
ghastly, but did he have to comment on it? Tears
threatened again. And she was not a crier. What
was wrong with her!

"Papa, yesterday you said you'd take me riding.
Are we going? Are we?"

"Yes," the earl said, his tone gentle. He stroked

Chad's head, almost unconsciously. "Finish your lunch, all of it. Even the peas. Then meet me in the library. All right?" He smiled at his son.

Jane's chest grew tight. The earl was incredibly handsome when he smiled like that, with such softness and warmth in his eyes. She felt her heart turning over, drumming. Lord—was she in love with him?

Was she in love with the man England had labeled the Lord of Darkness?

A man who had been tried for the murder of his wife?

"Come with me," the earl said to Jane, stroking Chad one last time. It was a command, his gaze expressionless and impenetrable now. Jane recovered from her monstrous thoughts. She had never been in love, did not know what it was like or how to determine if she was, indeed, afflicted with the phenomenon. She decided that, if she was in love, she would know it. Wouldn't she?

"Jane," the earl said from the doorway.

Jane did not want to go with him. She was sure he was going to berate her for her behavior the night before, and she had already berated herself enough. But when he used that tone he was not a man to be denied. Bravely, shoulders squared, mouth pursed, prepared to face any executioner, Jane followed the earl downstairs and into the library.

By the time they were there, Jane was feeling distinctly unwell again. Her head pounded mercilessly. She watched the earl pour coffee from a silver pot on his desk, then add whiskey to it. She started when he handed the foul concoction to her. "For me?" she squeaked.

The faintest of smiles touched the corners of his mouth. "It will help. Trust me."

She looked up at him and saw a soft light in his eyes. Immediately he turned away from her. Jane was sure she had imagined that look, but she hadn't imagined his words. *"Trust me."* The tone had been low, coaxing—enticing. She wanted to trust him, oh, she did. Her heart leapt at the thought.

She sipped the coffee and found, to her surprise, it was not bad. And when she had finished, she actually felt better.

"Trust me," he had said.

Jane realized that, despite it all, she did.

It was only her fourth day at Dragmore. Jane, feeling almost up to par after the earl's brew, was walking outdoors on the edge of the mansion's extensive lawns. She was already quite far from the manor. Stone-walled, rolling fields were on the other side of the grounds, marking its farthest boundaries. Sheep and their lambs dotted the hillside. It was a clear, cool day, the sky unusually blue and spotted with puffy cotton clouds. The air was fresh and invigorating. If Jane hadn't overindulged the night before and made such a fool of herself *and* if that redheaded floozy had not appeared, she would be in very high spirits, indeed.

But Amelia had appeared, and Jane had gotten drunk and made a fool of herself. If she fell in love with the earl, who was thirty-three, she had learned, and who did not even know she existed, she would suffer even more humiliation. She resolved not to join the earl and his mistress for supper, not tonight, not ever. Just like she would not fall in love with him. She had learned her lesson.

She was wearing the plaid dress she had arrived in, the one she particularly detested. The

hem was already muddy, for she had crossed the
gash in the lawn that the earl had made that
morning during his reckless gallop. Jane smiled.
The gardeners had been mending it industriously.
Each and every one of them had smiled at her
and said hello, all fifteen of them. Jane had
counted their astonishing number.

She lifted her skirt and climbed onto the stone
wall and settled herself down. A black-faced lamb
skittered away from her feet, to the safety of his
mother's side. Jane sighed and raised her face to
the sun. A red robin took wing from one of the
ancient oaks on her right. Jane admired it. She
then heard a harsh, heavy panting.

She tipped her head toward the sound, which
seemed to be emanating from the two huge oak
trees where the robin had been nesting, near the
wall. A strangled gasp sounded. Jane jumped to
her feet, concerned, and then she heard a woman's cries of ecstasy.

She backed away—but saw a flash of vivid magenta. She had assumed it was some farm work-
ers dallying. But the flash of magenta riveted her.
The fabric gleamed. No milkmaid wore magenta
silk. Curiosity might have killed the cat, but it had
never killed Jane. She had the worst, or best, suspicion, depending on how one looked at it. She
tiptoed toward the trees, trying to make as little
noise as possible.

Not that they would have noticed her if she'd
been a mad bull seeing red.

Lady Amelia Harrowby lay flat on her back, her
magenta skirts tossed to her waist, her plump
white thighs wrapped around the man's neck. He
was clearly a farmer, and he was pumping into
her. Jane had been raised in London. She knew
what the act entailed. But she had never seen it

performed before. She stared, mesmerized and fascinated.

Amelia's breasts were bared. She was thrashing and moaning, her hands on the man's shoulders, leaving red welts there. He was shirtless. Sweat slicked his broad, muscled back. He wore his pants, but they'd slid halfway down his narrow hips. His penis was big and red and slick as it plunged in and out of Amelia.

Jane couldn't move. A wet heat filled her, tightening her, swelling her. She imagined the earl—he would look something like the farmer, broad, muscular, big. Her breath stuck in her throat. Her heart raced. The farmer collapsed upon Amelia, who was screaming in pleasure. Jane realized with a start that they had finished, and she might be spied at any moment. But her feet were like lead. Taking a breath, trembling, she started to turn. She heard Amelia cry out in surprise.

Jane's gaze flew to the older woman and she saw her white, shocked face. A dozen thoughts raced through Jane's head, not least of which was: Did the earl know? What would he do if he knew? Somehow, Jane did not think he would be pleased to find out that his mistress was cuckolding him with one of his tenants. Jane did not smile. She was indignant, even outraged. Did the earl know what kind of tramp Amelia was? And how could she, Amelia, do this to the earl, when he was so lonely and in need of succor?

Amelia closed her eyes, gasping like a fish out of water.

Jane found that she was upset, even angry. The earl did not deserve this. And with her anger came newfound hope.

12

He hesitated before knocking twice upon her door.

"Molly? Come in," Jane said.

"It's not Molly," the Earl of Dragmore said, entering. Their gazes skittered, then locked.

She was the first to look away. He could not look away. Jane was sitting in front of her dressing table, brush in hand, her long, thick blond hair loose and flowing to her buttocks. The earl stared. It was a sight he'd imagined too often, and seeing her this way, in reality, made his chest quite tight. For a moment he forgot why he'd come.

Her gaze came back to his. "My lord?"

"Are you joining us, Jane?"

"No."

He was taken aback. He'd expected her to shy away from another supper with him and Amelia after last night's fiasco, but hadn't expected her blunt refusal. "Why don't you join us?" he said, his own tone flat. He didn't know why it was so important for him that she dine with them, but he was damned if she should hide up here in her room.

"I'm not hungry," she said, turning her gaze to the mirror. Still, their glances held in the looking glass. "I'm very tired."

She was impossibly beautiful like this, her face small and perfect, her lips sensually full, her cheeks tinged a healthy pink, the pale gold tresses floating over her shoulders and down her back. She did not seem quite the schoolgirl. Yet neither did she seem a woman full grown.

He felt the stirring, the incipient burning, of desire, deep in his groin.

"Join us," Nick said. It was a quiet command, yet it was a question too.

She looked at him directly, simply. "No, thank you."

Their gazes held. Hers was determined, his suspended. He recognized the extent of her will in this instance, and chose to bow to it. He nodded curtly, his gaze sweeping her one last time, then turned and strode out.

Amelia was waiting for him in the library.

He thought her face a touch too pale despite her cosmetics, and a touch worried. She smiled brightly at him, too brightly, and handed him a snifter of whiskey. "Hello, darling," she said. "I was just about to go looking for you."

He didn't respond, but moved to the open French doors and stared out at the twilight. He was aware of the slow, burning lust that was smoldering between his thighs. His reactions to Jane were getting worse. What the hell was he going to do?

Marry her off quickly, his inner voice said.

Or, take off to London, leaving her here.

Relief swept him. The second solution somehow pleased him. There was, he told himself, a lot
to do to arrange a marriage for her, and it
couldn't be rushed. He would go to London and
leave her here. A perfect idea.

"Darling?" Amelia came close. "What's wrong?
Is something the matter?"

He looked at her. She wore a stunning black
velvet gown, low cut and glittering with dia-
mantes. Her lips were touched with rouge, lightly,
as were her cheeks. She was a beautiful woman,
but he mentally compared her artifice with Jane's
natural, wholesome appeal. There was no comparison. "Nothing is wrong."

Amelia laughed. The sound was strained. The
earl looked at her sharply. She smiled quickly.
"Where is your little ward?"

"She is tired, upstairs."

"Yes, well, no wonder after—" The earl's look
stopped her in her tracks. "I happened across her
today, while I was taking a walk," Amelia said,
her eyes on his face. "Did she mention it?"

"No."

"Oh, well." Amelia turned away. Nick sensed
her relief. He wondered what she was hiding,
then dismissed the thought, for he did not really
care.

She came back to him, sliding her hand up his
white silk sleeve. "Darling." Her voice was
throaty. "I know what's ailing you."

He was annoyed. "Nothing ails me, Amelia."

Her hand tightened on his massive forearm.
"Never before have you turned me away from
your bed," she stated, low.

She was referring to last night. "I told you,"

Nick said, equally low. There was warning in his voice. "I was not in the mood."

Amelia did not drop her hand. Their gazes met, clashed. "You are always in the mood. You are a stud stallion. *I know you.*"

"Do you?" His tone was ironic. "Do not fool yourself," he said, a dangerous purring.

Amelia actually stamped her foot, flushed now. "You want her!"

The earl whirled. "What?"

"I see the way you look at her!" Amelia cried. "You want that skinny little blonde!"

His jaw clamped. His eyes blazed. "I do not."

She didn't just sense the danger, that she was pushing him too far, she felt it. Amelia's body was tight now, full, pulsing. "You want her," she hissed. "You wanted her last night. That's why you rejected me!"

"No."

"No?" She grabbed his arm and yanked his hand to her breast. "Prove it."

"Amelia," he warned.

"Prove it!"

He hauled her up against his body by her arms, hard. She did not whimper, but her breath escaped. "You want me to prove it?" he asked harshly, crushing her breast against the steel of his chest. He jammed his hard thigh between hers, and she gasped. "You accuse me of being depraved, Amelia, of lusting after a schoolgirl."

She saw the fury in his eyes. "I know what I saw."

"You saw nothing," he ground out, grabbing her hair, carefully coiffed, by her nape and wrenching her head back. She cried out. Her hair spilled free. He ground his mouth on hers brutally.

Amelia opened for him, and he thrust his tongue savagely inside her.

She clasped his powerful buttocks, pulling him closer, harder, against her. He was hard, but not like a rock, not like usual. She felt a searing frustration. He grabbed her breasts, lifting them from her bodice and taking one distended nipple between his teeth. It hurt—yet it also inflamed her.

She slid her hand from his buttocks to his thigh, then between them. She caressed the heavy sack hanging there. He did not make a sound, but she felt his response, the steel hardness thrusting against her hip. She ground her plump groin against him, then slid her hand around to the front of his breeches and began stroking the long, solid length of him. He bit her hard in response, and she gasped in both pleasure and pain.

She freed his thick, straining phallus expertly. She dropped to her knees, clasped his hips, and took the big, slick tip into her mouth. He still did not make a sound. Damn you, Nick Bragg, she thought. She had been with him enough to know she was losing the little power she had had over him.

Nick thrust past her lips. He despised Amelia and he felt it in every fiber of his being. He despised all women, he despised Patricia, who was dead. Maybe he would have killed her if she'd lived. The only woman he did not despise was Jane.

Jane. If this was Jane's hair in his hands he would come. The image was wrong, so very wrong, but it was so graphic and powerful, Jane taking him eagerly into her mouth, that a surge of desire more intense than any he'd experienced before swept him. Nick was on his knees, pushing Amelia onto her back. He did not, would not,

look at her. After flipping up her skirts, he slid
into her. She was wet and hot. He saw Jane as she
had been last night, languidly lying upon the bed,
breasts bared, head back, arching, offering her
pure, virginal breasts to him. He saw the lazy,
dark, languid light in her eyes. The sensuous invitation . . . The earl finished quickly.

He rolled away from Amelia, who lay panting
in satisfaction. He realized he did not just despise
his mistress—he despised himself.

13

"Whatever is going on in here? This racket is unbearable!" Amelia cried.

Jane didn't look at her. "Careful, John," she warned as he stood precariously upon a ladder in the yellow parlor taking down the heavy brocade drapes. Too late; the drapes fell, a goodly portion upon him, making him lose his balance. Fortunately, Thomas steadied the ladder just in time, preventing an accident. "Are you all right?" Jane cried anxiously.

"Yes'm," John said, grinning with embarrassment. He was just a year or two older than Jane.

"What *is* going on?" Amelia demanded from the doorway.

Jane sighed and turned to her. She gestured gracefully with one hand. "As you can see, we're cleaning."

Amelia's eyes narrowed.

All the rugs had been rolled up to be taken outside, swept, beaten, and aired. Likewise with the heavy, moldering drapes. Two maids had moved all of the furniture into the center of the room, the better to attack the gritty corners and cobwebs.

"John," Jane instructed, "ask Howard to help you remove all the furniture, except the piano, of course, into the drawing room so we can wax these floors."

"My, my," Amelia said. "We are the perfect housekeeper, aren't we?"

Jane turned. "I would not go around calling other people names, Amelia. They might call you something back."

Amelia had the sensitivity to flush. "There are names you could be called too," she shot. "I know all about you—Miss Barclay. You may be Weston's granddaughter, but he never publicly acknowledged you!"

Jane reddened, but lifted her chin. "My father did. And I am proud of who I am."

"Pride will not get you what you want," Amelia said, laughing. "Excuse me—it will not get you whom you want!"

The truth of that statement hurt. "But at least I have pride," Jane flashed back. "At least I don't stay with a man who practically accuses me of being a whore to my face!"

Amelia went white with fury. "At least," she hissed, "I make him happy when it counts! When the lights are out! You will never be woman enough for the earl!"

No matter how hard Amelia struck, nor how cruel she was, Jane could not threaten her with revealing what she'd seen. With innate dignity, she turned her back on the older woman. She realized then that the two maids, John, and Thomas were all frozen, having heard every word. She knew her cheeks were pink. Good Lord, did they all think that she coveted the earl? Nevertheless, she smiled at everyone and said cheerfully, "We will never get this room freshened if we all stand about gawking."

Immediately everyone returned to his task.

Amelia snorted.

"Annie, take everything off the mantel, if you please. It's as filthy as the rest of this room." Jane was aware, as Annie complied, that Amelia had stomped with all the grace of a cow out of the parlor. She realized her small hands were clenched into fists at her sides, and she relaxed them. That woman was a viper. How could he be so blind? Jane was trembling. How did Amelia know she cared about the earl? Would she tell him? Oh, Jane thought in despair, Amelia had no decency, she would tell him, laughing, and he would most likely be amused. *Amused.* If he should learn her feelings, as confused as they were, and be amused, Jane would die! And then she heard the front door closing, and Amelia's voice, no longer caustic, but sweeter than honey. "Hullo, darling. My, you look hot."

There was no reply.

Jane found herself at the door, peering down the corridor and into the foyer. The earl was striding toward her, Amelia hurrying alongside him. "Shall I tell Thomas you're ready for dinner, darling?" She cooed. "I've had him prepare a wonderful treat!"

Jane gritted her teeth, furious. She had supervised the day's menu—with the earl's foreign tastes specifically in mind.

He saw Jane; his stride slowed.

Jane found her chest unbearably tight. As on the day before, he wore tight, tight breeches—she

saw thick, powerful thighs and his heavy groin.
His shirt was half open and soaked through with
mist and sweat. His chest was slick. His hair was
damp and tousled. His eyes were bright before
their light was carefully extinguished. "Hello,
Jane," he said.

She smiled. Her eyes shone. "Good day, my
lord," she replied softly.

He didn't stop, but his gaze lingered, bringing
warmth to every fiber of Jane's being. Then he
was past. Amelia threw her a look of searing hatred. Jane didn't care, not in that moment. He had
spoken to her. He had been civil to her. Yesterday
he had been kind to her. He had been kind to her
the night before. And even though he had only
said hello, Jane had felt more, so much more.
And it wasn't a childish fantasy. Jane clasped her
hands to her breasts with a deep, deep breath. She
was taming the lion—she was gentling the Lord
of Darkness.

And then she saw the streak of mud he had
trailed through the house.

She sighed. Maybe he wasn't aware of what he
was doing. Maybe they didn't have mud in Texas.
Maybe he just didn't care. Either way . . . Jane
turned and started after the earl and Amelia. The
door to the library was open. Amelia was gushing
in delight over something. Jane froze. Amelia was
holding up a glittering necklace of gold and lapis.
Her expression was ecstatic.

"Thank you, darling, thank you!" she cried,
flinging herself at the earl.

Jane backed away. The earl was giving her
presents? Expensive jewelry? It shouldn't hurt,
but it did. It crushed her earlier joy. He was a
stupid, rutting boor of a man who couldn't see
past a pair of big breasts! And to think, to think

she had actually hoped to civilize him? To think
she had fancied herself falling in love with him!
To think she had thought he was coming around
and starting to care about her! She was a fool—as
big a fool as he! She could never compete with the
likes of Amelia!

Jane hurried down the hall and out the front
door. Bitter tears stung her eyes. The problem
was, it was too late.

She was already in love with him.

14

"What?"

"I am sorry," the earl of Dragmore said, without expression. "This is good-bye, Amelia. It's over."

Amelia stared, white-faced, the necklace dangling loosely from her hand.

"After dinner the coachman will take you to Lessing. There's a five o'clock train to London." He started to walk past her.

She grabbed his arm, her face ugly in its vicious fury. "You bastard!"

He stood very still. "I never said I wasn't a bastard," he said dryly. Little did she know she spoke the truth.

She slapped him across the face.

With the back of his hand, he rubbed his flesh, as if to remove her touch. "Now that you're calmer, please see to your things."

"You bastard!" she cried again, this time her voice breaking. "I love you!"

He raised a brow. "You don't love me," he said crudely. "You love this." He touched his groin briefly.

"That's not true! I do love you, I always have . . ."

"Spare me the theatrics." His voice cut like a knife. "It's over."

"It wasn't over last night!"

The earl looked at her. "Don't press me to say things I shouldn't have to say."

She shrank, then. "It's her. That little blonde. It's—"

"She is my ward," he said curtly. "I'm arranging a marriage for her. I am hungry. You may join me —but not to discuss this topic."

"Bastard." Amelia sobbed, and she ran out of the room.

The earl walked into the dining room and felt a twinge of pleasure at the sight of a third place set on the table—for Jane. "Thomas, I don't think Amelia will be joining us." He looked around, but Jane was not in sight. "Five minutes," he told his butler.

He bounded up the stairs. He felt renewed. Invigorated. Why? Because he'd recognized the fact that he despised his own mistress and had decided to get rid of her? Yes, that was it. Too bad he hadn't come to this conclusion a long time ago.

He remembered dinner with Jane the day before yesterday. He remembered her sweet smile when he'd poured her a glass of wine—after he'd been unspeakably rude to her. Her manners had been so perfect, so proper, while he had behaved, and looked like, a farmer. He recalled how her face had lit up like an angel's when he'd said hello to her just now in the hall. Something within him had lit up too.

He stripped off his shirt, throwing it on the floor. He strode into the water closet and began washing his torso, under his arms, his face. After toweling himself dry, he slid on a fresh, clean white shirt. Then he glanced down at his breeches, stained and dirty from his day's labors. With a sigh, he sat and yanked off his muddy boots. He donned another pair of pants, then he wiped off his boots, gave them a quick polish with his dirty shirt, and pulled them on. He hurried downstairs, his step lighter than it had been in a long time.

Jane had not appeared. Amelia's place had been removed. The earl paced a few minutes, aware of Thomas's curiosity, feeling ill at ease. He had never waited for anyone, not in four long years—he always dined alone. His face grew pink, high up on his cheekbones, giving him a sunburned look. "Thomas, where is Jane?"

"I saw her go outside, sir, and I don't think she's returned."

He realized she wasn't coming. And why should she? She probably expected Amelia to be present. She probably expected his own foul humor. The earl sat down, refusing to acknowledge his disappointment. He was used to dining alone. It made no difference to him.

Chad had his own Shetland pony, a fluffy black-and-white gelding that had been a gift on his fourth birthday. He was already a superb rider for his age. Like his father, he rode bareback with ease. It was a sight, the two of them. The earl on a lean, seventeen-hand hunter, his son on the fat, eight-hand pony. They were trotting through a cow pasture on their daily ride. Two wolfhounds ranged alongside them, sniffing at every tree and rock and gopher hole.

"Papa," Chad cried, "look at the log. Can I?"

A big old oak had rotted and fallen and lay sprawled in front of them. The earl studied the log; Chad pleaded with him. "Please, Papa, please? I can do it!"

The log was bigger than anything Chad had already jumped, but his son was ready for it. The boy rode as if glued to his mount, better bareback than with a saddle, his balance impeccable. "Wait here," the earl said, and he rode ahead.

The earl circled the log. When he had determined that the ground was safe, he came back, but not before breaking a branch off of the fallen tree. He handed it to his son. "Give him two swats, Chad."

Ponies had bad, variable tempers. This one was better than most, but the earl had no intention of taking any chances that the pony might decide to balk at the last minute and throw his son. Chad understood. He smacked the Shetland smartly on the shoulder once, to wake him up. His head came up, ears went back. Chad grinned, nudged him with his heels and smacked his flank. They set off at a canter.

"Keep him collected," the earl called, his chest tightening with pride. Chad rode beautifully, gathering up the pony beneath him, controlling the willful little beast, and then the two of them soared over the log as one.

Chad crowed with delight, stroking the Shetland and patting him enthusiastically. "Did you see? Did you see us?"

"Well done." The earl smiled. He rode round to his son. "Here, reward him." He handed his son a carrot and the boy leaned forward to feed the pony.

The earl's thoughts changed. Again. Where was she? He and Chad had left after tea. The earl of course did not drink tea, but for his son's sake, he observed the afternoon snack with the boy. Jane had not appeared. She had been gone for hours. Nick had to face his feelings, and he didn't like doing so. He was worried.

What if she had twisted her ankle and could not get back to the house?

What if she had been accosted by vagabonds?

He and Chad continued on. His son was quiet, having already told him all about his day. Every other sentence had been about Jane. Today she had shown him how to make a sling shot. They had been having a shooting contest, their target a row of bottles on a fence. He had won, he had said proudly. Tomorrow she was going to teach him how to talk through cans.

"Through cans?" The earl was dubious.

"Through cans," Chad confirmed.

It did something, hearing of his son together with Jane. It also made the earl think of how badly the boy needed a mother—not stern Governess Randall. Nick cut off his thoughts. One marriage—particularly his—was enough to last a lifetime.

They took a path through the woods on their way back to the stables. They rode in a companionable silence, their horses blowing softly. A late-afternoon sun had dissipated the day's heavy mist, and now it pierced brightly through the canopy of leaves overhead, glittering on the damp bark and foliage. The forest sparkled. Ahead of them a brook gurgled, followed by the sound of splashing and laughter.

"Someone's swimming in the creek, Papa," Chad alerted his father.

"Probably a couple of the tenants' boys," the earl responded, not caring. After he left Chad back at the house, he would have to search thoroughly for Jane. She could not just walk off and disappear for hours and hours without telling a soul where she was going.

They entered the glade that the brook crossed. The earl at first saw that he was right. A couple of boys stood knee deep in the water, fishing. He recognized Jimmy, the head groom's nephew, and his cousin, who was a few years older, maybe fifteen. And then he saw her.

He yanked his mount to an abrupt halt and stared.

Jane stood on the far side of the stream, in the shadows. Like the boys, she was in the water—but up to her thighs. Like the boys, she held a stick and line. Like the boys, she was soaking wet, from head to toe. That was where all similarity ended.

Her blouse and chemise were practically transparent. It molded her firm young breasts like a second skin. It left no doubts as to her gender, nor to her burgeoning womanhood. Her skirts molded her slim hips and her curved thighs and what was between them. She was practically naked.

"Jane!" Chad squealed. "Jane! Can I fish too? Papa—can I fish too?"

The earl was so stunned that he couldn't speak. Then the beginnings of hot, hot fury started its slow burn. He looked at Jimmy and his cousin, somehow, miraculously, controlling his rage.

Jimmy was only twelve, and the earl dismissed him. His cousin was another matter. The redhead stood near Jane, in the sunlight, not the shadows, and he was no boy. He was nearly full grown, tall and lanky, almost as tall as the earl. He had been saying something to Jane, grinning. She had been laughing. At Chad's voice, all conversation and activity ceased.

"Pop, let's go fishing!"

"No, Chad," the earl said unequivocally, and Chad fell silent. "Get out of the water, Jane."

Her smile faded. He saw her confusion. His heart was thrumming hard and fast. He watched her wade out. Her long, long legs became visible, the skirt clinging to every feminine inch as she climbed to shore. The redhead was staring too. Not with a little boy's interest. The earl saw him tug at his crotch.

"Shit," he said with an ominous growl.

Jane froze, just yards from him.

"This," the earl ground out, "is highly inappropriate."

She blinked.

He spurred his hunter to her, and before she could move, he reached down and hauled her up in front of him, as if she were no more than a sack of potatoes.

She wiggled. "Sir! I protest! You can't manhandle me—"

"No?" he said in her ear. Already he was aware of his mistake. Her perfect little behind was wedged between his thighs, not an auspicious place for it to be. Soon *he* would be tugging at his crotch. *"Sit still!"*

"I am not a child," she quavered. "To be treated like this!"

He clamped his arm around her waist, steadying her. "Then why," he muttered in her ear, "do you persist in acting like one?"

15

Jane was humiliated.

The earl had hauled her down from the horse with Thomas watching from the front steps, and then he'd hauled her inside and down the hall and into the library. He kicked the door closed behind them, and its reverberations boomed loudly through the manor.

The Earl of Dragmore was furious.

"I was only fishing." Jane gasped. The sound was strangled. He was actually red in the face.

"Fishing." He said the word as if she'd told him she'd been on her back, skirts up, the way Amelia had been. Jane skittered away from him as he took a step toward her, then his hands caught her, hauling her *again* to him, and turning her so her back was to his chest. He propelled her forward, and Jane found herself facing a huge mirror over a Louis XIV table. "What do you see?" he demanded.

Jane saw the earl's face above her, with its rigid angry lines. Their gazes met.

"Not me," he said through gritted teeth. He shook her once. "Look at yourself, Jane."

She obeyed, afraid not to.

Her face was white. Her eyes were wild-looking. Her hair was a wind-whipped mass, a third of it having escaped her braid. Then she noticed her blouse, and two pink spots bloomed on her cheeks.

Mostly she noticed her breasts.

They stood out like plump melons in the wet, clinging shirt. Her nipples were hard little points. She looked into the earl's reflection and saw that he had been remarking what she'd been remarking. His grip on her arms was so very tight. Her blush deepened. He released her and spun away.

"Have you no sense of propriety?" he grated.

She opened her mouth to reply—and shut it.

"Do you think you're twelve? Did you see the way that redhead was looking at you? Were you encouraging him? Another few minutes and he'd have had you flat on your back—your skirt to your ears!" the earl roared, grabbing her again.

"Propriety?" Jane gasped as he hauled her one more time up against him. Indignation rose full steam. "You berate me about propriety?"

"Did you hear me?" the earl cried, shaking her.

"Did you hear me!" she cried back. "Of course I wasn't encouraging him, we were only fishing!"

They glared. "Your behavior is in question here, not mine."

"But yours should be," Jane cried recklessly. "You're the one who tracks mud everywhere, you're the one who keeps a mistress publicly,

you're the one—" She stopped, knowing she had
gone too far.

The earl's hands shook. "What? Pray continue,
Jane." His voice was soft and dangerous.

"I'm sorry." She gasped, flushing.

"I'm the one who killed my wife?" It was a purr.

Jane started. "No! I mean, I wasn't even thinking that!"

"No? You would find fault with all of my behavior except the most critical?"

She bit her lip, desperately sorry for fighting
back and, apparently, hitting the earl where it
hurt.

He smiled, with no mirth, and released her. "As
an adult, I can damn well do what I want, when I
want, and frankly, my dear, I've long since ceased
to give a damn about propriety." His tone went
hard. "But you are another matter. Do you understand that, Jane?"

"That's not fair," she began.

"Don't you dare speak back to me."

"But you treat me like a child!"

"You are not a child, God damn it, didn't you
look in the mirror?" he shouted.

Jane blinked.

He paced away, pouring himself a stiff drink.
Jane felt a surging of excitement. "No, I am not a
child," she said softly to his back. "I am seventeen, and a woman."

He made a sound, not a polite one. "You are not
quite a woman—just close enough!"

Joy vanished. "I am not a child! When will you
realize that!"

"When you stop acting like one," he said cruelly.

She felt the heat of tears. Jane folded her arms,
upset, hurt. Then she saw where his gaze was,

upon her breasts again. He turned away quickly. But not quickly enough. Jane stood very still, thinking. He says one thing, she thought, but does another. He has noticed that I am not a child. Maybe he does not know how to be anything other than insulting. He is aware that I am a woman. He was looking at me. He was looking at me the way that silly redhead was looking at me.

She trembled. *He knows—he just won't admit it.*

He turned to her. "I want you to understand. As a young woman"—he stressed the adjective—"you cannot roam around the woods unescorted. There are unemployed riffraff everywhere these days. It is not safe."

She nodded, her eyes glued to his face. *He has finally seen that I am not a child!*

"And as for this afternoon, Jimmy's cousin may be younger than you but he is nearly a man, bigger than you, and nothing more than a farmer. When faced with temptation such as you offered, his needs will be more enthusiastic than his common sense. Do you understand?"

"Yes." She understood—she understood that now she had a chance.

He breathed a sigh of relief. He kept his regard carefully trained above her collar. "Supper is at eight."

Jane started. He was expecting her to dine with him. This was a far cry from his attitude when she had first arrived. Everything was a far cry from her arrival a few days past. She hid a smile. Maybe he didn't just expect her presence at his table, maybe he actually wanted it. There was one problem, and gracelessly she blurted, "What about Amelia?"

"Amelia is gone."

Their glances met, hers wide and elated, his hooded and unreadable.

Jane nearly skipped from the room.

The earl made a dashing figure in black trousers and silver waistcoat. He had not bothered to don a jacket, but Jane admired him just the same. He paused in the midst of a mouthful to meet her bold stare. Jane smiled. "You look very handsome tonight."

He choked.

Alarmed, Jane jumped up and began pounding his back. Outside, the hounds were baying. The earl reached for his water glass, Jane kept hitting him. The water spilled over his wrist. "Ooh!" Jane cried, ceasing to pound him. But her hand lingered upon his back, and she was standing so close to him her dress touched his left thigh. That was how the Earl of Raversford found them.

"Hullo, Shelton," he said cheerfully, walking in unannounced. He froze, taking in the scenario. "Well, what have we here?" He grinned.

Jane realized the impropriety of the moment and returned to her chair, her cheeks burning. The dark blond was regarding her openly, his handsome face admiring. "Aren't you going to introduce me, Shelton?" He grinned again.

The earl rose. "Damn it, Lindley, I forgot you were coming."

"I can see why." Jonathon Lindley's brown eyes were dancing. "I'd forget my own last name if I had her."

Annoyance flickered on the earl's face. "This is my ward. The Duke of Clarendon's granddaughter."

Jane stood to curtsy.

"I didn't know old Weston had any heirs other

than Chad," Lindley exclaimed. The earl made no comment. "Hullo." He took Jane's hand, bowing over it and kissing it. His mouth wasn't supposed to touch her skin—but it did.

She yanked her hand back as if it'd been burned.

Lindley smiled, but the earl's face grew tight. "Cut it out, Lindley," he warned. "She's seventeen."

"And private property?" Lindley turned to see the earl's black expression. He held up a hand. "Just kidding," he said somberly. His eyes were quizzical.

"You did not see what you think you saw," Nick explained stiffly. "I was—er—choking."

Lindley raised a brow.

"I was pounding his back," Jane admitted.

"Of course," Lindley said. He seemed to doubt them.

Thomas was setting another place. Lindley grinned affably at the earl. "Does this mean you have also forgotten the race this weekend?"

Nick scowled. He hadn't forgotten that he had intended to race his stallion No Regrets this Sunday. He had just put off the decision he was now making. "No. Damn it, Lindley, I meant to send you a message. Somehow it escaped me. I can't get away this weekend."

Lindley chuckled. "Of course not. I wouldn't budge either, if I were you."

"What in hell does that mean!"

"Easy, old man, don't take offense. Why don't we sit? Something smells awfully good." He smiled at Jane. "It seems I'm in the nick of time." His smile widened as he glanced at the earl.

Nick caught his meaning and shot his friend a warning look, which did not seem to affect Lind-

ley at all. After they were all seated and Lindley
served, the handsome peer turned to Jane. "So tell
me," he said amiably. "However did you arrive
here?"

The earl leaned back on the big, maroon sofa in
the drawing room, legs sprawled indolently in
front of him. He looked from Jane to his best and
only friend, Lindley.

Jane sat at the piano, playing beautifully, singing with the voice of an angel. It had been Lindley's suggestion, damn him. He was staring at her,
admiration in his eyes and on his face. It was obvious he found her very attractive. Damn him.

Nick had never been unhappy to see Lindley
before.

He looked at Jane. She was a vision. He looked
at Lindley. Lindley was a notorious rake. He had
dozens of mistresses. He admired all women of
passable charm. He was a born flirt. The earl had
seen him admiring many women the way he was
admiring Jane. She was too young for his attentions. He didn't like it, not one goddamn bit.

But he lost interest in Lindley. Jane was mes-
merizing him. He could not take his gaze from
her. She was so graceful, more graceful than any
seventeen-year-old—or any woman—had a right
to be. He thought of her today, in the stream. He
remembered the sight of her in her clinging
clothes, remembered how she'd felt in his arms
on his hunter. He remembered how she'd flirted
with him in the dining room.

He wanted her.

Physically. Now. He was stiff and erect. He did
not want Lindley to notice. He toyed with a small
pillow. Lindley was too enraptured to even notice
Nick's strange behavior. Pillows, indeed.

When Jane had finished, Lindley applauded enthusiastically. Jane smiled briefly at him, then turned to look at the earl. Their gazes met, held. "Very nice," he said thickly, ignoring the way Lindley was watching them. He lunged to his feet and left the room.

Nick poured himself a finger of whiskey in the library and listened to the hum of their voices. Jane's soft and sweet, Lindley's bold and flirtatious. Lindley then appeared, and Nick automatically poured him a brandy. Handing it to him, he said, "Don't flirt with her. She's only a child."

"A child? Come on, old man, you don't believe that, not for a minute. You can't fool me."

"She's seventeen."

"Seventeen and ripe for the plucking."

The earl stared.

"I'm joking. What's wrong with you?"

"You'd better be."

"You can't deny that she's very beautiful."

"No, I can't," the earl said. A silence followed.

Jane poked her head inside, cheeks pink enough to show she'd heard some, or all, of their conversation. "Excuse me, I'm off to bed."

The earl nodded, his gaze on her. Lindley kissed her hand. "Good night, Jane. Will we ride tomorrow? At eleven?"

"I hope so," she said, smiling. But she looked at Nick. "I think I need permission."

Nick hated the thought of them riding together, but Lindley was his best friend and, despite what he'd said, he trusted him. "You have it." He drained his glass.

"Thank you," Jane said, and with another good night, she left.

"You are testy," Lindley said. "Does this mean I'm intruding?"

"You are *not* intruding."

"No? Good. You know, I thought Amelia would be here. I saw her in London Monday last, at the Crystal Palace. She led me to believe she was coming this way."

"We're finished," the earl said.

Lindley was surprised. Then he laughed softly, looking at the door, where Jane had left. "Are you smitten, old man?"

"Of course not. She's seventeen!"

"Seventeen and imminently marriageable."

"Exactly," the earl said. "And I intend to marry her off immediately. Do you have any suggestions?"

16

The earl pulled out his watch and looked at it for the sixth time.

He was sitting astride his big bay gelding in one of the south fields, where a gang of laborers was mowing hay. It was half-past eleven.

He rode up to the gang's foreman and told him to give the men a fifteen-minute break. The day was unusually hot, with no clouds or drizzle. After voicing his approval for work well done, he turned his bay away. He decided to go to the north field to check the state of the stone wall begun earlier that week. He would ignore the fact that the stone wall was progressing just fine—he had seen it yesterday. He also ignored the fact that he would have to ride from one end of Dragmore to the other—in all likelihood passing Lindley and Jane on their morning ride.

"Are you smitten?" Lindley had asked.

Am I? he asked himself.

The question was disturbing. The earl had to

shove it from his mind. His responsibility was to
find Jane a husband. Every passing day made him
more aware of this, and how urgent it was. He
knew he could not leave her here while he went
to London alone, as he had thought to do. No, he
must get her married, the sooner the better. And
this meant he must take her to London.

The earl hated London. Truthfully, he wasn't
fond of cities in general, for he was a man of the
outdoors, a man who preferred physical labor to
sitting behind a desk. But he was a strong man, a
man of honor and duty. He had never shirked his
duty before, he would not now. Most of the nobil-
ity had left London for their country estates, but
in a month, in September, London would be a
whirlwind of parties, balls, masks, and fêtes as
the Season began. They would have to arrive before then. In order to launch Jane, the earl would
have to costume her properly. He would also have
to figure out a way to reinstate himself in Society.

And he would not feel dread.

Nick had never been comfortable among the
realm's peers. Not even as a boy, when he had
come to visit his grandfather three times and become acquainted with Dragmore and the life he
would one day assume. Even then, at twelve,
fourteen, and sixteen, he had felt dreadfully out
of place, as awkward as a gangling Great Dane
puppy in a china shop. The old earl had gently
corrected his manners and deportment, but Nick
had not been interested in learning. Even as a
boy, he had no use for such airs—they seemed
silly and a waste of time. He had been enthralled
with Dragmore, however. It was a ranch just as
his parents' home was a ranch, only here the cattle were tame, not wild Texas longhorns.

Outdoors, riding across the 25,000-acre estate,

inspecting the fields under cultivation, the herds of cattle, the dairy barns, the lambing pens, the blooded Thoroughbreds, here the earl was at home.

In a drawing room he was as likely to crush a china teacup merely by lifting it in his large hand or, worse, stumble when he tried to make a proper bow. Nick had long since foregone bows. He merely nodded his head.

As a boy he had suffered the usual teasing and taunting from the sons of the peers whom his grandfather introduced to him. They called him a barbarian to his face. When Nick efficiently dispatched one such name-caller by wielding a nine-inch knife, apparently from nowhere, to the youth's throat, his grandfather confiscated the weapon and told him he must never carry one again. Nick had never gone without a blade before. He had purchased another, but learned its usage must be discreet. To this day, the earl carried a blade in his boot, strapped to his calf.

And so the boys had only called him names when his back was turned.

Patricia had had no such compunctions.

It was an arranged marriage. Nick had stayed with the Union army until the winter of '65. He made one brief, last stop home, which was completely unsatisfying. There was a wall between him and his father now, due to his knowledge of his own tainted origins and his anger that Derek had lied. Yet Derek, always so open, had not mentioned the change in Nick's attitude. Nick knew both his parents thought that the long war had changed him.

He arrived in England the following spring, and one year later married the Clarendon heiress. Nick had been smitten at first sight. Patricia had rich, dark-gold hair, almond-shaped green eyes, and a voluptuous figure a man would kill to possess. She was a stunning beauty—and she knew it.

They spent very little time together before their marriage. He was disappointed with her coolness toward him, but assumed she was merely acting "proper," as the English were wont to do. He was afraid to kiss her—he who had been kissing women since he'd been fourteen. Yet he did, upon two occasions before their marriage. The first time she had let him, giving nothing back, her lips as cool and smooth as marble. The second time she had expressed her displeasure, reminding him that she was a lady and they were not married yet. She had said it so imperiously that Nick's ears had burned from the set-down. He didn't touch her again until after the wedding.

There were no fires to tap, at least, not for him. Patricia submitted to him passively. It was a stunning disappointment.

Nick was not just virile, he liked sex. It was probably partly due to how he was raised. His parents were very open about their love for one another, and his father was very open about his love for his wife—and how much he liked having sex with her. Derek's hands were constantly on Miranda, sometimes teasing, sometimes not. If he could, he'd drag her off to their bedroom or behind a haystack in broad daylight. The children, Nick, Rathe, and Storm, had heard Miranda cry on more than one occasion: "Derek! The children!"

Nick had foolishly thought that he and Patricia would have such a marriage.

When Patricia became pregnant, the truth came out. She denied Nick access to her bed, bluntly telling him she hated his touch. She even

shuddered as she spoke. Nick was deeply hurt—
but he refused to feel it. Without betraying his
feelings, his face a mask, he had turned on his
heel and left her, vowing never to touch her
again.

But after Chad's birth he had broken his vows.
He loved her. He wanted her. She was his wife
and it was her duty to obey him. He came to her,
she submitted. He tried to break down the wall
between them afterward, by talking to her. She
only wanted him to leave her bed and her room
so she could sleep.

He had been stupid in revealing the truth to
her. One day, half drunk and aching for just a
touch, or even a kind word, missing Texas, his
parents, God damn it, missing his father—who
wasn't his father—missing their closeness, he'd
gone to Patricia. She didn't deny him, but as always, making love to her was as exciting as fucking a board. After, looking at the ceiling, eyes
closed, feeling about to burst with despair, he
started to tell her the story of Chavez. He only got
as far as explaining he was one-quarter Indian.
Patricia was repulsed.

She began weeping hysterically, accusing him
of being a liar and a cheat. She wept over Chad,
whom she had shown little interest in, moaning
that she had given birth to a "breed." She had
tried to attack Nick with her hands clawed like
talons, hatred in her eyes. Nick had restrained
her physically, then left. Because of her horror
and shame, she told no one of his heritage.

Eight months later she ran away with her lover,
the Earl of Boltham.

If Nick had any feelings left for her, they died
when she abandoned him and his son.

But she was his wife. She was, more important,

Chad's mother. He went after them. He found them easily enough, at a tavern in Dover, about to flee to France. Boltham he challenged to a duel. Although handsome, the man was so inept Nick could not kill him. He only shot off his kneecap and crippled him for life. "A reminder," he told Boltham, "never touch what belongs to me."

Patricia he dragged back to Dragmore, ignoring her hate-filled glances and her sullen refusal even to speak with him. She would not appear with him in Society, fine. He hated Society. They would stay at Dragmore. He would never touch her again, he promised. All he demanded from her was that she be a good mother to Chad. Patricia refused.

She hated their son as she hated him.

If Nick hadn't hated her before, he hated her now.

But he did not kill her. Nor was he sorry she was dead.

She refused to leave her rooms. Nick did not care. Six months later there was the fire in the south wing. It was completely destroyed, except for the walls and the tower. Patricia's body was found, charred beyond recognition. All the staff had been asleep in their own quarters near the stables, alerted to the inferno only when it was too late. Her screams would haunt them a lifetime. Nick had not been home that night.

The earl's relationship with his wife was no secret. That she had left him, that he had crippled Boltham, that he had forced her to return to Dragmore, their savage fights, were all common gossip. Yet Nick never expected the local sheriff to arrest him for murder.

The trial rocked England to its very bones.

The small county courthouse was packed every

day, like a circus. All of London's finest came to
see the most shocking trial of the century of one
of their own peers. There were witnesses every
day for the prosecution. All of the Earl's "strange"
habits were brought forth—and it soon became
clear he was no Englishman, and never had been.

He drank immoderately. He smoked. He gam-
bled. He cursed openly. He was an avowed, unrepentant atheist. He was a profligate rake—and
had not been faithful to his wife.

Most of these charges were true, but in the face
of this character assassination, Nick did not try to
defend himself, not even on the question of his
fidelity—for he had been faithful to Patricia before she had left him. He sensed uncannily that
any defense would not matter. Society wanted to
believe what they were hearing; they wanted his
nonconforming blood.

His relations with his wife were aired publicly.
Servants testified that she had hated him from the
day of their wedding. That it had not been a marriage like any other. That he hated her, threatened her. That recently the countess had been
confined, or locked up, in her rooms. Witnesses
even said they'd heard he'd beaten her up. Of
course these leading statements were overruled,
but the damage was done.

He was violent. He had coldly, calculatingly
crippled the Earl of Boltham in the duel. He carried a knife, and used it with the dispatch of an
assassin. Even as a boy he had plied the knife in
violence against another young boy, who, now
grown, enthusiastically testified to that long-ago
day when they had been fourteen. That his wife
had been so appalled by him she had run away
from him was noted. The prosecution's observa-

tion that Patricia had run away in terror for her life was objected to by the defense and overruled.

In a society where morality, fidelity, temperance, and respectability were cherished, valued, and idealized, Nick was painted as a dark, drunken, womanizing, violent American brute. Yet in the end, there wasn't enough evidence to prove he had actually set the fire that had burned Patricia to death. More important, in the end, he paid a famous London madam whom he frequented quite regularly to testify that he had been with her all night. And he was acquitted of all charges.

He was acquitted of the charges, but not of his new title, for now they called him the Lord of Darkness.

It was an epithet that would haunt him the rest of his life.

17

ᏮᏮᏮ

He was tense and angry.

The earl was so tense and angry that he'd ridden his gelding back across the lawns at a gallop. Now he left the blowing bay drop-reined in front of the manor beside a bed of roses. He bounded up the stone steps. Where in hell were they?

The earl had traversed Dragmore from the south end to the north in the course of his day, and there had not been a sign of Lindley and Jane. He told himself his mood was not foul because of this, but, rather, because he was hot and sweaty and distinctly malodorous. Just where the hell had they been all morning?

In the corridor he bellowed, "Thomas!"

The butler was behind him, unruffled. "Yes, my lord?"

"Where is Lindley?"

"He is in the morning room with Miss Jane."

Nick felt something like daggers within him. He strode aggressively down the hall, then paused to regain calm. He heard her bell-like laughter, accompanied by Lindley's rich baritone. He stepped in. "How cozy," he commented. It was as close to a snarl as a human being could get.

They both froze, like two guilty culprits, which, clearly, they were. They were sitting on the same settee, very close together—Jane's skirts touched Lindley's leg. A book was spread across their communal lap, Lindley holding one end, Jane the other. Both heads had been bent close together. They had popped up at Nick's comment like a double-headed Jack-in-the-box.

Lindley grinned. "Hullo, Shelton. About time. We've worked up quite the appetite."

"Oh? Am I keeping you?" The earl's tone was cool. His gaze left Lindley. Jane was a pink-and-cream vision in a rose dress. Her cheeks were tinged with a healthy, outdoors blush, and her thick, pale hair was pulled back with one big velvet bow. Half of the tail spilled over her shoulder and down her right breast.

"Rough morning?" Lindley was sympathetic.

Nick didn't answer. He cut them with a look and strode to a silver butler's table, pouring himself—what the hell was it anyway? Lemonade? "What the hell is this?"

"Lemonade," Jane responded.

He shot her an ugly look.

"Look at this one," Lindley said, pointing. His hand moved to Jane's side of the book; his shoulder pressed hers.

"It's beautiful," Jane said.

They were looking at pictures, of what he didn't know or care. Could they possibly sit any closer? With disgust, he slammed his glass of untried lemonade down. Both heads popped up and swiveled toward him. Nick stepped closer and saw that they were admiring pressed butterflies, for God's sake. He turned and left.

He splashed his face with water and changed his shirt quickly, fuming. He did not bother with his breeches. Why should he? Lindley was impeccable—if she wanted a peacock to admire, she had him. If she wanted to smell spices and musk, she had him. He pounded back downstairs. He almost fell on his face in the hall, skidding to a stop and catching himself on the door jamb just in time—the floors were wet! "What is going on!" he exclaimed through gritted teeth.

Then he spotted the maid mopping the corridor. He righted himself to find Jane standing in the doorway, hands on her slender hips. "You are tracking mud and manure everywhere," she scolded.

He stared.

Behind Jane, Lindley muffled a laugh.

"So?" Nick challenged, bringing his gaze back to hers. She was, for some reason, angry.

"We are not in Texas. Maybe there is no mud in Texas. But you do have horses and cattle there, do you not?"

The earl felt himself start to blush.

"We have a guest," Jane said pointedly. "If he wanted to stroll in filth, he would go to the stables. This"—she gestured grandly, blue eyes flashing—"is not a stable."

He knew his face was burning.

Amazingly, she took his arm. Nick felt the contact to his very soul—hot and electric, he was jolted as if by lightning. But he did not have time to judge his own physical reaction. She led him into the parlor and to the window. "Look."

He looked at the lawn, specifically, he looked at the muddy runnel he had made with his horse.

He looked at Jane intently, searchingly. He did not look at Lindley. He was embarrassed. "Just what the hell do you care?" he asked, low, his gaze trained upon hers.

She did not flinch. "I care."

He flinched. Then, icily, he said, "It's my god-damn lawn and it's my goddamn house and if I want to track mud I will."

"Very well," Jane said. "That was spoken like a five-year-old."

His color heightened. Her gaze was blue fire. He jammed his hands in the pockets of his breeches and turned his back to her. He felt about five years old.

Lindley stood, clearing his throat. "How about some dinner? I think I smell roast beef."

Jane hadn't meant to berate the earl in front of Lindley. She had almost lost her temper when she had seen her sparkling floors tracked up, and then, when she had seen the lawn, well, that had been the final straw. The earl certainly knew bet-ter! Instinctively now she knew it was better to let the incident pass than to apologize. And, perhaps, the earl would start to think about what he was doing.

Jane dressed for supper with excitement. She wished desperately that she had an evening gown and jewelry, but she did not. (She would not dare wear another of her mother's gowns!) She wore her best dress, a dark rose, and let her hair fall free with a pearl-studded comb pulling back one side behind her ear. She pinched her cheeks and lips and studied herself in the mirror, eyes danc-ing.

Jane was discovering her power over men.

Last night she hadn't meant to eavesdrop. But

she had. Lindley thought she was beautiful—and so did the earl.

The Earl of Dragmore had admitted she was beautiful.

Yet it now became clear that even though he thought so, he still did not see her as a woman equal of him. However, Lindley did.

Lindley had defended her to the earl. Lindley thought her a woman. Jane knew it from her eavesdropping, and more important, she knew it from the way he looked at her and the way he flirted with her.

She was learning that a soft, intent look, lowered lashes, a sweet smile, could bring a warm glowing light to a man's eyes. Lindley's admiration was obvious and direct. Jane was used to admiration. She had been adored her entire life until she had left London to go to the parsonage. Finding this kind of love again was food for a starving soul. She felt that she could walk upon clouds!

And . . .

If the earl did not quite see her a woman equal to him, she would show him that she was—by flirting back with Lindley.

Jane glided down stairs, flushed with anticipation. Both men were waiting for her in the library, Lindley clad in evening wear, the earl in black trousers, shirt, and waistcoat. Yet it was the earl who stole her breath, who made her body tighten and pulsate with sexual awareness. However, Jane merely smiled at him. She beamed at Lindley.

"You are breathtaking." Lindley gasped, clearly meaning it.

Jane murmured something appropriate as he

kissed her hand warmly. Behind her, she heard the earl coughing as he choked on his drink.

"May I escort you?" Lindley asked warmly.

"You can always escort me," Jane said daringly, her voice throaty. She did not look behind her, but was aware of the earl's burning regard. "Anytime, anywhere."

Lindley laughed, thrilled.

The earl came up behind them, his presence looming and hot. "He will escort you," he said, "only when I allow it."

Lindley chuckled. "Relax, old man. What—got a case of jealousy, have you? Can't help it if she knows which of us is the handsome one." Lindley winked at Jane.

Jane gazed at him as if smitten, ignoring the earl. She thought she heard him grinding his teeth.

The earl said not a word throughout supper. Lindley regaled Jane with stories of India and the Philippines. Jane regaled Lindley with stories of her mother and the stage. She laughed, he laughed. The earl glowered.

"I need a whiskey," the earl finally muttered, shoving up abruptly from his chair. They had finished raspberry tarts, but it was rude nonetheless, for Lindley and Jane were still seated contentedly. Nick paused, making a caustic gesture. "My lady? Shall we adjourn to the parlor?" His tone was a mimickry of their own cultivated ones.

Lindley rose and hurried to pull back Jane's chair. Jane thanked him prettily. The earl snorted and strode away. Jane touched her hand to Lindley's sleeve. "It's such a beautiful night," she said wistfully. "It's a shame to sit inside and smoke and drink. Wouldn't you rather stroll in the moonlight with me?"

Lindley grinned, glancing over his shoulder, but the earl was gone. "You are either very smart," he said, low, "or very naive."

Jane looked at him innocently. "I have no idea what you're referring to."

He laughed. "If this is a game, I'm game. And if not, I'm enjoying myself immensely." He held out his arm. Jane took it, smiling. They exited the dining room and paused in the doorway of the library. The earl's gaze widened, then went black.

"I'm taking Jane for a breath of air, old man," Lindley said. "Have a cigar for me."

Under a maple tree, they separated. Jane lifted her face to the night, wondering if the earl would come after them. If not, well, all was not lost. She did like Lindley. It was exhilarating to find that she could captivate him so completely. He was handsome. Would he try to kiss her?

Her heart began to race. If he kissed her, what would she do?

She had never really been kissed before. She found she was both curious and afraid.

"You are very beautiful, Jane," Lindley said quietly, watching her.

"And you are very handsome," Jane said, meaning it. "And very nice."

"Thank you." Lindley raised his head to the moon. "Don't judge him too harshly."

"I don't."

"He's had a tough time of it."

"I know."

"I think you do," Lindley said.

"Did he . . ." Jane paused.

"No." Lindley's voice rang out, harsh in the night. "He didn't kill her, damn it, and very little of the gossip is true. And what is true has been totally distorted."

Jane whirled. "That wasn't the question! I wanted to know . . . did he love her? Patricia?"

Lindley relaxed. "I think you'll have to ask him that one."

Jane came closer, to lean against the same tree. She studied Lindley as he gazed back. Then she smiled and sighed. "I never believed it, not once I'd met him."

Lindley laughed softly. "Most people would believe it *after* meeting him."

She grinned conspiratorially.

His smile faded. So did Jane's, and the night became very quiet. Her heart began to pick up its beat under Lindley's warm regard. Jane knew, suddenly, that he wanted to kiss her, that he liked her. She felt a touch of fear, and a touch of excitement too. Mostly she wished it was the earl standing with her in the moonlight.

"Jane," Lindley said, his tone taking on a rough edge. He didn't continue.

"What?" Her voice was high-pitched.

He almost smiled, then grimaced. "I wish you weren't Shelton's ward."

"Why?"

He looked at her, half smiled. "Because you're very beautiful, and—"

"And?" Her eyes glowed, holding his.

He made a sound, like a laugh. "I'm out of my mind," he muttered. "Let's go back."

"Wait." Without thinking, Jane touched Lindley, her palm to his flat abdomen. He tensed. Jane froze, then, awkwardly, hopefully, asked, "Do you really think I'm beautiful?"

"Yes."

Their gazes locked. Jane smiled, aware of the

feel of him beneath her hand. "Do you want to kiss me?" It was a question, said more out of curiosity than anything else.

He inhaled, then took her hand in his, removing it from his belly but not releasing it. "Do you want him to kill me?"

"I've never been kissed," Jane said simply. "Not by a man."

Lindley stared.

Jane didn't realize it, but she swayed closer, fractionally, face upturned.

Lindley groaned. His hold on her hand tightened, and then he bent and kissed her once, briefly, on her parted lips. It happened so fast it was over before it had begun. Jane was disappointed.

"That's enough, Jane," the earl said tersely from behind them.

18

"It's not what you think," Lindley said.

Jane could see the earl clearly in the moonlight, clearly enough to know that he was enraged. Reflexively she stepped back from him, suddenly afraid for what she had done.

"If you were not my friend," the earl said through tight lips, "I would kill you."

"Nick—"

"Shut up!" His voice was thunder. "You are no longer welcome at Dragmore. Pack your bags and get out!"

A silence fell.

Jane felt as if the world were disintegrating beneath her feet. Lindley was the earl's one and only friend! She could not let this happen! God, she was so sorry! "It wasn't his fault," she managed breathlessly. "It was mine."

He whirled. "You shut up as well." To Lindley: "Move."

"When you're calmer," Lindley said, "we can discuss this—"

The earl hit him. It was an explosive blow with the speed of lightning and the force of a locomotive. He snapped back Lindley's head, knocking him against the maple. Jane cried out. Lindley staggered upright, holding his nose. The earl stood with thighs spread, fists ready, his face black. Lindley pushed off of the tree and, with a look, left.

"Oh, God!"

At the sound of Jane's moan, Nick turned to her. "You little flirt," he grated, sick inside, so sick. His hands found her shoulders of their own volition and he hauled her close, very close, lifting her off the ground so they were face to face. She didn't whimper, but she was white.

He wanted to hurt her the way she had hurt him. He wasn't thinking, he was only feeling.

"You little flirt," he said again, shaking her once. "I thought you were different, but you're not, are you? You're like all the rest, aren't you?"

"No." Jane gasped. Their faces were so close. She could see his eyes, and they frightened her.

"A man's kiss," Nick cried. "You want a man's kiss?"

She frantically shook her head no.

He shook her, then, with one arm, he yanked her against his chest, his other hand grabbing a hank of hair next to the scalp and anchoring her head viciously. She whimpered. His mouth came down hard and brutal upon hers.

He was savage in his attack, not waiting for any sign from her that he should proceed. His teeth clashed against hers, he forced her mouth open, thrusting his tongue through her lips. He plunged relentlessly into her mouth, again and again.

He slowly became aware of many things, one after the other.

Jane was soft and warm and more exciting than any woman he'd ever held. Every inch of her body throbbed against his. His kiss had, somehow, a will of its own, and it had softened. She was kissing him back. In fact, her tongue was dancing with his, entwining with his, stroking the inside of his mouth the way he'd stroked hers. And . . . she was clinging to him. Her hands were caught in his hair desperately. And she was wiggling her plump, sweet mons against the steel length of his erection.

Nick's hand left her hair and stroked down her back to her waist, hips, and the delicious curve of one buttock. "Jane," he whispered, agony in his voice. He pulled her closer against him. In response, she groaned a deep strangled sound, and then she wrenched her head free and buried her face in his neck, lifted one knee and wrapped it around his hip, trying to climb on top of him, instinctively opening herself, poising herself for him.

He needed her, desperately.

He wanted her, with every fiber of his soul and being.

In horror, he saw them then. The depraved brute and the innocent schoolgirl. Jane was moaning and whimpering into his neck, clinging, and if she lifted her other knee she would be astride him . . .

With supreme willpower, Nick threw her to the ground.

She lay panting, face uplifted. "Nicholas," she begged.

He stood panting, staring down, more horrified than he had ever been in his life. More afraid.

"God, what am I doing?" he cried into the night.
And then he turned and ran.

Jane managed to get to her room. Her dress
was soiled, her hair a tangled mess. She fell gratefully onto the bed, her heart still beating frantically. She covered it with her palm, hoping to still
it. She was in love.

And it was as much pain as pleasure.

She would never forget his kiss and the fire he
had set within her. Never. "Nicholas, I love you,"
she whispered, and then she started to weep.

She loved him but he didn't love her. As naive
as she was, she knew that. He had kissed her in
anger. Only in anger, and then the kiss had taken
on a life of its own.

But hadn't he been jealous?

Jane wasn't sure. As far as the earl went, she
was utterly confused. He was a dark, complex
man. And like all men, he could make love to a
woman without loving her.

Jane didn't want to be another Amelia.

She wanted to be his wife.

Seriously, realistically, she considered this. Was
it possible? And she knew it wasn't. She did not
doubt that the earl had no intention of marrying.
She could sense it. And even if he fell in love and
did marry, why would it be her? There were more
beautiful women in the world, many of them, and
the earl was a big catch.

Could she settle, then, for crumbs?

Could she be his mistress?

Jane wasn't sure. She only knew that she loved
him so much it hurt. She only knew that she
wanted him, to hold him, comfort him, to make
him laugh. And she wanted to be in his arms
again . . .

Remembering their heated kiss roused her blood—and her despair. He had so few friends. Maybe Lindley was the only one. Look at what she had done. She had destroyed their friendship. She was so sorry. If she had known, if she hadn't been so damn impulsive, so damn reckless—as always—she would have never flirted so brazenly. Jane hugged her pillow. She would have to reconcile the two men somehow. Oh, God!

"Nicholas, forgive me," she whispered.

The earl froze in the center of his library, where he was standing. He heard the carriage wheels crunching on the graveled driveway. His head turned toward the windows, and in the gaslit night, he watched as Lindley's coach pulled away from the front of the house. He knew a moment's insanity, when he had the urge to run out and stop him. He did not. He felt the pain, and he rubbed his chest, as if he could physically erase it.

Oh, God.

He sat down heavily, head hanging. Lindley had betrayed him. It didn't matter that Jane had provoked him; Lindley was older, he knew better. He had betrayed him. His best friend, his only friend. The man who had stood by him through the damn trial and all the ostracism since. "Damn you," Nick cried into the silent library. "Damn you!"

He damned himself.

He thought of Jane.

Jane, who, before his very eyes, was awakening to her sexuality, and God, it was hot, potent—dangerous.

He clenched his fists. She had been smitten with him, until Lindley had arrived. Then she had become infatuated with Raversford. She was an impressionable adolescent. Nothing more. Who would it be tomorrow? It had better be, he thought savagely, the man he would marry her to!

He would have to keep an eye on her. He would have to chaperon her. He could not trust her, not after tonight. She had begged Lindley to kiss her. She was a flirt. An accomplished flirt! And then she had kissed Nick back passionately when he had been trying to hurt her!

She was fickle and faithless.

He thought of Patricia and laughed aloud.

Patricia had been fickle and faithless too, but that was where the resemblance between the two ended. Patricia had been a lady, with ice in her veins. Jane was no lady. The duke's granddaughter—*maybe*—the actress's daughter, for sure. It explained her untutored, wild passion, her deep, deep sensuality.

"Jane." He tested her name, tasted it on his tongue. He dropped his head back on the couch as if the weight of it were too much to bear. With his hand, he began rubbing his chest. But the pain would not go away. It wasn't physical.

19

London

Jane stared out of the window and down Tottenham Court Road. The thoroughfare was well lit by gas lamps and busy with hired hansoms, other coaches, and even omnibuses pulled by teams of matched bays. Plastered residential homes with wrought-iron fences and slate roofs lined the streets. There were a few strollers about, but no gentry. Jane really did not care.

She glanced at the earl.

He was formidable and impassive, sitting beside her but well away from her, careful not to make contact with her with his knee or hand. He stared out of his own window. She could see the hard, set line of his jaw. He had barely spoken to her all day, and it had been Thomas who informed her that they were leaving for London just that morning.

"Today?" Jane had gasped, unsure she had understood. She was very tired, having been unable to sleep all night, haunted both by the earl's devastating kiss and her body's unrestrained response to it and by the falling out with Lindley. "I cannot possibly be packed and ready by this afternoon!"

"The earl said don't bother bringing more than a few essentials. He will be providing you with a complete wardrobe in London."

"Is he out on the estate?"

"Not this morning. He is in the library," Thomas replied.

Bravely or, at least, with an outward show of bravery, for inside she was quaking, Jane went downstairs and knocked. He looked up, saw her, and returned to his paperwork. "I'm occupied," he said brusquely.

"I want to apologize."

He did not look up. "Your apology changes nothing."

"I did not mean for things to go so far."

He ignored her. But she saw that his fingers were white upon his pen. "Please," she added in a whisper.

The pen snapped in his fingers. "We leave at four."

Jane huddled deeper in her corner of the coach. He acted as if he hated her. Possibly he did. Her heart was breaking.

"We're here," the earl said sometime later. The carriage had turned into Tavistock Square. Jane knew the square housed some of the most expensive homes in London, and she gazed upon the earl as he opened the door. For him to live here meant he was quite wealthy indeed. He turned to her and stiffly extended a hand.

She accepted it, eyeing him desperately. He

looked away, giving orders to the coachman regarding their baggage.

His town house was a huge, four-storied brick affair surrounded by high wrought-iron gates and sweeping lawns. It occupied the entire block. A massive line of oaks effectively screened the grounds from the curiosity of outsiders. Jane clutched her reticule and followed him down the brick walk. She was feeling lonely and wished she had had the foresight to ask to bring Molly. In a grand, marble-floored foyer with high, vaulted ceilings, an elderly woman told Jane she would show her upstairs to her room. Jane looked around and saw that the earl had disappeared. Very well, then, she would follow his example. She wanted nothing more than to crawl under the covers and be miserable.

The next day Jane overslept, due to another restless night. She was surprised therefore to find the earl still in the breakfast room with the *Times.* He looked up. Jane's heart was fluttering. "Good morning." She tried a smile, and knew it was fragile.

He nodded abruptly and buried his nose in his paper. He said, "As soon as you eat we have an appointment with a couturier."

Jane sat down, trembling. "We." He had said "we." He was taking her to a seamstress? She knew it was silly, but to have his company thrilled her—even if he was still punishing her for what had happened with Lindley.

And the day was filled with sunshine.

"May we drive through Hyde Park?" Jane asked, smiling eagerly once they were in his carriage with the bold black-and-gold Dragmore crest.

He tapped on the ceiling. "James, through the park and then on to Bond Street."

Jane smiled at him. He glanced at her and did not look immediately away. She was sunshine and laughter, he thought, shifting uneasily, uncomfortably. How could he hate her?

You depraved bastard, he told himself. You have never hated her and that is the problem.

Jane felt it, the softening. She was determined to bring him completely around. To make up for what she had done, to make him happy. She knew she could do it. If only he would let her love him.

"Look! Aren't they beautiful?"

The earl looked, saw the two riders on magnificent Thoroughbreds, the lady a vision in purple silk sitting sidesaddle. They both rode beautifully as they cantered through the park. There were quite a few riders about as well as curricles, gigs, and even a few strollers. "The chic time to ride in Hyde Park is before tea."

"It seems like such fun," Jane said wistfully.

The earl glanced at her, saw her longing expression. She felt his regard and quickly smiled at him; he turned away. But he was thinking carefully. She was an actress's child, she had been raised in the theaters of London. What had her upbringing been like? Her manners and airs were beautiful, flawless. Yet it occurred to him that she had been deprived of most of the pastimes open to high Society, for she was not truly a part of it. He found he was disturbed by the empathy he felt for her.

The couturier was ready for them. Nick explained, first, that Jane was his ward and the granddaughter of the deceased Lord Weston, Duke of Clarendon. She needed everything: riding habits in silk and velvet, satin tea gowns, evening gowns in velvet, brocade, and so forth. "And the smallest bustle, please," he said, knowing Jane would look ridiculous in an oversize one with her slender frame.

Not trusting Jane after the fiasco when she had appeared in the horrendous purple dress, Nick chose the fabrics for her—while she watched, wide-eyed. "This and this," he said, picking up delicate swaths of pale-blue and mint-green silk. "The silver for evening. These pinks, the rose." He squinted at Jane. "I think you can wear emerald and sapphire." He held up samples against her skin, trying to be immune to the worshipful look in her eyes. "Yes, these as well."

"How about the red?"

He looked at the flame-red dress and scowled. "Absolutely not. Maybe the wine. No red, no royal purples."

He left them then to hours of fittings. But her adoring gaze haunted him all through the day.

Jane was late for dinner due to the time it took for all the fittings. While she had been measured and pinned, the couturier's girls had altered several ready-to-wear pieces upon the earl's instructions. She dined alone on cold roast chicken and watercress salad. Her heart leapt when the earl appeared in breeches and boots. She smiled tremulously.

"Are you too tired to go for a ride in the park?" he asked flatly.

Jane almost fainted. "No."

"I'll be in the study."

Jane, no longer interested in food, raced upstairs to don a gray riding habit, hands shaking. She wondered if she should tell the earl she did not know how to ride, then decided against it. He would change their plans, and she would die rather than lose the opportunity to spend the afternoon with him.

Jane thought that her mount was an overly large thing. She studied the sidesaddle, then decided, What the hell? She was an actress, she understood the mechanics of riding, and everyone did it. How hard could it be?

Once in the saddle, her instincts asserted themselves and she held on for her dear life. The earl's voice, from behind her, made her realize what she was doing and how she must appear. She tried to relax and look casual. "He's a gentleman, don't worry," the earl said, his gaze sharp. "Are you afraid?"

Jane smiled brightly. "Of course not."

His features softened. "Let's go."

Taking a deep breath, Jane nudged her heels to the gray's sides and was surprised to find him ambling after the earl on his big bay hunter. Jane smiled. This was not so difficult. In fact, it was quite easy.

They rode down New Road at a sedate pace. The earl said nothing, and for once Jane did not mind. She was too busy accustoming herself to the feel of the horse's gait and learning how to use the reins to steer him. She knew she should pull on the right rein if she wanted to go right, but a brief experiment brought no results. Fortunately, her horse was following the earl. This was easier than trying to control him, so Jane settled for taking up the rear. Besides, that way she could openly stare at the earl, even if it was only at his broad back.

They entered Regents Park. Jane stared at a couple on horseback who were coming towards them. The woman wore a red velvet habit and an elaborate black hat with lace veiling. Her companion was impeccable in polished boots, breeches, and a hunter-green riding jacket. As they drew abreast, Jane craned her head to watch them, and realized that the two were doing the same to watch her and the earl. A moment later she realized that they were not interested in her. They were staring at the earl. He nodded politely. They instantly put their noses in the air and ignored him. Jane was appalled. She opened her mouth to say so, saw his fierce expression, and immediately closed it.

A curricle passed. Jane looked within and saw two men in suits and a woman in tweeds. Everyone looked at everyone, except for the earl, who regarded no one. The trio's undisguised curiosity gave way to elaborate shock. The woman gasped melodramatically, raised a gloved hand, and whispered loudly to her entourage. "It's him! The Lord of Darkness! You know, the one who—" The rest was indiscernible.

Jane's heart was pounding. She dared to peek at the earl. A vibrant shade of pink had stained his dark features, giving him the appearance of being sunburned. "I hate them," Jane cried aloud before she could think.

"Let's have a canter," the earl replied tonelessly, nudging his steed into a lope.

Before Jane could say "wait" or even consider how to approach this new predicament, her own nag was following suit. Jane, thankfully, did not scream. Instead, she hung on to the saddle for her dear life.

She forgot about the reins, and they fell from her hands to flap loosely against the gelding's neck. Her mount immediately became agitated, his gait increasing. The earl heard it and looked back—just in time to see a white-faced Jane slipping from the saddle in slow, slow motion.

"Damn it!" he cried, wheeling his hunter around roughly and then leaping off. He knelt in the dirt track by Jane, who was raising herself up on her elbows. She looked at the earl. Her cheeks grew pink.

"Are you all right?" he demanded. "Is anything broken? Are you hurt?"

"No, I think I'm fine." Her voice shook. She was lying. She was in imminent danger of having a heart attack!

Abruptly he ran his hands over her ankles, calves, and thighs, on top of her skirts. Jane went very still. A fire flamed in the wake of his hands. He slid his palms over her ribs and she stopped breathing. The underside of one breast brushed the top of his hand, and she said, "Oh!"

He froze, looked up, and stared at her.

His face was very close to hers. So close, if she leaned forward, they could kiss. Unconsciously, mouth parted, eyes wide, she swayed toward him.

He stood up quickly, brushing off his breeches. "You're all right," he said, his voice hoarse. He extended a hand, and it trembled.

Jane took it and was unceremoniously hauled to her feet. "Thank you," she managed.

"Why the hell," he said with a growl, "didn't you tell me you couldn't ride?"

She bit her lip. Her backside was throbbing. Tears stung her eyes from the sudden smarting— and from the tone of his voice. And because he hadn't kissed her and she had desperately wanted him to.

"We'll walk back," he decided abruptly, retrieving the reins of her horse, which was cropping grass near by.

"Is she all right, sport?" a fellow called from his horse, riding up to them from where he and his lady companion had been waiting and watching. "I saw it all, not a nasty spill, just—" He stopped in midsentence, staring at the earl. His eyes bulged.

The rider wheeled his mount away, returning to his lady friend. "It is he! It's Shelton!" They trotted away, with many backward glances and much whispering.

The earl's face was a mask. "So much for Samaritans," he muttered. "The best thing," he said, "is to get back on. If you don't, you'll always be afraid to ride."

"I know," Jane said meekly. Then she blurted, "They are hateful—every single one of them!"

"Welcome to London," the earl said.

20

He couldn't chase it away.

Inside, deep within, he felt dread.

Of course, the Earl of Dragmore refused to acknowledge such feelings. Just as he refused to dwell on the rudeness he'd encountered in Regents Park with Jane. Instead, he focused on the pertinent issue—how to get back into Society? For until he achieved this, he could not find Jane a husband.

But the dread was there, deep inside.

The Duchess of Lancaster was, he calculated quickly, now in her late forties. Ten years ago when Nick had first arrived in London with his grandfather, she had been a stunning, elegant woman. It mattered little that she was married, he soon found out, when she pressed her attentions upon him in an arbor at the Baron Ridington's country estate one weekend. Nick was only too eager to oblige her. He had kept obliging her through that entire fall.

He'd run into the duchess from time to time during his marriage, but not since the trial. Indeed, since the trial he had rarely come to London, residing exclusively at Dragmore. Now he found himself not just back in London, but faced with the formidable task of gaining an entrée into its social circles, and to do so, he stood awaiting the duchess in her parlor.

"You still ignore decorum," she said, entering.

He was startled, but hid it. Time had ravaged her. Where she had been an auburn-haired beauty at thirty-eight, now she was wrinkled, too thin, and graying. But Nick took her hand and bowed over it. He did not kiss it. "Forgive me."

She lifted his chin to look into his eyes. "A woman could never deny you when you speak like that."

Uncomfortable, the earl eased back.

"You should have left your card with the butler," the duchess told him. "And after you would receive an invitation from me to visit—if I decided to see you."

"I know. Claire, I could not wait."

They both stared at each other with this intimacy, a blatant reminder of the past.

"I heard you were back. Have you had enough of that isolated estate?"

"No. I need your help."

She raised an auburn brow. Its color was exaggerated. "I am about to swoon. The grand earl needs me? Whatever for?"

"I need to regain my place in Society."

"Ahh, yes, I should have guessed. I know you, Nick. You never gave a damn about Society, not then, and I suspect you don't now. Why?"

"I have a ward. I must find her a husband."

The duchess smiled, intrigued. "Who is she?"

"The Duke of Weston's granddaughter."

"I had heard there was some other offspring—from the wrong side of the blanket. So it's true!"

"It's true. Will you help me?"

She smiled again and touched his face. "One favor begets another." Her hand lingered. "I will help you, Nick."

"Thank you."

Her hand had moved to his strong neck. "You are still beautiful," she murmured. Then her tone became crisp. "Come this afternoon. At four."

The earl stared. "So there is a price?"

"I am a selfish woman."

"So I see." He walked to the door and turned. "But I am no prostitute."

"Nick—"

Shoulders rigid, he left.

Jane was excited. Her excitement was barely contained. On the plush seat in the earl's carriage, sitting beside him, she was wiggling enthusiastically. Hands clasped, she turned to him, her face wreathed with happiness. "I can't tell you what this means to me!"

The earl stared at her. They were on their way to the Lyceum to see Henry Irving perform. He was feeling very uncomfortable. His decision to go to the theater was calculated—he wanted Jane to be seen by the right people. He had not even considered how she would react to the prospect, while she apparently thought he was trying to please her. He wondered if he might be blushing slightly, but fortunately, it was dark in the carriage.

Jane was babbling on and on about Mr. Irving, who was a well-known actor. The earl barely heard. She was stunning tonight in her new

finery, a modest rose evening gown with flounces
and polonaise. She wore her hair curled and
hanging loose down her back. She was a vision,
an earthly angel, beyond description.

He thought of the Duchess of Lancaster and felt
sickened. So much for friendship. He should have
known better. No one did anything for nothing.
Jane touched his arm. The earl tensed.

"We're here," she told him excitedly.

He smiled slightly, unable to restrain himself.

Her smile answered his, and hers was uncontained.

The lobby was filled with the crowd. People
were milling, quickly exchanging a few words,
and hurrying to find their seats. Most socializing
took place during the intermission. The earl took
Jane's arm firmly. He spotted Lindley with a
young woman and another couple just as they
were entering the auditorium. He tensed.

"Look," Jane said, pressing close. "Lindley's
here."

He was aware of her body warm and soft
against his. Second, he was aware of her close
scrutiny. Mostly, he was aware of his body's flaming, uninhibited response. He cursed himself. *You
are in a public place, for God's sake!*

He maneuvered Jane apart from him. "Let's
take our seats."

As they took their seats in a private box, there
was a tangible hush in those around them. Then
he was cognizant of the whispers. "Ignore them,"
he told Jane.

Jane looked around with a fierce glare. "I cannot!"

"Sit." He gently pushed her down. "We are here
to enjoy ourselves," he lied. But he did not seat
himself immediately. He stood in the box, raking

the entire theater with his gaze, daring them all. Satisfied he had shown his courage and disdain, he sat. Jane was regarding him intensely.

His gaze skittered away from hers.

She placed her small, delicate, gloved hand upon his. "You are more man than all of them put together."

He did not know what to say. Was she flirting? Her tone was sincere. He shifted and stared at the curtains of the stage.

The earl was fond of *Hamlet,* yet he could not concentrate on the production, despite Mr. Irving's laudable performance. He found himself watching Jane. She was mesmerized with the drama, while he was mesmerized with her.

She laughed. She clapped. She *ohh*ed and *ahh*ed. She cried, she wept. She giggled, she shrieked. He could not take his eyes off of her. And he was glad he had brought her, even if it had not been for the right reason.

"Isn't it wonderful?" Jane cried as they made their way to the lobby for refreshments during the intermission.

"Quite," he said dryly.

"Have you been paying any attention to the play?" she demanded.

"Of course." He actually smiled at her.

She smiled back, knowing it was untrue, and then they both laughed.

Amazed, Jane saw two dimples appear in the earl's cheeks. Her heart turned over. Impulsively she reached for his hand and squeezed it. He jerked his palm away. She flushed.

Then she saw he was gazing at someone, and she looked too. He was regarding an older, elegant auburn-haired woman, expensively dressed and heavily jeweled. The woman was staring at them, then she raised a gloved hand to whisper to her companion. Her eyes never left them. It was obvious she was talking about them and that her words were unkind.

Jane moved closer, protectively, to the earl.

"Would you like some lemonade?" he asked stiffly.

"No, I'm fine." She hoped they could stand in this corner and be left alone for the entire intermission.

"You must be thirsty." His gaze was direct.

"I am not."

"I am." He took her elbow. Jane felt the dread. They moved into the crowd.

A path cleared before them. Everyone was staring and gasping and whispering. "Look, look, it's he! Dragmore!" ". . . Lord of Darkness. Who is she?" ". . . Weston's granddaughter. . . . Illegitimate" ". . . He killed his wife."

The earl's shoulders were squared, his face an expressionless mask. Jane fought tears. These people were cruel. She hated London. She hated them. She wanted to go home.

"They were in the park today, I saw them," someone said loudly. "He was kissing her, he was. Right in public!"

Jane halted, furious, and saw that the speaker was the rider who had stopped after she had fallen off her horse. He hastily looked away. The earl dragged her forward. "Ignore them," he said, but his face had that sunburned look.

"I hate them! Let's go home!"

"The performance is not over." He paused in front of the refreshment stand. The man he was standing behind in the queue turned slightly. It was Lindley.

Jane could have sworn his eyes were sympathetic.

The two men stared, then nodded stiffly. Lindley moved aside, but paused to bow before Jane and kiss her hand. "Hullo, Jane," he said softly.

With her eyes, she begged him for compassion for the earl. "Hello."

"Jonathon," a woman said in a whining voice.

Lindley smiled slightly and left. Jane turned to find the earl there, handing her a lemonade. His face was dark and he was drinking brandy. "Please let's go home."

"No," he said, and they went back inside.

21

The performance was long since over. The Earl of Raversford stood closeted with his sister, the Countess of Braddock, in her drawing room. They were fighting.

"You are out of your mind!" the blond countess cried.

"I am not out of my mind," Lindley replied calmly. "What is the problem?"

"It's the last minute! The party is tomorrow night!"

"You are a snob," he said cruelly.

She groaned with frustration.

"Invite him," Lindley said. "Invite Shelton. You can say that you only just learned of his arrival in London. Besides, it's the truth."

"Why must I be the one?" she cried. "You saw how it was tonight. Everyone cut him. John—"

"Have you no heart at all?" Lindley demanded. "He has not a single friend here!"

"And you have too much heart! After what he

did to you! And you his only friend! How can you still harbor a kind thought toward him!"

"You must be the first to invite him."

"It will be a disaster!"

"He is strong. He can handle it. Eventually the gossip will die and attitudes will change."

His tone changed, softened, cajoled. "Please, Mary. Please invite Dragmore. Only do not mention that I am behind it, for then he would not come."

She accepted defeat. "I will do it, but you are a fool. I cannot gain him acceptance in London. I am not powerful enough."

"I will gain him acceptance," Lindley said quietly. "*I* am powerful enough." Then his face darkened, and as an afterthought, he added, "But damn you, Shelton, you almost broke my nose."

The earl was no fool. He knew Lindley was behind his sister's invitation to her house party that night. Was Lindley trying to apologize for the liberties he'd taken with Jane? Nick still felt that his friend had betrayed him by kissing his ward, but he judged him less harshly than he judged himself. Thinking of what Lindley had done only reminded him of what he had done—and there was certainly no comparison. Lindley had been a gentleman—he had been a brute.

He was pleased that Lindley was offering some sort of olive branch, but he was not quite ready to accept it.

They were going to the party, however.

"I do not wish to go," Jane informed him that afternoon.

"We are going," the earl said, and that was that.

They were announced in the salon: "The Earl of Dragmore and Miss Jane Barclay."

A hush greeted this, with every head turned toward them. The earl held Jane's elbow and felt her trembling. His hand tightened in a reassuring squeeze, and he felt her relax slightly. They entered.

The countess came forth to greet them, dazzling in a black velvet gown and glittering diamonds. "Lord Shelton, how wonderful to see you again!" She smiled, but anxiety was written all over her face.

Nick bowed over her hand. "Countess. It's nice to see you as well. This is my wife's cousin, Jane Barclay."

The women exchanged polite greetings, and the countess took them over to a small group. "I do believe you all know Lord Shelton, and this is his ward, his wife's cousin. Lords Smythe-Paxton and Hubberly, Lady Edding and Lady Townsend."

"Good evening," the earl said, and the men nodded stiffly back. Their gazes were drawn to Jane like moths to a flame. She curtsied and managed her fragile smile. She looked like an angel in her gown of silver chiffon.

"Patricia Weston's cousin, eh?" Hubberly asked. He was a big, plump gray-haired baron. "I do believe I see a resemblance. Although Patricia, quite the stunner, could not compare to you, my dear."

Jane blushed, murmuring a thank you.

Lady Edding, dark and beautiful, stared rudely, first at Nick, then at Jane. "Barclay. Are you the actress's daughter?"

"Yes," Jane said proudly, lifting her chin. "My mother was Sandra Barclay, renowned throughout England."

The earl winced. He was still holding Jane's arm, and his grip tightened in warning. This was not the place in which to boast of such antecedents.

Lady Edding and Lady Townsend exchanged glances. "So you're the one!" the brunette said. Noses turned up, both women turned their backs on her and proceeded to have their own private, well-heard conversation.

"She was Edward Weston's mistress," Lady Edding said. "Imagine—bringing an actress's illegitimate child here! It's hard to say who is the more uncouth!"

"They were at the theater last night," Lady Townsend said eagerly. "I was not there, but the Duchess of Lancaster told me at tea today. He was holding her hand!"

Lady Edding gasped. Both women turned to look at Jane and the earl. Lords Hubberly and Smythe-Paxton walked away. Jane looked at the earl. There were tears in her eyes, but her voice was loud, clear, and rang out. "What unbelievable bitches."

The earl dragged her away.

"I do not want to stay!" Jane whispered furiously.

"Do not sink to their level," the earl hissed, equally furious.

"I cannot let them get away with their malicious slandering!"

"Yes, you can," he said through gritted teeth. "You will smile and be polite and beautiful and show them true gentility!"

"The way you do?"

"It's only words," he said.

"You must hate them too," Jane cried. "Isn't that why you never come to London?"

"I don't care enough to hate them."

"I don't believe you."

They stared, fierce gazes locked. The earl finally broke the standoff. "Believe what you want. It doesn't matter to me."

"Why not?" Jane asked desperately. She touched his sleeve. "I know you. You are kind, you are good. It is these people who are rotten!"

The earl started visibly, and then a mask quickly settled upon his features, chasing away and hiding any emotions he might have had. "Come." He inclined his head toward the crowded room.

"Please, let's go home—to Dragmore."

Their gazes held. "No," he said finally. He was thrown off balance again, this time by her reference to Dragmore as home. "We are staying. I am going to find you a husband, Jane."

Her gaze darkened. "I don't want a husband!"

"Every woman wants a husband."

Jane opened her mouth to protest, when she heard a woman behind them. "Scandalous," she said. "Utterly scandalous."

The earl started to steer her away.

Jane dug her heels in furiously.

She turned around to stare at the speaker—the Duchess of Lancaster. The woman ignored her, and continued to regale her circle of half a dozen men and women. "I saw it myself. He did not take his eyes off her the entire performance."

"Unbelievable."

There were murmurs of assent.

"She is his ward, his wife's cousin," the duchess said viciously, turning to stare at them. "He is depraved."

The earl met her gaze. He did not so much as flinch. His face was a mask—but his cheeks had a sunburned cast. He was aware of Jane stepping in

front of him, as if to shield him with her little
body.

"You are depraved," Jane hissed. "Wicked and
depraved! All of you!" She grabbed the earl's
hand. "Let's go!"

"I'm afraid we now have no choice." He bowed
toward the duchess. He was smiling sarcastically.
"Good night, madame. It was a pleasure."

22

The earl was drunk.

He sat sprawled on the sofa. He did not care.

God, what had Jane done? They would never be welcome in Society now, not after tonight. And he would never find her a husband.

Good, he thought savagely.

He decided he was drunker than he'd realized.

Jane, a blue-eyed angel in silver chiffon. "I know you," she had cried. "You are kind and good!"

Kind and good?

He almost laughed, but the sound choked on itself.

The evening was a vivid tapestry in his mind. All the gilded, perfumed elegance and glamour. Their taunts echoed now, tormenting him. *He could not take his eyes off her . . . depraved . . . depraved . . . the Lord of Darkness . . . He killed his wife . . . holding hands . . . depraved . . .*

God! He was sick of it, sick of the persecution, sick of being everyone's scapegoat, sick and tired —damn them all! When would it end? *When?*

"God!" he cried aloud. "It will not end, it will never end—for it's the truth!"

He lunged to his feet, thinking of Jane, her innocent beauty and his decrepit lust. And even knowing it was wrong, he was tormented with wanting her still as he saw her as she was— young, fresh, innocent—trying to defend him, for God's sake! He took the decanter and emptied it.

And when he found the sofa again, he buried his face in his hands. His shoulders trembled, but he did not weep.

Jane could not sleep.

He was down there somewhere beyond her door, alone.

She leaned against the windowsill, staring out into the starlit night, her hair loose, a thin cotton and lace nightgown drifting over her body. People were hateful. She had never realized there was so much cruelty in the world before. And even though the earl's face had been a mask of indifference, beneath that façade, he had to have felt something.

Was he hurting? Right now, was he in despair? She knew him for what he was, a lonely man in need of warmth and love. How she wanted to give him what he needed.

She wanted to weep, for him.

She turned to look at the door. It was late, but she doubted he was asleep. When they had returned from the party, he had gone directly to the library without even a good night. Perhaps he was still there. Maybe she could get him to talk. Talk-

ing with someone who cared would do him a
world of good.

Jane could not stop herself from checking on
the earl—she had to.

She slipped on a matching cotton robe, hugging
it closed, and padded down the hall. The house
was eerily quiet and very dark, making her nervous. She did not know this mansion as well as
she knew Dragmore, but she found his study. The
door was ajar, light spilled out from within. He
was here, then. Feeling a rush of anticipation,
Jane pushed open the door.

He had been here. The library was silent, but it
smelled of cigars. An empty decanter and glass
sat on the table in front of the sofa. His black
evening jacket was on the floor, his tie upon a
chair next to it. The doors leading to the patio
were open, and Jane crossed the room to close
them. She turned off the lights and left.

She was disappointed. He had gone to bed.

And then she decided she did not care. She
wanted to see him—she *had* to see him.

The master suite was on the first floor, on the
other side of the house. Jane made her way cautiously in the dark. She prayed she would not run
into any servants, making up stories to explain
her presence if she did. She did not. She had
never entered this wing before, so she did not
know exactly where his rooms were. But the light
gave them away.

The door to his living room was wide open.
Jane entered cautiously, blinking. He was not
within, but again she smelled cigars, and this time
whiskey as well. She found half a glass on the side
table by the chaise.

No respectable woman would do what she was
going to do.

Jane knocked on the door to his bedroom. There was no response. It was firmly closed, but she thought she saw a light beneath. Boldly she knocked again. Nothing.

She opened the door.

He lay sprawled on the bed on his back, a sheet pulled to his waist, one arm flung across his eyes, as if warding off the dim glow from the lamp by his bedside. He was sleeping.

Like a moth drawn to a flame, Jane approached.

He was beautiful.

Jane paused beside him, unable to take her gaze from him, studying him raptly as he slept. His face, with its strong nose, sensual mouth, and high, high cheekbones, was not relaxed in sleep. It was drawn with worry, and even now he stirred, groaning. Pain flickered across his features.

"Oh, Nicholas, darling," she whispered, and her hand slid into his hair. "Sleep, darling, sleep, everything will be all right."

He went very still. Jane froze, afraid she'd wakened him, but then he sighed, visibly relaxing. Her hand moved through his thick, black hair, stroking, caressing.

She stared unabashed at his bare upper body. He was a big, powerful man. He had the shoulders, chest, and arms of a carpenter or a woodcutter—but without any fat. He was sculpted with flat planes of muscle and rigid bands of sinew. There was a sprinkling of hair on his chest between his nipples, and it trailed down his belly to disappear beneath the sheet. Startled, Jane realized he was stark naked under the thin covering, and she stared, fascinated.

He moaned, tossing restlessly. Jane touched his

forehead, murmuring unintelligibly, as if to a
babe. The sheet had slipped, revealing his taut
lower abdomen and lean hips. Fire raced along
the nerves of her body. She slid her hand to his
neck, his shoulder, and down his sculpted arm. "I
love you," she told him. "Nicholas, I love you."

His face was creased with worry, and he turned
onto his stomach with another distorted sound.
Impulsively, ignoring the warning bells that were
going off in her brain, Jane went round the bed
and climbed in, tossing off her robe. She snuggled
close and took him in her arms. It was heaven, to
hold him thus. He snuggled his face into her neck
with a very childlike sound. She stroked his nape
and back, marveling at the feel of him, hot and
hard and magnificently male. She kissed his forehead.

He nuzzled her neck, his lips against her skin.
His arm moved around her waist, and he pulled
her tightly against his torso, crushing her breasts.

Jane stopped breathing. Every nerve and fiber
of her being was alive with sensual awareness,
throbbingly so, demanding more. She knew she
should leave him. Soon, she told herself. Just a
little more. She wanted just a little more time to
be together like this. Her own hand slid down to
caress his waist. She trembled.

He groaned. His big palm was sliding now
along her back, at first slowly, sensually, then
with the stirrings of urgency. He nuzzled her
neck. His hand began exploring her derriere.

Jane froze, heart pounding. He was clearly
asleep, and she should make her exit now. Jane
couldn't. His hand was slipping over one high
curve, lazily, intently, and it was delicious. Jane
gasped with the pleasure. He was kneading her
buttock insistently now, and he moaned, a deep,

sexual sound. Jane was trembling. Her knee was practically upon him, her thighs parting of their own will. He urged her leg across his hips and then ran his hand down the back of her thigh. Jane heard the sound coming from deep within her throat—and barely recognized herself. Then she gasped as his hand came back up—beneath her gown.

And then she could not think. His palm on her bare buttock was heaven. She was shaking, on fire. His fingertips brushed the joining of her legs and rear. Jane moaned, hooking her leg around his waist, boldly pressing toward him. Suddenly he pulled her onto her back and was on top of her, pressed against her from breast to ankle, his mouth on hers, hot yet soft and lazy. And against her belly he was hot and hard and not lazy at all.

Jane no longer thought of leaving. She was a prisoner to what he was doing. She opened her mouth, wide, eagerly, and when he thrust his tongue within, she met him fiercely.

He knew it was a dream.

But it was the best dream Nick had ever had, and he did not want to wake up. But to make sure it was Jane, he looked at her, saw her passion-glazed face, the full, parted, wet lips. "Jane." He groaned. She was beneath him, soft and lush and shaking with need. He dove upon her mouth again, shaking now in his excitement, wishing with the back of his mind that he hadn't drunk so much so he could enjoy the dream more. His hands stroked her from her waist to her hips. He urgently kneed her thighs apart, to settle his heavy, stiff penis there, where it belonged. She gasped and arched against him.

Groaning in the combination of pleasure-agony, Nick found her breasts, nuzzling them

fiercely. The cotton fabric was in the way; he tore
it abruptly apart. Lifting one firm breast, he eagerly took its small nipple in his mouth and began
sucking voraciously. Jane writhed beneath him.
Her nails clawed down his back. He felt her
hands on his buttocks, stroking frantically. And
he could not wait.

Raising up, he thrust against her.

She cried out.

Vaguely, even though it was a dream, he remembered she was a virgin. "Sorry," he whispered, panting, reaching down, his hand shaking.
He rubbed the full wet folds of her femininity.
She cried out. He could not wait. Parting her, he
eased in, then thrust fully, hard, into her.

Jane clung to him as he plunged again and
again into her. The pain had been brief and mo-
mentary. She tried to move in tandem with him,
but it was impossible, he was like a crazed bull,
beyond control. And she felt the volcano within
her, building, insistent, about to erupt. "I love
you." She sobbed. "Please, please . . ."

"Jane," he cried out, tensing on top of her. He
collapsed, panting. She felt something wet and
sticky between her legs. Breathing harshly, she
clung to him, kissing his wet hair again and
again. He kissed the side of her neck.

Her body was alive, desperately yearning for
something fierce and unknown. She moved her
hips experimentally beneath him, hoping to encourage him into another bout of passion. But he
was soft now, slipping out of her, his arms tightening around her. He rolled to his side, pulling
her with him. "Jane," he said.

Was he awake? Jane froze, peered at him, and
saw he was still asleep. As they held each other,

she stared at the ceiling, sanity returning. Oh, God, she thought, what have I done this time?

Then she decided it did not matter. She loved him. She had wanted him. It had been wonderful. Now she would never, ever leave him.

23

The earl awoke with a feeling of deep, deep satisfaction.

Surprisingly, despite the huge quantity of alcohol he'd consumed the night before, he had only a minor headache. Smiling, he remembered the dream—making frantic love to Jane. His smile disappeared. The pain began then, incipient, raw, from knowing he was a degenerate even in his subconscious. He tried telling himself it had only been a dream, and then someone soft and warm snuggled against his side.

Nick's eyes flew open.

He stared aghast at Jane.

Jane, sleeping in his bed.

With dawning horror, he jerked upright, the sheet falling from the both of them. The first thing he saw was her long, lovely naked legs—her nightgown was twisted up around her thighs, revealing the bottom of one buttock. Then he saw the bed—the splotch of blood on the pristine white sheets. He looked down at himself and saw that his member was stained as well. With an agonized cry, he shoved her to her back and saw the blood between her thighs.

"Ahh, God!" he cried. "What have I done?"

Jane blinked at him sleepily.

He was standing, naked, panting. He looked at Jane and she shrank against the headboard wide-eyed now. He tried to recall exactly how it had happened. He remembered getting drunk in the library. He remembered the dream. He remembered coming to bed alone—or had he been so drunk he did not remember abducting her? He turned his back to her, shoulders drooping with defeat. He saw his own ravaged face in the mirror. "God, what have I done?"

She touched him.

He jumped.

She was an angel in her white nightgown and her splendid platinum hair. His gaze, horrified, riveted upon her bodice. It was ripped from the neck to the waist. *Had he raped her?*

"It's all right," she told him, big blue eyes wide and earnest. "I wanted to be with you." She smiled tremulously.

"You are a fool," he cried. "And I am perverted, sick, sick." Bluntly he said, "I don't remember what happened. Did I rape you?"

"No!" Her smile was at first hesitant, then it began to shine. "It was wonderful!"

He stepped back, as if struck. "Did I abduct you?"

She stared. Then, in a small voice: "No."

"I don't understand."

She faltered. "You were sleeping. I only wanted to comfort you, hold you. But you were so beautiful, I—" Seeing his black expression, she froze.

"I was sleeping? What are you saying?" he roared.

"I didn't think when I climbed into bed, I just wanted to hold you, and when you started kissing me, I . . . I . . . couldn't stop . . ."

Relief was instant, flooding him. He hadn't raped her, he hadn't abducted her. Then the fury came. "You got into bed with me? While I was sleeping? And you let me make love to you? Damn you! Damn you!" he roared.

She flinched as if struck, then backed away. Tears filled her eyes.

"Ahh, shit," Nick said, turning away, leaning on the bureau. He had to think—he couldn't think. And then he heard someone in the hall. He whirled. He had to protect Jane's reputation at all costs.

"Quick! Get into your robe! Don't make a sound!"

He sent the maid off on a false errand, then rushed back into the room. He whipped the bloody sheet off the bed, balling it up. He would have to rinse it immediately, then spill red wine upon it. "You get back to your room," he ordered Jane in a deadly voice. "And make sure no one sees you leaving this wing. Do you understand?"

She nodded, her face crumbling, a child on the verge of tears.

"And you await my summons there," he said with a snarl.

The earl was sick.

It didn't matter that she had come to him, although he thanked the God he did not believe in that he had not abducted her. What was done was irreversible. He had ruined her. He almost wanted to kill Jane. She was utterly reckless, impulsive, thoughtless! So much for propriety, he thought savagely. She did not have a proper bone in her body!

He recalled, too perfectly now, her passion as she writhed beneath him. No, she had not a proper bone in her *entire* body!

Nor did he. For with the memory came hot desire. He hated himself for wanting her again.

He could never find her a husband now. He would not even consider it. His own fate had been sealed, as had hers. He would, of course, do his duty and marry her.

You are kind and good.

He furiously shoved the echo of her words away.

He paced his sitting room. Anger was in every taut stride. He did not want to marry. He did not want a wife. Especially he did not want Jane as a wife.

Again, he thought of her uninhibited passion. When his body started to respond, he pushed the thoughts away. This was no reason for marriage. He could fuck anytime, anywhere. Damn her!

He sank onto the settee. And he felt it then—the fear.

For some unfathomable reason, Jane imagined herself in love with him. She had a schoolgirl's crush. He knew well enough that soon this would disappear. Reality would replace fantasy. She would see him as he was, the way Patricia had seen him. Patricia had not even known of Chavez, yet she had thought him uncouth and perverted in his appetites. Soon Jane would too. She would hate him . . .

The Earl of Dragmore was afraid.

Abruptly he stood. What did it matter what she thought? He was older, wiser. She would be his wife, bear his children, obey him. If she hated him, it did not matter. If he repulsed her, it did not matter. He was not the same man he had been five years ago. He had since grown a thick, impenetrable skin. He could handle seeing her eyes, now filled with adoration, glazed with disgust. Besides, there was no choice. They were getting married.

Yet the fear was there, cloying.

He knew that if he loved her, she would hurt him.

The earl was uneasy, standing near the door, now closed, just within Jane's bedroom. Jane was nervous too. She stood anxiously by the bed, hands clasped, her eyes luminous upon him. "I'm sorry!" she blurted before he could speak.

He ignored her. "We are getting married."

Jane gasped.

"Hopefully," he continued, his tone impassive, "you are not pregnant. We will marry as soon as decorum allows, so as not to seem hasty."

Jane was trembling, and a smile transformed her face. Her eyes shone. She loved him—and now she was going to become his wife! None of her other dreams mattered anymore, only this, her marriage to the earl and the life they would share. Her smile broadened. Did this mean he loved her?

His face grew dark. His tone was distinctly dangerous. "You look pleased."

"Oh, I am," Jane cried.

He reached her in a stride and grabbed her. Jane cried out. "Was this a seduction, then? Are you nothing more than some scheming little fortune hunter? Did you plan all of this, right down to the final act where I took your damn virginity? You were a virgin—were you not?"

He was shaking her, hurting her. Jane's eyes teared, but from the hurt in her heart, not his hands upon her flesh. "No, no."

He stared at her, trying to assess the truth.

"I love you," she told him. "That's why I want to be your wife."

He laughed, tossed her away. "Love?" He snarled. "You do not know the meaning of the word. Love does not exist, except for fools. What you feel is a child's adolescent infatuation and, to be crude, pure lust."

She felt as if her world were crumbling, brick by brick, beneath her very feet. "It's not true."

"No?" he taunted. "You would tell me about love, about lust, about men and women?"

She hugged herself. "Why are you doing this?" she whispered. "Why do you want to hurt me?"

"Why do you think?" he shouted. "Goddamn you, did I ask for a ward? I already have a son, I do not need another child to look after! Did I appear to be in need of a wife? Did I?" He roared.

Tears crept down her cheeks. "You don't want to get married, do you?"

He laughed caustically. "Top of the class, Jane."

She turned away, her heart breaking. "You don't love me."

He didn't answer, and it was answer enough.

She looked at him through thick tears, her vision blurred. He was dark and hard and angry. "Why are you marrying me?"

"Duty. One thing I have always done is my duty."

"You hate me." She gasped, stunned.

He stared, then abruptly turned and slammed out of the room. The walls shook.

Jane sank to the floor, tears pouring from her eyes. He was marrying her because of duty and honor and other such nonsense. He did not love her, not even close. He hated her. She had seen it in his eyes.

That night she left him.

The earl found the note the next day when Jane did not appear for dinner and the maid said her bed had not been slept in. It was brief and to the point and emotionless:

Dear Nicholas,
I do not want to marry either. I told you I am going to be an actress. I will be eighteen in October, and I hope you realize that I am quite old enough to take care of myself. I know you can find me if you choose, so I will not hide my whereabouts from you. I will be with my dear old friend Robert Gordon, the manager of the Lyceum. Please realize that this is the best solution for the both of us.

                                         Jane

His vision was swimming.

Nick was shocked to realize he had dampness on his cheeks.

He crumbled the letter, crushing it.

And the pain was unbearable.

She had left him.

Jane had run away rather than marry him. He had known all along that it would come to this. When given the choice, she had chosen what all women would choose—not to spend a lifetime with him.

He remembered everything then, and the memories were torture. The first time he had seen Jane, with her aunt Matilda. Her trepidation had been vast, while she was sweet and innocent, like an angel, her eyes big and blue as she stared at him. He saw her as she played with Chad, he saw her white-faced in stunned surprise as she fell from the old nag in Regents Park. He saw her in glorious fury as she told the Duchess of Lancaster that she was wicked and depraved. He recalled how she had laughed and flirted with Lindley. He recalled how she smiled at him. And he recalled the night before last, now, more clearly than ever before. Her frantic response to him, her body arching and twisting beneath his, her hands claws upon his back. He still wore her marks. Her heat, her sweetness.

Mostly he recalled last night, his cruelty and her stricken, hurt expression, the tears welling and slowly falling.

He knew then that it was too late. What he had fought from the beginning had happened. He loved her. He loved her as he had never loved anyone before, not even Patricia. But it did not matter.

She had run away from him.

She did not want him.

Hadn't he known all along that this would happen?

Jane had left him. It was over.

He closed his eyes. The pain was unbearable.

II

Fallen Angel

LONDON 1876

24

The applause continued.

Jane's heart surged. As she curtsied again, alone on the vast stage, a vision in shimmering blue chiffon, the crescendo increased, and Jane thought that this once the ovation would become thunder, that this once it would become endless. But already, and she had only just taken her bow, she heard the pitch dropping. Still smiling, Jane inclined her head and left the stage.

Her smile disappeared. From elation came the dragon of despair. She felt it choking her. Would she ever get a standing ovation as her mother had?

Would she ever be as good as her mother?

"Jane, darling, you were wonderful!"

Jane managed a smile for Robert Gordon's benefit. He was beaming, and he hugged her soundly. It felt good, and Jane clung briefly.

He was middle-aged with graying hair and a mustache. He gave her a searching glance, then

swept her into her dressing room. Jane dropped
down on the dark-red velvet love seat, feeling the
drain now, as Robert popped open a bottle of
champagne. He handed her a glass. "You were
wonderful, Jane," he said levelly.

She looked at him, her eyes big and blue amid
the white stage makeup, her lips rouged, cheeks
flushed the color of ripe strawberries. "So you
say."

"Jane." It was reproving. Jane sipped the champagne and closed her eyes, head back. "You are
very talented," Robert continued. "We've only
been running three weeks, and London loves you!
The performance tonight was nearly sold out!"

Jane opened her eyes. "But it will be the same
tomorrow, won't it, Robert? They'll say I am quite
talented, especially for one so young. Then they'll
wonder—will she ever reach the grandeur of her
mother?" Jane suddenly set the champagne flute
down with force. "I'm tired of being compared to
my mother! Tired of it!"

Robert came to her and put his arm around
her. "You *are* young. You *are* good. Give yourself
time."

Jane rubbed her eyes. "I'm just tired, Robert,
forgive me." She stood and walked to the dressing
table and began to remove her stage makeup with
Pond's cream and cotton. Robert left her. When
she had finished, she released her hair from its
chignon and tied it back in a simple tail. Robert
returned with his arms full of roses. Jane had to
smile.

"Do you want to see the cards?" he asked.

"Are they all amorous?" Jane returned.

"Of course."

Jane laughed, shaking her head. "I'll take the

flowers home." She glanced around. "There's no place here for any more."

And there wasn't. Roses in vases were everywhere: upon her dressing table, on the butler's table, on the side tables by the sofa. At least in this one respect she was similar to her mother, Jane thought. She had many admirers, not that she cared. Nor did she even care to know who they were.

They went out the back entrance, to avoid a few men who were waiting in front of her dressing room, hoping to catch a glimpse of her and have a few words. It was that way every night. At first Jane had been flattered, then amused. Now she accepted the attention and admiration as a part of her celebrity, as she did the appellation "Little Angel." Apparently someone had remembered that she had been called "Sandra's Angel" as a child and had been too glad to revive the nickname. She was glad they had dropped her mother's name; the cross would have been too much to bear.

They had avoided the busy mobs and traffic on Picadilly Circus where the Criterion Theatre was located; the street out back was silent and nearly deserted. The Criterion had been built only two years before as an annex to the popular Criterion Restaurant. Things had changed. All of London's theaters were now booking long-running performances, instead of troupes that had a variety of acts in their portfolio. Troupes no longer traveled about England and performed, and the companies changed when the performances did. It made more sense, as evidenced by the popularity of the play Jane was acting in now, James Albery's comedy, *Pink Dominoes.*

Jane sat with a shawl around her shoulders in Robert's coach. There was still a bite in the air in the evenings, even in mid-June. She was very tired from her performance, and Robert understood, as he always understood, and he said nothing. Impulsively Jane reached out to squeeze his hand, and he squeezed hers back. Jane didn't know what she would have done without Robert.

Not how she would have survived, but how she would have lived after leaving the Earl of Dragmore.

Robert had still been at the Lyceum almost two years ago, and Jane had found him instantly. Her world was still intact, shattered but intact, because she expected the earl to come claim her. Not out of love, but out of duty. Yet deep inside her soul, deep within her heart, she had the fantasy that he would chase her because he realized, at that last moment, that he loved her and could not live without her. But he hadn't come.

And then her world had shattered like crystal glass. For he hadn't come.

Robert picked up all the pieces. Jane stayed with him, grieving, her heart broken. He encouraged her to come to the theater with him, and after a few months of serious depression, Jane found her heart again in her love of the stage. And she began to smile once more; the tears came less.

She just wished she could hate him, and knew she never would.

Jane had a small town house on Gloucester Street. Originally she had stayed with Robert, but soon both deemed that arrangement inappropriate. The apartments were small and three-storied, plaster over yellow brick, in a modest but fresh neighborhood filled with shady elms. She even had a small yard in the back in the Mews with daisys and black-eyed Susans and a swing. One of the stagehands had painted it for her, a pretty shell pink.

"Robert, I'm very tired," Jane said, hoping he wouldn't want to come in.

"I know. I'll come by in the morning." He looked at her.

Jane gave him her cheek, and he kissed it, his mouth lingering. "Good night." She flashed him her smile, the one everyone said was so angelic. Then she slipped out of the cab and through the wrought-iron gate to the house.

Molly was waiting. "Evenin', mum, more flowers?" A merry grin split her face. "How was it?"

Jane smiled. "Good. Here, take these, please."

Molly laughed at Jane's tone, taking the armload of roses. "I've got roast beef still warm in the oven, mum."

"Maybe later," Jane said, watching Molly leave with the flowers. She smiled. It had been impulse, asking Molly to come with her that night so long ago when she had run away, but the maid had instantly agreed. She had never been farther than Lessing, and the thought of going to London had been immeasurably exciting to her.

Jane hurried upstairs, kicking off her high-heeled slippers and quietly opening a bedroom door. One small nightlight was on, illuminating the room. There was a small bed, the headboard painted pink and blue and white. Blue and yellow clowns graced the wallpaper, holding pink ribbons. A few dolls lay scattered about, and a new, white-and-black wooden rocking horse grinned at

Jane from the center of the room. Jane moved to the bed, its sides up, to look at her daughter.

She smiled, because Nicole did that to her, made her unbelievably warm and happy—and unbelievably protective.

No one knew about her.

No one was going to take her away from Jane.

Jane knew, without a doubt, that if *he* knew, he would claim her and take her away. Just the thought made her sick with despair—and furious with maternal anger. If he had come after her when she had run away, then the child would have been theirs together. But he had forfeited all rights. Nicole was hers. Hers. And he was never going to take her away from her. *Not ever.*

Molly understood and Robert understood. They were the only ones who knew her secret. It was a terrible thing to live with, like a dragon breathing fire, to know that one day her secret might be found out and that one day he might come and take Nicole away from her.

Jane refused to feel any sympathy for the Earl of Dragmore. She refused to consider his right to know. She refused to consider his feelings—and the kind of father he would be. He had Chad. Nicole was hers.

She heard it then, Molly racing up the steps. She was coming too fast, something was wrong. Jane straightened, one last glance at her year-old daughter, wanting to touch the dark curls but resisting. She quietly left the room, closing the door and leaning upon it. Molly appeared, breathless, wild-eyed. Jane's body tensed in anticipation. "What is it? What's happened?"

"Oh, good Lord!" Molly cried, white-faced. "There was a knock on the door and I looked out the window, but it's so dark, so when I saw a gentleman on the stoop I thought it was Robert come back! Or I'd never have opened the door!"

Jane's heart stopped.

"But it ain't! Mum! He's here!"

25

Jane thought her heart had truly stopped. Somehow, she recovered. "Send him away!" she hissed. "Tell him I'm not home! Now!" And already she was planning her escape.

For escape she must.

Sanity fled. She only knew that he was here. Was he coming for Nicole? Did he know about his daughter's existence? God, if so, he would chase them to the ends of the earth! She would grab the sleeping baby and they would flee now, out the back, as they were, into the night.

Molly whirled to go, but froze as heavy footsteps on the stairs sounded. She shot a desperate glance at Jane. Too late—he was coming! Jane knew she could not let him come up. She must buy time. She rushed forward, shoving past Molly, and started down the dark stairwell—to come face to face with him.

"Lindley!"

The Earl of Raversford stood on a lower step,

and they were eye to eye. Hers wide, stunned; his wide, warm. Relief surged, then fell abruptly away. "Are you alone?" she demanded.

"Yes. Jane, I—"

Jane sagged against the wall. Her heart was slamming, and sweat had gathered beneath her breasts. "How did you find me?"

Still on the stairwell, they stared. "I'm sorry," Lindley said. "I've upset you."

"No, it's all right." Then she had a horrifying thought. If Lindley knew her whereabouts, did he? Jane pulled herself together with great effort. She must be calm, collected. "Forgive me, Jon. Where are my manners? It was just such a shock. Come, let's go downstairs."

"Forgive me," Lindley said, turning and back-tracking. "But I had to come, and I guessed you might not want to see me. I apologize for my forwardness."

Downstairs, in the light of the foyer, away from Nicole's room, Jane could breathe easier. She sighed. "You're forgiven." She meant it and smiled, although her heart was still racing from the scare she'd had. And so were her thoughts. Was the earl close by? Did he too know where she lived? Had he sent Lindley? What would Lindley do if he found out about Nicole? "Come into the parlor."

"Thank you," Lindley said.

Jane paused as he went in, then grabbed Molly and whispered fiercely, "Stay with her. Don't let her cry!"

Molly nodded and raced upstairs.

Jane composed herself before entering. Lindley studied her openly, eagerly, with appreciation. Jane let him, waiting. "Well?"

"You're not a schoolgirl anymore," Lindley said softly.

Jane didn't blush. "No, I'm not."

Lindley's smile disappeared. "You're so beautiful, more than before, I think. On the stage tonight, Jane, you took my breath away, I swear it. I had to find you, to at least say hello and find out how you've fared."

"I'm doing well, as you can see," Jane said. "I have everything I want." She shrugged, moved gracefully to the sideboard. "A brandy, Jon?"

"Everything?"

Her back was to him. She stiffened. "Everything. I'm on the stage, my dreams have come true." *Liar!* her mind screamed.

"I'm glad," Lindley said softly.

Jane handed him a brandy, taking a small sherry for herself. Lindley's gaze was warm, unceasing. "So," Jane asked casually. "Who were your companions tonight? Anyone I know?"

"He wasn't with me," Lindley said quietly.

Jane met his gaze, then dropped hers. Her fingers tightened upon the glass she held. She wanted to ask where he was. And mingled with relief was disappointment. She refused to acknowledge it.

"He is at Dragmore," Lindley stated, watching her.

Jane shrugged indifferently. Yet she found herself thinking an unwelcome thought: *How is he?*

"How did you find me?" she asked quickly, hating her heart for being a traitor to her mind.

"I followed you." Lindley's smile was sheepish. "There were two dozen gentlemen waiting at your dressing-room door, and I knew I had not one chance." He grinned. "I made a few discreet

inquiries, heard about the back exit, saw you and
your friend leave. So I followed."

"Shame," Jane said, but she smiled.

Lindley studied his snifter, his fingers long, his
hands graceful but masculine. "What happened,
Jane?"

Jane went tense.

"I'm sorry, I'm intruding. Nick wouldn't say
much. A few days after my sister's party I went to
his town house to make peace, if I could. It was
closed up, and I assumed the two of you had left
for Dragmore. A month later I was in Sussex and
I stopped by there. And you were gone. Nick said
you'd gone back to your mother's friends in London. He wouldn't say another word on that topic.
In fact, I sensed my life might be in danger if I
pursued it."

Jane managed a charming smile; after all, she
was an actress. "There wasn't anything else to say.
I was not going to get married, and that was that.
This"—she gestured grandly—"is my life."

His gaze searched hers. It was too probing, too
inquisitive, and Jane had too many secrets, so she
looked away. When she was certain her secrets
were well hidden, she smiled and met his gaze. "I
hope you will keep my residence discreet. From
everyone."

Lindley's stare was direct. "Are you hiding from
someone, Jane?"

"Of course not."

"It's funny, but I know Nick as well as anyone
does, I think. Although that may not be saying
much. I find it difficult to believe he would let you
return to the theater."

"We fought like cats and dogs," Jane said
calmly. "And this is the result."

"Of course." Then, abruptly, he said, "You've

changed, Jane. I'm not sure what it is, it's not
your just being older, more mature. I sense something . . ."

"Of course I've changed," Jane said. "I'm not
seventeen, I'm nineteen. I am no longer quite so
naive—I understand life." Too well, she might
have added, but she didn't.

Lindley studied her again, too closely, so she
looked away. She felt the bitterness and sadness,
and did not want him to see it. "Did you enjoy the
performance?"

"Immensely," he said easily. "You're a wonderful actress, Jane."

"Wonderful," she echoed. Unbidden, she
thought of the applause tonight, enthusiastic but
not wild. Tomorrow, of course, the critics would
laud her performance, and laud her. A great
beauty like her mother, they would say. Some had
even said she was more beautiful. But will she
ever be the great actress that her mother was?

Unbidden, she imagined him in the audience,
dark and silent, expressionless, watching her as
she soared in her performance.

She shifted uneasily. So many questions clam-
ored in her heart, in her soul. Mostly she wondered how he was, and why.

Why hadn't he come after her?

Why?

26

Lindley told himself not to be a fool. Yet that next morning he sent her a bouquet of white lilies. Their pristine paleness pleased him and reminded him of Jane.

He wondered at the events that had changed her and made her a woman with secrets.

He wondered what Shelton would do if he knew he had seen her.

Lindley was torn. He was not a fool, and never had been one. He clearly remembered that summer almost two years ago. He remembered Jane's eyes, big and blue and able to see no one but his friend, Nick. He remembered Shelton, dark and angry, more so than usual, and he knew Nick had been attracted to her too. It was still amazing to him that Nick had let her go to the theater.

Unable to help himself, telling himself they were just friends, Lindley sent Jane a note, asking her if he could take her to tea. The invitation was politely declined by her maid.

Another invitation was also declined, and not one to rely on dismal chance, Lindley went to her cozy home on Gloucester Street three days later. He was not infatuated, he was too worldly, yet he was intrigued and he had thought about her quite a lot. He was shown into the parlor, and Jane appeared, looking both stunning and innocent—an impossible feat, he thought—in a rich wine gown.

"Hello, Jon." She was polite but cool. And there was caution in her eyes.

"Hullo, Jane." He took her hand and kissed it. Unlike the first time, she did not flinch as if burned, and he wondered how many admirers she'd had. And lovers? It was a rude thought, one he'd had before, and he shoved it away. Yet he was certainly not the only man to be intrigued. She was a charming, disturbing combination of innocence and worldliness, and he didn't know what to make of it. "Jane, I have the feeling you don't want to see me." He, of course, expected her to politely refute this, and then he'd charm her into seeing him.

"What is the point?"

Surprised, he could only stare.

"Why have you come?"

"Jane, you're a beautiful woman and an old friend—or at least it feels that way. Why shouldn't I want to see you?"

"I have no time in my life for anything other than my profession," Jane said firmly.

"I find that hard to believe," Lindley said easily, but he was hurt by the rejection. He was not used to it.

It must have showed. Jane's eyes softened, and she touched his hand lightly. "I'm sorry. I'm being terribly rude, when you've never done anything but be kind to me. Shall we walk in the park?"

"How about Covent Gardens?" he suggested, grinning, the hurt gone.

Jane flashed him her beautiful smile. "All right," she said.

Two weeks later Lindley knew Shelton was back in town from the gossip. He felt a stirring of guilt, but told himself he was ridiculous. It was ridiculous because it had to do with Jane, whom he'd seen four or five times. And whom he was planning on seeing again.

She was wonderful company, all light and laughter, and she was beautiful. He had stopped kidding himself that he wanted to be with her as old friends. He wasn't in love with her, which was good, because it wouldn't do for him to fall in love with an actress when one day he must marry from his own class. Still, she was his friend, and he hoped that soon she would become his mistress.

But, because she was a lady, and so young, and her innocence was a tangible thing (and he was confused by just how experienced she was), he hadn't even tried to kiss her. Now, on his way to greet Shelton, Lindley had a disturbing thought. Jane was only nineteen. Was she still technically Dragmore's ward? If so, he knew he'd forfeit his life if he made love to her. The thought was as shocking as cold water thrown on his face.

He hadn't intended to mention Jane to the earl, but now he wondered if he'd better sound out the sensitive topic. How did one tell one's best friend that he wanted to make his ward, now a stage actress, his mistress? It was all terribly complicated.

The earl was glad to see him. "I was wondering when you'd bother to come by," he said, the barest of smiles turning up the corners of his mouth.

Lindley grinned back. "You know where I live, old man."

"But knowing you," Nick shot, "you're abed with God knows whom until God knows when, and God forbid I should disturb you from your philandering."

Lindley laughed. "And how's Amelia and Genevieve and who's the Spanish dancer? Therese?"

Ignoring all sense of decorum, the men had coffee liberally laced with cognac and cigars at 10 A.M., proceeding to catch up on news, pertinent gossip (only), and their own affairs. They had long since reconciled from the time when the earl had thrown Lindley off Dragmore, although Lindley sensed, always, that something had changed between them and that it would never be quite the same again. He knew Shelton well enough to know that he did hold a mean grudge. He also knew Shelton had forgiven him for taking liberties with Jane. Forgiven, but not forgotten.

"I've seen her," Lindley said an hour later.

"Who?" the earl asked, inhaling deeply on his cigar. "Amelia?"

Lindley shook his head, polishing off the last of the strong coffee. He had a pleasant glow, no doubt about it. "Jane Barclay."

For an instant the earl stiffened, eyes wide. Then he dropped his gaze, sipped his coffee—and his cup and saucer rattled when he set it down. Lindley frowned.

The earl said nothing. His face had become impassive, impossible to read. Still frowning, Lindley said, "She's quite good, old boy. I saw her on the stage. The critics like her too. And beautiful! A stunner! Even Patricia never had what she had—

it's the innocence and the sensuality. I guess you
did the right thing, letting her take to the stage. I'd
say she's quite the natural. Whether she's as good
as her mother, now, that I doubt."

The earl looked at him, his eyes black, and
Lindley thought that he was angry. Yet there was
no reason for him to be, so Lindley guessed he
was wrong. But there was tension now emanating
from the dark figure sitting near him. "You sound
as if you're in love with her," the earl said flatly.

Suddenly wanting to squirm, Lindley denied it
vigorously. "Don't be mad. I've a dozen mistresses, as you well know."

The earl inhaled deeply. "Did she see you?"

Lindley hesitated. Now was the time to come
clean, if he was going to tell all. He said, "We
spoke after the performance."

The earl said nothing, his gaze drifting to the
windows, staring out at the tree-lined square. It
had begun to rain, a thick drizzle.

"Is she still your ward?" Lindley asked bluntly.

"Technically," he said.

Lindley felt it then, an intense disappointment.
He would have to be friends with her, no matter
how strong his romantic interest. At least until
she came of age.

And there was still another question. "Are you
going to go see her? She plays at the Criterion."

Savagely the earl ground out his cigar. "No." He
lunged out of his chair. "I'm meeting Amelia at
Harrod's and taking her to dinner. Care to come?"

Politely Lindley declined. And he felt relieved
with the earl's answer.

27

Inside the auditorium, it was dark and quiet, the audience spellbound, and on the stage, bathed in light, Jane performed.

He stood very quietly, his spine rigid, his back to the doors leading to the lobby. He made no move to find a seat, and he made no move to leave. Indeed, even though it was the third and final act, he had only just arrived. He stared, unable to peel his gaze away from the actress, just like everyone else in the theater.

Beneath his breath, the Earl of Dragmore swore crudely.

God, he hated her!

After all this time, he had thought he would feel nothing. That he would be cold and indifferent. Yet it was not cool indifference flowing through his veins, but hot anger. He trembled with it.

Hearing about her yesterday, he had not been able to stay away.

She was beautiful—as Lindley had said. She

was a contradiction, both angelic innocence and
carnal sensuality. His lips sneered, and he wondered how many lovers she'd had since him. He
told himself he did not care, and this time, he
cursed aloud.

"Shhh," fifty people hissed at once.

He ordered himself to leave, but he did not.

And when she was particularly funny, and everyone around him roared in mirth, he did not
laugh. He did not even smile.

She had left him.

He had loved her—and she had left him.

As intense as his anger had been in that moment, his despair had been worse. Yet he had not
let her go to London alone and fending for herself. He had sent a runner immediately to Gordon
at the Lyceum, to ascertain that she had arrived
safely and was cared for. That assured, he had
given in to his fury and hatred, spending his days
in dark, angry despair, seeking solace in a bottle,
closed up alone in his library. After a few days he
returned grimly to the living, to run Dragmore.
The anger and hurt faded to manageable proportions, and by a month's time, he felt nothing at
all.

He met with Gordon once, to determine the extent of the responsibility he owed Jane. For she
was still his ward. Gordon assured him Jane was
no burden, that he loved her as he would a daughter, having loved her mother as a friend. Not satisfied, the earl made arrangements to support her
financially. He did not see Jane, indeed, made
damn sure they met at Tavistock Square to avoid
this happening. And then he put her out of his
mind.

Except, sometimes, in the lonely darkness of
the night, she came to him and, half asleep, he

reached for her—but it was only a dream, and she was not there.

The play was over, and Jane was taking her bow alone before the crowd, which was roaring its approval. The earl stood frozen, his gaze never wavering from her. She was beaming, ecstatic, and when someone pelted her with red roses, she laughed, picking one up and waving it at the audience. He felt a chink in the armor of his hatred. Her joy was nearly contagious. Desperately he wrapped the cloak of burning emotion more tightly around himself, standing more rigidly, fixing a look of loathing upon his features. She disappeared backstage amid shouts of "Angel! Angel! We want Angel!"

Angel, he thought savagely. Witch was more like it. And he clenched his fist so hard it hurt.

In the lobby he paused, the crowd flowing around him, giving him the usual wide berth and even wider stares. Those who did not see him were chattering animatedly, with laughter interspersed and many comments of praise for Jane— especially among the men. Nick could feel his heart throbbing with dark intent. In fact, he became aware of his entire body pulsating, alive and heated. He knew he should just drag his damn feet to the main doors and leave the goddamn theater. Instead, he abruptly turned and went backstage.

Jane was flushed and smiling. She knew that tonight she had been better than ever, and she could not wait to read the critics tomorrow. "Jon," she cried, whirling, her chiffon floating around her, "have I ever been better?"

Lindley grinned. "I don't think so, darling, never."

Jane turned to Robert Gordon. "Have I?" she
demanded. "Have I?"

"Never," Robert assured her. "Maybe tonight
calls for a special celebration."

Her laughter was rich, warm and undeniably
infectious. "I feel like dancing!"

"This can easily be arranged," Lindley said eagerly, catching her hand and pulling her to him.
"Shall I take you dancing, Jane? And to supper?"

Jane looked at him flirtatiously, her mood too
impossibly good, her elation making her float like
the angels in the clouds above. She opened her
mouth to reply, knowing she was flirting and
knowing she should stop, when from outside the
door came the sound of thunder.

And then again thunder boomed, as someone
banged once, furiously, and the door shook.

Everyone inside the room froze, then Gordon
started forward, frowning angrily. Jane reacted
with instinct—and intuition. "No!" she shrieked.
"Don't open it!"

"Who is it?" Gordon called rigidly. "No need to
break the door down, man!"

"It's the Earl of Dragmore" was the frozen reply.

Jane went white.

Seeing this, Lindley's hands went to her shoulders. "It's all right."

"No! It's not," Jane cried frantically, clinging to
Lindley. Then, to Robert: "Don't open it! Don't let
him in!" She had one coherent thought among the
knifing panic, and that was to escape.

"Jane." Gordon frowned. "We must be civil—"

But Jane was already across the room, her fear
giving her wings, and at the back door. "Delay
him," she cried to the two men in a whisper. "Delay him, tell him I just stepped out and I'll be back

—please!" Neither man could deny her appealing
look. And then she rushed out, the door drifting
shut behind her.

The thunder came again. "Open the goddamn
door, Gordon," the earl demanded. "Now—before
I break it down!"

Gordon and Lindley exchanged glances.
"Maybe you'd best do as he suggests," Lindley
said, shooting a glance at the door Jane had escaped through. He didn't like her reaction to the
earl, not at all.

"Let's give her another minute," Gordon said,
low. "Although why she—"

Thunder boomed, wood cracked, and the door
flew in off its hinges, the earl's shoulder behind it.
He righted himself, his face a grim mask of determination—and then he saw Lindley. Anger
blazed. His gaze swept the room, seeking Jane.
"Where is she? I know she was here—I heard
her."

"She'll be right back," Gordon said calmly.
"Damn it, Shelton, there was no need to break
down the door!"

But Nick wasn't listening. He was staring furiously at Lindley. "What the hell are you doing
here?"

Lindley smiled easily. "The same thing as you—
I came to see Jane."

They stared at each other.

The earl looked around again, taking in the soft
Aubusson carpet, the plush settee, the rosewood
butler's table, the dressing table and gilt mirror.
He eyed the many vases of flowers, and the Chi-
nese dressing screen—black with inlaid gold and
opal dragons. His gaze lingered on a wispy blue
satin robe hanging upon it. Then he saw the other
door, near the dressing table, and in a stride he

reached it and flung it open. He stared down the black hallway. Then turned.

"She left," he said, his tone low and barely controlled.

Neither Lindley nor Gordon responded.

With a violent cry, the earl's arm swept out, and he savagely cleared the table of its contents, sending a vase of roses and all Jane's toiletries smashing to the floor.

A shocked silence followed.

The earl broke it. "Where is she?"

Lindley didn't move a muscle, but Gordon grimaced.

"Where is she?" When Gordon didn't respond, the earl leapt. He threw him against the wall, pinning him there. Gordon cried out. "Tell me, damn it, before I break your neck," the earl shouted.

Lindley hauled on the earl from behind, trying to drag him off Gordon. "Stop it, Nick, damn it, stop it!"

The earl froze, Lindley's assault no more bothersome than an attack of gnats, and then he slumped, freeing Gordon. He leaned against the wall, forehead pressed there, shoulders slumped. Gordon skittered away. "I'm sorry," the earl said heavily. "I'm sorry."

28

Jane was not able to sleep all night. Her thoughts were filled with him.

She lay awake staring at the ceiling, waiting, listening, for the sound of a carriage or a horse. Her chest was so tight it hurt. She was so stiff she hurt. She was sure he would come after her.

But he didn't.

Just as he hadn't come after her two years ago.

At first, panicked in the darkness, she was sure the only reason he could have had in coming to see her after all this time was Nicole.

But how had he found out? No one knew about their daughter, no one except herself and Molly and Gordon, and Jane trusted the other two with all her heart. Yet she did not underestimate the earl, not for a second. He was shrewd. He certainly wasn't coming to say hello—or take up where they had left off. She refused to acknowledge the bitterness that rose. Only one thing became clear: He could not know. She grew calmer

as dawn approached. No, he could not know. But
he had been so angry. She had heard it in his
voice. Yet she recalled only too well that the earl
was an angry man. It took so little to light the
fires that burned within him. Such dark fires.

She would not feel compassion.

Today she did not play outside in the yard or sit
on the pink swing with her daughter. They stayed
inside, just in case he did come. Hiding. Despite
the voice of logic, she was afraid.

Holding Nicole after breakfast, Jane debated
what to do as her daughter explored the ribbons
in Jane's hair. If she were a true mother, she
would quit the Criterion and take Nicole away
and just disappear. But Jane didn't think she
could do this, not yet, not unless there was absolutely no other choice. Maybe she should send Nicole and Molly to Brighton for a short vacation,
just until things died down. She could confront
the earl, demand what he wanted, surmise if he
knew about Nicole—yes! This was what she
would do.

Leaving Nicole playing in the parlor for a moment, Jane hurried into the kitchen, just next
door. "Molly, pack up a few things. I want you to
take Nicole to Brighton for a week."

Molly's eyes widened, then she squealed with
delight, having developed a fondness for travel
once she'd discovered it. Jane explained why, and
the two women walked out of the kitchen together, making plans.

A man filled the doorway of the parlor, his back
to them. He was rigid.

Jane froze, hands clutched to her breast. "Jon!
How did you get in!"

He whirled, eyes wide, stunned. "The door was
open, wide open."

Jane hurried past him to her daughter, who was sitting and playing with a silver box she must have somehow knocked down. She knelt, sweeping Nicole into her arms.

"My God," Lindley said.

Rising, holding her daughter fiercely, Jane said with outward calm, "Molly, please close and lock the front door."

Molly was red. "I'm sorry, mum. When the milkman come, I must have left it ajar."

"It's all right," Jane said, her gaze bonded with Lindley's.

Lindley stared at Nicole. Jane kissed her hair, rubbing her cheek there. "I think you should go, Jon," she managed. She felt it, her world beginning to cave in. She was trembling.

"I had to see you today," Lindley said stiffly. "I had to see you. I couldn't sleep all last night, thinking about what happened at the Criterion yesterday. Thinking about how afraid you were to see him. Do you know he broke the door down?"

Jane said nothing. Tears slipped down her cheeks, and she closed her lids tightly.

"Now I know why. It's his, isn't it?"

Jane held the toddler closer. "No."

"She has black hair, almost as black as his. Her skin isn't dark, but it's not as fair as yours. And her eyes are not blue and not gray, but somewhere in between. But you know what the give-away is? Her cheekbones. High, wide—like his. How old is she? Let me think—thirteen months?" Suddenly his face went hard. "That bastard!"

Jane felt the panic. "Please! Please, Jon, if you care at all—you mustn't tell him!"

Lindley stared. "He doesn't know."

"If he finds out he'll take her away from me, I know he will!"

Lindley said nothing, not moving a muscle.

Jane put Nicole down, wiping her eyes, but the tears kept coming. "Please, Jon, he has Chad, and —I love Nicole. Please don't tell him. I'm so afraid. I won't have a chance if he knows, even if I run away to India. Please." She sobbed, her control breaking.

Lindley went to her and swept her into his arms. She wept upon his shirt front, and he held her, stroking the hair at the nape of her neck. "Don't cry, Jane, please. I won't say a word. Shh."

Jane clung to him, shaking. She lifted her tear-stained face. "Promise me?"

Lindley felt the swift stabbing of doubt, and Jane saw it. Her face crumbled. Lindley groaned, hugging her harder, burying his face on the top of her hair. "I promise," he said harshly, knowing he would regret it.

And then he forgot about regrets. Jane was soft in his arms. Her breasts were crushed against his chest. She smelled of lilies. Her hair was silk. Not for the first time, he was assailed with desire, the heat building rapidly in his loins. "Jane," he said harshly. He should move away, yet he could not.

"You are so good." She sniffed, her face buried in his shirt. "So good, so kind."

"Damn kindness," Lindley said. He tipped her chin up and kissed her, hard.

Jane froze. Lindley's mouth moved voraciously over hers, testing, tasting, demanding. When he prodded her lips with his tongue, she opened slightly, enough for him to thrust in. He realized through a hot-red fog that she was not responding, just allowing him to kiss her. He was so thick against her belly he wanted to explode. Somehow he pushed himself away from her. He gave her his back to regain control.

When he turned again Jane was watching him, a squirming Nicole protectively cradled in her arms.

"I'm sorry," Lindley said. "But you know I want you, Jane."

"I thought we were friends," Jane said softly.

"We're friends, but I want more."

"I can't give you more."

"Because of him?"

Jane shook her head. "No. Because I don't love you."

"Do you love him?"

She didn't hesitate. "No."

Lindley shoved his hands in his pockets. "I suppose that makes me feel a bit better."

"Jon." She came to him and touched his cheek. "I need your friendship. I've come to count on it. Don't—don't walk away, please, not now." Her voice was tight and high.

"God, Jane, I wouldn't!" He touched her hair, and felt his need again. "But I'm a man, Jane, and I won't lie to you anymore. Do I have a chance?"

"What do you want?" she asked sadly. "A tumble? A mistress? I know you don't want me as your wife."

He felt ashamed, and reddened.

"I thought so," she said softly. "Once I thought I loved someone and I gave myself to him freely. If I ever love again, I will do the same, but not until then—not for sport and not for gain."

His shame increased, and maybe it was then that he started to fall in love with her. "I will always be here for you," he said. And he knew, as he said it, that it was the truth.

29

🔥🔥🔥

Now that he had glimpsed her once, he had to see her.

He dared not question why. And the old burning rage was back.

He had stayed abed late, unusual for him, because he had not even entered it until dawn. He had a headache from the whiskey he'd consumed, and he blamed it on the blue-eyed blond witch they called Angel. How appropriate, he thought with a grimace as he buttoned up his shirt, the Lord of Darkness and the Little Angel.

"What time is it, darling?" Amelia asked, sitting up and baring her large breasts. She yawned, knowing he was watching her in the mirror, posturing for him.

He grimaced again. He had fucked her savagely last night, with no consideration for her feelings. Of course, he did not give a damn about her feelings, and she liked rough sex. He turned, leaning against the bureau, openly studying her. Amelia smiled with lazy invitation, stretched again, and let the sheets fall to her plump thighs. She spread them slightly.

She was getting fat, he thought with disgust. Or had she always been overripe? She reminded him of a cow in that moment, and he could not dispel a mental image of Jane. He had only seen her from afar, but she had been slender and impossibly sensual, a siren beckoning all from the stage. He tried to remember why, after breaking it off with Amelia two years ago, he had ever bothered to renew their relationship. She had run after him the next time he had been in London, that fall, and he hadn't much cared who was warming his bed that night. Convenience, he supposed, summed it up then, and summed it up now.

"Come here," Amelia purred, stroking the bed by her thigh.

He turned and left abruptly, not bothering to close the door.

"You are a boor," she shouted after him, frustration in her voice. "More boorish than ever!"

He ignored her. If she didn't like it she could leave; in fact, he hoped she would leave. He ordered his carriage brought around as he sipped strong, hot coffee, suddenly too tense to eat anything. He was going to see Jane. But first he would have to find her.

He was regretting the decision he had made almost two years ago when he had undertaken to support her financially, through Robert Gordon. Then he had made it clear he did not want to do more than provide the monthly allowance, that under no circumstances did he want to be bothered with any details about Jane *at all*. So during the past two years he had written the checks and had not heard a single word from Gordon. The bottom line was that he did not even know where she lived. And now he would have to waste time finding out.

The earl's first stop was Mayfair. Thinking about Lindley in her dressing room brought back the anger he had felt when he had found him there. He intended to confront Lindley, but he had already left for the day and was not expected back until after tea. Nick wasn't sure Lindley knew where Jane could be found anyway. It depended on the question that was arousing his ire: Just how well did they know each other? Were they lovers?

He would kill Lindley if they were.

He calmed himself as he trotted down the steps of the big brick town house Lindley had recently built for himself. He told himself he would not kill Lindley for being seduced by that little hussy. She had probably climbed into his bed when he was asleep and drunk, as she had done to him. No man could resist in such circumstances. Besides, it was not his affair. She was his ward, yes, but only technically. She had chosen her life—one without him. So be it. He provided money and she could damn well fuck whomever she pleased, Lindley included.

He was not calm.

He knew where Gordon lived, but he was also not at home and not expected back until after the theater that night. The earl did not leave a message.

No one at the Criterion knew where she lived, and the earl was sure they were all telling the truth. He realized that she hid the location of her residence. It seemed a bit odd, but recalling all her fervent admirers the night before, he decided it was reasonable.

The trail was dead, for now. He debated hiring a detective who could, within a few days, find out all the details he wanted to know. This was a waste, and he dismissed the notion immediately. He would return to Lindley's at five to see what he knew. If this proved fruitless, he would catch Jane before her evening performance.

She would not escape him again.

The two men stared at each other.

Tension filled the room.

Finally Lindley spoke. He looked Nick in the eye. "I don't know where she is."

The earl stared back. "Are you seeing her?"

Lindley hesitated. "She is just a friend."

The earl was angry. "Then you must know where she lives."

"I do not," Lindley said firmly, too firmly.

"You're lying." Nick was incredulous. "You're lying to me."

Lindley didn't answer, grimmer now.

"Damn her!" Nick exploded. "Will she come between us again, destroy the one friendship important to me?"

"I'm sorry," Lindley said. "Damn it! She made me promise not to tell! How can I break my promise?" His gaze was imploring.

The earl paced. He turned. "I will find out. Keep your promise. Are you fucking her?"

"No."

The earl knew his friend well enough to know when he was telling the truth. He felt it then, the relief.

"Why do you care?" Lindley asked softly. "Not because she is technically your ward."

"I don't care," the earl stated flatly. "I only wanted to know the facts."

"Well, I do care," Lindley said. "I care about Jane. She is warm and special and she deserves to be happy. Leave her alone, Shelton. For some damn reason she doesn't want to see you. Just leave her alone."

The earl turned his back on Lindley, his strides hard and long, exiting the room, the house.

"I wish I could come with you to Charing Cross, darling, but I can't," Jane crooned, hugging Nicole. Anxiously she looked at Molly. "You have everything? Money, the extra blanket, sweaters?"

"I have everything, mum, don't worry," Molly said, reaching for Nicole. They stood outside on the front stoop of Jane's house. A hired hansom waited in the street to take them to the depot at Charing Cross. To avoid the scrutiny of her neighbors, an elaborate hat and veil hid Jane's face and hair.

Jane hugged Nicole again. "Good-bye, darling, it's only for a week." She gave her daughter to Molly, kissing the woman's plump cheek. "Send me a telegram when you arrive, and every day as well. Just don't mention Nicole, only that everything is fine."

"Yes'm. Don't worry, mum, everyone goes to Brighton."

"Yes, yes," Jane said nervously. She kissed them each again, then watched Molly and Nicole, small valise in hand, heading through the gate to the cab. She felt a sense of loss, her anxiety acute, but knew she was only being a foolish mother parting with her baby for the first time.

And she would not think about tomorrow.

Tomorrow she would confront the Earl of Dragmore.

30

He waited outside the theater, across the street, in plain sight but shielded slightly by the many passersby and the shadows of the awning over a pharmacist's. He guessed she would arrive from the side street instead of Picadilly Circus, and he was right. What he had not guessed was that she would be protected by bodyguards.

Stunned, furious, the earl watched Jane exit the coach accompanied by three men, all big and burly with revolvers and clubs, clearly detectives. They disappeared into the back entrance of the theater. Gordon was with them.

At least Lindley was not.

He had not a single doubt that she knew he was after her and that the guards were there to protect her from him.

What was she so afraid of? Did she think he would hurt her? Almost two years had passed since she had crawled uninvited into his bed. He grew grim. Uninvited? Hah! He had wished her there the entire short time she had been at Drag-more and he damn well knew it! She might have seduced him, but he had been a willing victim, and he had not a doubt that had she seduced him while he was wide awake and sober as a judge he'd have been willing then too.

But two years had passed. Why was she afraid of him?

What was she hiding?

This was not the Jane he had known, who was open and honest and direct and guileless. This was a woman keeping secrets. A desperate woman—he had heard the fear in her voice last night before she had fled from her dressing room.

His curiosity, his suspicions, were aroused.

Patiently he waited.

And when she left hours later, still accompanied by the guards, he followed on foot discreetly. The earl was in magnificent form, and he had no trouble keeping up. In fact, he enjoyed the hunt, the chase. He kept to the shadows and out of the streetlamps, trotting tirelessly. His years growing up in the wilds and his Comanche blood were paying off.

His glee was savage when she alighted from the coach at a town house on Gloucester Street. He had not a single doubt that this was where Jane lived. This was her kind of home, cozy and cheerful, honeysuckle creeping along the iron fence, the shutters painted yellow, the door a royal blue, purple pansies spilling from the window boxes. She entered the house and her escort remained outside, bidding her good night. The detectives returned to the coach, Gordon with them, and the carriage pulled away.

The earl could not believe his good fortune.

He strode impatiently up the walk and knocked

on the door. A moment later it opened, Jane saying "Robert?"

And their gazes locked.

His held triumph, hers recognition, then shock, then fear. She tried to slam the door in his face, but he was too fast. He rammed his shoulder into it, then effortlessly barreled through. Jane cried out in despair, his force knocking her back against the wall. He straightened, his heart pounding as if he'd run a race. Her blue eyes were wide and riveted on his. "What do you want!"

With an outward display of calm, he closed the door. He turned back slowly. His ears were ringing, his breath short. He looked at her.

God, she was beautiful.

"What do you want!" she cried again.

"I don't know."

She stood frozen against the wall, like a hare cornered before the hounds.

His gaze slipped from her white face. She had changed, filled out, become lush with maturity. Her bosom was fuller, straining against her low-cut gown and spilling over it. Her waist seemed tinier, perhaps in contrast. Her hips were rounder, softer. Before she had been coltish. She was still slender, but so perfectly curved his groin began raging.

He hated his lust.

He hated her for what she did to him.

"Maybe," he said, sneering, "I want what Lindley wants."

She stiffened. Her chin came up, her eyes blazed. "Get out!"

He smiled, a dangerous, mean smile, and stalked past her into the parlor. His gaze swept it. He heard her coming up behind him. He moved away, down the corridor, opening the door to a back room, which obviously belonged to the maid.

"What are you doing?" Jane demanded. "You can't just come into my home as if you own it!"

He shot her a look. "But I do." He moved past her, to inspect the small dining room and kitchen.

She followed, furious. "What do you mean, you do! I pay the rent, this is my house, and if you don't leave I'll call the Peelers on you!"

He paused once again in the foyer, leaning against the wall negligently, arms crossed. "Do you pay the rent, Jane? Or did Gordon set you up here?"

She flushed. "It's none of your damn business!"

"The kitten has grown claws," he said.

"This kitten would like to spit in your face!"

"Gordon set you up here," the earl said calmly. "I pay him a monthly allowance—for your rent and keep."

She stared, shocked.

He lost his negligent stance, standing, looming over her. "What? No thank yous? Oh, how could I forget? A woman who skulks away in the dark of night without a good-bye would not be the type to say thank you. The one thing," he said viciously, "that I know is my duty. Did you forget, Jane, who your guardian is?"

"You have been giving Robert money?"

"Since the day you left."

She turned away, distraught. "How much? How much do I owe you?"

"Nothing."

She whirled. "How much, damn you! How much do I owe you!"

He was shocked because she was crying. "Two thousand pounds at the end of this year."

Jane gasped. Two thousand pounds was a fortune—and had she known, she could have lived in a much more lavish place than this house.

As it was, she earned just enough to pay the rent and provide the necessities to maintain Nicole and herself. Robert was always trying to give her a few extra pounds, and always buying her the luxuries she could not afford. No wonder he had been able to be so generous—it was with the earl's money! She was certain that Robert hadn't told her about the allowance because he knew she would refuse it. Jane had no doubt that by now he had put away a tidy nest egg for Nicole and herself.

She bit her lip. She did not have the money to pay the earl back. Not now. Not yet. Maybe, in another year, she would be making such a sum. But not this year. "I don't have it," she said woodenly.

"It doesn't matter."

"It does matter!" she flared. "I don't want anything from you—do you understand?"

"Once you said you loved me." He laughed. The sound was harsh. "Now you hate me."

She didn't refute him. She just stared, eyes glazed with tears.

He felt it then, the terrible stabbing pain. Once, when he had been about to marry her, he had told himself he would be indifferent to her hate, should she one day detest him. But he was not indifferent, oh no. He touched his chest, rubbed it. The pain did not go away.

"Why have you come?"

"Curiosity," he said, shrugging. "Have no fear, I will not come again."

"Good," she flung. "Because you are not welcome here. Your curiosity is satisfied, I presume. So—leave."

He tore his gaze away from her with difficulty. Yet his feet would not move to the door. Instead, he stood unmoving, his gaze going past her to the open door of the parlor. He was strangely unwilling to leave.

And he could see Jane's touch everywhere. The parlor was warm and cozy, bright and cheerful. The walls were a fresh yellow, the drapes cream. The rug was a bright floral. The couch was spring green, comfortably upholstered, and even the baby's shirt she was knitting was a pretty pink. There were wildflowers in the vases, not roses, but . . .

Baby's shirt?

His gaze flew to the knitting left on a chair. The shirt was pink and finished except for one tiny sleeve. His heart had constricted; now it began to slam forcefully against his ribs. He strode within, lifted the knitting. "What's this?"

It was a demand. He turned, saw that she was whiter than a ghost. His gaze pierced hers. "It's Molly's," she said. "Molly has a child."

He stared at her. His first thought was to wonder if the child was his, but the odds were low, as Molly had a lascivious appetite. Then his gaze narrowed, his heart slamming again. "Molly, your maid, sits in your parlor knitting for her child?" And he thought about her fear and the secret he'd known she was hiding.

Jane flushed. "Why not?" She shrugged gracefully.

She was lying, he knew it. For the first time since he'd stepped within her house, she was calm and composed. "I want to see the child," he said.

"Why?"

"Why? The brat could be mine."

She flushed again. "You know Molly. She has—er—a fondness for men. Trust me, it's not yours."

Her voice was very firm. His smile was cynical. "Humor me."

"They're not here."

"Oh? Then you won't mind if I look around."

She ran after him. "Stop! This is my home! I shall call the Bobbies!"

He ignored her, pulse pounding, and pushed open the door to Molly's room. He turned on a lamp. As he'd thought, there was no crib within, not even another cot for her baby. "Where does the child sleep?"

Jane was white. She did not answer.

He wanted to strangle her.

Furious, he ran up the stairs. This time she remained frozen below. He threw open the first door on the left, turned on a lamp, and saw that it was Jane's room. Just for a moment he stared at the bed, covered in a white, lace-trimmed quilt. Then he strode across the hall. He heard Jane scream, pounding up the stairs like a madwoman. He reached for the door. With a savage cry, like a female warrior, she grabbed his hand with both of hers, her nails tearing into his flesh. "No! Leave! I want you out of here now!"

He found her wrists, making her release her clawlike grasp, and he pushed her against the wall. She was panting, bosom heaving, her face red with fury. When he released her she attacked him. With her nails poised like talons, she went for his face, and succeeded in scratching him from temple to jaw.

He exploded. He wrestled her arms behind her back, pinning her to the wall. To his dismay, and fury, he was huge and erect against her belly. She writhed wildly, once, inflaming him further. Then, abruptly, she went still.

Tears filled her eyes. She was panting. His own breathing was harsh. He felt a tremor assail his body. He still wanted her, more than he had ever wanted any other woman. His face was close to hers, and he leaned closer to kiss her.

"I hate you."

He froze, then smiled, baring even white teeth. "Well said." His smile was gone. He yanked on her, pulling her harder against him, wanting her to feel his aching, agonized tumescence. She began to tremble. He decided he'd enjoy her fear. Let her think he'd rape her, the bitch! The lying deceitful two-faced philandering bitch! "What are you hiding, Jane?"

She stared and said nothing.

He held her for a second more, waiting for her fear to grow, but it didn't. Instead, he felt her stiffness fading, and as she relaxed, she looked at his open shirt, at the dark, wet skin of his chest, inches from her mouth.

She was a temptress, a woman of wiles, attempting now to distract him. He heaved away from her. He heard her choke. He entered the room, flicked on a lamp, and stared.

A nursery.

He took it all in, the clowns on the wallpaper, the rocking horse, the dolls, the pretty painted headboard. The bed was empty.

She had a child.

He turned, slowly, heart clamoring. "Who is the father?"

She stood in the doorway, a pale wraith. "Robert."

He had thought it might be his, hoped it was his, and the pain of her having another man's child struck him with such force he staggered backward. "You're lying." But even as he spoke, he knew that the odds of his being the father from one time in Jane's bed were minute. The pain increased.

"It's Robert's," she said, and tears spilled from her lashes. She began to cry.

"Where is he?"

"Robert lives—"

"Where is the child?"

For one moment she looked at him, her eyes filled with despair, and then she crumbled against the door jamb, weeping. "God forgive me," she cried. "I can't do this, I can't! Robert isn't the father, you are."

31

Stunned, he did not move.

She wept, hugging herself.

A child. He had a child, Jane's child. The shock faded. Understanding flared. The enormity of her deception—her lies. He wanted to kill her.

She sensed it, because she stopped crying and took a step back.

"Were you ever going to tell me?"

Jane did not answer. It was answer enough. The earl came toward her, reaching for her, his temper raging. She didn't move. If she had, he probably would have gone after her and hurt her. But her frozen fear made him sane, or was it her desire for punishment? He stopped, letting his hands fall to his sides. "God!" he cried, the sound agonized.

"I'm sorry," she whispered.

He whirled. "Where is he?"

"She is in Brighton with Molly."

It was a daughter—his child was a daughter.

Jubilation soared, mixing with the pain of her betrayal. "A daughter," he said softly. "What is her name?"

Tears filled Jane's eyes. "Nicole."

It was like a blow to his gut, and he could not breathe. Jane turned away from him, shoulders slumped. Defeat etched her posture. He forgot himself. In that moment he wanted to go to her and cradle her and comfort her against his big body. But he didn't move. "I will go to Brighton and get her. Where are they staying?"

Jane snapped around. "No! I will go! You wait here!"

She was afraid of him still, and he did not understand why. Nor did he care anymore. He only wanted to see his daughter. "You perform tomorrow," he said coldly. "You cannot go. I will leave immediately. Where are they staying?"

"No, no, no!" Jane cried.

He was tired of her games, and he moved past her and down the hall. Brighton wasn't large and he would find them. She ran after him. "You can't go at night!"

He didn't bother to reply.

She stumbled on the stairs. "Can't you wait until the morning? We can go together!"

He paused in the foyer. "And what about tomorrow's engagement?"

"I will cancel it," she said frantically.

He took her chin in his hand and held her face immobile. He squeezed only enough to apply pressure that indicated his mood. Her lips parted on a breath.

"Do you think I want your miserable company another minute?" He snarled. "Like all women, you are a selfish liar. I can't stand the sight of you." He released her. "Stay away from me," he warned. "And I mean it, Jane."

He flung open the door and disappeared into the night.

His words immobilized her.

I am not selfish, I am not a liar, she thought, the tears falling again. She sagged against the banister, her strength suddenly gone. And then the truth of his words hit her with such force it was painful. She had lied, she had been selfish. She had cheated him of his daughter.

"God forgive me," she whispered.

And then her urge to protect her daughter took over.

She had to stop him. She had to stop him from finding Nicole. He would take her and she would never see her again—especially the way he felt about her now. There was the heartbreaking pain again, that he should hate her so, but she shrugged it off. He had never cared for her, not ever—in fact, if she collected all her memories it was as if he had always hated her. So what did it matter that he hated her still?

Only Nicole mattered.

Jane grabbed a cloak and ran outside. Once she was on the deserted street she realized her predicament. She would have to walk a good distance to a major thoroughfare to find a hansom at this time of night. And she was a woman, alone. At this hour only thieves and prostitutes were about, and the homeless. Her neighborhood was a decent one, with no such riffraff, but a few blocks away were the worst dregs of society. Jane hesitated only briefly.

Her daughter gave her courage.

As she walked, half running, she thought frantically of how to stop the earl. She must go to Brighton directly, take Nicole and run. But she did not have enough money, she needed help. She thought of Robert and dismissed him. Gordon would cave in to the earl easily. All along he had disapproved of her keeping Nicole a secret from him. Lindley. Lindley was big, strong, and not afraid of the Earl. And he was rich enough to help her.

It was frightening traveling through London on foot at night. She passed prostitutes on street corners and beggars asleep or passed out on front stoops. She stopped once to hide from a gang of unruly, roughneck teenagers intent on vandalism, her heart in her throat. And she passed two burglars picking the lock of a mercantile shop.

Where were all the Bobbies this night?

Finally she found a cab, and an hour after she had left her home, she arrived at Lindley's.

Jane did not pause despite the fact that it was two in the morning. She banged on the massive front door, pulling the bell repeatedly, creating a racket. From around back, dogs started barking. Lights came on. First in an outer wing, then upstairs, then all around the house. Jane kept banging. She realized she was starting to cry. She prayed that Lindley was at home. The door was opened by a sleepy-eyed, consternated servant, his jacket unbuttoned as he'd shrugged on his clothes with haste.

"I must see the earl!" Jane cried, barreling past him. And then she saw him, trotting down the stairs in a wine-colored, paisley men's robe.

"Jane!"

"My lord, forgive me, this woman—" the servant began.

But Jane had rushed to Lindley, and he swept

her into his arms. She clung. "What is it? What's happened?" Lindley cried.

Jane gripped his lapels. "It's him! The earl! He found out about Nicole and now he's gone to Brighton to get her! Please! You must help me, I beg you!"

Lindley stared, comprehension slowly beginning. He put his arm around Jane. "We'll talk in my study. Richard, bring us some tea and toast."

"You don't understand! There is no time to lose!"

Lindley led her into a large, magnificent library and steered her to the couch, pushing her down. He sat beside her, taking her small, cold hands in his. "No, I don't understand. Take a few deep breaths, Jane, and explain what has upset you so."

Jane closed her eyes briefly. "Jon, I sent Nicole to Brighton with Molly. I was afraid the earl had found out about her—why else would he have suddenly tried to see me? But he hadn't! I don't know why the sudden interest in me. He came to my house tonight. He found out about her. Now he's gone to Brighton to get her. You must help me! Please—will you?"

"Of course I will. But I still don't understand."

"He will take her away from me, don't you see?" Jane pleaded. "I must get to Brighton first, take Nicole and hide." She gripped his hands. "I need your help. Will you come with me, help me, lend me money to go to France?"

He stared.

Jane closed her eyes again, in frustration and prayer.

"Jane, this is not the way to act. Has Shelton said he'll take Nicole from you?"

Jane looked at him. "No."

"Then—"

"But he will! You know the kind of man he is! And he hates me so!"

"All right," Lindley said. "We will go to Brighton. We will get Nicole. But then you and Shelton must talk."

Jane opened her mouth to protest, then closed it. One step at a time. They would go to Brighton and get Nicole. Let Lindley think she was willing to talk to the earl. Once she had Nicole she would run—to India if she had to.

Lindley smiled, squeezing her hand. "We will leave first thing in the morning."

"We must leave now! Please!" Again she gripped his lapels.

Her face was so close, he could have kissed her. And, unable to restrain himself, he did, briefly, softly, once. "All right. It seems I cannot say no to you."

Jane slumped against the couch, relieved. It was what she had been counting on. Yet when they arrived in Brighton by midmorning, it was too late. Nicole and Molly were gone.

By the time Jane and Lindley arrived back in London late that afternoon, Jane was white-faced and gaunt. No amount of reassurance from Lindley as to the earl's intentions could reassure her. Her frame of mind worsened when she was told at the Shelton residence that the earl had not been seen since yesterday evening, and his whereabouts were unknown.

"He's taken her to Dragmore," Jane moaned.

Lindley grimaced, for it certainly looked that way. "Go home, Jane, eat something and get a good night's rest. Tomorrow we will go to Dragmore and talk to Shelton. What the hell is wrong with him!"

"He wants to hurt me," Jane flashed. Then she groaned again, sinking deeper into the plush seat of Lindley's coach. Lindley ordered his driver to take them to Gloucester Street.

"I want to go to Dragmore tonight," Jane said, turning to Lindley. She placed her hand on his forearm. "Please? I need only to get a few things."

"Jane, you're exhausted. You'll make yourself sick."

"I don't care. My daughter is at stake!"

Lindley fought with himself, and lost. "All right. But we need fresh horses, for these are finished. Get what you need. But for God's sake, Jane, have a hot soak and eat supper. I'll pick you up later."

Jane agreed, compromising. "Thank you," she said seriously, gratitude in her eyes. Again she touched his arm.

He touched her chin, lifting it. He waited, and she did not flinch away. He knew it was only gratitude, but he hoped it was more, and he took advantage despite better intentions. He leaned forward and kissed her, for a long moment, sensually, softly. Jane didn't respond, but she didn't pull away either. "Give me a chance," Lindley said, drawing back.

She didn't say anything.

The coach stopped in front of her plastered house. Lindley walked her to the front door and waited until she had unlocked it. "I'll pick you up at ten," he told her.

"Thank you so much," Jane said huskily, kissing his cheek. He smiled and left, and she closed the door behind him.

"Mum, where have you been!"

Jane jumped, stunned, to find a joyous Molly behind her. "Is Nicole here?"

"Nicole is upstairs, asleep," the Earl of Drag-more said, from the doorway of the parlor.

Jane went white.

"Where have you been?" His tone was casual.

Jane stood very still. Her heart was racing wildly. "Mum?" Molly questioned. "Are you all right?"

Jane sagged against the door. He hadn't taken Nicole to Dragmore. He hadn't stolen her away. He had gone to get her—and had brought her back here to Gloucester Street. Slowly, her eyes filling with tears of fatigue and relief, Jane slid down the wall to sit on the floor.

"Mum!" Molly cried, kneeling. "What is it, are you ill?"

Her exhaustion was so great, she could not move. She closed her eyes, her head against the door, and managed to shake her head negatively. She felt Molly's hand on her forehead, seeking a fever.

He hadn't tried to abduct Nicole.

She felt the earl's arms as he lifted her. Jane tensed, opened her eyes, and tried to protest. His face was white, his body big, solid, hard, and warm. All thoughts of protest died. Jane let her lids fall shut and leaned her cheek against his chest, her chin touching the bare flesh exposed by his open shirt. She smiled.

He hadn't tried to steal her daughter from her.

The earl stood outside Jane's bedroom door, the waiting endless. What was wrong? Was she ill? And why the hell did he give a damn! He re-minded himself of her deceit, but still, he re-mained glued outside her door.

Molly appeared, and the earl strained to see past her into the bedroom. Jane was curled up on the bed, fast asleep, her profile toward him. Platinum hair spilled from the bed to the floor. She looked like an angel and his entire body tightened at the sight of her. Molly shut the door in his face.

"How is she? What's wrong? I want you to go and fetch a doctor," Nick said.

Molly smiled. "She's just tired is all. She went all the way to Brighton and back, my lord."

"What!"

Molly nodded. "Didn't sleep a wink, she said. She's fine, just worn right out."

"Why in hell did she go to Brighton when I told her I'd get Nicole?" the earl asked, turning away. Wisely Molly didn't answer.

The earl ran a hand through his hair. He felt some of the tension draining from him. He'd expected to confront Jane today with his decision. Now it would have to wait. He tried, for the hundredth time, to imagine her reaction when he told her. Anger, tears, stubborn opposition? Inanely, he pictured her face lighting up with joy.

He grew grim. Why was he indulging in foolish fantasies? Jane clearly hated him—and he bore her no fondness. She was a liar and a cheat, and he would never forget it. She had tried to keep him from his daughter, from his flesh and blood. She was his enemy, and he would remember this well.

She was also the mother of his child.

He refused to feel the thrill.

He paced to the nursery and looked in. His daughter was sleeping peacefully, but the earl did not smile. No, Jane would not be happy when he gave her his decision. He had not a single doubt that she would fight him tooth and nail when he told her they were getting married.

And it was just too bad.

32

🔥🔥🔥

Jane was not surprised when she awoke the next day and found the Earl of Dragmore in her house. Spotting his gloves and riding crop left carelessly on the table in the foyer, Jane's heart leapt. "Molly!"

The maid came running from the kitchen. "Good mornin', mum. Feelin' better?"

He was not in the parlor. "Quite, thank you. Where is Nicole? Where is the earl?"

"Out back."

Swallowing, feeling heated, Jane hurried into the kitchen. She paused at the screened door leading to the back garden, opening it but not going through. An impossible sight greeted her.

The big earl dwarfed the little pink swing. He looked positively silly sitting in it. In fact, it was distinctly possible that he'd break it if he continued to use it. He held Nicole in his arms, moving the swing back and forth with his muscular, breeches-clad legs. Nicole wiggled and made noises and said a few words, including her favorite one—"Mama."

Jane couldn't help it. She smiled. Warmth stole through every fiber of her being. Worse, tears filled her eyes, blurring them. She was unbearably touched, and suddenly so ashamed for keeping father and daughter apart.

It was clear that he wasn't taking her daughter from her. Was it possible that he would just ask to be able to visit as he willed?

She must have made a sound, for the earl looked up, saw her, and jumped to his feet. Nicole squealed in protest. The earl's face had taken on that sunburned look. His gaze melded with Jane's. "I was just giving her some air," he said defensively. "She likes the swing."

Jane carefully wiped the smile from her face. "Yes, she does," she said levelly. But, God, her heart felt as if it would burst with nameless need. Politely she said, "Would you care to come in and share breakfast with us?"

He was startled. His eyes flashed silver, and then he came forward, Nicole wriggling like an imp in his arms.

Today he wasn't angry and Jane wasn't threatened. She was very, very aware of the earl. Of his size—she had forgotten how tall he was. Of his strength—she had forgotten how broad were his shoulders, how thick his legs. Of his power— he filled up the tiny yard, and as he approached, his presence overwhelmed her. She had forgotten how handsome he was. His silver eyes, the thick, slashed brows, the high, high cheekbones, the hard, square jaw and straight, flared nose. He was a magnificent man. And he still ignored decorum.

His shirt was casually buttoned halfway. His chest and the black hairs there were visible. She

noticed a sprinkling of gray ones as well. His
breeches had dirt on the knees—had he been
playing with Nicole on the lawn? And they were
tight, as tight as she remembered, hugging his
form, hugging everything. She glanced at his
groin before she could stop herself, and quickly
turned to let him and Nicole pass inside.

Color had flooded her. And she was warm, so
warm. God, she ached. She remembered, too perfectly, yesterday evening. His body, pinning hers
to the wall. His strength, his power—his heat and
hardness.

She still wanted him.

The realization was a shock.

Lips pressed together, Jane followed them into
the cheery blue-and-white kitchen. "Molly, the
earl will be joining us." She gestured for him to
follow her to the dining room. She would not
meet his gaze. She took Nicole from his arms and
set her in her baby chair. Nicole laughed with
happiness, clapping her plump hands. She loved
to eat.

Jane sat in her customary place at the head of
the small table, which sat eight. The earl awkwardly sat on her left, across from their daughter.
Neither spoke. Jane fiddled with Nicole, talking
with her, while the earl folded his muscular arms
across his chest and watched impassively.

She couldn't help the thought. It was as if they
were man and wife. If only he had wanted to
marry her . . .

He couldn't help the thought. If she hadn't left
him, they would be married, and sitting here as
man and wife right now . . .

Molly served them buttermilk pancakes with
fresh berries and cream. Jane ignored her own
plate to help her daughter eat. The earl finished

his food, watching them constantly, the only conversation between mother and daughter. He
shoved his plate away. "Eat," he said to Jane. "I'll
do it."

Jane froze, holding a spoonful of pancake to
her daughter's mouth. She did not look at the
earl. "It's all right, I'll eat afterward."

The earl got up, came around the table, wedged
between them, and took the spoon from Jane's
hand. He smiled at Nicole. "Aren't you hungry,
darling?" he coaxed softly. "Open for Papa."

The sound of his voice, the heat of his nearness,
and the sight of him feeding their daughter assailed Jane with such powerful desire she
couldn't move or breathe. Nicole laughed and the
earl fed her a spoonful. Jane looked at her plate.
This was intolerable. Would he ever speak to her
in such a warm, low tone?

She toyed with her food. The earl continued to
coax Nicole into eating rather than playing, and
Nicole responded better to her father than she did
to Jane or Molly or anyone else. Finally the earl
set the spoon down and looked at Jane. "There's
something I would like to discuss with you when
you're finished." His tone was level and boded
neither good nor bad will.

"I'm through," Jane said, rising. "Molly! Please
take Nicole."

The earl walked into the parlor and Jane followed him, trying not to stare at his broad back
and small hips and worse, lower. He reached behind her to shut the door. His stare was hard.
"We're going to get married, Jane."

Jane couldn't believe her ears.

"No objection? Good, this is better than I'd an-
ticipated," he said easily, still pinning her with his

gaze. "We will be married next week, and you and Nicole will move into my London flat."

Jane recovered. Her very first reaction was a primal elation, which was quickly swept away by rationality. Jane was no longer naive, and did not even pause to think he was marrying her for any reason other than their daughter. Did she want to be married to this man, who had broken her heart? Who would marry her again out of duty? The answer was a resounding no.

But, logically, she considered Nicole and what was best for her. And knew the answer was still no, for the earl had been providing abundantly for her when he didn't even know about his daughter, and he could certainly continue to do so. She grew angry. "No."

"It wasn't a proposal," he said in a mocking tone. "I was telling you what we are doing."

She gasped at his audacity. "You cannot force me to marry you! I have no wish to marry you—I have no need to marry you. I am not marrying you, and that is that." She turned to go.

He reached over her shoulder and placed his palm flat on the door, preventing her from opening it, should she try. She did not. "Please remove your hand," she said calmly, although she was beginning to perspire and tremble.

He turned her around, and she gasped again. "You have no choice. Look at the bright side, it will be best for Nicole."

"Best for Nicole! What do you mean, I have no choice? I am telling you, I refuse to marry you." She was shouting.

"Have you forgotten?" he said softly, so softly she had to strain to hear. He smiled. "I am your guardian, Jane, and you are under age. We are getting married next week."

Understanding dawned. Horrified, Jane could only stare. He was going to marry her whether she liked it or not—she had no choice.

The earl had left. Jane sank down into a plush chaise, still shocked. She knew the earl well enough to know that if marrying her was within his power, and this was his desire, he would accomplish it no matter who objected, no matter the cost. She did not stand a chance.

Her head began to pound with the beginnings of a headache. She rubbed her temple, trying to think, trying to sort out her feelings and what must be done.

Only one fact was clear. He had broken her heart, bastard that he was. And she wasn't indifferent to him, not at all. To the contrary, at the very least she was physically attracted to this man. And she still suffered bouts of compassion for him. To be married to him under these circumstances would be intolerable. He would probably break her heart again.

She tried to hate him. She couldn't, but she was angry, so very angry, and so damn frustrated . . .

There was one single bright spot to the entire rotten tangle. Nicole would have a father and would not grow up a bastard. Maybe this was for the best. But what about their relationship?

Suddenly Jane was swamped with the realization of just what marriage entailed—and she was terrified.

She would be his wife. Caring for Chad and Nicole, caring for his house, caring for him. An image of them in bed together assailed her. Shaking, she rose abruptly and went upstairs.

The earl had said he would come back tomorrow to see Nicole. Tomorrow was not soon enough.

Jane changed her clothes and was on her way to Tavistock Square. She was so determined and so preoccupied she did not have a smile for Thomas when he let her in and ushered her into the morning room to await the earl.

She paced. She was flushed, her blood pounding. Her fists were clenched tightly at her sides. When the door opened Jane whirled. The earl smiled. "So eager to see me that you couldn't wait until tomorrow?"

"Eager? Not quite," she said coolly. She marched to the door and slammed it behind him. He regarded her with interest.

"I realize that we are getting married no matter how strongly I object," Jane said. "True?"

"True." He watched her.

"We have not discussed the terms of the marriage."

He raised a brow.

"Firstly," Jane said, "I am continuing my work. You will not interfere in my career. Is this understood?"

"You may have your goddamn career," he said easily, but his eyes were diamond hard. "We will reside in London during the run of your performance. However, you will take a few months off between each performance to come to Dragmore and behave as a mother should."

Her fists tightened. "Are you insinuating that I am lacking as a mother?"

"I am merely pointing out that Nicole is your first priority."

"So far I have been the best of mothers, even while working full time."

"It is impossible to be the best of mothers while

working full time." He smiled irritatingly with superior knowledge.

There was no point in banging her head against this wall. Jane fumed. "Are we agreed then? I perform until the run is finished, then return to Dragmore for two months?"

"Three."

"Two!"

"Three. Do not test my generosity, Jane."

"You are a bastard," she hissed, meaning it.

He shrugged. "Next?"

"We shall have separate bedrooms."

His expression did not change. He appeared unperturbed. "It's the fashion."

"No, you do not understand. You are not welcome in my bed. You will not touch me."

He stared.

She smiled and it wasn't pretty. "This is your idea. Therefore it will be only a marriage of convenience for Nicole's sake. You may do what you will elsewhere, but do not bother me."

He folded his arms. The smile was back, ugly and hard. There was no smile in his eyes. "Do you think I lust after you? You may have a child, Jane, but you're still nineteen, and as far as I am concerned, barely out of pinafores."

God, it hurt. She lifted her head high. "And you shall not interfere in my private life either."

His arms fell, fists clenched, and he took a step forward. "Just what is your private life, Jane? Rather, who? Lindley?"

"It is none of your business," she told him fiercely.

He eyed her with such revulsion she knew then that he did hate her. Fists still tight, he smiled meanly. "Fine. Enjoy your paramours. But I de-

mand discretion. I will not have Nicole humiliated by a slut for a mother."

"Nicole?" Jane scoffed, trying to ignore the pain
his slander brought. "Or yourself?"

"Why would I be humiliated? To be humiliated
I must care." He stalked to the door, paused. "Any
other considerations?"

Tears threatened to rise, and Jane willed them
away. She would not cry now, not in front of him.
"No."

"Good." With hard strides he left, thumping
down the hall and out the front door, shouting for
his coach.

Jane began to tremble. She moved to the window, saw him waiting rigidly for the carriage,
and tears filled her eyes. Bastard! He was selfish
and ruthless and completely insensitive, and he
certainly despised her. But it was for the best. If
he didn't hate her so much, she would soften toward him and maybe come to love him again as
they spent a lifetime together as man and wife.
God forbid! To love such a man could only bring
heartbreak. The dark burning fires that flamed so
deeply within him came from a tortured soul, and
she doubted they could ever be extinguished.

Jane turned away, pulling herself together. She
was a survivor. If she had survived his rejection
almost two years ago, she could survive this as
well.

33

It was only natural that he would tell his best friend that he was getting married. Nick entered an exclusive men's club on St. James's Street. His membership at White's had survived the trial because of Lindley's firm patronage, support, and, Nick suspected, generous bribery. Inside it was all dark wood and even darker carpets. He found Lindley sitting with two men, a baron and a viscount. Lindley spotted him. "Shelton! Come join us."

"Thank you." The earl dropped down into a big padded leather chair. A white-coated waiter materialized, and Nick ordered his usual Scotch whiskey.

He was bitter and angry and he knew it. His emotions roiled like hot lava in a volcano. The dialogue he'd just had with Jane—his wife-to-be—was fresh in his mind. "A toast," he said, smiling, lifting his glass. The three men joined him. "To the actress, London's Little Angel—soon to be my wife."

A shocked silence greeted this. The baron looked at the viscount. Nick laughed, imagining their gossip already. The Lord of Darkness (who had killed his wife) was marrying the Little Angel —the actress! Weston's bastard granddaughter!

And soon Nicole and his relationship to her would be no secret. More scandal was inevitable. He did not care. Not for himself, at any rate, and certainly not for that witch, Jane. (Separate bedrooms—hah! As if he'd touch her with a ten-foot pole!) He cared only about Nicole, and by the time she was old enough to understand it would have long since faded into oblivion.

Lindley was white. "Is this a joke?"

The earl drained his glass, thumped it down. "What's the matter, Jon? You thinking of marrying belowstairs?"

Lindley just sat and stared.

"I say, old boy," the baron said, attempting a smile, "this is quite the trick!"

"I'm sure," Nick said dryly. He suffered their falsely meant congratulations, except for Lindley, who said nothing. The baron and viscount finally left—no doubt to impart what they had just learned. Nick looked at his friend. "What? No handshake, no smile, no joy to equal my own?" The words came out terribly twisted.

"It's because of Nicole," Lindley said heavily. "Isn't it?"

Nick looked at him. "How in hell—"

"I found out recently. She made me promise not to tell you. I'm sorry, Nick, but she twisted me around her finger, and once I gave her my word I couldn't go back on it."

"You son of a bitch," the earl managed, shocked. "You weren't going to tell me I had a daughter? You? My only goddamn friend?"

Lindley rubbed his face. "I was going to try to persuade Jane to tell you herself," he said.

That eased some of the pain, but a bitter residue was left nonetheless.

"You don't have to marry her," Lindley said. "You don't have to go that far. She . . . wants to marry you?" His tone was fearful.

The earl felt a soaring jealousy and suddenly disliked his friend intensely. "I am marrying her. I am adopting Nicole and raising her in my household. And no, Jane does not want to marry me, so you can relax. She hates the very idea."

Relief was visible on Lindley's features. "But if she isn't willing—"

"She is my ward. I gave her no choice."

Lindley was horrified. "Surely you won't marry her against her will!"

"No?" Nick laughed. "Try me, damn it, just try me." He lunged to his feet. "Tell me something, Lindley. Am I marrying your mistress?" His lips were twisted in a parody of a smile.

Lindley just stared up at him, then finally shook his head. "No. No."

The earl turned away abruptly. For the first time in his life, he did not trust Lindley. He doubted him and was sure that he was lying. He wanted to smash something. Preferably her.

She didn't want him.

As he waited for his coach to be brought round, he was assailed with the inescapable fact. She didn't want him. Like Patricia, she despised him. Like Patricia, she had left him. Like Patricia, she had hurt him. And once again, he was entering the shackles of marriage to a hate-filled spouse.

But this time he did not love his wife. This time he despised her too.

34

They went directly from the wedding ceremony, attended only by Molly and Lindley, Nicole and Chad and Governess Randall, to the house on Tavistock Square. All of Jane and Nicole's belongings had been packed that week and sent over earlier that day. In deference to Jane, who was Anglican, a minister had presided at the ceremony. Jane was too numb and weary from the past week, too filled with anxiety and frustration, too bitter, to even consider this small display of sensitivity on her groom's part.

Now Jane held Nicole tightly and stood in the hallway upstairs in the master wing of the town house. Her husband, who had not smiled even once, who even now appeared angry and glowering, was beside her, hands shoved deep in his pockets. One of the servants was moving a final trunk into her rooms. Jane ignored the earl, although she felt his gaze upon her, and stepped within her sitting room.

It was large and luxuriously appointed, not that she had doubted it would be anything less. There were two doors leading from it, one on either side of the room. Her apprehension was great. Jane moved across the thick Persian carpet to open one, which led to her bedroom, dominated by a damask-canopied bed. With a quick glance around, she stepped back into the sitting room, where her husband now stood, frozen like a statue. She ignored him, although her heart was beating mercilessly, and found that the other door opened onto a marble-floored water closet complete with pedestal tub and running water. Where was his bedroom? Surely he remembered their arrangement?

"Satisfied?" he queried sarcastically.

She faced him squarely. "Where are your rooms?"

He smiled mockingly. "Changing your mind already, Jane?"

She lifted her nose in the air. "To the contrary. I want to make sure the door between us is locked."

His gray eyes flashed. Without a word, he turned and strode out, slamming the door behind him. Nicole started to cry.

"Hush," Jane said, caressing her hair. "It's all right. He isn't mad at you." She was stricken with remorse for her cruelty and wished she had a heart of iron to fortify herself with.

That afternoon she took dinner alone, her husband having disappeared. Jane was too proud even to ask Thomas where he had gone to, and told herself she did not care. She ran into him in the hallway that evening after her bath. She was in a dressing gown, getting ready to go to the theater for the night's performance. She needed a glass of milk to settle her stomach. She was always nervous before a performance, but never had her nerves been so taut. She told herself it was because of this past week—attendance was dropping at the Criterion every night. The play had only been running six weeks, and this was not a good sign. Only once last week had the house been nearly full. Robert had told her he was afraid the show had peaked and was on its last legs.

Jane was not ready to finish the run. Never had she been so good in her role. Although the critics had not seemed to notice her improvement—in fact, they had barely mentioned her all week, and only to compare her beauty to her mother's. Worse, she had an agreement with her husband— if the performance closed down, she would have to go to Dragmore for the next three months. This she absolutely dreaded.

They met on the stairs, she going up, a glass of milk in hand, he coming down. At first they were both startled to see each other. Then he nodded; she nodded. They passed without touching, making an obvious effort not to, and without a word. He was dressed elegantly for an evening out. It was tense and awkward between them. Jane did not feel like a wife, not like the mistress of the house. She felt like an unwanted guest, an intruder. She wondered where he was going— worse, with whom?

That night she had never been better—but she played to only half a house.

Afterward Robert consoled her in her dressing room. "Jane, you are growing dramatically as an actress. I can see you improving with each performance."

"Then how come nobody is coming?" She was tired and she slumped in front of her dressing mirror. She did not want to go home to the earl's house. She wished she was going home to her own cozy house on Gloucester Street.

"Every show has a life of its own," Gordon said. "Don't worry, we can find you another role as soon as this closes."

Jane just looked at him. She was too weary to explain to him she would have to take a three-month "holiday."

That evening Jane gave Gordon a lift home in the Dragmore carriage with its black-and-gold crest. Before exiting, he leaned to her. "Is everything all right, Jane?"

She knew to what, and to whom, he referred. She managed a smile. "I suppose so."

"If you need anything," he said earnestly, "don't hesitate."

Gratitude flooded her. She was so lucky to have a real friend whom she could rely on. "Thank you."

Shortly after, Thomas let her in, impeccable despite the hour, which was just short of midnight. While he served her a light supper, Jane had to casually ask if the earl was asleep. Thomas's expression was carefully blank. "No, my lady."

Jane was careful to stare down at her carrots as she forked them. "He is in the library, then?" Not that she cared where he was.

"He is still out," Thomas said.

Jane was very tired, but decided to read for a while after checking on Nicole. She sat on a chintz-covered chaise in her sitting room, the door slightly ajar. She had learned that afternoon that his apartments were just down the hall from

hers, and it would be impossible not to hear him
when he returned, for he would have to pass her
rooms. Of course, she was not waiting up for him,
nor did she care when he came in. She found herself listening to the night, however, not reading.
And there were no footsteps upon the stairs, no
carriage wheels spinning on the gravel outside.
Annoyed, Jane snapped her book shut and
glanced at the malachite-framed clock. It was 2
A.M.

Yet when she finally heard the carriage, the
horses, and voices outside her window, which
was open, she reached for the clock and brought
it close to gaze at it in the starlight. She could
dimly make out its face—it was four-thirty.

She rolled onto her stomach, feeling an acute
stabbing that was distinctly hurtful. Of course he
had mistresses, of course he would see them. It
was not her business. Indeed, she had given him
her permission to do as he chose. But why, oh
why, did it have to hurt so much?

Jane never slept late despite her vocation and
usually arose around eight. She did not expect to
see the earl, recalling how at Dragmore he was up
with the sun and gone shortly thereafter. Of
course, in Sussex he was not out all night long
with paramours. Therefore, it should not have
stopped her in her tracks to see him sitting at the
big gilt dining table with the London *Times*.

Her heart skipped a few beats. He barely
glanced at her. There were two other settings on
the table, one used and abandoned. With a start,
Jane realized Chad must take breakfast with his
father. She had seen him yesterday to say hello,
and had been stunned at the difference two years
could make. He was quite the seven-year-old imp

now, and he had been delighted to see her and
thrilled to have her marrying his father. At least
one member of the family was happy with the
circumstances, Jane thought grimly.

She sat on the earl's right. He said nothing, just
cracked his paper once. To not even exchange
civil good mornings was too much as far as Jane
was concerned. "Good morning," she said, not
looking at him and pouring herself coffee from a
silver pot.

He grunted.

Jane helped herself to a croissant. As she but-
tered it, not looking at him, she said, perversely,
"Did you have a pleasant time last evening?"

"Very."

Bastard, she thought, buttering the bread with
vigor now. He laid aside his paper and penetrated
her with a look. "And you?"

"Just wonderful," she said calmly. "May I?" She
gestured to the *Times*.

He leaned back indolently in his chair, which
reminded Jane of a throne with its high scrolled
back and clawed arms. Jane took the paper and
searched for the theater reviews. A headline in
the social column screamed out at her: LORD OF
DARKNESS WEDS LONDON'S ANGEL! She gasped, fixing him with big blue eyes.

He smiled. "What's the matter? Aren't you used
to notoriety by now?"

His tone was hurtful. Deliberately, calmly, she
closed the paper and set it back where it had
come from, near his right hand. "Exactly what
are you insinuating?"

"Am I insinuating anything?"

"I think so."

"You tell me."

"I think, sir, that you are a boor."

He laughed. His teeth were so very white. "So I've been told." He rose abruptly to his feet. *"Bon appetit,* Jane."

35

𝕤𝕤𝕤

Jane was ecstatic. She had been ecstatic all evening, since first peeking out at the audience for the night's performance. It was packed. The house was full. And knowing this, she had played to them with all the passion in her soul. Now, the final curtain lowered, Jane curtsied to the sound of the house's applause.

Yet it was no standing ovation. Also, it was curiously lacking in thunder, in resonance, in enthusiasm. There was something restrained about it, something polite. Jane sensed a great gap between herself and her audience, one she could not understand, yet as she bowed again, she did not let the smile slip from her face. With the house so full, why was this ovation so routine, so lacking in passion? A rose fell at her feet. Automatically, gracefully, she retrieved it, waving and blowing a kiss to the front rows. A man in the aisle below center stage called her nickname fervently, "Angel, Angel!"

Jane turned to go, spirits starting to sink. And then she heard a clear shout: "Where is the Angel's Lord of Darkness?" This from a woman heckler.

She froze briefly, half turned away from the audience, then continued from the stage, slipping behind the curtains. And there she stood stock still, hearing the chant of "Angel, Angel," but she also thought she heard his name—Darkness, Dragmore, Darkness, Dragmore . . .

Oh, God!

She clutched herself, suddenly terribly afraid.

"Jane, you were fantastic," Gordon cried, taking her hands.

Jane's soul was numb, although her mind was functioning. Someone, or some persons, had been shouting his name—her husband's name. Hadn't they? She hadn't imagined it, had she? No! Impossible! She was a professional actress, and such ribaldery would not occur here. She was imagining things.

The press were waiting for her in the corridor in front of her dressing room, and her heart leapt in anticipation. She knew them all now, and managed a big smile, still shocked, but her gaze was anxious, searching from one to the other. She saw avid, leering interest—at least, she thought she did.

"Jane!" cried the man from the *Star*. "You were great tonight! So marriage suits you?"

A woman shoved past. "How did you two meet? Was it love at first sight? Aren't you afraid of him?" And she shuddered theatrically.

Jane recoiled.

The *Star* reporter pressed forward. "Why the secret marriage? When did he propose? When did you two decide to get married? Did he kill his wife?"

"Enough!" Jane cried, suddenly aghast and sickened. She used Gordon as a buffer to hurl through them and into the sanctuary of her dressing room.

But the woman's voice carried. "Did he kill his wife? Aren't you afraid he'll tire of you and kill you too?"

Gordon slammed the door in her face.

Jane stood frozen, shaking. She was as pale as death. "Oh, God!"

"Forget it," Gordon said decisively. "It's not a big affair. It's just not every day that a famous actress marries a notorious lord."

Jane was clutching her throat. "They're bloodthirsty barbarians," she whispered. "And the audience—did you hear them? They shouted his name tonight."

"Curiosity—" Gordon began.

"Curiosity!" Jane screeched, hysterical. "They came tonight because of curiosity! Am I a circus now?" Tears filled her eyes. "I've worked so hard, so damn hard, I've paid my dues, more than paid, and they come to see the Lord of Darkness's new wife! Not to see me, Jane Barclay!"

"You're exaggerating," Gordon said. "Calm down, Jane."

"Attendance has been dropping steadily. Yesterday we got married, this morning it was plastered all over the papers! 'London's Angel Weds the Lord of Darkness!' " She cried bitterly. "They only came to stare at a freak show tonight! I knew something was wrong when I heard the applause!"

Gordon rubbed her shoulder. "You are exaggerating, Jane. Maybe a few of them came to gawk,

but most came for the performance." Yet his voice
held a note of doubt.

Jane swiped at her eyes with the back of her
hand, pulling away. "I hate him," she whispered.
"He's ruining me!"

Gordon said nothing.

Trembling, angry, distraught, Jane sat and began abruptly removing her makeup. She ignored
the sherry Robert handed her. "How will I overcome this?"

"It will die down in a few days," Gordon told
her. "You'll see."

Jane stared at her pale reflection in the mirror.
This, at last, made sense, and offered hope. She
rubbed her temples. They throbbed.

"You'll feel better once you get home," Gordon
told her. "After a good night's rest."

Jane laughed. "The last place I want to go is
home! The last person I want to see . . ." She
clenched her fists. She was so mad, so upset, and
she was still shaking.

"How about some supper then?" he suggested
gently.

Jane wasn't hungry, but she was too upset to go
home and face him and his house. She turned to
Gordon with relief. "Thank you, Robert. That is a
wonderful idea."

Gordon took her to one of their favorite restaurants on Hay Market. It was dimly lit and cozy,
the chef and owner Parisian, the food uncom-
monly good, and popular with theater-goers and
late-night revelers. The maitre d' knew them and
took them promptly to a table in a back corner.
Jane was used to receiving looks in public places,
and had never been quite sure if it was because
she was beautiful (as everyone claimed) or be-

cause she was recognized to be the stage actress.
Yet here, at Chez Oz, where she dined at least once
a week after performing, she had become an accepted patron, and most of the clientele paid her
little attention. Yet tonight was different.

Heads craned her way. Voices hushed. Silence
formed a wake behind her, only to spume gossipy
whispers. Jane heard *his* name, damn him, and
hers, and felt heat suffuse her face. She kept her
head high, avoiding all eye contact. Gordon
seated her, flustered.

"I'm sorry," he apologized.

She only looked at him, although her seat faced
out upon the restaurant. "As you said"—she
shrugged with feigned indifference—"it will die
down."

"You are a trooper, Jane," Gordon said, smiling.
"Like your mother."

Tonight Jane was not in the mood to be compared, once again, and by her best friend, to her
mother. She turned her head away, glancing casually around. With her fingers she toyed with her
water glass. And then she saw him, and she froze.

She had not thought the evening could get
worse.

Sitting a few tables away, in the very midst of
the dining room, was her husband. *With Amelia.*

Jane stared at them, stunned. He was magnificent in black tails and tie, and Amelia was ravishing in emerald taffeta and diamonds. They made
a gorgeous couple. She realized her heart was
beating painfully; worse, he was staring back at
her. Jane felt the heat return to her face, and,
damn him, the need to cry came hotly behind her
lids.

"I don't believe it," Gordon cried, outraged.

Jane turned away, seemingly calm and poised,

and placed a hand on his arm. Her smile was sick. "Please, Robert, do not interfere. It makes no difference to me whom he sees, as long as he stays away from me." Her voice was suspiciously shaky.

"He is a son of a bitch," Gordon said, low and furious.

"Absolutely." Jane would not look at him, at them. She knew she was still beet red, and now she understood the lurid interest her entrance had aroused. She wondered who she hated more, the earl or Amelia.

"We'll go," Gordon said, starting to rise.

Jane restrained him. "We will not." Somehow she smiled. "I am in the mood for a Montrachet and some Dover sole." She leaned close, and her eyes flashed. "He shall not chase me away!"

Gordon signaled to the maitre d', then grimaced. "They're leaving," he told Jane, who would not look in their direction again. "Prepare yourself, they're coming this way."

Jane hated him. Her heart pounded painfully, yet her will was iron. Casually, gracefully, she turned to watch their approach, with elegance and seeming disinterest.

The earl paused beside her, Amelia behind him. His face was expressionless. "Hello, Jane," he said, gazing at her. There was such power in his smoldering regard that Jane could not look away. He took her hand and kissed it, making lingering contact with her flesh, as if savoring the touch. "How was the show?"

So he would play polite games even as he made a fool of her publicly! "Don't pretend you care!" she spat, blue eyes blazing. He hadn't released her hand, and a brief tug failed to dislodge it. She knew they were making a scene, and she did not

want to appear aroused, so she refrained from
further attempts at freeing herself.

He stiffened, released her palm, and pulled
Amelia forward. He nodded at Gordon. "We were
just taking our leave," he said, his face a mask.

Amelia was smiling with unfettered glee. "Why,
hullo, Jane! This is a surprise! Imagine, you and
your friend running into me and mine! What a
small world! Nick insists we should leave, but we
haven't even eaten yet, perhaps we should all dine
together?"

Jane knew she would never survive a supper
with the earl and his flaming floozy. Color was
rising high upon her cheekbones again. Then the
earl gripped Amelia's elbow and rudely yanked it,
causing her to screech like a crow. He never took
his gaze from Jane, and the burning intensity
there confused her. "Good night," he said. "I will
see you shortly at home."

"Will you?" Jane said snidely. "I doubt it." She
sniffed.

He gave her a look and then turned away, dragging a gleeful Amelia with him.

"So much for discretion," Jane said, a sob
catching in her voice.

"Jane, let's go. Staying here is masochistic."

"No," Jane said grimly. "No, no. The last place I
am going tonight is home."

36

🔥🔥🔥

"You're not going to come in?" Amelia gasped.

"Not tonight," the earl said calmly as they stood on the doorstep of her brick town house. His carriage awaited him in the gas-lit, cobbled street beyond the small front garden and wrought-iron fence.

"Darling, really," Amelia said, wrapping her arms around his neck and pressing her lush body against his. "Don't be so moody."

He unwrapped her, removing her from him. "Good night, Amelia."

She grasped his hand, halting him as he turned to leave. "Are you going to be faithful to her?" she cried, her face white and angry in the lamplight. There was no question that she was referring to Jane.

A cruel look crossed his features, and he gripped her chin hard. "My wife has nothing to do with this."

"No? Somehow, I doubt it! I think you have a tendre for her!"

The earl laughed, white teeth gleaming. "Don't think to provoke me into your bed, Amelia."

"Let me provoke you," she said huskily, reaching to touch his flaccid penis through his trousers, rubbing it gently.

He removed her hand, ungently. "Do you ever have anything other than sex on your mind?"

"You didn't come in last night either!"

"I'm sure that strapping twenty-year-old groom you make eyes at can accommodate you, Amelia," the earl purred.

"Ooh!" She gasped, recoiling, yet shock and fear of discovery flared in her eyes.

He grinned. "Don't ever underestimate me, my dear," he said, low. "And never play me for the fool." He turned his back on her and strode down the walk.

"You bastard!" she hissed. "How dare you insinuate such a thing!"

His laughter, soft, mocking, assured, drifted to her as he climbed into the carriage with the Dragmore crests. "Home, Eddie," he called, not glancing back once at his furious mistress.

Tension reared itself in the earl. He sat stiffly, staring straight ahead at the opposite seat with its plush black leather upholstery, yet he saw only Jane. Jane pale, shocked, hurt. Impossibly beautiful, as fragile as an angel, as innocent. Something that felt like a knife twisted in his guts.

He did not want to hurt her.

Ever.

But she had hurt him. Had lied, deceived him, cheated him of his daughter. She had left him too, after he had offered marriage—after he had realized he loved her. She had never loved him, he realized now. She had merely harbored an adolescent crush upon him, one that had passed readily enough. Again there was the stabbing of an old, old pain.

And there was jealousy.

She only appeared innocent, and he reminded himself of this fact vigorously.

He did not like her relationship with Gordon. Gordon was only fifty, a trim, elegant man, and maybe, once upon a time, he had been like a father to Jane. The earl did not believe in fairy tales. Jane was now a ravishing woman, and any man with one eye could see that, and no man could be immune to her intriguing combination of innocence and sensuality. Including Gordon.

Was he one of her lovers?

And what about Lindley? Had Lindley lied? He and Jane were awfully close, weren't they?

The earl knew he was torturing himself, but he couldn't help it. When he had offered Jane marriage after discovering Nicole's existence, he had never even dreamed it would be upon the terms she insisted on. To the contrary—he had envisioned her in his bed, naked and wet and writhing beneath him while he slaked his endless lust for her. He had envisioned giving her more children, beautiful blond, blue-eyed dolls. Yet instead, he was keeping company with his oversexed mistress while Jane kept company with her own paramours.

His fist crashed down on the seat beside him. He was rigid now, seething, agonized. Damn her —he hated her!

He wanted to go back to Amelia and fuck her. Prove his manhood, prove his own disinterest in his wife. But he knew he would not, *could not,* knew he was only fooling himself if he told himself he did not want Jane. Oh, he wanted her, all right.

But never would he prostrate himself to her.

Never would he beg for her favors.

Never.

He lunged out of the coach when they arrived at the house on Tavistock Square. Thomas had dutifully waited up for him. "Is my wife here?" the earl asked abruptly.

"No, sir," Thomas said.

Nick cursed and paced into his study. It was only half-past one. She was still at the restaurant, undoubtedly. He should either go to sleep or go out again. But he did neither.

He threw his jacket and tie on the sofa, where they slipped to the floor, and unbuttoned his shirt. He paced restlessly, like a caged lion who scents the kill but is not freed to hunt it. Tonight half a glass of whiskey sufficed, he could not contemplate more. He put out three cigars, barely touched. It was hot and humid this night, and his skin was damp and sticky. He removed his shirt with a growl, a lion pricked by a thorn, and balled it, threw it aside. And his flesh, his flesh was pulsing with anger and jealousy and unfulfilled need.

It was three-thirty before she returned.

Three-thirty.

The earl heard the long-awaited sounds of the coach, the horses, the hounds, and finally her sweet voice thanking a servant who let her in. Fists clenched, he loomed in the doorway of the library, backlit by the swelling lights from within. She jumped upon seeing him.

He stared at her rudely. Her hair, he saw, was still caught up in the chignon, not a hair out of place. Her face was pale, eyes wide and bright, lips unswollen. Her low-cut dress was immaculately in place, perfectly buttoned, perfectly adorned. He found his gaze lingering upon her breasts and he imagined them filling his hands. When he jerked his eyes back to hers, he saw that color had crept along her cheekbones.

"Where the hell have you been?" he demanded harshly.

She started, then her blue eyes flashed. "That, my lord, is none of your affair!" She sneered his title.

"Oh, it's my affair all right," he said softly, dangerously, stepping closer to her. She backed off a step. "Where in hell have you been!"

"Where have you been?" She lifted a pale eyebrow regally.

He grabbed her before she could dodge him, catching her small wrist, so she could not flee. "Answer me, Jane." His tone was ominous.

"I was with Robert Gordon, as you well know!"

"Where?" he said with a snarl.

"It's none of your concern!" She tried to free her hand and failed.

"As your husband, every goddamn breath you take is my concern."

"We have an agreement," she cried. "Or have you forgotten?"

"Forgotten?" he purred, pulling her closer. She gasped when he drew her so close their breaths mingled, her skirts touching his knees. "How could I ever forget?"

Just for an instant, Jane couldn't reply. His face was so close. Dark, deadly, his eyes silver with fury and hot, glittering passion, his mouth so sensually curved, parted, and so near hers. She could even feel the heat of his slickly damp, bared torso. He wanted her, she knew it. He was going to kiss her. Her heart was thumping its way right out of her breast.

"I could never forget."

His words scorched their way right to her heart. She tried to twist free, failing. "Obviously you haven't forgotten," she cried. "Obviously you are making good use of our 'agreement.'" Images of Amelia rose to torment her further.

"Very good use," the earl agreed.

"Let me go!"

"Is he good?" the earl asked cruelly. "Does he please you, Jane? Can an old man like that even give you orgasms?"

Jane gasped, recoiling.

He yanked her hard to him, wrapped one steel arm around her waist, crushed her breasts to his naked, wet chest, and kissed her brutally. Jane felt panic on the heels of her shock. He was all steel strength, and he was so dark and angry, that her struggle was futile unless he chose to release her. Yet even as her mind grappled with panic, the feel of his damp skin on her partly bared breasts caused her nipples to harden with agony, caused shafts of need deep within her. Then he pulled his mouth away from hers. "You would kiss him but not me, your husband?"

Jane was furious. She had had enough. And that he would think she and Robert lovers was unbelievable. Yet she had only to recall him and Amelia to know she would not deny it. "Let me go," she said with forced calm.

"I don't think so."

As she stood imprisoned in his embrace, her body hot and pulsing in response to him, her control snapped. "Perchance," she said too sweetly, "Amelia doesn't satisfy you?"

He froze.

"If she did," she cried, "you would not have so much energy left over to torment me with! Or is it just your style to leap from her bed to mine? Is this perhaps the new fashion? Is it the fashion nowadays to parade one's mistress in public before one's wife—within days of the wedding?"

In that instant his grip tightened, and she saw both pain and anger wrenching on his face. She stood very still, her heart slamming; and he released her abruptly.

Jane backed away, breathing hard. The earl slumped against the wall, a mocking smile distorting his beautiful mouth. "Go back to your lovers, Jane," he said wearily. "I don't want you."

As if doused with water, the fires of her rage dimmed and died. As her pulse slowed from its mad gallop, her eyes never left him. With her heart, she wanted to tell him the truth; with her heart, she wanted to go to him, touch his brow, smooth the pain away, and somehow take away what had been said and start over. But she responded with her mind and with her pride. Tears welling, lips pursed, she backed away, found the stairs, and fled up them into the refuge of her room.

37

Jane came downstairs thoroughly · exhausted from a sleepless night. Although finally dozing sometime after dawn, she had overslept as well, and it was half-past nine. This at least gave her some small degree of satisfaction, for surely the earl would have retreated to his library and papers, or left the house, by this hour. After the cruel words they had exchanged the night before, Jane did not want to face him. She came to an abrupt stop in the dining-room doorway when she saw him seated at the head of the long gilt table. Her heart lurched.

He didn't look at her. Nicole was in her baby chair, on his right, playing with a spoon and croissant. He was sipping coffee and reading the *Times*, apparently having overslept as well. Had he also passed a mostly sleepless night? Jane realized she was slightly breathless, and despite their fight she couldn't help but remember, of all things, his hard body pressing hers and the heat and strength of his mouth.

Determined, then, and angry with herself, Jane sailed forward, toward Nicole. She cried out at the sight of her mother approaching, finally causing the earl to glance indifferently her way. Nicole waved the spoon happily, banged it once, then began to gnaw it.

"No, sweetheart," the earl said, taking the spoon from her despite her vocal protests. " 'Tis unseemly to chew the silverware."

Nicole began to cry.

Nick stroked her hair and placed the croissant in her chubby hand, but she ignored him, dropping it. Jane paused, waiting to be summoned to the rescue, yet feeling no satisfaction—just a wrenching in her heart at the sight of father and daughter together.

"Sweetheart, the croissant was baked today," Nick cajoled with a smile. His voice was low and melodious, and Nicole suddenly stopped shrieking to stare at him as he smiled and bit off a third, chewing gustily. "Want to share Papa's?" he asked.

"Papa," Nicole cried, chubby hands flailing. Nick handed her the croissant, which she now claimed greedily. "Mama!" she shrieked triumphantly, waving the pastry at Jane.

The earl returned to his journal, apparently immersed in the news. Jane came forward to greet her daughter with a hug and a kiss. She sat on Nicole's right, her gaze flitting toward her absorbed husband. He had treated her abominably last night, not to mention humiliating her in public with his fat floozy; and now he was apparently ignoring her. She decided to ignore him as well.

. Tossing the *Times* aside, he called to Thomas and ordered the carriage brought round, then summoned Molly, now officially Nicole's nurse. "Have Nicole dressed for a ride in the park," he said, standing.

He finally looked at Jane. He nodded curtly.

"You're taking Nicole to the park?" Jane managed, flustered by both his intention and his nearness. Standing he towered over her, his legs braced, and there was no denying the strength of his thighs so obviously delineated in the snug breeches.

"I assume you have no objections?"

"Of course not," Jane said, suddenly wistful. She imagined them all together in the open carriage on this beautiful morning, her, Nicole, the earl. She wanted to join them. She waited for an invitation—but it did not come. The earl, instead, nodded again and left.

Jane had lost her appetite, if indeed she had ever had one that day. Molly had taken Nicole to dress her more warmly, as it was cool this morning, and she was left alone in the vast dining room. Should she ask if she could accompany them? Suddenly it seemed like the most marvelous idea, an outing in the park, and they could even take Chad away from his studies. Her heart was pounding, yet she did not have the courage to move from her chair.

Ten minutes later she heard the coach leaving, and she bit her lip, foolishly feeling like crying.

What was wrong with her?

The earl might be a bastard as a man, but as a father he was superb—yet this knowledge wasn't new. So why should she be so distraught now, just because he'd taken his daughter for a ride in the park? Why should she be so touched? Because it was not the thing—no other peer would dream of doing something so inelegant, so unsophisticated, as to take his tiny child for a drive. It was touching. And she was his wife, the mother of his child, yet she wasn't welcome to join them.

And she felt the guilt then too for having denied him his daughter in the first place.

"My lady," Thomas intoned from the doorway, "you have a caller."

Jane rose, brow lifted.

"It's the Earl of Raversford," Thomas said, a touch disapprovingly.

"Have you told him he just missed the earl?"

"Yes. It's you he's come to see. I showed him to the morning room."

Jane instructed Thomas to bring tea and cakes, and hurried forward, surprised and both worried and glad that Lindley had decided to visit her. She hadn't seen him privately since the earl had decreed that they would be married, and not being a fool, she knew he had been told as promptly as she of the intended marriage and had thus stayed away. Yet why would he come to her now?

Lindley stood gazing out the windows at the lawns and flower beds. He turned at her footstep, and his eyes lit up at the sight of her. Jane found herself glad to see him, and she smiled eagerly. "Jon, I'm so glad you've come!"

He came forward and took both her hands, his regard warm and penetrating. "You are, aren't you? How are you, Jane?"

She motioned for them to sit. "Well, I suppose," she said, avoiding his gaze.

Lindley lifted her chin. "You look tired, as if you haven't slept," he said softly. He didn't remove his fingertips from her face.

Jane blushed. She wanted to confide in him, but she would not. She could not betray her husband by sharing the problems in their life, no matter how much she needed a friend. "I had a bad dream."

Thomas entered, looking dour as he rolled in the silver butler's table with refreshments. Lindley dropped his hand, Jane sat up straighter. She was pink now, and wondering exactly what Thomas thought.

"Can I bring you anything else, my lady?" Thomas asked, his eyes having lost their customary blandness.

"No, that is all for now," Jane said, feeling guilty. But for what? She hadn't done anything except greet an old friend. The problem was, she could tell that Lindley still harbored affection for her.

It was going to come out sooner or later, the earl supposed. So it might as well be now.

They had passed many carriages and riders since entering the park, all of whom turned to stare at the Dragmore carriage with its bold black-and-gold crests. Nick sat in the backseat of the open curricle with Nicole on a baby chair beside him, Molly on the opposite seat facing them. Nicole played with a rattle and laughed and shrieked happily. Those who passed them all did double takes at the sight of the baby in the Earl of Dragmore's carriage, their curious stares turning to open gawking. The earl ignored everyone, and when he grew tired of the seating arangements, he did not hesitate to put Nicole upon his knee. She was thrilled with this, and quite outspoken in her pleasure.

A carriage finally, purposefully, pulled alongside them. The earl was not surprised; to the contrary, he had expected someone to be brave enough to come up to him for the past half hour.

This gig bore the Hadderly colors, and Nick found himself facing the young countess, a newlywed, and two of her friends, a baron and another young lady. "Good morning, my lord," Countess Hadderly hailed brightly, her eyes wide at the sight of Nick and Nicole.

"Good morning," the earl replied politely. He ignored the trio's rude gaping.

"It's quite the day for a drive," she continued gaily.

"Quite."

"I do say, is that a baby upon your lap?"

The earl refrained from making a sarcastic comment and decided to let her off the hook. "This is my daughter, Nicole."

"Daughter!" It was gasped in unison by both women.

"B-but—" The lovely countess was flustered. "I had no idea you had a daughter, sir."

The earl felt like saying "Neither did I," but wisely did not. Suddenly the countess made the connection, and her eyes widened like saucers. "Her mother is your wife?"

"That is the usual, is it not?" the earl said calmly.

The countess looked as if she would choke upon the news.

"Good day," the earl said with a polite smile. He rapped his crop upon the door for the driver to increase his speed, and they left the other party behind.

Well, it was done. Nicole could not be kept a secret. She was his daughter, and one day would come into Society as was her right. He was glad she was too young to be aware of the scandal that was forming even now. When she was old enough to understand, it would be long since past. He lifted his gaze to find Molly watching him reprovingly.

He almost explained himself to the maid, but instead gave her a sharp stare, causing her to blush and drop her gaze. The earl then ordered the driver to return to Tavistock Square.

38

The first thing the earl saw upon his return was the Raversford carriage outside his home in the driveway, the coachmen chatting as they waited for Lindley. Every fiber in his being went tight at the sight. He handed Nicole to Molly and stepped down, then dismissed his driver, following the maid and his daughter inside.

Molly took Nicole upstairs while the earl stood frozen in the foyer. He could hear the tinkle of Jane's laughter drifting through the hallway. Happy laughter. The kind of laughter he did not hear in his own presence. He turned grimly to Thomas. "How long has Lindley been here?"

"Since just after you left, my lord," Thomas said with a sniff of obvious disapproval.

He felt the surging anger. "You told him I had just left and would not return for an hour?"

"He wanted to see the lady Jane, my lord," Thomas said.

The anger increased. And with it, jealousy and

suspicion. So Lindley had come to see Jane, had he? It was damn convenient that Raversford had shown up while he was out. Had Lindley waited to see that he had left before coming? He pushed the rude thought away, telling himself to get a grip on his wayward suspicions. But damn if he'd be cuckolded in his own home by his own best friend!

He strode into the morning room.

They were seated on the same sofa, of course, about a foot apart. Lindley was telling a merry tale and Jane was all smiles. It was quite cozy, quite familiar. At his entrance, Lindley froze in midsentence, and Jane's smiles abruptly ceased. Glad to see him, were they? The earl bared his teeth. "Hello, Lindley."

Raversford stood. "Hullo, Shelton." He didn't smile either.

"This is a surprise," the earl drawled sarcastically, his glance sweeping from Lindley to Jane. She was impossibly fetching in a pale-pink morning gown with her hair delicately put up, loose strands floating around her face. She was flushed too. From his kisses?

"Would you like some tea?" Jane asked politely.

"I'm afraid to interrupt," he said bitingly, pinning Lindley now with his regard. "I am interrupting, aren't I?"

Lindley shoved his hands in his pockets. "You're not interrupting, Nick," he said quietly.

"No? Funny, but this tête-à-tête seemed just that, made for two." His eyes flashed silver.

"Don't be a fool," Jane flared, standing. "Your best friend came to pay his respects. I am your wife, and you were out. Should I have turned him away?"

"Should you have, Jane?" the earl demanded.

Lindley looked uncomfortable. "I think I'd best be going."

Good idea, the earl wanted to shout furiously, but he did not. His gaze skewered him. "Suddenly in a rush? Please, stay. My wife seems to enjoy your company." He mocked.

"I have several appointments," Lindley said. He bowed over Jane's hand. Fortunately, for his sake, he did not kiss it. He nodded uncertainly—guiltily?—at Nick, then left.

Jane clenched her fists, cheeks pinker now. "You were unbearably rude!"

"Rude? I invited him to stay longer."

"You chased him away!"

"Did I upset your plans?" he asked dangerously.

"Plans? I don't know what you're talking about!"

"No? Why are you so angry—because Lindley left? Or because I returned?"

"You boor! I am angry because you've treated your good friend despicably. Because your behavior was unspeakably rude!" Jane cried.

"And why do you care how I behave?" He wanted her to reply that she did care about his behavior—because he was her husband. But he was disappointed.

"Why do I care? Because Lindley is our friend —and a guest in our home!"

"So Lindley is your friend too, Jane? Ah, how could I forget, he was dancing attendance on you before we wed. How could I forget? He knew where you were, and would not tell me. Knew of Nicole, and kept it from me. So intimate, weren't we? Or is it aren't we? And for how long has he been your *friend?* "

She gasped, recoiling. "You are disgusting!"

He clenched his fists to keep from grabbing her. "How long has he been your friend, Jane?"

She clamped her mouth hard together, eyes blazing, chin high, and stared him down.

"I will not be cuckolded in my own home," he said through gritted teeth, gripping her by the shoulders.

She wrenched free, panting. "Don't touch me!"

"But he can touch you? You *let* him touch you! And what else have you allowed?"

She slapped him, a whiplash across his face.

He was shocked, motionless, as stunned as she was. An absolute silence knifed between them.

Then Jane gasped, her lips trembling, and she backed away. "I-I'm sorry."

He smiled, a menacing curve of his lips. "Too late," he said, and he grabbed her.

Her cry of protest was cut off by his mouth. He anchored her in an ungiving embrace of steel, jamming one rock-hard thigh between hers, his mouth forcing hers open, his teeth cutting hers, his tongue raping her. She could not even whimper beneath his onslaught. He clasped one buttock and hauled her even harder against the steel ridge of his erection. He heard her choke in protest even as his grip loosened and one hand slid down her back, stroking. His mouth softened. She softened. He felt her lips open, felt her tongue touch his tentatively. With a groan he pulled her into his mouth, sucking her, devouring her. She pressed fiercely against him, her lips locked to his. His palm, rubbing her buttock, eased beneath it, caressing her and urging her to ride his muscular thigh.

He had no thoughts, no coherent ones, that is.

His mouth still merged with Jane's, he dropped to his knees, bringing her down with him onto the floor. She went unresisting, her small hands clutching his broad shoulders. And when he pushed her onto her back, her thighs opened wide, letting him settle himself against her as he pleased. It was unbearable. He was going to explode now, soon.

"Jane!" he cried, burying his face in her taut neck and reaching, trembling, for her skirts. Her panting was harsh and arrhythmic in his ear. When his hand touched her bare knee she gasped. When he slid his palm up her thigh on the inside she whimpered, thrashing, spreading her legs more and arching her pelvis wildly. He cupped the mound of her femininity boldly and found her drawers soaked. Soaked for him. It was his undoing.

"Jane, Jane," he heard himself chanting, slipping his fingers beneath the silk, touching her.

She cried out, clinging to him, arching convulsively, shaking with need.

He could not wait. He reached for his breeches, yanking them open, and heard her, clearly. "Nicholas! Nicholas!" It was sobbed, a plea.

He found her mouth as he freed his rigid organ, and then he was thrusting home. It was excruciating, unbearable, hot, tight, as tight as the first time, and he knew he was lost.

"No," he cried, plunging into her. "No, no, I don't want to come, not yet . . ." And then he came, spewing into her, pumping, pumping endlessly. And through the haze of his ecstasy he heard her cry his name and felt her contract violently around him, again and again.

39

Jane became aware of the floor, hard and hurtful beneath her.

And the earl, who was hard and warm on top of her. His face was still buried in her neck, his breath hot and wispy on her skin. She could feel his lips against her throat, damp, and the thudding of his racing heart on her breast. He had her arms gripped firmly in his powerful hands, and she could still feel him inside her.

Oh, God!

She felt it then, the rushing tidal wave of tears behind her lids, hot, threatening—imminent. The urge to weep was overwhelming. Jane struggled as she'd never struggled before—she could not cry in front of him. Not now.

The earl abruptly rolled off her, onto his back, and was momentarily still. Jane had not known that so much pain remained in her heart. If she didn't control herself, she would soon be sobbing hysterically in a flood of grief. And why? Because she loved this beautiful, angry man? Because he had married her for their daughter's sake, not out of love for herself? Because he had hurt her once, two years ago, so devastatingly? Because now he had taken her in anger and jealousy and lust? She did not know. She was confused and distressed, in an emotional quagmire.

And she sniffed, daring to wipe away more tears before he should see them.

The earl suddenly lunged to his feet. Jane heard him cross the room and close the door. She was too upset to care that it had been open. She turned her head away, and more tears crawled down her cheeks. She felt his gaze upon her.

"God," he said, the sound choked. "Jane? Did—did I hurt you?"

She was afraid to even try and speak; she shook her head no. She did not dare turn to look at him, not with her wet face.

"I'm sorry," he said harshly.

It was the agonized tone of his voice that brought her to her elbows to stare. He had now turned his gaze aside. His profile was etched in rigid lines of tension, haggard, pain-filled. He was rubbing his chest as if his heart hurt him. "I'm sorry," he said again, and in his voice she heard it all—the cruel self-flagellation.

She started to protest, unable to bear the sight and sound of him like his.

He looked at her and his gaze widened. "Why are you crying? Shit!"

He gave her his back, leaning on a chair, the muscles in his back and arms straining rigidly. "How can I ask such a stupid question!" Still, he would not turn to face her. "I'm sorry. It won't happen again—I promise."

"It's not your fault," Jane told him, getting to

her feet. He would not face her. She hesitated, wanting to comfort him. "Both of us are responsible adults. I did not deny you."

He didn't move. She heard him curse. She could see the tendons straining in the back of his neck. Hesitantly Jane approached and laid a palm on his waist. He flinched as if struck. "Don't touch me!"

Jane withdrew, hurt.

"I promise you," the earl said harshly, turning to look at her. His eyes were silver with pain and some form of deep, internal punishment. "I'll send Molly to you."

And then he was gone.

Jane did not see the earl the rest of that day. It was as if he were avoiding her. With the incident in the morning room past, she began to think more clearly. There was no question that he had broken their agreement, even if she had been a willing party once he'd started kissing her. Yet she could not be angry. She had only to remember her own ecstasy in his arms, and his own agony after, to keep any wrath at bay.

And Jane worried about him.

What dark obsessions tormented him? What dark fires burned in his darker soul? And why, why did she have the terrible urge to heal him and make him laugh and smile?

Even when she arrived at the Criterion for the evening's show she could not shake him from her thoughts. Robert informed her that they had another full house. This momentarily distracted her.

She knew her performance was off that night, and knew it was because of him. She did her best but could not lose herself in her role. In the back of her mind there loomed a hot memory she could not shed. And after, after the polite, scattered applause, the press attacked her outside her dressing room once again.

"Is the child yours?"

"Why keep it a secret?"

"He took her to Regents Park today and admitted she is his. Any comment?"

"Is it true you were Dragmore's ward in the summer of seventy-four?"

"Wouldn't that mean you are still his ward?"

"Did he abuse his position? The child *is* yours?"

"So you were what—seventeen that summer?"

"Why didn't he marry you then?"

Jane escaped into her room, with Gordon slamming the door behind her.

She was frozen, stunned, unable to move. Unable to breathe.

"Good Lord!" Gordon cried. "My God! The impertinence! Jane, are you all right?"

Her hand fluttered to her breast. Her eyes were wide. She was still unable to move. And she was whiter than death. "Oh, God, what next?"

The earl could not find solace in brandy.

"Darling, what ails you tonight?"

He did not hear his mistress. Amelia huffed with frustration. They were in her parlor, Amelia dressed for an evening out, the earl in his breeches, boots, and shirt, the latter open halfway, untucked and wrinkled. There was a shadow on his face, but it was nothing compared to the shadow in his eyes. He had drunk half a bottle of whiskey, but he wasn't drunk. To the contrary, he was stone-cold sober.

"Fuck," he said viciously, and he sent the bottle sailing onto the Turkish carpet on the floor.

"Nick!" Amelia cried, furious. She bent to pick up the bottle.

"Leave it," he ground out.

She stood, hands on her plump hips. "You are a bastard tonight. Are we or are we not going to the Sinclair soirée?"

He looked at her for the first time in an hour. He despised her, always had. Yet he was here—because he must stay away from his wife.

At all costs.

"You go," he said with contempt.

"Why do I put up with you!" Amelia stormed out.

Nick clenched the arms of the chair until he heard the frame crack. He had taken Jane in anger today, in violence. He had raped her.

Like Chavez.

He was just like Chavez.

His heart was hammering painfully. But more painful was the searing memory of her delicate, oval face, flushed from his mouth and skin, and the tears spilling down her cheeks.

How could he make it up to her? How?

By staying away from her. Maybe he should leave her in London, while he went to Dragmore. But could he run from his wife forever?

Could he run from himself?

"Jane, I'm sorry." He groaned. "Never, ever did I want to hurt you."

It was just past midnight. The earl heard Amelia giving instructions to her maid as she left for the evening. He felt relief at her departure. Just past twelve; Jane's performance had ended. Would she be going home directly, or go out with Gordon? Or Lindley?

Tonight there was no jealousy, just more pain.

It didn't matter. Whether she went home or not,

for he had to stay away from her. The earl got up and sprawled on the sofa, an arm flung across his forehead, staring at the painted fan on the ceiling. He could only think of Jane, Jane. On the stage, dynamic, angelic, beautiful. Jane shy and trembling, as when they'd first met. Jane in his arms, hot, carnal, crying his name.

He closed his eyes. He was so tired. He knew he never could sleep. But when he opened them again, it was almost four, and Amelia was bending over him, cooing in a way he particularly detested.

"Darling, you are so tired! Come with me, up to bed." She stroked his hair.

He sat up, instantly awake, ignoring her pawing. Then he stood, looking around for his jacket. He found it on a chair and shrugged it on.

"You're going?"

"I'm very tired," he told her, heading for the door.

Amelia followed on his heels. "I am going to take another lover!"

He almost smiled, but to himself, for he did not even turn to her. "You already have other lovers, Amelia," he said, stepping out into the night. He didn't look back as he strode to his carriage.

Jane filled his thoughts again, and he was afraid. He didn't like her being on his mind like this, did not trust himself anymore to be able to stay away from her. He had hurt her once, would he hurt her again? Would she ever forgive him for what he had done? And did it even matter if she did?

Once home, as he climbed the stairs, he became very aware of drawing nearer to her. He paused on the second-floor landing. Just down the hall she was there, in her room, asleep. He was tense with the knowledge, the certainty. Tonight she was not out with a paramour.

Nick paused outside her door, then opened it. Silently he crossed her sitting room and entered the bedroom.

Moonlight spilled in through the open windows. A breeze lifted sheer curtains and the lace hangings on the canopy of her bed. Her room smelled of lilies. She was asleep, on her side, curled up like a child.

Unable to stop himself, he approached.

She was a sleeping angel—his sleeping angel, his wife.

His wife, whom he had hurt, violated, in the grossest way. The pain filled him again, choking him. He felt hot tears behind his eyes, and knew the strongest urge to cry since being a boy.

"I'm so sorry, Jane," he whispered.

She did not move. His hand, of its own accord, touched a tress of her hair, and then it slipped deeply into the mass to touch her head. She sighed.

"Forgive me," he whispered, kneeling beside her. His face was close to hers. "I'm sorry. Jane? Will you ever forgive me?"

There was no response. Had he expected one?

"I love you," he heard himself say, and he wasn't shocked by his admission at all.

"Jane, I love you," he choked.

And then he got up and left.

40

🔥🔥🔥

Jane awoke unhappy.

It was early, not even eight, but she couldn't stay abed, even though she hadn't been able to sleep until after three. And he hadn't been home yet. As she dressed she found herself equally depressed and upset. He had made love to her only yesterday afternoon, yet last night he had been with one or another of his mistresses. The thought of him with Amelia was unbearable.

And then there was still the foul aftertaste of what had happened at the Criterion last night after her performance.

Jane expected to find him in the dining room breakfasting, and she was not disappointed. This morning he looked up, his gaze hooded. Chad, who was about finished, called out an enthusiastic greeting. "Good morning," she said to the boy, tousling his hair and kissing his cheek as she passed. He beamed.

She found the earl regarding her. Jane was

shocked at the circles beneath his eyes. He looked as tired as she was, and she felt herself start to soften. With a distinct effort, she reminded herself that he had not come home last night until very, very late. She hugged her daughter and sat.

"Good morning," the earl said.

"Good morning." Jane was just as polite. Their gazes cautiously met, and both flew immediately apart.

Nicole was making a mess of bread and jam, up to her elbows in strawberry preserves, so Jane busied herself with rescuing her daughter from further disaster. She was aware of the earl watching as she scolded the baby gently. Nicole gurgled happily, then began banging the tray table. "Red, red," she shouted.

"What does she want?" Chad asked, nose wrinkled in disgust.

"You must eat it, not play," Jane admonished, handing her a new slice of toast and removing the sticky crumbled mess. "More bread."

"Papa, may I be excused?" Chad was already standing.

The earl's smile was gentle, and it reached his eyes. "Yes."

Chad started to run, but the earl called him back. Sheepish, Chad gave his father a hug, then started to dart away again. "Chad! What about Jane?"

Chad grinned, raced to Jane, gave her a kiss and fled at a run.

"Study hard," Jane called after him.

Nicole was jamming the bread into her mouth with gusto.

"She has a good appetite," the earl remarked.

Jane's gaze flew to his, skittered away. "Like her father." There was silence, and she began blushing, thinking about the earl's many appetites—his manly ones.

The earl toyed with the *Times*, darting more looks at her. Jane studiously began filling her plate with food she did not want. Out of the corner of her eye she glimpsed his strong, big hands, and she clearly recalled how they felt on her flesh. She tried to recall his infidelities as well, but was too unnerved to become angry.

"May I?" she asked, pointing at the newspaper.

"Of course," he said, handing it to her. He busied himself with pouring a fresh cup of coffee, then, on an afterthought, filled her cup for her. "Sorry." He was blushing faintly, high on his cheekbones.

"It's all right," she said shyly, thrilled at the gesture.

Their gazes met, held. The earl was the first to glance away.

Jane nibbled toast and sipped coffee, thumbing through the *Times*. She was very aware of her husband and paid scant attention to the newsbreaking headlines. Until a bold typeface in the midsection caught her eyes, and then she gasped.

FALLEN ANGEL!

It was a screaming headline. The story was accompanied by two separate illustrations of her and the earl. Jane scanned the page and saw that it boasted all the sordid details of their stormy relationship. That she had been, and was, his ward, that she was the mother of his year-old illegitimate daughter, that they were just married, that he consorted with his mistress and she with her manager and "very good friend."

"What is it?" the earl asked sharply.

"Look!" Jane cried, pale, choked. "Look at this!"

The earl took the paper she shoved at him and began to read. He grew dark and grim.

"Last night they badgered me with disgusting questions about you and me, about Nicole, about the past!" Jane said vehemently. "And the night before as well! The show was ready to close, but since our marriage we've had two full houses. But they don't come to see the play! They come to see the Fallen Angel! I'm no longer an actress—I'm a freak show!"

"I'm sorry," the earl said harshly. "God, I'm sorry!"

She turned on him, letting loose all her frustration and anger. "How could you!" she cried, standing. "How could you take Nicole to the park yesterday? How could you!"

"Jane, she's my daughter."

"You could have warned me! We could have figured out what to do! Did you do it on purpose?"

"Nicole is my daughter. Not some damned secret to be kept hidden from the world! If I want to take her out I will!"

"I'll never overcome the scandal! My career! I'm ruined!"

The earl was on his feet too. "What would you have us do? Hide? The way you were hiding?"

"Yes!" Jane shouted irrationally. "Yes! If you don't care about humiliating me"—she thought of Amelia—"then at least spare a concern for your daughter!"

"Nicole is my concern!" the earl shouted. "I'll be damned if I'll deny her her place in this goddamn Society! It was her I was thinking of—this I can assure you!"

"Yes." Jane was bitter. "You would think only of Nicole—and not of me!"

"Nicole is my daughter. I had every right to publicly claim her."

"And ruin me! But you don't care, do you? You've never cared!"

He froze then. "It will die down. There's nothing else for them to dig up."

"Die down," she echoed grimly, flushed now. "That's easy for you to say. You're not the one who's ruined!"

He flinched. "Think again."

Jane's senses returned. He was as much a victim of the scandal as she was, maybe even more. After all, he'd been her guardian. They would blame him at least as much, if not more, for her downfall, for seducing her, his underage ward.

"I should have never married you. Damn it, I was selfish. I wanted Nicole, I didn't think!"

That hurt—the confession that he'd wanted his daughter. She saw him pace away, rigid with self-condemnation. She suddenly regretted all her words and accusations, even if it hurt to know he cared only about Nicole and not about her. She thought of how he had lived with scandal for the past six years—with scandal and darkness. She hurried to him. "I'm the one being selfish. Forgive me. I can handle this. You're right. It will die down."

He turned to her, eyes mocking. "What? A change of heart?"

She regarded him steadily, with compassion. She wanted to touch him, hold him.

Anger flared in his eyes. *"Don't pity me!"*

"I don't!"

But it was too late. He was already striding furiously from the room, and the doors slammed behind him like thunder.

41

🔥🔥🔥

The earl was determined to go out.

He eyed his reflection in the mirror as he adjusted his tie, black against the snowy whiteness of his shirt and the silver of his brocade vest. He slipped on a dinner jacket with tails. It was two days since the scandal had broken, three since he'd lain with his wife. They'd been avoiding each other with purposeful determination—he had only passed her in the corridors coming and going. She had not come down to breakfast since their fight.

He should be glad, but he wasn't. He was angry, and maybe even depressed.

He had his own sources, so he knew the theater was packed every night since their marriage, just as he knew Jane was right—people were going now to see her, the Fallen Angel, to feast with their own eyes upon the Lord of Darkness's wife, the mother of his bastard. Sometimes she was heckled by the audience, usually after the final curtain, but once in a while during an act. The press would still be hounding her if it wasn't for him. He had assigned two manservants to Jane, to keep them away from her.

He wanted to help her, but he didn't know how.

He eyed himself with distaste in the mirror. She'd had only to marry him to find the devil's tail and descend with him into sheer hell. She was his wife and, being such, was brought down with him. Had he foreseen the consequences, he would have never married her, despite Nicole, because it was killing him to watch her suffer so staunchly. He could bear the unbearable burden of scandal and ostracism, but Jane was fragile, no matter how brave. And she was kind and good. She did not deserve what he had brought down upon her.

That he was the instrument of her ruination tortured him.

He sighed heavily and left the room. His strides slowed as he went down the hall, getting slower still when he heard Chad laughing. The sound came from her sitting room. Then he heard her voice, the words not yet distinct. Slowing even more, he finally hesitated, just beyond the partly open door.

" 'But what shall we do?' Gretel cried. She was afraid of the witch.

" 'Don't worry,' Hansel replied. 'I have a wonderful idea. We'll take stones, Gretel, and drop them behind us to leave a trail so we can find our way!' " Jane read animatedly.

"He's smart," Chad cried excitedly. "It's what I would do!"

"Is it?" Jane asked, affection in her tone.

The earl swallowed heavily. She was reading a fairy tale to his son. Unable to go on, he stepped closer, to peer into the room.

Jane continued reading. She was seated on the watered silk settee, her legs bent beneath her. Nicole was in the crook of one arm, sucking her thumb contentedly. Chad sat on the floor at her feet, leaning against the sofa, gazing up at her raptly. A blooded Labrador puppy that the earl had given him on his last birthday gamboled around his feet.

The earl could not breathe. He listened to Jane's sweet, soft voice, his gaze fixed upon her. Her hair was loose, falling over her shoulders in glorious disarray. Nicole decided to suck on a hunk, but Jane didn't seem to notice or even mind. She was so beautiful. She was such a wonderful mother.

He closed his eyes briefly. He was on his way to a party, with Amelia. Opening them, he knew such a lump of longing he could not swallow it. He did not want to go out. He wanted to go inside Jane's room, sit on the end of the settee at her feet, and listen to her read to their children. He wanted it so badly it hurt.

Yet he was afraid. Nothing could make him enter that room. Nor could he force his feet to move to continue on his way.

And then she looked up, as Chad shrieked at something she'd read, and she saw him.

Her expression was wide-eyed, and she stared.

The earl didn't move, he couldn't.

"Papa!" Chad shouted, bouncing to his feet. He ran to the earl and hugged his thighs, then tugged on him. "Come, listen to the story about the witch!"

The earl stared at Jane, his heart pounding in his ears. She was motionless, like a small, mesmerized bird. She did not invite him in.

He felt the acute disappointment washing over him.

He found his ability to function, and he ruffled Chad's hair. "Sorry, son, I have an appointment."

Chad pouted briefly, then raced back to his spot on the floor at Jane's feet. Color was suffusing her face, and she dropped her gaze to the book. "Have a nice evening," she said, strained.

"Thank you," he returned, equally strained. "You too."

His limbs were wooden, but he managed to turn and leave. And as he went downstairs he listened intently to her voice until he could hear it no more.

Jane couldn't shake the incident from her mind. Had the earl wanted to join them? Should she have invited him in? She felt guilty that she had not, guilty and cruel, yet he had told Chad he had an appointment. Appointment! Hah! With that damned tart Amelia, undoubtedly.

It hurt. It hurt too much to even think about, yet Jane could no more turn off her thoughts than she could stop a flood. She had never dreamed marriage to him would be so painful.

She was tired, exhausted in fact, from the stress of the past few days, both of living in high tension with the earl, even though they rarely saw each other, and of living with the scandal that London was still thriving on. There had been another packed house, although not quite full this time. The hecklers had been worse than ever tonight. Some drunken men in a front row had been taunting her with epithets throughout the final act. Jane had ignored them, but their cries for her to be their Fallen Angel had truly shaken her. She slumped on the sofa in her dressing room at the Criterion.

"I know just how to cheer you up," Lindley said, entering the room.

Jane suddenly felt tears come to her eyes. Tears of self-pity that his presence had brought instantly.

"What's this!" he cried, dropping down besides her and taking both of her hands. "Jane, are you crying?"

She sniffed and fought the tears and the urge to unburden herself and tell him all of her troubles. "No, no, I'm fine. Just tired."

He touched her temple, smoothing away hair. "It's the godawful scandal, isn't it?"

Jane nodded glumly.

"It will pass."

"So everyone says."

He stared at her, and she knew he wanted to ask her questions, intimate ones, about her life with the earl. But Lindley was a gentleman, and still holding her hands, he sat straighter. "Let's go to a party."

"I can't," she said immediately. "I'm too tired."

"Ah, but this is no elegant soirée. This is artists and bohemians and students and it will be full of wine and food and fun. Trust me," he added, his brown eyes sincere.

Jane suddenly smiled. "How do you know artists and bohemians, Jon?"

He grinned. "I'll never tell."

She thought about going home—while he was out with Amelia—and was suddenly determined to have fun, to enjoy herself, to live. "All right! Just let me remove this makeup and change."

*   *   *

The party was in the cellar of an old building near the Thames on the Strand. The cellar was some sort of avant-garde café, Parisian style. As they descended rickety wooden stairs, a raucous din could be heard. Lindley had Jane's arm, for she was wearing high-heeled red shoes, to help her down. They pushed through a glass door on the bottom landing.

The interior was crowded and smoky and dimly lighted. Many small tables were packed within, all apparently full. All the aisles were crowded too. Jane saw that the crowd was half Society, elegantly dressed for an evening at the theater or opera or private soirées, and partly young students in casual tweeds. There were even a few women in bloomers, smoking cigarettes. A stunning African woman stood by a piano singing to a tune beat out ebulliently by a mustachioed player. A few of the bohemian couples were dancing enthusiastically and wildly near the piano, between the tables and the diners.

Jane's fatigue fled. She looked at the grinning Lindley and laughed. "Let's dance," she cried impulsively.

Lindley was delighted. He pulled her into his arms and whirled her about in the aisle. It was no sedate waltz, this, but something spontaneous and rhythmic and quite original. Someone at the table crowding them began to clap, and others joined in.

The song ended and the woman began another one, this one soulful and melancholy, the beat slow. Lindley didn't hesitate, but moved Jane into his swaying, barely moving embrace. Jane stiffened. "Jon, what are you doing?"

"You said you wanted to dance," he replied gruffly.

Jane could feel every inch of his body, the way he was holding her. She wasn't sure she liked it. She thought of the earl and felt guilty. Yet she was so alone, and she needed somebody. To be held intimately like this was wrenchingly wonderful. She started to relax.

"You're so damn beautiful," Lindley whispered, his breath warm on her cheek.

Jane didn't know what to say, so she said nothing.

When the song ended, Lindley let her pull away. Jane was both embarrassed and agitated from the intimacy they had shared. "Shall we find a place to sit?" she asked uncertainly.

"We can try," he said, taking her hand. He started to lead her forward, but a couple barred their way in the narrow aisle. The man was large and dark, and although at first indistinguishable amid the dim illumination, the flickering candles and foglike swirling smoke, so very familiar. His stance was rigid. It was the Earl of Dragmore.

Jane could not believe it.

His gaze was a furious silver, locked on Lindley. Lindley broke the strained silence. "Hullo, Shelton, Amelia."

It was then that Jane saw the redhead. As usual, Amelia looked voluptuous and beautiful—and she was grinning. "Hi, Jon," she purred.

The earl looked from Lindley to Jane. Jane met his gaze, her apprehension immense. She knew he was enraged to find her there with Lindley, yet he was there with Amelia. What a pretty coil, she thought, suddenly sick and miserable. Her instincts were to preempt any eruption from occurring. "Hello, Nicholas," she said quietly. He flinched as if shot at the sound of his name. "Amelia."

The earl's regard burned her. "Are you enjoying yourself, Jane?" His tone was biting.

She looked at him, eyes wide. "No. I have quite the headache."

Amelia snickered, glued to the Earl's side and pressing closer. "Maybe you should go home, to *bed*," she said snidely, implying that Lindley would be in it as well.

"You're quite right." Jane turned to Lindley. "Would you take me home? I don't feel well from all this smoke and noise."

"Of course," he said promptly. Then he looked at the earl. "Unless, of course, Nick wants to escort you back."

Jane suddenly froze, her heart clamoring with sudden hope.

The earl's lips curled up, baring his white teeth. "She came with you, she can leave with you. I have other plans."

Jane closed her eyes briefly. His cruel words hurt. If only she could hate him. She took Lindley's arm and they made their way out through the crowd.

So she didn't see the earl start after them, only to stop as abruptly, wrestling with some inner demon.

"Let them go." Amelia pouted.

"Shut up," he said, his eyes never leaving their departing forms. He took another strained step forward, then cursed viciously, raking a hand through his hair. He stared after his wife, until she disappeared through the door.

And the demons howled deep within him.

42

Jane said nothing during the drive back to the house on Tavistock Square, and Lindley, after a few attempts at conversation, let her be. He handed her down from the carriage and walked her to the front door. Thomas let them in.

Lindley hesitated in the foyer, clearly reluctant to leave. "Don't let him get you down, Jane. You deserve only happiness," he said, low. Thomas was hovering in the alcove as he put away Jane's velvet wrap.

Jane managed a shrug. "I'm fine, really I am."

"How about a brandy?" Lindley suggested. "It's still early."

"Jon . . ."

"For God's sake, Jane, am I your friend or not? You know you can trust me! And he's out with Amelia."

Jane nodded and ordered Thomas to fetch them some pâté and cold roast chicken. He grunted, moving off with obvious displeasure.

Lindley followed Jane into the parlor. "He used to like me," he said dryly.

"At least *he* is loyal to the earl," Jane said.

"You care for him, don't you?" Lindley said, amazed. "Even after all he's done to you."

Jane colored, sitting at one end of the oversized sofa. "He is my husband. As such, I am loyal too."

"Damn your loyalty," Lindley cried, sitting near her. Jane tried to skitter away but couldn't, as she was already at one end of the couch. He grasped her hands. "He does not deserve your loyalty," Lindley snarled with passion.

"Please, don't."

"I thought I knew Nick, but I don't!" Lindley stated savagely. "To flaunt that whore publicly while newly wed!"

Jane cast her eyes down. This sore, sore spot brought her close to fresh, yet old, tears.

"Ahh, Jane, I'm sorry." He pulled her hands against his stomach. "I didn't mean to upset you."

"It's all right," she said softly, not looking up. "We have an—an agreement."

"What kind of agreement?"

She looked at him. "I've allowed him his paramours," she said, not steadily. She inhaled. "Don't trouble yourself over me, Jon."

He touched her face. "Trouble myself over you?" He laughed. "Jane, darling, I love you, and knowing how unhappy you are is making me miserable!"

Jane was stunned.

"It's true," he said, low, kissing her hands, one after the other. "I love you. You deserve better. You deserve love, not cruelty. God—" He kissed her hand again, this time keeping it pressed to his cheek. He looked at her. "I want you, Jane. I want you."

She tried to pull away, and sensing her agitation, he let her go. Immediately she jumped to her feet and moved away. "I already told you," she said. "I cannot be your mistress."

"Why not? He has Amelia. And others. Why not? I can make you happy." Lindley stood urgently. "At least I would die trying. Let me try. Give me a chance."

She shook her head numbly. "Don't you see? When I make love with a man, it's just that— love." Her tone dropped. "I'm sorry, Jon, but I don't love you."

He was very still. "I know," he finally said. "But I think you would come to love me, if you let yourself."

"I'm married."

"Damn!" He paced away, then turned. "But you don't love him, Jane."

She bit her lip, staring at him with wide eyes.

"Oh, God! You do!"

She moved away, feeling unspeakably sad. "I'm sorry, Jon. Please, just be my friend."

"I had better go," he said harshly, the hurt clear in his tone.

Jane pursed her mouth so as not to cry. She watched him leave abruptly. He wouldn't look at her. She felt so bad for him. Why was life so unfair?

Thomas arrived with a trolley table set for two, pushing it into the middle of the room. "I shall be dining alone, Thomas," Jane told him, taking her seat. She helped herself to a glass of white wine and sipped it as Thomas uncovered the platters, then left. She wasn't even hungry—just unbearably tired and thoroughly miserable.

Jonathon Lindley, in love with her, and she had hurt him. The earl with Amelia. The scandal. And here she was, so alone and so lonely. She suddenly wished Jon hadn't left.

And as it turned out, she wasn't as alone as she'd thought.

"No appetite?"

She gasped to find her husband leaning in the doorway, his expression mocking. "I—I didn't hear you come in."

He smiled without warmth. "It's in my *red blood*," he said, moving into the room. He stripped off his tie and let it fall onto a chair.

"What?"

Another sarcastic grin. "Maybe someday I'll tell you a tale." He tossed his jacket on the same chair; it slipped to the floor. "A true tale," he said, prowling closer.

Jane didn't move, watching him carefully. She could not take her eyes from him. There was a coiled energy in him, and it was menacing. In that moment he reminded her of a panther, stalking his prey. Stalking her. And a hot, hot memory of him pressing her to the floor and plunging into her assailed her.

He paused by the table, inspecting it. "Dining alone? Why is that? The table's clearly set for two."

Jane looked at him. His eyes glittered.

"Don't tell me." He laughed, the sound mirthless and harsh. "You were expecting me."

"Would you care to join me?" she managed. Her heart was beating wildly. She could feel her blood pulsing in every fiber of her being. Suddenly she was aware of her body as never before—of her legs in their sexy high heels, the fullness of her hips in the fitted gown, her breasts straining against the low bodice. She was flamingly, agonizingly alive.

"How kind of you, dear wife," he said, abruptly hauling out a chair and sitting. "As it turns out, I've yet to eat. Shall I serve you as well?"

"Please," she whispered helplessly.

He served her chicken and cold carrot and raisin salad, pâté and warm toast. Then he served himself. She watched his strong brown hands, his long, lean fingers. She stared at his downturned face, at the strong jaw, the hawkish nose, the sensuously chiseled lips and high, harsh cheekbones. He looked up, bared his teeth. "Don't wait for me."

She toyed with her food.

He attacked his.

Jane could not eat. She was aware of him cleaning his plate fiercely, with the same kind of thick, raw energy she sensed he harbored in his body. He finished, shoved the plate away, and raised his glass. "To you, wife."

She didn't move. He drained it. When he set it down, his glittering eyes went to her bosom.

Jane could not breathe. She would be fooling herself if she denied what she was waiting for now—his touch. She wanted him. Despite all the hurt and humiliation, despite Amelia, now, right now, she wanted him to take her in his steely arms and make hard, hot love to her.

Their gazes locked. Jane leaned slightly forward. She willed him to come to her. Instead, he lunged to his feet with a savage curse and strode from the room.

Disappointment left her trembling.

She sat still and unmoving for a long time, trying not to think. He did not want her, he'd probably just bedded Amelia. It hurt. It hurt so much. Slowly she rose, taking her glass of wine with her. She moved to the French doors and stared unseeingly into the night, blind to the moon and the stars. Then she went upstairs.

At her door she paused, her hand on the knob, not opening it. She knew he was two doors down the hall. Her body was flaming from the thought. She would just go to say good night. She would not, she told herself, make any forward moves, but she would give him an ample opportunity to come to her.

She decided not to knock. She pushed open the door to his bedroom. He was standing in the middle of the room, shirtless, trousers unbuttoned and belt open, an unlighted cigar in hand. His gaze whipped to hers.

He was all gleaming bronze skin and thickly packed sinew. He was a beautiful male animal. She drank him in.

"What do you want?" he said harshly, taking one rigid step toward her and going no farther.

She tried to breathe evenly, and failed. "I—I just wanted to say—say good night." Jane swallowed, her palm pressing against her own abdomen, her breasts rising and falling visibly.

"Damn," he growled. "Damn! Didn't Lindley satisfy you?"

The question barely registered, and then she dismissed it. She only knew that if he didn't touch her she would die. And if he did touch her . . .

"Didn't he?" the earl roared, fists clenched, taking another step forward. His body shook. His skin glowed in the lamplight.

"No," Jane whispered. Her gaze fell from his hot eyes to his flat belly and into the vee of his open trousers. His sex bulged against his underpants. She met his gaze. "Lindley is only a friend."

He stared, his muscular chest rising and falling now too. "Jane," he said thickly. "You're asking for it. If you don't leave—now—you're going to get it."

Jane didn't break their eye contact. And she didn't move.

He struggled visibly with himself.

"Nicholas," she said softly, and boldly stepped forward to touch his hard belly.

For one instant he gasped, and they both stared at her small white hand low on his dark abdomen. Then he covered her palm with his, groaning, pushing it down into his trousers. He filled her hand through the underwear.

He caught her up, kissing her wildly, carrying her to the bed. She didn't release him, but began to stroke his thick length, hard and fast. He threw her down, pressing on top of her, anchoring her head with her hair, tearing at her mouth. Jane slipped her hand into his briefs and gripped him. He was sticky, sliding easily in her grasp.

He gasped, arching on all fours, thrusting into her palm. "Jane," he cried, their gazes meeting.

"Please." She moaned. "Please!"

He pressed onto her, tossing up her skirts, tearing off her delicate French lace panties. At the feel of his fingers against her heat and wetness, Jane sobbed. And she guided him against her.

He thrust home. They cried out together, strained together, rose together, fell together. He plunged savagely and she met him savagely. Jane suddenly gripped the headboard, keening, and a moment later the earl collapsed with his own cries on top of her.

43

Jane didn't move as the earl rolled from her to lay
on his back beside her. His arm touched hers.

She listened to his slowing breathing as her
own uproar subsided. With returning calm came
such a forceful floodtide of emotion Jane was immobilized by it. Again she felt the urge to weep.
And this time she knew with utter clarity that it
was because she loved the earl.

Two years ago she had loved him with a schoolgirl's naïveté and infatuation. Now her love was
something more, something deep. She recognized
that his absence in her life prevented her from
attaining fulfillment and completion. There was
still the stunning physical attracton that had been
there from the start, but there was more, so much
more. Jane knew she needed him. She needed his
strength, his protection, even though she was a
wholly capable and independent woman. And
Jane knew he needed her. She knew, with utter
clarity, that she could chase away his demons,

heal his heart, that she could bring light and ease into his life. Oh, how she wanted to do so!

How she wished he would touch her, hold her.

How she wanted to touch him, hold him.

She didn't know what to do, and she wanted to do something. She didn't know what to say, but something must be said. She was absolutely determined that they would not go back to separate beds and that the earl would get rid of his mistresses. Gently she must ease him down this path.

And make him love her. Just a little.

I'm a fool, she thought. She knew how hard the earl was. Knew he would never love any woman, and certainly not her. But maybe, one day, he would come to care for her as his friend, supporter, and wife.

Recklessly Jane rolled onto her side to snuggle against him, her face to his shoulder, breast to his arm, knee to knee. He went stiff.

Jane was rigid too. But she did not back down. Her lips were against his damp skin and she pressed them there. She felt him relaxing then, and abruptly he shifted toward her and pulled her into his embrace.

He kissed her. It was slow and leisurely, yet it brought a new sensual onslaught. His hand slid down her back in a soft, tender caress. Jane touched his ribs, explored them, while their tongues mated. The earl broke the kiss, pulling her partly beneath him, rose up so he could look down into her face fully. Jane gazed back steadily. She wanted to smile, but just couldn't.

Finally he spoke, low and husky. "You're so beautiful."

And she did smile. "So are you."

This turned up the chiseled curve of his mouth. "I'm not sure that is a compliment."

"Oh, it is."

His gaze darkened. There was something profound and sincere in his eyes, something deep and desperate, yet Jane could not decipher what she saw, and sensed. He kissed her hungrily, then rained kisses upon her face and throat and chest.

It was as if he could not get enough of her, or as if he were afraid that this moment was just that, only a moment and there would be no more. Jane felt his fear, his need. It fueled her response to his lovemaking.

After, they lay entwined together in each other's arms. Jane's heart was bursting with joy and breaking with sorrow. She loved this man, and the pain of loving him was nearly unbearable. Yet bear it she knew she would.

He would leave her now, she thought miserably, as he shifted onto his side. Yet he groped for her, hauled her again into his embrace, and kissed her once on the shoulder. Jane realized that the earl had fallen asleep.

Tears came to her eyes. She snuggled close unabashedly, watching him sleep, the lines of ravage upon his face softer now. Her heart tripped heavily. She prayed he would not wake up, prayed he would spend the night with her in its entirety.

For Jane was determined. From this day forward they would be man and wife in all senses of the word.

When Jane awoke to bright, midmorning sunlight, the bed was empty and the earl was gone.

She cuddled deep into his pillow, smiling. She had barely slept all night, unable to do more than doze beside him. In the middle of the evening he had awakened to go to the W.C. Jane had thought he was leaving her, adjourning to his study. She had feigned sleep, vastly disappointed. Yet he had only gone to the toilet and then he returned, climbing into bed beside her and hauling her into his arms. His kisses began on her neck, his hands gentle on her buttocks. Soon they were making love again.

Jane laughed, stretching like a cat. The earl was a magnificent man. Handsome and virile and smart—and she was in love.

Would he come to her tonight?

If he went out with Amelia she would be devastated.

She had an urge, but it was too brash and bold for this stage of their relationship. It was too soon to invite him to sup with her after her performance. She would have to come home and hope he was here, waiting for her.

Downstairs, Thomas informed her that the earl was already gone for a business appointment, and Jane was disappointed. She felt as if she were merely living for the next time she saw him, and told herself to stop being such a besotted fool. Yet she could no more deny her heart than she could take wing and fly. Indeed, it was as if she flew through the day, floating on clouds, her thoughts filled with him.

As was becoming customary, Jane gathered Chad and Nicole after their early supper to read to them. She chose another fairy tale, and had just begun when she sensed his presence and looked up. Purposefully she had left the door wide open.

The earl stood in breeches and tweed jacket, his tie dangling from his hand. His gaze dwelled solely upon her, steady, unflinching, unfathomable.

"Papa!" Chad shouted, running to hug him.

"Papa!" Nicole echoed, imitating her brother. She waved a hair ribbon in her chubby fist.

Still with eyes only for Jane, the earl's hand found Chad's back. Finally he tore his gaze free. "Hello, son."

"Want to hear a story?" Chad asked enthusiastically.

His hand in the boy's hair, the earl looked up, again at Jane, this time with a question in his eyes.

Jane, sitting on the settee, legs tucked beneath her, Nicole on her lap, smiled softly. "Please, join us."

His gaze leapt. The earl shrugged off his jacket, tossing it onto a chaise where, of course, it fell to the floor. Chad was dancing gleefully around his father, then dropped to his place at Jane's feet. The earl eased onto the settee by her bent knees. Their gazes met, locked.

Jane's heart lodged somewhere in the vicinity of her throat. She wanted to touch him, lean forward and kiss his cheek. But she did not dare.

"Hello, sweetheart," he said gently to a happy Nicole. He lifted her onto his own lap, the baby shouting with excitement.

"She loves her papa," Jane noted, heart pounding. He was so big he dwarfed the sofa, crowding her. His thigh touched her knee.

The earl smiled a rare smile, with real pleasure. Two dimples appeared to accompany it. "Yes, she does," he said, and then his silver gaze lanced hers again. Jane knew he was thinking about last night—just as she was.

"Jane," Chad shouted, tugging on her skirt. "Come on, don't forget the story!"

Jane tousled his hair, smiling, and opened the book on her lap. She began to read.

44

🔥🔥🔥

Jane handed Thomas her cloak. Quietly she asked, "Is the earl at home?"

Thomas smiled. "He's in the library, my lady."

Jane's heart danced. Trying to hide her own obvious pleasure, she touched the heavy knot of hair at the nape of her neck, then smoothed the silk of her bodice. She was wearing an emerald-green gown that she knew did especially wonderful things for her face and figure, and she hurried to the study. He sat on the couch with a journal, whiskey, and cigar. With more elation, Jane saw that he was wearing trousers with a paisley smoking jacket—and a gentleman never wore his smoking jacket out of the house.

He looked up, a light flaring in his smoky gray eyes.

"Good evening," Jane said, suddenly nervous.

"Good evening," he replied. His tone was polite, but his eyes were not. They devoured her, every inch, finally lingering upon her bosom, shock-ingly revealed by the low-cut dress. He set the journal down. "And how was it tonight?"

"Fine," she said. "You're not going out?"

He gave her a slight smile. "I found all the proferred engagements uninteresting." His look was sharp.

Jane bit back a smile. "May I . . . ?" She trailed off shyly.

"Please," he said quickly, leaping to his feet. "A sherry?"

"That would be wonderful," Jane said, coming toward the sofa. He went to pour her a glass. Jane sat down gracefully, choosing deliberately not the middle of the couch, but not the end either. He returned, handed her the glass, and sat, somewhere in the middle of the sofa—almost touching her skirts.

"Shall I ask Thomas to serve us a late supper?"

"You haven't eaten?" Jane was surprised, and wondered, daringly, if he had waited for her.

He colored slightly on his high cheekbones. "I was very involved in reading," he said lamely. "It escaped my mind."

"I am famished," Jane lied. She had no appetite, but would certainly find one, anything to linger with him!

The earl rose and rang a bell, then, when Thomas appeared, ordered him to serve what he would on the trolley table. Thomas departed, positively beaming. Jane sipped the sherry, eyes lowered, her body tense.

The earl sipped his whiskey. They seemed at a loss for conversation.

"Did you—" Jane began.

"Was it—" the earl said simultaneously.

They both smiled, each waiting for the other to continue. "Please," the earl said.

"Did you have a satisfactory business meeting?" Jane asked.

"Yes. I'm investing in an East India import-export company."

"Oh. And what do they import-export?"

"Spices, oils, silks, rugs, the usual exotica," the earl told her.

A new silence, no less awkward, descended. The earl broke it carefully. "And how was the performance tonight?"

Jane sighed. "No more full houses. We had about two-thirds attendance tonight." She set her sherry down. "The novelty is wearing off, and I'm afraid that soon we shall be closing this run."

"I'm sorry," he said.

Jane shrugged. "It's part of the business. Every show has a life of its own—legs, we call it. I guess we shall be adjourning to Dragmore, then?"

"Yes, I guess so. Unless there is a reason you wish to remain in London?"

Jane thought of being at Dragmore, away from all of Society and the horrible gossip, away from Amelia and her likes, and she was suddenly eager to go. They would be a family—just the two of them and the children. She wished they could depart tomorrow. "No," she said, deliberately hiding her enthusiasm. "I promised, and Dragmore is fine. Besides, it will be good for the children."

"Yes," he said, "I think so too."

Their gazes cautiously met. Then they boldly held. His glittered like hot silver, stealing Jane's breath and making her chest tight. Softly he said, "You are ravishing in that dress."

Jane was about to say thank you when Thomas wheeled in the trolley table, replete with covered dishes, set with silver and crystal. The earl followed her to the table, then pulled out her chair

before she could do so herself. He smiled at her
surprise, seating her before sitting himself. He
gestured for Thomas to pour the wine and begin
serving them.

He could not take his eyes off Jane.

She was stunningly beautiful, and tonight,
more than ever, she glowed with that innocent
carnal sensuality that was such an intriguing contradiction. The earl had no desire to eat. All he
wanted to do was watch Jane, listen to her voice,
be with her.

She'd haunted him throughout the day.

As had the memories of their passionate night
together.

The earl had had no intention of going out that
evening. Not with Jane on his mind, in his very
soul. He'd hoped she'd come home directly from
the Criterion, and had been ill-pressed to hide his
profound elation when she had. Maybe, just
maybe, like himself, she wanted to be with him.

Would she invite him to her bed tonight?

He ached for her, even now, sitting at the table,
the napkin barely disguising his arousal. He
would gladly die a dozen deaths just to be in her
arms again tonight. All day he'd been tormented
with wondering if she'd changed her mind about
their "agreement." About the separate bedrooms.
Yet he was so afraid of her answer that he could
not, would not, ask.

He knew he was being selfish, but he wanted
the play to fold, and soon. He wanted to take his
family, his children, his wife, to the peace and
solitude of Dragmore, where he could be alone
with them, with her. The thought was exhilarating.

Yet he tried to chase it away, because he wanted

Jane to be happy, and he knew the stage was her joy.

He tried to eat. He barely managed, and noticed that she too had little appetite. He kept thinking about what would happen after the meal. Different scenarios played themselves out: They would walk upstairs, pause at her door, she would say good night, and then disappear into her rooms, alone.

Or she would pause, blushing, not quite able to meet his gaze, and her voice, low, timid, indistinct, she would ask him if he cared to come in.

Or, better, her look would be direct, bold and sexy and suggestive of all the carnal pleasure they would share, and there would be no words. He would follow her in, her invitation silent, and she would turn, and then he would fall wildly upon her . . .

The earl shifted, thoroughly uncomfortable now. The meal could not be finished soon enough. Yet he dreaded its end too, dreaded the possibility of rejection.

Jane sighed, laying her knife and fork carefully side by side, indicating she was through. The earl promptly pushed his plate away, calling for Thomas. As the butler removed their dishes, the earl gazed at Jane's bent head, at her small hands resting on the linen tablecloth. She wore only one ring, a ruby that had been her mother's, and no bracelets. He was determined then to buy her jewelry. She looked up, her gaze wide and uncertain although unwavering, and gave him a small smile. The earl wanted to grab her and crush her in his arms.

"Coffee, my lady? Would you care for some fresh raspberry tarts?" Thomas asked.

"No, thank you," Jane said, "nothing more."
Her glance drifted to and settled upon the earl.

His chest was tight—everything was tight. He
waved Thomas away. "That will be all for tonight,
thank you." He rose, went to Jane, and drew back
her chair. His hands brushed her shoulders.
Tremors traveled along his spine from the slight
contact.

"Well," Jane said, with a small smile.

"Would you like another drink?"

She bit her lip, her blue eyes upon him. "No, I—
I think I—I'll go upstairs."

He stared at her in the following silence, then
nodded. With his hand, he touched her back as
she moved forward, ahead of him.

It took an eternity to ascend the stairs to the
second floor. The earl's heart was beating thickly,
out of control, even uncomfortably. Would she invite him in? Would she? The question echoed, tormented, consumed him.

At her door she paused, her back to him. He
stood behind her, waiting. She turned slightly and
looked at him with a tremulous, uncertain gaze. It
was not an invitation. Yet it was not a rejection.
They stared at each other for endless moments.

The earl heard himself say, thickly, "Do you
want me to come in?" And in the ensuing seconds
time came to a standstill.

"Yes," she whispered finally, blushing pink.

Joy suffused him. His gaze went bright like
lightning, and he smiled. She smiled too. The earl
reached past her and pushed open the door, and
together they went in.

45

As sleep faded, Nick reached for Jane.

His hand found only the warm space on her side of the bed, and it lingered there, while his consciousness returned. With it came recollection of the night before and that morning, when, a few hours earlier, he'd awakened her with his hands and mouth, to make love to her again. The first time had been frantic, the last soft and easy. He was stirring now. Amazingly, he could not get enough of her and he wanted her again.

He opened his eyes to look up at the peach silk tenting of the canopy above his head, listening for her, for the sounds of her return. A smile lazily appeared, softening his features, easing the harsh lines around his mouth. He didn't think he'd ever felt so wonderful, so calm and relaxed, so replete. Hurry back to me, Jane, he thought. I want you, darling.

He closed his eyes. Was he brave enough to tell

her how much she meant to him? That without her there was only darkness and despair? That she was the sunshine and laughter in his life? That he loved her?

He was a coward. He was afraid to let her know the enormity of his feelings for her.

And then he heard the distinct sound of retching.

The earl was already out of the bed as the harsh sound came again from the water closet. Grim and concerned, he rushed forward, to find Jane on her knees, hugging the bowl, her face pale and tinged green.

"What is it?" he cried, acute panic knifing him. He knelt beside her, taking her into his arms, and she leaned against him wearily. "Jane, you're ill!"

"It will pass, I think," she mumbled into his chest.

He stroked her hair, then froze, as the significance of her morning illness struck him. Morning illness. He separated himself from her to stare at her, tense and hard now, sick and furious. Didn't women become ill like this a month or so after conceiving? Not within a few days. She suddenly dove for the bowl again, retching.

He steadied her and, after she had finished, helped her rise. He watched her as she rinsed her mouth and washed her face and hands. For once he was, impossibly, immune to her naked body, so slim and slender, yet so perfectly curved. She turned to him, with an embarrassed smile, then saw his expression and froze. "Nicholas? What is it?"

He smiled, but it was only a bitter twisting of one side of his mouth. "Maybe you had better tell me."

"What's wrong?" she asked, anxiety in her tone. She touched his arm, he jerked away. "What is it!" she cried.

"You're pregnant," he said flatly, eyes cold and emotionless. "And it certainly isn't with my child."

Jane stared.

"Whose is it?"

"My God," she said, touching her chest, and then she started to smile.

His frown became a scowl. "Who is the father, Jane?"

"I am not pregnant," she told him. "It's an impossibility—unless the child is yours."

"You seem pregnant to me, and you wouldn't have this morning sickness so quickly from my seed!"

"You ninny!" she cried. "I told you, it's impossible that this is morning sickness. There has been no one but you, Nicholas. I have a flu, that's all."

His heart clenched. He gripped her shoulders. "What are you saying!"

She touched his face. "There's been no one but you."

"I don't understand."

"I've never been with another man, Nicholas, ever."

He stared, swallowing hard, stunned.

She smiled beautifully, touching his face again. "If I am pregnant, darling, it's from the past few days or that time in the library. It's that simple."

"God." Nick groaned. "Jane, this is the truth?" He was hoarse, barely able to function.

"Yes."

She had never been with anyone but him. Never given herself to anyone but him. Had been loyal to him. He swept her into his arms and held her fiercely, rocking her, while hot tears stung his eyes. I love you, he thought. God, I love you!

But he could not say the words.

And then he wondered if she loved him. His heart beat painfully, exuberantly. She must! Why else would she have been faithful to him all these years? God, she must!

And suddenly he was no longer damned, but blessed.

Nick buried his face in Jane's hair, clinging to her.

"Nicholas," she whispered, her hands roving his back. "What is it?"

He couldn't speak. So he just held her.

Two evenings later, the earl made his way backstage to his wife's dressing room. Once again he had sat in the nearly empty theater through her entire performance, unable to take his eyes off her. She mesmerized him as she performed, and he knew he was sorely infatuated with her.

A dark man with spectacles was just leaving her room as Nick entered. He was the Criterion's manager, and he nodded abruptly at him. Gordon was with Jane, looking somber, but the earl had eyes only for his wife. She sat on the sofa, pale and taut, surrounded by hundreds of white roses, which filled the dressing room. His white roses, and he smiled at the thought.

"I'll leave you two alone," Gordon said. "Good night, Jane, Shelton."

"Nicholas," she cried intensely after he'd gone.

Instantly he came to her, took her hands, kissed them. "Darling, what is it?"

"You won't have to send me any more flowers,"
she said simply.

"You're closing?"

She nodded, her eyes large and luminous.

He hugged her, and she rested in his embrace,
eyes closed. "There'll be other shows, Jane. And
you were wonderful. I can personally vouch for
that."

She sighed. "I think you're not exactly objec-
tive." The brief smile faded. "It's just so sad when
the show closes. It's almost as if someone has
died."

He stroked the hair at her temple. He had
wanted nothing more than to take her and their
children to Dragmore, but now he changed his
mind. "We will stay in London," he said. "We
won't go to Dragmore."

"What!"

He smiled gently. "I'm realizing how much acting means to you. Find another show. It's all
right. Forget that lousy agreement we made.
You're as wonderful a mother as you are an actress, and you've certainly proved you can be both
at once."

Tears filled her eyes. She clung to him and
started to cry.

"Jane." He was numb. What had he done? He'd
only wanted to make her happy. "Darling, if I've
done something wrong . . ."

She shook her head, sniffing, nose red now.
"You are an angel, Nicholas," she said softly.
"Your offer is superb. You are superb."

He tried to hide his pleasure at the compliment,
and failed. "Well." He shrugged, but he was smiling.

"I happen to want to go to Dragmore," Jane announced, stroking her finger along his jaw. "I

want some time alone with you and the children. Do you mind?"

"Mind?" He nearly shouted. He laughed, swept her against him. "Jane," he said, low. "No one's ever called me an angel before!"

46

Jane stood in front of the dressing table in her bedroom, a dreamy smile on her face, as Molly helped her button up the back of her dress. She had overslept, sinfully. Yet she hadn't gone to bed until dawn. Her smile increased. She was remembering last night.

The earl had taken her for an intimate, elegant dinner at one of London's finest restaurants. From there they had gone dancing at the Regency, then strolled along the Thames, hand in hand, and after . . .

Jane briefly closed her eyes. Just thinking about his lovemaking brought an instant tension and need to her body.

"There you go, mum," Molly said. "My, ain't you a sight this morning! A stunner if ever you were one, if you don't mind me sayin' so."

Jane smiled, regarding herself openly. Her eyes were a dazzling blue, sparkling boldly, her cheeks flushed naturally, and, indeed, she was striking this day. "I don't mind," she said softly, while inside her soul was singing. She reached for her pearl-inlaid hairbrush, then paused, noticing a small wrapped, beribboned jeweler's box next to it, with a card.

Molly saw it too. "Another one!" She gasped.

Jane tried to frown, and failed. She opened the gilt-edged card. As had all the others, it said simply "To my wife, Jane, from Nicholas." She shook her head. Inside the box was a choker of diamonds that must have cost thousands of pounds. Molly gasped.

In the past week, since their reconciliation, he had given her a stunning sapphire ensemble, a breathtaking bracelet of rubies, emeralds, and diamonds, an exquisite rope of pearls. Not to mention all the white roses. And now this, worth a king's ransom. He was surely out of his mind!

"He must love you very much," Molly breathed, awed. "Ain't you gonna try it on?"

Jane did not exactly have to be coerced, and Molly helped her don the necklace. It consisted of three tiers and a large teardrop point. It was much too much—where would she wear it?

"Where is the earl?"

"He's still in the dining room." Molly grinned. "He slept late too."

Jane blushed. She hurried downstairs, her heart tripping, and trying to control it.

As usual, the sight of him stole her breath. His dark head was bent over something he was reading. He was utterly magnificent, bronze and ebony, and when he looked up, his eyes flashed silver. Then he saw the necklace and he smiled. "Good morning," he said, his tone intimate and sexy, conjuring up memories of their many shared moments of heated passion.

"Nicholas," she tried to chide.

He was standing, coming to her, taking her shoulders and giving her a quite improper kiss. Jane lost her head, of course, and returned it, and it was he who set her apart as she clung to him. "Maybe we should go back upstairs," he said, teasing.

Incredibly, had he been serious, she would have needed no persuasion! "Nicholas, you must not give me any more gifts!"

"You don't like it?" he asked, hurt.

"I love it," she cried. "But this is insane! I don't need so much jewelery, and if you keep this up you'll be bankrupt!"

He threw back his head and laughed. "Let me worry about our finances, Jane. Dragmore is quite in the black, thank you."

"Please," she said, as he seated her. "Please, no more gifts."

"I cannot give you my word," he said, his grin mischievous, and Jane knew she had lost. She wondered if Molly was right. If he loved her.

As he poured her coffee, automatically adding cream, she saw he was reading a letter. "Who is it from, Nicholas?"

She felt the easy carefree attitude evaporate. Seriously he replied, "It's from my parents. In Texas."

Jane sensed something amiss and did not understand. "How wonderful. What news?"

He smiled then, slightly. "It seems my roguish brother has finally been snared—by a suffragette, no less. He got married this spring."

Jane knew a little bit about Nick's younger brother, Rathe. She had been told that he was charming, handsome, and a very successful businessman, as well as an unrepenting ladies' man.

But, apparently, his womanizing days were over. "It must be a romantic story," she said, a touch wistfully. "He doesn't sound like the type to have fallen for one of those Bloomer girls!"

Nick's smile was wry. "No, he doesn't, does he." Then he growled, "The little bastard! He must be in love—not to write me himself!"

"You love him very much," Jane said softly.

High up on his cheekbones, the earl reddened. "He's my brother," he said gruffly.

"And your sister? The one in San Francisco? Storm?"

"Happily married, two kids, just moved into another mansion." Nick smiled. "Probably still making Brett crazy with her wild ways."

"She's wild?"

He softened. "She was quite the tomboy, Jane, and totally stubborn. How she ever became the lady she is today is quite beyond me."

"You miss them."

He avoided her gaze.

"Let's go visit."

The earl looked at her, saying nothing, but Jane saw something dark and disturbed in his eyes; worse, she felt it. "Shouldn't Chad meet his aunt and uncle, his cousins, his grandparents?"

The earl toyed with his knife, eyes upon the table. "Yes."

Jane said nothing. What was amiss? She didn't want to pry, not yet, their relationship was too fragile, yet she sensed his need and desperation— that there was something deep and malignant which needed healing.

The earl sighed, the sound heavy. "I've been thinking about taking Chad to Texas. It's his heritage as much as Dragmore." His gaze, pain-filled, touched Jane's. "It's where I was born and raised."

Jane said nothing.

"It's been a long time," the earl said thickly, and Jane knew he was talking about himself and the last time he'd been to his parents'.

"Are your parents well?"

"Yes." He managed a rough smile. "They want me to come home. They've been begging me to make a trip west for years."

"It sounds like they miss you very much," Jane said. "Do you want to go?"

He hesitated, turned to look out the window at the immaculate lawn. "Yes. No."

Jane touched his hand, covering it with her own. "Whenever you want to go, I will be ready."

His gaze held hers, filled with relief and gratitude. "Thank you."

47

Later that night, the earl paused in the threshold of his wife's room. She sat reading in bed, a vision in diaphanous white French lace, her long platinum hair cascading about her. She had left one lamp on, so the room was dimly illuminated. She was Beauty Incarnate, and he loved her.

Sensing his presence, she looked up and smiled, laying aside her novel.

He did not smile back. He could not. Nor did he come forward. He stared at her. And inside, his nerves were so taut he thought he must vomit immediately.

"Nicholas?" Worry edged her voice. "What is it?"

He had to know. He had to know if she would reject him as Patricia had. He dared to hope that she would not when she learned he was partly Indian. Yet he would never forget Patricia's horror and hysteria. He had loved Patricia then, yet it was nothing compared to what he felt for Jane. If

Jane was repulsed, as a part of him was sure she would be, he did not know what he would do. He could not find any armor against the scorn and revulsion he was afraid would surely come when she learned this part of the truth. He would not reveal more than this, he could not. And even now he wished he could turn and walk away, without testing her. But he had to know.

"Nicholas!" Jane was sitting up straight, her face pale. "What's wrong! You're frightening me!"

He came forward slowly, like a somnambulist, pausing by the post at the foot of her bed. He stared at her. Would she reject him?

"What is it?" Jane begged.

"There's something I want to tell you," he said flatly, no emotion or turmoil in his tone.

"What?"

"My father is a half-breed," he said, waiting for her reaction.

She blinked at him. "Excuse me?"

"My father," he said, raising his voice. "Derek Bragg. He is a half-breed, half Indian, half white man."

Jane's eyes grew wide.

"That makes me," he said roughly, "one-quarter breed. Do you understand?"

Wide-eyed, she stared.

He waited, unable to breathe, the urge to vomit intense, for the rejection, the scorn, the revulsion.

Suddenly she smiled, then bit it back. "Oh, I had a funny thought, but now is not the time to be amusing. Nicholas, come here."

"What was your thought?" he said stiffly, ignoring her summons. She would make fun of him now. This he hadn't counted on.

Her lips curved up. "So that is why you're so dark!"

He blinked. "Excuse me?"

She got up and came to him, placing her hands inside his robe and sliding them over the bronze skin of his chest. "Why you're so dark." She lifted her gaze and grinned wickedly. "I think I like dark men."

His heart began to hammer loudly. "You're not disgusted?"

"Of course not," she said softly, touching his face. "Why should I be?"

He could barely believe it, and was stunned.

With a smile, she slid her hand down his torso, around to his hip, and then clasped his hard buttock. "I definitely like dark men!"

He growled, lifting her up into his arms. "You had better like only this dark man," he said fiercely, and then he kissed her, hard, voraciously, raping her with his mouth. She clung.

He carried her to the bed, pushing her down, coming down on top of her. He was shaking with need—and relief.

Jane managed to tear her mouth free of his rampaging one, stroking his thick arms. "Nicholas, it's all right," she said. "It's all right."

He pressed her into the mattress, burying his face in her neck, and he groaned, the sound long and low and a release of deep inner torment. She stroked his hair as he trembled on top of her, his body hard and rigid and searing. Then he lifted up. "Let me love you," he whispered harshly. "Let me love you, Jane," he begged.

She caught his face and kissed him fiercely back, wondering at the dampness there.

The earl lay on his back, looking up at the canopy tenting them. Jane was on her side, snuggled against him. They had been talking about leaving for Dragmore early the next week.

"Jane," the earl said, turning his head. "Are you sure you wouldn't rather stay and work in London?"

She kissed his shoulder. "You are a dear. No, I am determined to go to Dragmore." She grinned. "And you know how stubborn I am."

He smiled, his gaze fond. "Are you stubborn?"

"Since I was a child," she said. "When I decide to do something, I do it."

"Like haunting the village bully? What was his name?"

"Timothy Smith," Jane said. "He deserved it! But that was nothing! Do you know that once I won a hundred pounds at the men's club, Boodle's?"

"What?"

Jane laughed. "It was a dare—that I could not get into Boodle's. I was fourteen, it was just before I left the acting company to live with Matilda and Fred at the parsonage. A few young actors thought they'd really got me with this dare. Of course, I won." She wrinkled up her nose with disdain.

"I don't believe it."

"I did. I disguised myself as a boy and went in with two old lords with a reputation for liking young boys. They thought I was their entertainment for the night and they were just thrilled. They never guessed I was a girl. Nobody bothered to stop me from gambling at the tables—I think everyone found a young lad trying his luck quite amusing."

The earl groaned. "And after? How did you escape your lecherous benefactors?"

"By running away," she said simply.

A silence ensued. Jane cuddled closer, caressing the earl's flat, iron-hard belly. He stared up at the canopy. "I have a story," he finally said quietly.

Jane glanced at him to see that his eyes were closed.

"There was a young woman, newly wed and newly widowed. She was ravishingly beautiful but very delicate—more so than you. In fact, she had been raised in a convent in France." He paused.

Jane gazed at him curiously, wondering what kind of story he was telling her, and why. He still had not opened his eyes.

"She lived on the frontier in Texas. While traveling there from France, overland in Mississippi, she had accidentally met a man. A Comanchero. He was stricken with her beauty and he wanted her. In fact, he succeeded in kidnapping her before her first marriage, but a Texas Ranger rescued her before she was harmed." He paused again.

Jane shifted. She wanted to ask if he knew this woman, and was certain he did—but did not dare interrupt. His tone was so flat, so devoid of emotion, that it frightened her.

"Her first husband died—was killed actually, in a typical brawl. The frontier was full of violence back then. She married again—to the Ranger who had rescued her—immediately. It was not unusual, because a woman could not survive alone in the wilderness. One day, when he was on duty with his regiment, their home was attacked by Comanches, and she was taken prisoner.

"The leader of the attack was the same Comanchero Chavez."

Jane could not refrain from speaking. "Oh, God. What happened?"

"He raped her," the earl said flatly.

"Did—did he kill her?"

"No. Fortunately, weeks later, the Rangers found their camp and destroyed it, rescuing her. The Ranger who was her husband killed the Comanchero, mutilating him first."

Jane shuddered. "This is an awful story. Nicholas?"

He opened his eyes, to stare up at the canopy. "She had a child nine months later. It was not the Ranger's. It was his."

Jane pressed close, sensing his need, and stroked his hip. "And?"

He shrugged. "That's all. It's just a typical frontier story."

Jane was confused. Why had he told her this terrible tale? "What happened to the child?"

The earl hesitated. "I don't know."

She nuzzled his shoulder. "Why did you tell me this?"

He turned to her, his gaze dark and unreadable. "I grew up in this frontier where violence rules and only the strong survive. This is where I come from."

Jane shuddered. She touched him. "Is it still so savage?"

"No. Somewhat untamed, but not like what I've just described."

"Do you know the woman?"

His gaze moved over her features. It was a long time before he answered. "Yes."

"That poor woman," Jane said, suddenly inexplicably moved. "Did—did it destroy her marriage? To the Ranger?"

He shook his head. "No. He loved her, still loves

her, more than life itself, I think. And she feels the same way about him."

Tears came to Jane's eyes. "How romantic! Love triumphs after all."

"Why are you crying?"

Jane shook her head. "It's a terrible story, but even more beautiful too because of the tragedy they overcame."

The earl said nothing, just stared at her. Then he leaned forward, wiping away her tears with his big, calloused thumb. Surprised, Jane saw that his eyes were glistening. "Nich—"

"Sshh," he said, claiming her mouth with barely leashed power, and then he claimed her body as well.

48

🔥🔥🔥

Summer had come to London in all its first glory.
It was a beautiful day, red robins singing high in
the elm trees, the sky blue and cloudless, the day
warm enough to go with the thinnest of garments
and no coats or wraps. The bold Dragmore carriage rolled through Hyde Park, pulled by its
team of magnificent bays. The earl and Jane sat
side by side, their bodies touching from shoulder
to hip to knee. Nicole was in her mother's arms,
unusually quiet, and Chad sat on the seat facing
them, waving to all those they passed and remarking excitedly upon any and everything.

"What a wonderful idea," Jane said to Nick, her
gaze lingering upon his handsome face. She was
sure her love for him was easy to read and quite
obvious to everyone.

"Governess Randall wasn't exactly pleased," the
earl said. He had taken Chad from his studies.

"To hell with her," Jane returned, her manner
prim.

The earl laughed and took her hand, squeezing it. "Sshh, not in front of the children."

Jane made a stricken face, and the earl laughed again. He did not release her hand. Jane settled more comfortably against him. They both ignored the many gaping, gossiping riders and coach passengers whom they passed.

"Papa," Chad cried excitedly. "Can we go for a ride in a boat?"

They were approaching the lake, and a few rowboats were evident, ladies lounging amid the lace of their dresses and parasols, the men in striped shirtsleeves rolled casually up, rowing steadily.

"I don't see why not," the earl replied. He turned to Jane. "It's up to your mother."

Jane held his gaze. His words thrilled her, and she impulsively leaned forward to plant a light kiss on his mouth. "Of course it's all right."

The earl blushed, looking quite pleased. "Jane," he said a few moments later, as the carriage stopped in front of the green, shingled boathouse, "do you remember that story I told you last night?"

Jane glanced at him curiously. "Of course I do."

Chad interrupted, asking if he could go look at the boats. The earl nodded and his son rushed from the carriage. The earl and Jane made no move to follow. He stared at her. "That woman, Jane," he said. "She is my mother."

Jane gasped.

"I am the boy."

Jane stared, her thoughts racing, her grip on his hand tightening instinctively. "Oh, Nicholas, what an awful cross to bear!"

He stared at her.

"Darling," she cried, using the endearment for

the first time, "have you been punishing yourself all these years for something you were not responsible for?" She touched his face.

"It doesn't bother you?" he asked thickly.

"It hurts me to see you hurt," she cried. "How could they have told you this terrible story!" She was suddenly furious, as all the implications settled in. This was the dark torment burning in his soul that she had sensed and seen signs of so often.

"They didn't tell me," Nick said quietly. "I found out just before I left for the war. They don't even realize that I know the truth. My father"— and he hesitated—"Derek, I mean, he doesn't know I found out the truth. That he is not my father, that Chavez is."

Jane clutched his hand. The hurt in his tone was there, thick and palpable. "Darling, I'm sure he loves you like a son. You are his son! He raised you your entire life."

"He is a great man," the earl said.

Jane suddenly, intuitively, understood. "He is your father, Nicholas," she said stubbornly. "You are the man you are today because of him. You must see him," she cried. "This is awful, surely he senses something amiss. You must tell him you know!"

"Jane," the earl said. "You don't think I am like him?"

Jane knew who "he" was—the Comanchero. "You are kind and good. Don't you ever say such a thing again!"

"I almost raped you," he said, very low. "And, God, when you were only seventeen and just a schoolgirl, I wanted you. It was all I could think of. It was depraved."

She covered his mouth with her palm. "We

wanted each other, like men and women do who share the attraction we have for each other. It wasn't depraved, Nicholas, it was destiny. Our destiny."

He pulled her into his embrace. "God," he cried, his face against hers, "what did I do to deserve you?"

"No, Nicholas," Jane said, threading her fingers through his hair. "It's the other way around. What did I do to deserve you?"

Their gazes met. His was glistening, but so was hers.

The earl took a deep breath. "Well," he said, coughing. "Shall we?"

The footman was waiting at a discreet distance. The earl signaled him and let Jane precede him from the carriage. They caught up with Chad and Nick tousled his hair. "Come on, son, you can help me choose a boat."

"I can?" Chad shouted, thrilled. He ran to the boats, the earl following. He paused to glance back. "Wait here, Jane." His words were innocuous but his look was not. It was shimmering with deep, deep emotion. "We'll only be a few minutes."

Jane nodded. As the earl went to make arrangements, her mind was whirling with the significance of what she had found out. And with it came the determination to cleanse him forever of his guilt at being Chavez's son and to help him learn, and believe, that he was the magnificent man he truly was. And, equally important, she would bring father and son back together again.

Jane was happy. It was the beginning for them all, the first day of the rest of their glorious life together. They would leave the dark past behind. Now was the present, shimmering with love and passion, and awaiting them was the future, its promise even more glorious.

The afternoon upon the lake passed too quickly amid much laughter and affection and camaraderie. As the Dragmore carriage sped home, Jane found herself imitating Chad, who had fallen asleep on the earl's left, his head upon his father's shoulder. Her own cheek pressed his other shoulder, and her lids were so very heavy. The earl's palm stroked her arm, and she started to doze.

"We're home, darling," the earl said in her ear. "Chad, wake up, son."

A sleepy entourage emerged from the carriage, Nicole starting to howl and squirm in Jane's arms, Chad holding the earl's hand. Thomas greeted them at the door with Molly, who rushed forward to take Nicole. The butler was as white as death itself.

"Thomas, what's wrong?" the earl said sharply.

Jane became fully awake, to see that Thomas was in a rare frenzy, eyes popping as if he'd seen a ghost. "My lord," he cried. "It's your wife!"

"My wife?" the earl said, glancing at Jane. Jane suddenly pressed closer to the earl, sensing danger.

"Not the lady Jane." Thomas gasped. *"The other one."*

The earl stared, then his eyes narrowed. "You are making no sense, Thomas," he warned.

"It's Lady Patricia," Thomas cried. "She is here!"

"What?"

"She is here, in the parlor, alive—not dead!"

And then a stunning blond woman appeared from behind Thomas, her bearing regal and disdainful. With a glance, she took them all in, Chad,

Jane, Nicole and Molly, the earl. "Hello, my lord," she said coolly.

"My God," Nick said softly, stunned.

Jane stared at the beautiful woman—his wife. And then the ground came rushing up to meet her and, blessedly, she knew no more.

49

Before sweeping Jane up in his arms and rushing with her into the house, the earl directed a searing look of disbelief and hatred at Patricia. "Thomas," he shouted, "bring tea and whiskey, cool cloths and smelling salts."

He pounded into the study. He lay Jane down upon the sofa as if she were made of fragile china, smoothing hair away from her forehead. "Jane," he said, low, soft. "Jane, wake up."

And then, although there was no sound, he felt her animosity and contempt and he turned to see his first wife standing in the doorway, staring at them. "How quaint," she said.

"You bitch," he bit out, and turned back to Jane.

"Papa!" Chad came running in, white-faced, Governess Randall on his heels. "What's happened to Jane? Is she dead?" He started to cry, although manfully trying to hold back the tears.

"She's only had a little faint," the earl told him. "Chad, be a good man and go upstairs with Ran-

dall. Jane will be up shortly and you'll see she is
fine. You've missed enough studies as it is today."

Although reluctant, Chad allowed the governess
to take his hand. He followed her out, with many
backward glances at Jane. Jane moaned. The earl
touched her face, coaxing her back to consciousness. "Wake up, darling," he murmured. "Jane,
wake up."

Thomas entered with the damp cloths and li-
quor. "The tea will be just a moment more," he
said, handing the earl a whiskey. He ignored Patricia quite royally.

Jane eyes fluttered open.

The earl propped her up. "You've had a shock,"
he said grimly. "We all have. Here, sip this," he
said, guiding the glass to her mouth.

Jane took a draft, coughed, turned away pro-
testing and saw Patricia. She froze.

The earl whipped his head around furiously.
"You may await my summons in the parlor," he
said through gritted teeth.

Her eyes blazed, but she was also afraid, and
with a negligent shrug she exited.

"Oh, God!" Jane cried, sinking back down and
covering her face with her hands.

"We'll work it out, Jane," the earl promised, but
there was a note of desperation in his voice.

She sat up. "I want to go to my room," she managed. Her face was stark white, and she turned
her agonized blue gaze upon him. "How can she
be alive? How?" she cried. "And why has she come
back now?"

"I don't know," he said tautly. "I don't know."

The earl closed the parlor door behind him,
leaning against it. Hatred blazed from his eyes.

Seated like a queen in the center of the couch,

still every bit the beauty, dressed richly in gold silk and brocade, Patricia Weston met his stare steadily, a tiny smile of superiority turning up the corners of her mouth.

"This is unbelievable," the earl said. "Have the past six years been amusing, Patricia?"

She made a moue. "Apparently they have been quite amusing for you."

He clenched his fists. "Why have you come back? And where the hell have you been?"

"I've been in America, mostly," she said, as if discussing a two-week holiday. "And I came back for what's mine." Her green eyes hardened.

"You mean Clarendon?" The earl laughed. "Clarendon is Chad's. And I have a wife."

"Do you? You don't mean that little tart? *I* am your wife, she is merely a mistress. Legally speaking, that is."

"You goddamn bitch. You think to take your place as my wife in my home, in my life? Well, think again!"

"We can find a mutually satisfactory arrangement, Nick." Patricia smoothed her skirts. "I will reside elsewhere, of course. Our paths need never cross. You must only furnish me with a reasonable allowance and my inheritance, which I left behind in my haste to flee you six years ago."

"I will gladly give you the ten thousand pounds that is your estate," the earl spat. "I have no need of it." The enormity of the dilemma facing him confronted him squarely, painfully. "God!" he cried, realizing with anguish that his wife was Patricia, not Jane.

"Don't worry, you may keep her. It suits me, in fact. But of course you cannot live with her," Patricia said. "It would be too indiscreet."

He whirled. He wanted to strangle her. "Maybe

I should do what everyone accused me of doing all those years back," he growled. "Maybe I should kill you!"

Patricia paled.

"Don't," the earl warned, pacing forward. "Don't you dare to give me ultimatums."

"I'm sorry," she said, eyeing him with fear.

"Did you know I was tried for your murder?" He was shaking with fury. He saw the flash of fear again in her eyes. "You were in hiding, pretending to be dead—while I was almost convicted!"

"I didn't know."

He was sure she was lying, he saw it in her eyes. "You unbelievably selfish, self-centered bitch. Am I to assume you were with Boltham? He left for America after the trial, did he not?" Again, he did not need her answer. "You didn't shed one tear over your son, did you?" he snarled.

"Chad is yours," she said, shoulders squared, head held high. Distaste twisted her lips. "Every bit yours."

He compared her to Jane, beautiful, big-hearted Jane, and could not believe he had ever loved her. "Who died in the fire?" the earl shot.

"My maid, the Irish girl." Patricia shrugged. "The silly twit fell in her haste to flee and hit her head. I had to leave her behind."

"Did you start the fire, Patricia?"

"No."

The earl knew it was a lie.

She shrugged. "You cannot prove anything."

"You would go to such extremes to escape me? And you feel not a jot of guilt for that poor girl who died?"

"I hate you," Patricia suddenly hissed. "I've always hated you, from the moment we met! I did what I had to! I would do it again!"

The earl had a sudden idea. "Who has seen you? Other than the servants? Who knows you are still alive?"

"No one who knows me," Patricia said. "Except Boltham, of course."

"I will give you more money than you can possibly spend," the earl said vehemently. "But I want you to get out of this country and never come back. Do you understand?"

Patricia smiled. "So you can live with your new wife as if I am really dead? Forget it! I am tired of America. Boltham bores me. And he is penniless too. I want my place back in Society. I am not leaving. I am tired of being an anonymous English noblewoman!"

"You selfish bitch," the earl said.

It was over, wasn't it? It was over before it had really begun. Their life together. His wife, *his first love*, was back, to claim her rightful place at his side. Why else would she appear? Jane hugged her pillow and wept.

Fate was so cruel, to bring her and Nicholas together then wrench them apart. How, how would she survive?

And they weren't even married. His wife was Patricia, she was just his paramour in the eyes of God and the law. Jane sobbed harder.

Did he still love Patricia?

And now what?

"Jane," the earl said, entering without knocking.

"No," she managed, clutching the pillow even tighter. She lay curled in a ball on the bed. "Not now."

"We have to talk," the earl said.

"Go away, go to her! Go to your real wife!" Jane cried hysterically.

He sat beside her, the mattress dipping, and pulled her against him. She fought him. "I don't want to go to her," he said thickly. "Jane, we must be calm. We must talk."

She did not release the pillow. Her ears were ringing, her temple throbbing, and everything was so *unreal*. She was so afraid. "I don't want to talk. Not now." Did he still love her? Why was he so calm?

"Jane, don't let her tear you up like this. It *will* be all right," he vowed. "You will see. We shall work it out."

It was impossible and she knew it. There was nothing to work out. Patricia was his wife and she was not. Patricia had come back because she was his wife. Hadn't she?

"What does she want?" she heard herself say, her voice sounding strange and far away. Although she knew the answer, she prayed, she hoped, to hear something else.

For a long moment he did not speak, and she caught a glimpse of something like desperation in his eyes. But then there was only firm, steel resolve, and she knew she had imagined seeing any other emotion. "Please, Jane," he said. "Don't torture yourself. Trust me. You know I will always take care of you and Nicole. Always. We will find a solution. I promise."

Jane almost laughed, hysterically. She had known it, sensed it, the moment she first saw Patricia. There was only one solution. Obviously Patricia had come back from the dead to resume her role as his wife. That left one role for Jane—as mistress. Nicholas would "take care" of her. Jane knew she could not relinquish Nicholas to another woman, especially not to his first love. She could not, would not, be his mistress, after being his wife. She balled up her fists. And just when he was starting to love her a little!

"Don't cry," the earl said shakily. "She's gone, for now, anyway, to Clarendon. She won't be staying here, regardless."

Jane lifted her face, gripping his shirt. "Make love to me, Nicholas," she said desperately. "Make love to me now."

"Jane," he protested.

Her fingers clenching his hair, she pulled his head down and kissed him with all the desperation and love she felt. He did not resist, then began to respond, her hunger feeding his. Jane pulled him down on top of her, tearing at his shirt, the buttons flying off. He kissed her fiercely, crushing her breasts.

It was going to be the last time, and she knew it.

"Come to me," she screamed, biting his mouth. "Come to me, Nicholas, now!"

"Jane!"

She wrenched open his trousers, yanking at them, baring his thick manhood. The earl gasped as she bit his jaw, her nails raking down his back. "Nicholas!" she screamed, weeping.

He tossed up her skirts and impaled her.

Together they strained in desperation, the one to the other, their hot tears mingling on their cheeks. And after, Jane could not cry anew, for she had nothing left to give.

The earl stroked her face and hair, holding her. "We will work it out," he said again.

She tried to smile, and failed.

50

🔥🔥🔥

The earl had summoned his lawyer. Now he stood miserably, tautly, in his study, unable to calm down. He began pacing with agitation. Damn the woman! He couldn't help wishing that Patricia were really dead. Thinking about her infuriated him.

He heard Jane's voice in the hallway as she asked Thomas for a carriage. The earl was already at the door, and there he froze.

She slowly lifted her gaze to his.

He stared, not at her, but at her trunk and valise, the blood draining from his face—and from his very soul.

"I cannot stay here, Nicholas," Jane said calmly.

His gaze was wild. "You are leaving me?"

"It's better if I go back to Gloucester Street," she said, her mouth trembling.

"You cannot go!"

"I cannot stay here," she cried, her face even

paler than his. "I am not your wife anymore,
Nicholas—or have you forgotten?"

The pain was unbearable. "Jane, I told you, we
will work it out."

"Oh, yes," she said bitterly. "There is certainly a
solution! An obvious one." Tears filled her eyes.
"But regardless, she is your wife, and I cannot
remain here."

"Don't go," he said hoarsely.

"Think! Think about the children! We cannot
immerse them in another scandal, my God!" And
her mouth crumbled as the tears fell freely now.

If it were only him, he would not care about
another scandal. But now he had Jane and the
children to think about, to protect. It would be
the height of indecency and immorality should
she remain in his household with Patricia back
from the dead. Still, it did not make it any easier
to bear—it did not ease the godawful pain.

"I—I had better go," Jane said into the raw silence.

The earl said nothing. He watched her move
away, wondering at the magnitude of heartache
he was feeling. But then he consoled himself—she
was only going to Gloucester Street, and as she
had said, there was an obvious solution. Where
the hell was his lawyer?

Nick strode outside after her. Jane was ascend-
ing into the carriage, Molly and Nicole already
within. He caught her from behind and turned
her for a fierce, searing kiss, one of possession.
She did not respond, as if numb and shocked.

"I will come to you tomorrow," he promised
her.

Her eyes teared again. "Good-bye, Nicholas."

"Tomorrow, Jane," he said firmly, then watched

as the carriage rolled down the drive, through the iron gates, and into Tavistock Square.

His lawyer, Henry Felding, was a tall, thin, somewhat nervous man. However, he was quite brilliant. He arrived a quarter hour later. "Where have you been?" Nick ground out.

"I'm sorry, my lord, but the traffic is nigh on impossible at this hour. How is your wife?" Felding asked politely.

"My wife, damn her soul, has come back from the dead!"

Felding was openly shocked.

"My first wife," Nick said through gritted teeth. "Patricia Weston Shelton. She is alive, and in London."

Felding sat down. "Oh, dear," he said.

"Oh, dear is damn right." The earl pulled a chair up and sat, leaning forward aggressively. "Am I still legally married to her? She disappeared six years ago and was assumed dead, as you well know."

Felding wiped his face with a handkerchief. "Yes, I recall all that hoopla. And yes, she is still your wife, both legally and in the eyes of the church."

Nick cursed savagely.

Felding blushed.

"And where, pray tell, does that leave Jane?"

"I am afraid Jane has no status, not legally, that is."

"I want a divorce."

"An annulment would be a matter of course," Felding said, brightening now. "As the Lady Patricia is still alive, the church will readily annul your marriage to Jane."

"No. I want to divorce that faithless, selfish bitch—Patricia. Start the proceedings now!"

Felding gasped. Divorce was not just rare, among the upper classes it was almost unheard of and certainly a last, dire resort. Worse, it was immoral and scandalous. "Are you certain?"

"One hundred percent. How long will it take?"

"Usually there is a bit of a wait, nigh on a year."

"Damn."

"But"—Felding brightened again—"in this case, with your wife having abandoned you, and being thought dead, with you having taken a second wife, and there being issue thereof, I imagine we can speed things up quite a bit."

"Good," the earl said savagely. "Good!"

"I will begin inquiries immediately," Felding said, taking out a pen and notebook and scribbling some notes.

The earl went to his desk and returned with two envelopes. "This is for you—a bonus for a job well done in advance," he said.

Felding blushed. "Thank you, my lord, but it's really not necessary. . . ."

"And this is for whomever you judge worthy and helpful. I want this done as quickly as possible," he said, handing him the second envelope. Both were full of thousands of pounds.

"This will certainly expedite matters," Henry Felding said.

It was just past eleven when the Dragmore carriage with its bold crests pulled up to the front doors of Clarendon.

The Clarendon estate was in Kent, some five hours by coach from London. It sprawled over twelve thousand acres, most of the farmland leased to tenants due to the mismanagement of the various dukes. The mansion itself had been built in the Tudor style during the reign of Henry

VII, and added on to subsequently during the end of Queen Elizabeth's reign, and then time and again. As such, it was a huge, sprawling, confused affair—quite ghastly, in fact. Nick had never been impressed by the place.

He was determined to inform Patricia of his plans and get any confrontation over with. He had traveled all evening to do so. He alighted from the carriage purposefully and was greeted by pale, sweating servants, no doubt still in the same state of shock that he'd been in when Patricia had materialized upon his own doorstep earlier that day. He reckoned that she had probably arrived five or six hours ago.

"My lady is asleep," he was informed somewhat disdainfully by the butler, whose name he could not remember.

He stood arrogantly in the grand hallway, a cruel smile on his lips. "Then awaken her. I expect her downstairs and in the library in fifteen minutes. If she is not there then, I shall come and get her myself. Even if I have to drag her from her bed."

The butler scurried off.

The earl strode down the hall, flinging open doors, looking for the library. He was greeted by a grand ballroom, a music room, a small withdrawing room, a vast parlor. He finally found the room he was looking for and poured himself a French Bordeaux. It had aged well.

Patricia appeared in twenty minutes, not fifteen, and was not the least sleepy-eyed. "What is the meaning of this?" she demanded haughtily, sure of herself in her own domain.

He eyed her in her velvet robe. "I have news I wish to discuss."

"Here? Now? In the middle of the night?"

"Here, now, in the middle of the night. I am divorcing you, Patricia."

She went white.

"I give you fair notice now. Although I shall point out that you do not deserve any fairness from me, I have no intention of being shackled to you for the rest of my life. You will have your estate and a healthy allowance, but Clarendon is Chad's. I will allow you to reside here until his majority, however."

"You miserable bastard!" she hissed. "I don't want a divorce! The scandal! However will I survive?"

"Patricia, you are surely not thinking clearly," he said. "You have already created quite the scandal, by resurrecting yourself from the dead."

"But I have the perfect story! How I escaped the fire but lost my mind from the horror of it!" she cried wildly. "I will be Society's Darling, you shall see!"

"Frankly, I don't give a damn," he said. "You cannot stop this divorce, not after abandoning me and your child."

"But I lost my memory," she said with a sneer, eyes cool and calculating now.

He turned to her, smiling. "Do you wish to come up against me? Do you think you can possibly win?"

She just looked at him smugly.

His smile increased, showing white, even teeth. "Patricia, if I do not get this divorce, I shall make your life a living hell."

She stared, nostrils flared and eyes dilated.

"Once you despised me—for my red blood." His teeth showed white again, and he took a step toward her. "That same blood still fills my veins. My ancestors used to covet blond scalps like yours, Patricia. They used to hang them, raw and bloody, from their belts."

She went white.

"I daresay," he said, his grin genuine now, "my father had a scalp or two to his credit. Did you know that, Patricia?"

"You're lying," she whispered, shocked.

His response was a snarl. "You had better pray that I succeed in attaining this divorce. For if I do not, there will be no agreement between us, no separate residences. I will be a husband in every sense of the word, whenever I choose, regardless of your sensibilities. If you resist me I will rape you. I will spend the rest of our marriage making your life hell on earth."

Tears came to her eyes. "Bastard!"

"I mean it," he said, and he did.

"Take your divorce then, take it!" she cried. "I shall tell everyone my story, and they will sympathize with me and I shall find a new husband! One who is not some half-breed Indian!"

"I have no doubts you shall land on both feet, head held high," he said easily, and then he bowed. "I shall keep you informed of the progress of the proceedings."

The earl arrived at the house on Gloucester Street just as dawn was brightening the sky from black to mauve gray.

He paused on the sidewalk. It was a gray, misty morning, a thick fog blanketing the neighborhood. The house seemed closed up, deserted, utterly quiet. Of course, it was his imagination, for Jane and his daughter were there, soundly asleep within. He started forward, eager to tell her the good news and to beg her to hang on, just for a little while until they got through this trying period.

Soon he would be divorced, and he and Jane would remarry.

His heart tripped at the thought. Yet he grew sober as he strode through the wrought-iron gate and up to the bright-blue door. Something pricked at him, making him uneasy. It was so damn quiet! He noticed that all the bright-yellow shutters were closed. Surely this was what was throwing him off. He strained to hear a sound, perhaps Nicole, who woke up notoriously early in the morning. But there was nothing, nothing at all, not even the day's first birdsongs. Yet he knew he was a fool, for it was only the crack of dawn, and only the milkmen were up now.

He rang the doorbell, shifting impatiently. Surely Molly was already awake, preparing breakfast for her mistress. There was no answer, and the earl rang again, once, twice, three times. He tried to peer through a window without shutters, but the curtains were drawn.

He had a terrible pang.

He banged now, hard. "Molly! Open up! It's the Earl of Dragmore!"

There was no response, as if the house were utterly deserted.

But that was impossible, he thought, hurrying round to the back. The little yard where he had sat with Nicole on the pink swing was already overgrown. He tried the kitchen door, but it was locked. Yet the shades were up and he could look in. The kitchen was barren, perfectly tidy—it looked as if it had not been used in a very long time.

Something sick welled within him.

They were not here. He knew it in that lightning moment.

Determined, eyes wild, the earl looked around and picked up a stone. He smashed the glass pane of the back door, knocked out the jagged pieces recklessly, then slipped his hand through and turned the lock from inside. The door swung open.

He rushed into the empty, immaculate kitchen, into the dining room, where dust coated the table, and bounded up the stairs, two at a time. He flung open the door to Jane's room, calling her name. The room was empty, the bed perfectly made and unslept in.

Eyes wide and disbelieving, he flung open the closet—to find it starkly bare as well.

She wasn't there.

She wasn't there, hadn't been there, wasn't coming there.

The comprehension was shocking, and as if in a trance, he went to the window, pushed back the curtains, and stared out into the fog.

Where was she? Where had she gone? And, dear God, why?

He howled into the dawn then, the sound anguished and wolflike. She had left him. Once again she had left him.

"Jane," he cried, eyes squeezed shut. "Jane, Jane, you cannot leave me! You cannot leave me again!"

But there was no answer.

Around him, the house was utterly still and silent.

"Why!" he shouted, fists clenched. "Why!"

III

Paradise Reclaimed

NEW YORK 1876

51

Fall had come early to New York City. As Jane hurried across Fifth Avenue, her cheeks were stung red from the new nip in the air. Already the big oaks lining the park were turning, their leaves red and gold. Squirrels were already gathering their winter provisions, scurrying amid the trees. The sky was blue and cloudless, the sun shining with faded brilliance. An early snow was in the air. Jane did not pause to admire the scene.

In fact, never had her spirits been so low.

Oh, God, she thought again, for the dozenth time, how will I deal with this as well?

It had been hard enough leaving England, hard enough leaving him. Yet she had had no choice. To stay in London as his mistress—the obvious solution—would have been to die a slow death. Loving him so thoroughly, Jane could not share him with another woman—worse, with the woman he had loved once and so completely before herself. Having been his wife, Jane could not now be only his mistress.

She had not meant to leave so abruptly, nor had she meant to go to America. She had gone with Molly and Nicole to the little house on Gloucester Street, numb and shocked, not even able to cry. The house was empty, barren, offering no sense of warmth or coziness. Jane had stood in the parlor amid the rolled-up rugs and covered furniture, everything so immaculate and bare with all her personal treasures gone, and she'd known she could not stay. If she stayed, she would succumb to Nicholas. If he begged her to be his mistress, she would not be able to deny him. She had never been able to deny him. She had decided to go to Paris.

And, of course, she needed money.

At her urgent message, Lindley had come instantly. And it was Lindley who persuaded her to go to New York, not France, with him, as he was on his way there for a business trip. He had been planning on leaving in ten days. Jane had told him she would go—provided they left that day, or the next, on the first available ship. She could only guess that he had agreed because he really did love her, and he wanted to get her away from Nicholas as quickly and surely as possible.

Jane hurried into the Regency Hotel on Sixth Avenue. She was not overwhelmed by the huge marble columns, the high frescoed ceilings, the vast crystal chandeliers, or the endless Persian rugs. She had become accustomed to such grandeur. As she hurried up the stairs to their adjoining suites, a refrain repeated itself in her head.

Should she tell him?

Should she tell Lindley? And what about Nicholas?

God, how she missed Nicholas!

Her heart was broken, yet every day she was faced with an onslaught of fresh, raw pain, despite the passage of the past month. This time, she knew, she would never recover from Nicholas's love.

Jane entered her own suite, throwing down her packages. She'd been shopping. She had just sat down on the sofa when the polished mahogany door attaching her living room to Lindley's opened, and Jonathon came in. "Jane! I've been worried! You said you'd be back hours ago."

She barely looked at him. "I took a long walk in the park."

"A long walk?" He was skeptical. Then he came and sat beside her. "What's wrong? You look like hell."

She abruptly made the decision to tell him and blurted, "I'm pregnant!"

He stared, shocked.

Jane felt the tears rising. "Damn, damn, damn!" she cursed, not caring. Then she was instantly contrite. "Oh, I take it back, of course I want his baby!"

"I don't believe it," Lindley breathed.

"He must know," Jane said, her heart wrenching with the memory of how she had denied him Nicole. "I must tell him. I will write him a letter."

"No! He'll come after you!"

Jane looked at him sadly. "I won't write him today, Jon. In a few months, when he no longer wants me, then I will send him a note."

Lindley opened his mouth, then closed it. He touched her shoulder, rubbing it. "What can I do?"

"Nothing." Her smile was small, rueful.

"Do you want to cancel supper tonight?"

Jane regarded him, her heart twisting with worry. They were to dine tonight at Rathe Bragg's. Rathe was Nicholas's brother. He was, of course, friendly with Lindley, having met him numerous times when he was in London visiting his brother. Lindley and Rathe had bumped into each other one day at lunch at a men's club, and Rathe had invited Lindley to have dinner with him and his new wife, Grace. Jane had not wanted to go. Of course, Rathe did not know she had been his brother's mistress and was the mother of his child. Still, Jane wanted to stay away from him, sensing danger in the relationship, even if it was only a casual acquaintance. But Lindley talked her into it. Just one evening with nice people, Jane, he had said, you deserve it, and she had gone. Unfortunately, or fortunately, she and Grace had instantly become fast friends. Now, two weeks later, Grace knew everything there was to know about Jane, as Jane did about Grace, so rapidly had their friendship grown. Except Grace only knew that there had been a big love in London—not that it was her brother-in-law. Jane had not told her anything about her relationship with Nicholas, carefully avoiding that period of her life. Jane knew that both Rathe and Grace thought her to be Lindley's mistress—and they were both utterly charming about it.

Jane suddenly wanted to go to dinner. She wanted to confide in her friend—everything. Of course, she could not, she would not. But she could at least discuss some of her predicament, and cry on her best friend's shoulder. "No, I want to go, I want to see Grace."

But Lindley wasn't listening. He was staring at her intently. "Jane," he said, "there is a solution."

Jane blinked.

"Marry me."

"I can't!"

"Of course you can! Shelton is married to Patricia. Face it, Jane, face it! Damn, I hate seeing you like this! Patricia is his wife. Now you're pregnant and alone. And we are friends. Most important, I love you and will gladly care for you—and be the father to your child. Do you want this child born a bastard?"

Jane flinched. "I don't know, I must think."

"Think." He leaned close, touched her cheek. "I am here for you. I think I've proved it many times. You know you can count on me and trust me."

He got up and departed to his own rooms. Jane watched him leave. Then she bit her trembling lower lip, her cheek dropping to the sofa back, hugging the big throw pillows. Should she marry Lindley?

Oh, God! What else could Fate possibly have in store for her?

"Oh, Nicholas," she whispered. "Did I do the right thing?"

52

🔥🔥🔥

"Darling," Grace Bragg said, her smile semisweet and semiwicked, "why don't you take John into the den and do whatever it is you men like so much to do when you're ensconced in your all-male citadels that prohibit the fairer, more enlightened sex? Smoke and drink and all that interesting, intellectual—it must be intellectual—male conversation?"

The tall, voluptuous redhead was bending over her husband, a smile on her beautiful face. He was still seated, quite indolently, at the dining-room table, as were Jane and Lindley. Rathe, a big, muscular, devastatingly handsome man, was visibly surprised, his blue eyes wide, his expression startled. Grace nuzzled her cheek to his. "Darling, you could even gamble a bit."

With one strong arm, he suddenly caught her around the waist, imprisoning her in an intimate position. "Is my wife trying to get rid of me?" he asked, low, laughter sparking his eyes, his mouth near her ear. "Is my impossibly liberated wife trying to encourage my antiquated, chauvinistic stereotypically male pursuits?"

Grace had the grace to blush. During their stormy courtship down south in Natchez, she had, on one or two occasions (or more!), accused him of male arrogance and other philistine attributes. Now she smiled even more sweetly and more wickedly. "Darling, don't look a gift horse in the mouth!"

"Is this the wild, rabble-rousing suffragist I married?" he teased. "Or are you someone else, a look-alike? Has there been a stranger in my bed recently?"

She smacked him playfully, drawing free of him, winking at Jane, who was regarding their close, uninhibited relationship wistfully. There was so much love and affection and respect between them. But then again, Grace was such an admirable woman, so strong in her convictions, and so well educated and intelligent. While Rathe appeared to be the ideal husband. Not only was he handsome, virile, and magnetic, he was a very successful businessman and he clearly worshiped her.

"All right, I take the hint," Rathe announced, rising. He winked as well. Big dimples accompanied his smile, causing a pang in Jane's heart at the resemblance between the brothers. Yet this was the only resemblance. Rathe was a golden-haired, blue-eyed man, always smiling, teasing, in love with the world and himself and his family. Jane's anguish increased; how could one brother be so sunny and carefree and the other so dark and tormented? Yet with her, Nicholas had begun to change, to smile and laugh and even to tease. God, she missed him.

"C'mon, Lindley, let's pursue some antiquated, male-oriented pastimes," Rathe was saying.

"Sounds good to me." Lindley grinned, squeezing Jane's shoulder as he passed. Rathe had the aplomb and insouciance to swat Grace's behind rather forcefully as he went out, causing her to gasp, jump, and blush a fierce red, in that order. Her gaze met Jane's sheepishly, then she laughed. "He is impossible, that man!"

"You are so very lucky," Jane said huskily.

"Very lucky," Grace agreed softly, her palm touching her abdomen. She was just starting to show the signs of her pregnancy. Her expression grew serious. She closed the dining-room doors, then returned to the table and sat in Lindley's place, next to Jane. "But you have a good man too."

Jane just looked at Grace.

Grace smiled. "Tea or coffee? How about some more of this sinful chocolate cake?"

Jane accepted both and had just taken a bit of the cake, which was sheer heaven, when Grace abruptly said, "What's wrong, Jane? You look as if your best friend died."

Jane laid down her fork. "I'm pregnant."

"Oh," Grace said. "Oh."

Jane pushed the cake away. Grace knew about Nicole—adored her, in fact—and Jane knew she suspected Lindley wasn't the father, because of the baby's coloring, but she had been too polite to even ask. In fact, it was amazing that the Braggs had accepted her into their home knowing she had a fatherless baby, as if she were Lindley's wife, not, as they thought, his paramour. But they were real people, without a single snobbish thought between the two of them. Besides, after they'd become friends, Grace had confessed she'd been Rathe's mistress for a while—although not exactly willingly. Jane had been shocked. "He forced you?"

Grace had grinned. "Well, coerce is a better word. Actually, he took advantage of my dire circumstances." Then she'd amended herself. "Really, I'm making Rathe sound like such a cad. He was sort of a cad, I admit. However, he did want to marry me. I refused."

Jane had been shocked. Grace had laughed. "I was in love with him but stubbornly refusing to admit it," she'd confessed. "Can you believe I told him I'd rather be his mistress, that way I wouldn't be stuck with him forever?"

Jane could barely believe it, her eyes popping at Grace's daring insolence. "You should have seen his reaction." Grace had laughed.

Now Grace covered Jane's hand with her own. "Does Jon know?" She meant about the pregnancy.

Jane looked up at her. Obviously Grace thought she was carrying Lindley's child. "It's not his," she said tersely.

Grace's eyes went wide.

Jane's filled with tears.

"Oh, I'm sorry, that was so thoughtless of me," Grace cried, squeezing her hand. "Jane, I am not judging you!"

Jane shook her head unable to speak, and wiped her eyes with the napkin. "No, you see, Grace, what you've thought all along isn't true. I am not Lindley's mistress." Grace stared again—they had never discussed this openly. "I am only his friend," Jane confessed. "He does love me, and he does want me. Today he even asked me to marry him. But, you see, I love someone else."

"I see," Grace said.

Jane fought the sob choking her. "I love Nicole's father," she said softly. "He is in London. He is married," she added.

"I'm so sorry," Grace cried. "That bastard! That typical, rotten, selfish, philandering, rutting bastard! That—"

"Grace!" Jane cried. "He is Rathe's brother, Lord Shelton, the Earl of Dragmore!"

Grace gasped.

The two women stared at each other, Grace's flush of fury fading to sheer white, Jane's nose red, eyes shiny. "We thought his wife was dead," Jane said miserably. "And he married me. But not out of love, but because he found out about Nicole. Yet I love him so. When his first wife reappeared, I couldn't take it, I couldn't. He wanted me to be his mistress, but after being his wife . . . I ran away!" Jane began to cry. She tried not to, but it was impossible.

Grace got up and swiftly hugged her. "Sometimes men are such insensitive boors," she said. "Get it out, Jane, all of it," she said, recovering her calm. "You will feel much better, and you can trust me."

Jane regarded her. "I was only seventeen when we met," she said unsteadily. "And I fell in love with him that very first moment. He was so big and dark, so powerful, even menacing. And his eyes, they were silver, so cold—yet so hot." She paused, lost in remembrance of that time in the dusty parlor at Dragmore. She decided to tell it all. "They called him the Lord of Darkness . . ."

53

🔥🔥🔥

Rathe Bragg sat on the edge of the big, four-postered bed in his and Grace's silk-walled bedroom, shirtless. His thickly muscled torso gleamed in the gentle gas lighting from the chandelier. Now his expression was amazed, even stunned. "Nick's mistress! Grace! Nicole is my niece!"

Grace was pacing in a filmy nightgown and robe, one of the many intimate gifts her husband constantly bought her, her long, magnificent red hair loose and cascading to her hips. "Poor Jane!" she cried. "Do you think your brother really asked her to be his mistress when Patricia came back?"

Rathe grimaced. "It's certainly possible. And knowing Nick, with Nicole involved it's even likely. He would want to see mother and daughter frequently, I think. I can't believe this!"

Grace sat down hard next to him. "What are we going to do?"

Normally, Rathe firmly opposed his wife's

schemes, for she was, he had to admit (fondly), a fervent busybody once aroused to a cause. This occasion seemed to warrant some interference, however. "So she's carrying Nick's child," he mused, "and she loves him."

"I didn't tell her he is on his way here," Grace said intensely. "Should we tell her that Nick is coming?"

"I wonder if he's bringing Patricia," Rathe responded obliquely. "He didn't say in the telegram —but we'll find out soon enough. I imagine he should be here any day."

Grace abruptly rose to pace again, like a restless tigress. "Rathe! I feel guilty knowing Nick is on his way and not telling Jane! She has already suffered so!"

Rathe got up and went to her, clasping her shoulders and pulling her back against his chest. He held her there, kissing her neck. "Darling, if she knows he's coming she'll run away. Let's let nature take its course. They need to resolve their affair one way or another. Jane's running away left it open. Maybe she even wants Nick to chase after her. And Nick certainly has the right to know about the child."

"What if she decides to marry Lindley?" Grace asked, twisting to face him.

"That's her right," Rathe said simply. "After all, Nick is married." He grimaced and cursed graphically. "God, I can't believe that bitch is alive! Too bad!"

"Rathe!"

"She made my brother miserable and you know it," Rathe said vehemently. "She nearly destroyed him! What if he'd been convicted of her murder?" Then he looked intently at his wife. "I don't think this is a coincidence, Grace, do you?"

She regarded him levelly. "I was wondering the same thing. Jane appears here, and Nick is on his way—when he's never been back to America since he took up his inheritance at Dragmore."

"He's coming after her," Rathe said firmly, and their gazes locked in understanding.

Grace wrapped her arms around her husband's waist. "Maybe he loves her," she said softly. "Maybe you're right. He is chasing her—and she wants him to, even if she doesn't know it consciously."

"Maybe he does," Rathe returned. "If he didn't, would he run after her like this?"

Suddenly they smiled at each other, understanding exactly what the other was thinking—that they were doing the right thing in not telling Jane that Nick was coming and in bringing the two together. "Oh, we're terrible!" Grace said.

"We?" Rathe protested, but his dimples were deep. "This is your scheme, I'm just an innocent accomplice."

"Darling, the terms are a contradiction."

"You are a contradiction," he murmured, kissing her. "So smart, and so beautiful."

"And you," she said throatily, kissing him back, "are unrepentant. Haven't I reformed you yet?"

"Keep trying," he managed to gasp.

The divorce would be final when he returned.

It was a happy thought in an otherwise grim day. The Earl of Dragmore stared out the window of the rented hansom at First Avenue. It was a rough ride, due to the cobbled street. He barely noted how New York had grown in the ten years since he'd left the States, he was too preoccupied. He and Chad had just arrived on a passenger ship and were on their way directly to his brother's home on Riverside Drive.

He intended to scour every hotel until he found them.

He still could not believe she had left with his best friend—he still prayed, desperately, for a reasonable explanation.

He knew, or he thought he did, that Jane cared about him. No woman could be such a superb actress, could she? He winced at his thought, because Jane *was* an actress, and he had forced her into marriage with him. What they had shared was good sex, nothing more. Instantly he corrected himself. They had shared a grand passion, one he certainly had never experienced with any other woman before.

And then he remembered her reading to Chad and Nicole in her sitting room, their outing in Hyde Park, boating on the lake. He remembered their breakfasts, Nicole dominating with her outlandish temper, and he remembered dancing until dawn. They had shared more than even a grand passion.

And even though she had left him, again, lied to him and left him, run away with his best friend, stolen his daughter—he still wanted her.

He still loved her.

Of course, if she was Lindley's mistress he would kill him, and he hoped then he would be so disgusted he would no longer want Jane. Anger vied with need, and the result was a coiled, confused desperation.

As soon as he had discovered that Jane had fled, he had hastened to Robert Gordon's, expecting to find her there. Gordon had informed him that Jane had left for America. The earl had been shocked.

"She loves you very much," Gordon had said bluntly. "And Patricia's return has killed her."

Was it true? Did she really love him?

His plans to follow her were delayed because he decided to take Chad for that long-overdue visit to meet his grandparents. Soon he found out that Lindley had also gone to America, on business. The coincidence was impossible, and he was enraged. Gordon confirmed that they had gone together.

"Is she fucking him?" the earl had shouted, at that moment wanting to kill them both.

"I told you, she loves you!" Gordon was hot to defend Jane. "Lindley has always been her friend, even if he is in love with her himself. But Jane is not that type of woman, and if you don't know it, you should!"

He did know it, didn't he? She had given herself to him when she was seventeen and had not given herself to another man in the years since. Until perhaps now, in anger and in hurt . . .

He could not bear the thought. And as much as he felt he could kill if this was the case, another side of him, the dark desperate side, would forgive her anything if only she would return to him.

His brother's home was a red brick mansion set high on a hill, surrounded by brick walls topped with a wrought-iron curtain. Nick smiled wryly as the cab turned through the open gates. Rathe had certainly done well for himself, he mused, not just a little bit surprised. His brother had always said he was doing rather well in his business affairs, which consisted of many diverse investments across America, but Nick had had no idea that he had done this well. Tall, stately pines from upstate, undoubtedly, graced the long sweeping drive. Beside him, Chad was bouncing in his seat with uncontained excitement.

Nick reached out to touch him, his own heart starting to thud.

It had been just a couple of years since he'd seen Rathe, but even that was too long. This thought led to another. If two years was too long to be apart from his brother, how about the more than ten that had passed since he'd seen his parents? He felt a surge of old anguish, but it was duller now, the old hurt and betrayal having recently faded. Because of Jane. He knew he was doing the right thing in returning to America. First he would find Jane and settle matters between them. He was not going to Texas without her. And then he would take Chad west, to the ranch that was just as much his heritage as Dragmore. To see his grandparents, his grandfather.

And it was because of Jane. He knew that a year ago he wouldn't have even considered a trip to Texas. A year ago had been before Jane. Before she'd given him her love and warmth and incredible courage, before she'd reminded him, shown him, what love meant, what a family meant. Now it was almost hard to believe that he'd put off this trip, this resolution with *his* parents, with *his* father, for so long. But in a way he understood. Before Jane, nothing had really mattered. She had changed all that; she had changed his life.

The hansom stopped by the immense, flat tiers of pink granite steps leading up to the imposing teakwood front doors of the mansion. Nick paid and thanked the cabbie, and stepped out after his son. At that precise moment, Rathe came through the front doors, beaming and dimpled, his blue eyes dancing. Behind him, Nick saw a beautiful tall redhead, obviously his wife.

"Nick!"

The earl smiled a genuine smile, revealing his own dimples, so like his brother's. The two men embraced, clinging for just a moment, then drew apart, embarrassed. The earl was blushing slightly. "God, it's good to see you," he said, smacking Rathe's shoulder.

Rathe punched him back. "My brother, the earl! And who's this? No—this can't be Chad? You said he was only six!"

"Seven!" Chad cried, grinning. "Are you my Uncle Rathe?"

"You bet!" Rathe swung him up into his arms and Chad squealed. "Want a ride, champ?" he asked. When Chad responded enthusiastically, he set him on his broad shoulders. "Nick, this is my wife, Grace."

Grace smiled with genuine warmth as Nick kissed her hand. "I'm so glad you've come," she said softly.

Nick studied her openly. "I'm so glad my hell-raising brother finally found his match," he said at last.

Grace grinned; Rathe groaned. "You don't know the half of it!" he exclaimed. "How was your trip? Nick, we have some company, I hope you won't mind."

"Not at all," Nick said easily, following his brother with his son on his shoulders into the house. His attention, however, was caught by Grace, who had given Rathe a warning look, her own gaze worried.

"It's someone you know," Rathe continued easily, swinging Chad to the ground in the doorway of a small, intimate parlor and taking his hand.

Nick's smile died as he glanced past his brother.

His heart actually stopped in midbeat, and he stared, stunned.

Jane, impossibly beautiful and impossibly pale, sat alone on the sofa and stared back, equally shocked.

54

He had come to New York to find Jane, but he had never expected to find her in his brother's house. For one long moment he could not speak or move, he could only stare.

Jane rose nervously to her feet, clutching her gown in her fists, her eyes as big as saucers, her face whiter than a ghost's. It was then that Lindley came forward from the tall, draped windows, his stride hard, his face set. He moved toward Jane, as if to protect her.

The earl didn't think. He rushed forward, swinging. Lindley ducked, and the earl's blow, containing enough power to kill, merely glanced off his temple. But it knocked Lindley off balance and to his knees. The earl went after him like a maddened bull, dragging him up by his suit lapels. Grace cried out in protest clutching the wide-eyed Chad. Rathe was rushing to them, grabbing his brother from behind and trying to tear him from Lindley. "Nick! Damn it, stop!"

Jane stood frozen, hands clutched to her breasts.

Nick burst free of Rathe's hold as Lindley backed warily away, panting. "I'll kill you if you've so much as touched her, you son of a bitch!" Nick roared. His face was red, the veins standing out rigidly in his temples, his throat corded. "I will kill you, do you hear?"

Rathe grabbed him again. Furious, Nick spun free. "Stay out of this," he warned his brother, who instantly stepped back, not out of fear, but out of sudden understanding and respect.

Chad broke free of Grace's grasp to run to his father. "Papa! Papa!"

The earl caught him. "It's all right," he said firmly. "Go with your aunt Grace. Jane and I have something to discuss."

Chad was reluctant, but Grace came forward to take his hand and lead him out, despite his many backward glances.

The earl moved to Jane, fist raised with frustration, but clearly not raised at her. "Did he touch you? Are you sleeping with him? Are you?"

Jane shrank back. "No." It was a barely audible whisper.

"You've done enough," Lindley shouted from behind them. "Leave her alone—can't you see that you've practically destroyed her?"

The earl whirled, but Rathe was between the two of them before further violence could erupt. Jane swallowed. "He is only my friend," she managed, her voice quavering.

Jealousy was red and hot, a haze blinding him now that he had found them together. "How good a friend, Jane?" he demanded. *"How good?"*

"He is not my lover!" she cried, a flush rising to her face. "How dare you even ask! How dare you

—when you have Patricia running your household and warming your bed!"

That froze the earl, and he stood there panting, his shoulders straining the seams of his jacket, sweat beading at his temples. Jane was panting too, facing him, her breasts rising and falling rapidly above the low, lace-edged bodice of her gown.

"Jon," Rathe said quietly, yet there was authority in his tone, "let's leave them alone."

"You knew he was coming," Lindley hurled. "Yet you didn't tell us!"

"He is my brother—and the father of Nicole."

"I am not moving," Lindley stated. "Jane, we don't have to stay here and take this abuse. Let's go back to the hotel."

Jane bit her lip, tears coming to her eyes, and she nodded. But she only took a step before the earl grabbed her, hauling her to him. "You lied to me! You told me you were going to the house on Gloucester Street! Instead you left me!" His voice broke, agonized. "Damn you, Jane, how could you?"

"How could I not?" Her voice quavered. "How could I not? You expected me to remain with you as your mistress and send you home to Patricia every night? This I could not, and cannot, do!"

He stared, then he shook her. "Did I ask you to be my mistress?" he shouted. "Did I?"

"You said there was an obvious solution!" she cried back. "You said you would take care of me! Did you or did you not?"

He released her, incredulous. "You fool! Do you know me so little? Jane, I—" He stopped, unable to continue. He wrenched away and wiped the sweat from his brow. And Jane stared at his back, hope so plainly etched on her face that Lindley

allowed Rathe to lead him from the salon, closing
the doors on them both and leaving them alone.

Jane waited, unmoving.

He turned to face her. There was a suspicious
film on his eyes. "I didn't just come here to bring
Chad to his grandparents," he said, low.

She swallowed. She gulped down tears.

"I cannot let you go from my life, Jane. I cannot."

"I will not be your mistress," she said, and then
her face collapsed and she moaned. "Oh, damn
you, Nicholas! Why couldn't you let me go? Why?"

She sank onto the couch. "Leaving you was the
hardest thing I've ever done, but staying with you
will surely kill me, a little bit every day." She
stared at him out of glazed eyes. "But you know
what?" Her voice quavered. "I would rather die a
little bit every day with you than live without you
in a world that would be frozen and barren and
lifeless."

She closed her eyes, his widened. "All right,"
she said heavily, her voice breaking. "You win. I
love you too much, you see. I will return with
you, I will be your mistress. For as long as you
want me, I will be yours."

He cried out and dropped down beside her,
wrapping her in his arms. She began to cry. So
did he. "Jane, you fool! I am getting a divorce!
How could you think anything otherwise?"

"What?" She pushed a bit away, blinking,
cheeks tearstained and nose as red as a cherry.

"It will be final very shortly. Patricia already
knows. How could you not have understood what
I meant when I said there was an obvious solution?"

"A divorce?" She gasped.

"Jane—did I hear you right?" He brushed hair

from her cheek. His hand trembled. His own cheeks were as damp as hers. "Did you say you love me?"

"I've always loved you, Nicholas," she said simply. "From that first moment when we met in the parlor with Aunt Matilda."

He crushed her to him, hard, his power raw and agonized and so immense, Jane knew, in that moment, that he loved her too, with an intensity she had never dreamed of.

"Will you marry me?" he whispered humbly. "Jane, please, will you be my wife?"

"Yes, Nicholas, oh, yes." She wept, clinging.

They rocked each other for a long time, his lips pressing against her cheek and temple and hair again and again, until she turned her mouth up to his, and blindly, their lips met in mad desperation. It was a long, hot, hard kiss filled with the power of love.

"I love you," he finally said. "Jane. Jane, God, I love you."

She understood what it cost him to say it, she could hear it in his low, barely audible, strained tone. He cupped her face to look at her. "Jane, I've never said it before, not to Patricia, not to anyone."

"I know," she said, attempting to stall the tears.

He fought himself too. "I—I never felt this for her, it wasn't like this. What I feel for you—I can't live without you," he managed, raw.

She sniffed, brushed a tear from his eyes, while finally letting her own flow unchecked. "Does this mean you forgive me for my stupid impulsiveness once again?"

He laughed through the blur of his vision. "Darling, I can forgive you anything—as long as you never stop loving me."

She smiled then, impishly. "Stop loving you? That, Nicholas, would be impossible."

55

West Texas

Jane had never quite had a ride like this before.

Dust filled the coach, and she'd long since given up holding a kerchief to her nose. She'd grown used to the thick taste of grit on her tongue. If the carriage had springs, they were broken. She was jarred by every rut and pothole, which meant that despite Nicholas's supporting arm around her, she was tumbling around like a pair of straight die. Chad clung tenaciously to the seat opposite where he sat, his eyes wide and round as saucers as he stared at the rugged passing landscape. "Papa," he asked again, for the dozenth time, "are you sure there are no Indians?"

Beside her, just for a moment, the earl relaxed, and a hint of a smile touched the corners of his mouth. "Well," he said levelly, "maybe just one or two renegades hiding up on that ridge."

If possible, Chad's eyes grew larger. "Wow!"

Nicole was the true trooper, enjoying the mad-
cap ride, shrieking with delight every time they
all went into the air, as if it were nothing more
than being tossed by her father. Molly was a distinct shade of apple green, nearly oblivious to her
charge's howling pleasure.

No, she had never had a ride quite like this one.
Jane was gripping the earl's palm as she rode the
bucking stage. And he was clenching her hand
back just as tightly.

His face was taut, as taut as his grip on her.
Jane knew he was filled with anxiety, in the
clutches of his own inner turmoil. She leaned
close to kiss his cheek. Briefly he smiled at her,
squeezing her hand. And then his gaze turned out
the window, his jaw so tight he surely must be
grinding down his teeth one by one.

"I'm sorry about this, Jane," he said. "Soon the
railhead to the D and M will be completed, probably in the spring. But until then, the only way to
my parents' ranch is via stage from San Antonio."

"It's all right," Jane said softly, covering his
palm in hers with her other gloved hand. "At the
least, this is a unique experience, especially for
the children. And the country is magnificent."

It was. A sage- and mesquite-studded vista
rolled away from them in shades of purple and
green. In the distance, jagged mountains etched a
mauve line across the bluest sky Jane had ever
seen. Never had Jane had the feeling before of
being so insignificant, or of being in the midst of
God's land. The power and majesty of this huge,
raw, wild country stretching before her was overwhelming and scintillating.

And her husband was a part of it.

"D 'n' M just up ahead," yelled the driver from
outside, above them.

Eagerly Jane and Molly and Chad all rushed to peer out the windows for a glimpse of the Bragg ranch. Only the earl sat unmoving. Jane was disappointed when what looked like a small but busy town greeted her. They roared down a wide dirt street, and she glimpsed brick storefronts and homes with gardens and white picket fences. Then they pulled to a stop in front of a small shop. Its sign, hanging lopsided from a chain, said JOE'S POSTE STAGE STOPS HERE.

Jane looked at the earl, who was rigid and still. "Why, this isn't a ranch, it's a town!"

Nick could not manage a smile. He looked at her numbly. He was sweating. "Rathe said the ranch had grown. None of this was here when I left in sixty-five."

Jane was worried by his tone and his expression. She took his hand again. "Darling, it will be all right."

He held her gaze. They hadn't discussed the situation between him and his father again, not once in the past two weeks since their reconciliation. Nick had not brought up the topic, and Jane, although wanting to, was afraid it was too sensitive for her to mention. But now she saw the naked worry in his eyes, and her heart wept for him. She touched his cheek as the door opened and Chad bounced out. "Darling, everything will be fine, you will see."

Molly exited with Nicole, who was having a temper tantrum because the ride had ended.

Nick gripped her hand hard. "Do you think so?" he asked hoarsely.

"I'm sure," she managed, unnerved by his fear and anxiety.

And then from outside a voice boomed: "Are you Chad Bragg?"

"No, sir," Chad piped. "I'm Chad Bragg, Lord Shelton."

"Lord! No—I don't believe it!"

"It's the truth—you can ask my papa!"

Suddenly Chad shrieked, and Jane saw through the window a big leonine man in his early sixties lifting the boy high in the air. "I am Grandpa Bragg!" he shouted.

"Derek! You'll frighten him to death! Put him down and introduce yourself properly!" a woman cried in affectionate exasperation.

Jane twisted to face her husband. He was still clinging to her hand, and he was as pale as she had ever seen him. "They're here," she said simply.

He took a deep breath. "I know."

He couldn't stay in the coach forever. Not that he wanted to. It was just that he was feeling so choked with emotions—ones he hadn't quite expected—that he was paralyzed. He hadn't seen his parents in more than ten years. Love and joy were washing over him in incredible proportions, but so was fear. Raw, bitter fear. For even as he was reunited with his family, there was the knowledge of the confrontation he would instigate—immediately. And then he would learn the truth he had avoided so desperately for so long.

He tried to tell himself it no longer mattered. He was an adult, not a child, and he had Jane and his children and Dragmore. So it didn't matter that he was not Derek's son. It didn't matter that Derek's real children were Rathe and Storm, that he loved them, and not him, Nick. Nick knew Derek cared, of course, but he couldn't possibly love the child of a man who had raped his wife. The problem was that no matter how hard he told himself he did not care that Derek did not really love him, the truth was he still loved Derek as a father—for the man was his father in his heart.

Slowly he climbed out of the coach.

Derek barely looked a day older than when Nick had last seen him. He was as tall as Nick, and once he'd been as broad or even broader with thick, powerful muscles. Now he'd slimmed down a bit, but he was still an unusually powerful man. With his typical unrestrained, uninhibited exuberance (Derek always did what he felt like when he felt like it, Miranda often scolded), he was staring incredulously at the delicate gloved hand Jane had offered him.

"What's this?" he roared, laughing, revealing white, even teeth. He turned to grin at his wife who held Chad's hand, a petite, slender, elegant woman in her early fifties. "My God, Miranda, does she remind you of someone?"

Jane turned to look at Miranda, confused.

Miranda took her hand. "Forgive him, he's overcome. But it was a compliment—I think he was comparing you to me when I first came to the frontier."

Jane took the woman's hand, then was embraced in a light hug. A moment later she was enveloped in a bear hug that could easily squash her—and she was lifted off her feet. When Derek put her down, she was blushing beet red.

Nick almost grinned. Derek liked his wife, and eventually Jane would get used to his enthusiasm. Then his father saw him, and Nick froze.

But Derek didn't. "Son!"

When his father reached him to embrace him, hard, Nick closed his eyes and fought the childish urge to cry. His father released him. "God, look at you." Impulsively Derek clasped his shoulder.

"Look at you! You were a man when you left, but not like this."

"Hello, Father." The word just popped out. Nick felt himself blushing.

Derek threw his arm around him, and tears filled his eyes. "Shit!" He roared. "I'm like an old woman. God, son, you've done well for yourself—two beautiful children and a beautiful wife . . ."

"Derek!" Miranda reproved, but she was weeping and she threw herself at Nick. She clung to him, a tiny woman, and Nick clung back until it was unseemly and he forced them to separate.

"Hi, Mom." He managed a grin. He hoped his own eyes weren't tearing.

" 'Hi, Mom'! I haven't seen you in over ten years and you say 'hi, Mom'?" Her voice was broken, and she wiped tears delicately away with a lace handkerchief. "Oh, Nick! It's so good to have you home!"

Nick was very quiet, and had been all through the ride to the D and M and through the sumptuous dinner Miranda had waiting for them. Jane knew his parents had noticed—because the two had exchanged clear, concerned glances. Now they all sat at the oak dining-room table after finishing homemade pie and thick, strong coffee. Molly had taken Nicole for a nap, despite her protests (and her grandparents'). Chad was restlessly squirming. Derek had promised to take him riding and show him the ranch. "When are we going, Grandpa?" he asked excitedly.

"Can Grandpa finish his coffee?" Derek returned, grinning.

"Chad," Nick and Jane reproved simultaneously. Nick picked up his mug, so Jane continued. "Let your grandfather finish his meal and enjoy his son's company. Wouldn't you want to be with your papa if you hadn't seen him in more than ten years?"

Chad bit his lip, then nodded slowly. "Ten years is a long time, isn't it?"

"Very," Derek interjected.

"Okay, we can go riding tomorrow," Chad announced. "But may I go out and play, Papa?"

"Of course," Nick said, but as Chad leapt up, he eyed him sternly. Obedient to the unspoken command, Chad gave Jane a hug and kiss, then his father. "And what about your grandparents?"

"Sorry," he mumbled, but then he ran to Derek and Miranda before racing with a whoop out of the room.

"You have a fine son," Derek said, smiling.

Miranda, sitting beside Nick, touched his arm. "Are you happy, Nick?"

He looked at Jane intently. "Yes."

"I'm so glad," Miranda said, a catch in her voice.

Nick gazed at his mother briefly, then turned to his father. "How come," he demanded, "how come you lied to me?"

56

"How come," Nick said, his voice hoarse, "neither one of you told me the truth?"

Jane was stunned he'd bring it up now, so abruptly, and she froze.

Derek looked quizzical but then suddenly sober. He moved his coffee aside. "Never told you what truth?"

"The truth!" Nick's voice rose, his eyes flashed. He stared at his father. "How come you lied to me?"

Derek straightened. He stared back, shocked. "I'm not a liar—especially not to my own son. What are you accusing me of?"

Jane, sitting between father and son, put her hand on Nick to restrain him.

He ignored her. "But you did lie—and I'm not your son."

Derek's confusion was obvious. "What the hell are you ranting about? What's—"

Miranda's gasp cut him off. She was whiter

than white, clutching her breast, staring horrified at Nick.

Nick looked at her. "I found out the truth the day I rode off to fight in the war."

"Oh, Nick," Miranda cried, gripping his arm. "Why didn't you come to us then?"

"What in hell?" Derek cried, standing.

"Chavez," Nick said, lunging to his feet.

Derek became deadly pale, and he gripped the table for support. "Oh, God."

"Chavez is my father," Nick continued ruthlessly. "You lied to me—all these years!"

"How did you find out?" Miranda moaned.

"We were protecting you," Derek said heavily.

"We didn't tell you because it was pointless!" Miranda cried. "Pointless and cruel!"

"My life here has been lies!" Nick shouted.

"My love for you isn't a lie," Derek said, so softly, so hoarsely, he brought an absolute silence to the room.

Nick gripped the table too. He stared at Derek. Waiting, beseeching.

"That's the truth," Derek said. "Nick, the day you were born I took you in my arms and loved you as my own. That's the truth."

Nick stared at the table, his vision hazing. "Shit. It's not possible. How could you love the son of a man who raped your wife? How?"

"Chavez paid for what he did," Derek said savagely. "You are my son!"

"Rathe is your son!"

"No more than you."

Nick just stared.

"I don't love him more," Derek said urgently with sudden insight. "In fact, it killed me from the very beginning that you were the one who had to go to that goddamn England and take over that damned inheritance—it killed me! Rathe was suited for it, not you. This is where you belong, where you've always belonged, here, at my side, on the D and M, the way it used to be . . ."

"Really?" Nick was hoarse.

"Son, do you want to see my will? I've left all of this to the three of you equally. A parent doesn't love one child more than the other, yet, Nick— you were our first. In a way, that makes you special, always, to me and Miranda."

Nick hung his head. He felt Jane's hand on his back. He heard his mother speaking.

"Nick, you know your father isn't a liar, and you know that he is a warm, loving man. Don't doubt his love for you! The day you left for England he wept." At Derek's startled look, she smiled through her own tears. "Yes, darling, I knew. I decided to leave you in privacy." She touched Nick. "We both grieved, and we comforted each other. We didn't want you to go, Nick. Do you want to know the truth? The truth is, if my father hadn't been an earl, Derek would have left you the D and M, instead of leaving it to the three of you equally. We always thought you were the most like your father, and you know what? Because Derek and I never questioned his being your father, or his love, we sort of forgot the truth, and it didn't seem strange that you should be so like Derek—more so than your brother. You're the one who is happy working the land, you're the one who is a homebody, a family man."

Derek moved around the table, but stopped short at Nick's side, not touching him. "You should have come to me immediately—not ten, no, fifteen years later! God, Nick, when I think of what you've been through . . ." He choked.

Nick looked up. "I was afraid."

"How could you have doubted me?" Derek asked, his eyes glistening.

"I don't know," Nick managed.

"Do you—do you still doubt me?" Derek asked.

"No."

His eyes brimming, Derek smiled and pulled his son into his embrace for a big bear hug. Just for a moment, Nick clung, and then the two separated, both embarrassed.

"I should wallop the hell out of you," Derek tossed out.

And, nose red, Nick laughed.

It was the happiest sound Jane had ever heard.

Arm in arm, hips brushing, they walked along the ridge at sunset overlooking the D and M. Below them, on the right, were the many timbered buildings of the ranch—the main house, the barns, the smokehouses, the bunkhouses, the tool sheds and tackrooms. On the left, in the distance, were the many rooftops of the little sprawling town. Above them, a golden eagle soared, and they both paused to watch.

"You know what?" Nick said, his tone lighter than Jane had ever heard it, his body relaxed against hers, "I feel like that bird."

Jane cuddled closer into his side. "Like a bird?"

He smiled down at her, his eyes warm and unshadowed. "I feel like that eagle. I feel so light, so free, that I could fly, soar, along these mountaintops."

"I'm so glad, Nicholas," Jane said.

His hand stroked her shoulder. She said, "They are very special people."

"Yes, they are."

"Quite the couple."

"Absolutely." Nick suddenly chuckled. "Derek thinks you're like Miranda. It tickles him to death!"

"He can't get past our accents, is all," Jane teased.

"He knows a lady and a beauty when he sees one," Nick said, lifting her hand to kiss it. "Mmm, you taste good."

She kissed his shoulder, eyeing him. "You taste like horse."

He laughed, a roar she had never heard before, one suspiciously like his father's. "Really? You just don't know what to do seeing me in blue cotton and denim pants and cowboy boots!"

"I think the outfit is—er—interesting," she said. Then she looked at him askance. "I think the pants fit you too well, Nicholas."

"Too well?" He grinned. "And why is that?"

"They're rather . . . provocative."

He laughed, another roar, and lifted her up and swung her around. She shrieked and clung, and when he put her down, they were both breathless and giggling like children. They started walking again.

"It's amazing," Nick said, "how this ranch has grown. Do you know when I was last here there was no town, just two little cabins that two of the hands built for their brides and a general store."

"Really? Why, I even saw a bank this afternoon."

"You're right, Derek does have a bank."

"It's your father's!"

Nick nodded, smiling. "Rathe talked him into it. Everything you see sprang up to support the ranch—Derek has two hundred employees working for him. Many have families and live in the town. Families need a postal office and shops, restaurants, a bank. The new railhead will bring even more business. Derek told me they're electing a mayor this spring."

"So this is genesis," Jane said. "It's incredible, Nick, when you know the entire story—how Derek brought Miranda here when it was nothing but a wilderness—he made this all for her and you and Rathe and Storm."

"With his own two hands. My father is quite a man," Nick said, with obvious pride.

"And your mother quite a woman—to come from a convent in France and manage to thrive here!"

Nick stared down at the ranch. "This was quite the homecoming, Jane."

"I'm so happy we came. I'm so happy you and your father had this out."

"So am I. I feel like a whole person again. But you know what's funny?"

"What?"

"Even though this is home, and it always will be, it's not the way it used to be."

"What do you mean, Nicholas?"

"I mean"—and he smiled at her—"I am very aware of the fact that Dragmore is patiently awaiting our return."

Jane's heart swelled with joy. "You miss our home, Nicholas?"

"Yes, I do. I really do. Dragmore is in my blood, Jane. I don't know how it got there."

She gripped his hand. "It's half your heritage too, Nicholas."

They were silent for a long while, both lost in their own thoughts, but both thinking of Dragmore—of home.

"If you want," Nick said, "we can return sooner. We don't have to stay the six weeks we promised."

"Do you want to go back earlier?"

"No. There's so much catching up to do . . ."

"Good," Jane said, leaning close. "Because we don't know when we will come again, especially now." Her hand touched her abdomen and rested there.

The earl pulled her against his side, his expression soft and adoring. "Just think," he whispered, "next April I'll be bouncing our baby on my knee."

"I'm glad you're so happy."

"Deliriously so. How does six sound?"

Jane froze. "Six?"

"Six."

"Six, er, what, Nicholas?"

He kept a straight face. "Six children."

Her eyes widened, he whooped and hugged her. "I can compromise," he whispered in her ear.

"Good," Jane said, relieved. "We'll settle on ten, then."

He roared. His arms still around her, his laughter subsided, and they gazed out at the panorama spread before them, each cherishing their own special thoughts. The golden eagle took wing again and soared above them.

"Can you think of a name?" Nick suddenly said.

"What?"

"The town has no name. Derek asked me to think of one—every one he likes, Miranda hates, and every one she likes, he hates." Nick suddenly chuckled. "Derek wants to call it Mirandaville!"

"Oh, no!" Jane agreed, laughing. "We had best come up with something!"

Nick took her hand, pulling her close against his side. Jane looked down at the town sprawling with its frontier fervor amid mesquite and sage, and she thought of how Nick's father had come to this land when it was raw and virgin, how he and his wife had tamed it, turned it into this lush, thriving Eden. "Truly," she murmured, "it was genesis."

Acutely attuned to her, Nick frowned. "You want to name it Genesis?"

Jane laughed, pressing closer and smiling up at him. "No, Nicholas, darling. It's very simple. This"—and she gestured grandly at the mountains behind them, the plains ahead, at the spectacular orange and purple sunset splaying across the Texas sky—"is Paradise."

"Paradise," Nick said, and he smiled. "Do I detect a bit of wit, Angel dear?"

"Wit?" Jane laughed. "Never—my lord."

And so it came to be. Paradise, Texas, was born from a little bit of wit and a whole lot of love.

EPILOGUE

Dragmore, 1877

Summer was tardy in its arrival, and there was nothing gracious about it. The sky could not be bluer, yet there was more than a hint of dampness in the air. The vast Dragmore lands undulated a glistening green, dotted with sheep, and the trees overhead provided thick, fresh canopies of new foliage, yet the road from Lessing was muddy and scarred from spring's steady rains. The Dragmore coach with its bold crests hit another pothole, sending a cascade of mud up from its wheels, dousing some poor rider upon his mare. Within, instinctively, the earl took Jane's arm and steadied her.

Jane was remembering another time in almost the same place. The memory was poignant. She was remembering a young girl sitting in a hired coach next to her stiff, unsympathetic Aunt Matilda, on their way to Dragmore for the very first time. Then it had been summer too, the hills had been damp and glossy like now, only she had been so very afraid. Of the future, of the Earl of Dragmore. She bent to drop a kiss upon her baby's forehead as she held her, and then she smiled at her husband. He, however, was gazing raptly at the countryside.

"Papa!" Nicole shouted. "Papa, papa! Dragmore, where is Dragmore?" This was one of the first larger words that had been added to her vocabulary while abroad.

Chad, who had been leaning forward to stare eagerly out the window, turned irately to his sister. "Right here, silly. You don't even know what Dragmore is!" He scoffed. "Does she?" He turned to his father. "She's too young to remember. She's just pretending to know what she's talking about!"

The earl was preoccupied, but he tore his own gaze from the coach windows as they entered the long winding drive that would take them to the house. "She'll probably remember bits and pieces," he said quietly, and turned to watch out the window again.

Dragmore. It had been so long. Once abroad, they had spent several months with Nick's family in Texas, then had left the children with their grandparents to take a honeymoon after their marriage. They had gone visiting his sister, Storm, and her husband, Brett, in San Francisco. A truly idyllic month in Hawaii had followed, and then they had decided to wait out the rest of Jane's advancing pregnancy in Texas. But now, within moments, they would be home. *Home.* He tasted the word, tested it, and finally said it aloud. "Home."

His wife, holding his hand, squeezed it. He looked at her, all his preoccupation vanishing, his gray gaze instantly softening. He smiled; she smiled. "It feels good, Nicholas," Jane said softly. "Doesn't it?"

"Yes," he answered. "It does."

His hand tightened on hers. It was incredible, but his pulses were pounding with anticipation and excitement soared in his veins. This *was* home. He was coming home. He felt it in every fiber of his being, and the feeling was both exultant and peaceful. Jane reached over and planted a kiss on his cheek. He smiled at her, and it reached his eyes.

"Look," Chad shouted. "Look!"

"Look," Nicole screamed. "Look!"

Chad gave her a dark glance, she laughed.

Jane and Nick leaned forward and saw the turrets of the mansion and its dark bold outline. As they got closer, they could make out the pink roses creeping along the gray stone walls everywhere. And then Jane gasped.

"My God!" she cried. "The south tower, it's gone!"

The earl grinned slowly.

The burned-out south wing had been completely razed—it had ceased to exist. And in its place the lawn was green and inviting, although a little bare, without any trees or gardens. Jane turned to her husband, stunned.

"I decided last fall to get rid of that, er, ruin."

She started to smile.

"Instead of deciding whether and what to rebuild there, I merely had them put in the lawn. I didn't even have them plant any gardens. We can rebuild the tower, if you like, or add an extension to the house. Or even a patio." His grin flashed. "I decided I had better consult my wife before doing any redesigning."

"That was wise," Jane agreed, beaming. "Oh, Nicholas, what a wonderful surprise."

"I rather thought so, myself."

The carriage had come to a stop. Chad leapt out, while Molly, who had gone in a coach ahead of them, and the footmen received Nicole and the baby. Jane and the earl alighted and, as one, walked past the house and to tne new lawn where the south wing had once been. Hand in hand they stood there, not saying anything, just feeling the moment.

"It feels peaceful now," Jane said softly. "Peaceful and light. There are no old spirits, no dark passions, haunting here anymore."

The earl lifted her hand to his lips. "Nor are they lingering in our hearts or in our heads."

Jane's eyes misted.

"Thank you, darling," he said.

Reckless abandon. Intrigue. And spirited love. A magnificent array of tempestuous, passionate historical romances to capture your heart.

Virginia Henley

☐ 17161-X	The Raven and the Rose	$4.50
☐ 20144-6	The Hawk and the Dove	$4.99
☐ 20429-1	The Falcon and the Flower	$3.95

Joanne Redd

☐ 20825-4	Steal The Flame	$4.50
☐ 18982-9	To Love an Eagle	$4.50
☐ 20114-4	Chasing a Dream	$4.50
☐ 20224-8	Desert Bride	$3.95

Lori Copeland

☐ 10374-6	Avenging Angel	$4.50
☐ 20134-9	Passion's Captive	$4.50
☐ 20325-2	Sweet Talkin' Stranger	$3.95
☐ 20842-4	Sweet Hannah Rose	$4.95

Elaine Coffman

☐ 20529-8	Escape Not My Love	$4.99
☐ 20262-0	If My Love Could Hold You	$4.99
☐ 20198-5	My Enemy, My Love	$3.95

Experience the Passion and the Ecstasy

Heather Graham

☐ 20235-3 Sweet Savage Eden $3.95

☐ 11740-2 Devil's Mistress $4.50

Meagan McKinney

☐ 16412-5 No Choice But
Surrender $3.95

☐ 20301-5 My Wicked
Enchantress $3.95

☐ 20521-2 When Angels Fall $3.95